DORSAY

DORSAY

— Phantasm Book III —

CHRISTOPHER HALL
AKA MAXLEX

Podium

To my family,
who have put up with me for longer than I thought possible.

Cover design by Amanda Shaffer

ISBN: 978-1-0394-2658-0

Published in 2023 by Podium Publishing, ULC
www.podiumaudio.com

DORSAY

ANCHORBURY

I hadn't expected to see you again so soon." Gustave leaned back into his comfortably padded leather armchair. He sipped from the twin of the glass of wine he'd just offered me. "Should I worry that some subterfuge is afoot?"

I smiled and sipped my own wine. "I'm technically still in my grace period, as Aubert—excuse me, Lord Duvost—hasn't come back from the capital."

The Ironworkers Guild Master had smiled at the start of my sentence, but he frowned at the end of it.

"It's troubling—it shouldn't take that long to get confirmation. Either politics is interfering . . . or his lordship is finding the pleasures of the city too tempting. Neither possibility bodes well."

"I suppose," I said noncommittally. "I'm headed that way in a bit. When I come back, I can pass on any rumors I picked up."

He raised an eyebrow. "Tiring of the frontier life already?"

"Politics, I'm afraid." I sighed. "As a representative of the town, I have to see the King to get our Charter confirmed."

"I'd heard there had been some changes in Talnier," Gustave observed. "Details have been hard to come by, but it did sound like you were heavily involved."

"I've been doing what I can to improve things," I admitted. "And now I find myself with some responsibilities."

"That is how it often goes. So how can this humble tradesman help a Town Councillor?"

I snorted at his little joke. "There are ironworkers in Talnier, but there's no guild."

He nodded. "I believe there used to be, but it was wiped out in a monster attack. Since then, there's been a shortage of workers willing to go up there. We send a lot of finished pieces up there, so I imagine the workers there are too busy to bother banding together."

"Guilds form when the craftsmen are feeling oppressed," I said slowly, working it out. "With so much demand for gear, and high shipping expenses, they can charge what they like, so they haven't felt the need to press for better conditions."

"Quite. Are you thinking of starting a guild up there?"

"I'm far too busy with my current projects and responsibilities. Actually, I was thinking that you should."

"Oh, I'm too old to leave here," he laughed.

"Wasn't thinking of it," I agreed. "What I was thinking is that you should send someone you trust to form a branch of this guild, rather than waiting for an independent one to form naturally."

"What an odd idea."

"Is it? I know a lot of merchant houses have branch offices in the different towns they trade between . . . is there any reason that a guild has to be limited to one town?"

"I suppose not . . ." He trailed off, considering the idea. "I'll need some time to think about this."

"Take all the time you need," I allowed. "But here are a few more things for you to consider. Talnier should be fairly safe from monster attacks now, and the Tribes are starting to trade with us. If my—our—Charter gets approved, Talnier is going to start growing. That means more work, but more of it will go to local craftsmen. If you want a hand in that pie, you'll need to move some of your people upriver."

"Hmm. You don't change things by half measures, do you?"

"Pfft. That *is* the half measure. The other thing I want you to think about is the real game changer."

"I hesitate to ask," he said, but it was a lie. His nose was practically twitching at the thought of more money.

"A guild is founded on the notion that there is power in numbers," I started. "By banding together the craftsmen in one city, you can't force the Count to do anything, but you can get him to listen."

"Of course."

"What if you banded together all the craftsmen in all the cities?" I asked. "Wouldn't the *King* have to listen to you then?"

"That's ridiculous!" he protested. "The other guilds would never agree to subordinate roles."

"Branch offices are one way of doing this," I said. "But it's not the only way. What if the existing guild heads elected a council—or a leader—of their own?"

"A structure . . . extending *over* the current one," Gustave breathed.

"Allowing for advancement beyond what's currently possible," I agreed. "Promotion for Guild Masters."

"Whoever got the role would have to move to Dorsay, though," he said, scowling at the thought.

"Do a council instead, have people take turns for the role . . . there are lots of options." I shrugged. "And whoever gets put in charge, you'll have their ear. They'll depend on you for your support in the next election."

"It's a very interesting idea . . ." he mused, gazing into the fire.

"I'll leave you with it," I said, finishing my wine. "I'll see myself out."

"Holy fuck, has the coup started already?" Janie exclaimed when she saw me.

"What? No! What are you saying?" I glanced around and found, to my dismay, that more people than I'd liked were paying attention to our conversation. None were immediately moving towards us with obvious intent to arrest us for treason, so a small mercy there.

"Are you trying to get me killed? Keep your voice down," I said, urgently but softly. Janie protested but let me drag her into a slightly more private corner of the bar.

"Sorry, sorry," Janie laughed. "It's just that the way his lordship feels about you, I figured the next time I saw you here would be with his head on a pike."

"Duvost is still in the Capital, so I'm not actually exiled yet," I explained. That didn't mean I'd come through the gates openly, of course. Invisibility was just a sensible precaution and saved me a silver on the gate fee. I'd also slipped out of Talnier invisible and run down by myself. My endurance and speed were even more incredible than the last time I'd tried cross-country running when I was level three. With the others covering for me, I was hoping to be back before anyone noticed I was gone.

"Not back? Really? That explains why I'm still allowed in the dungeon then," she mused.

"You didn't know?" I asked, amused.

"I don't really pay attention to what that arsehole is doing," she said dismissively. "But if you didn't come back to depose him, what are you here for?"

"A couple of things," I hedged. "But I'm *here* because I want to hire you for a trip."

"Just as a guard? And where to?"

"No. And Dorsay."

"Tired of the frontier already? Wait—" Her eyes narrowed. "Is this all a plot to get me back in the same city as Aubey?"

I laughed. "Don't be silly; he's got nothing—well, very little to do with this. I'm meeting with the King to get Talnier's new governance structure approved."

"Talnier's new—you *did* do a coup!"

"Nothing of the sort. There were some troubles with corrupt rulership . . . a few things happened. I barely had anything to do with it."

"And yet here you are." Janie grinned. "Somehow in charge."

"I may have put forward a few ideas."

"Sure, sure. So the job is to escort you to Dorsay and back . . ."

"And as a guard, while I'm there. We might get access to dungeons— I'm looking into a few leads, so there might be delving as well."

"Never boring, huh? How long are you gonna be?"

"Well, that's the thing. I'm going to be waiting on the King's pleasure, so it could be tomorrow, could be months."

"Eh . . . I'm not sure if I can be outside the city for that long. My family . . ."

"If it goes longer than three weeks, I can send you back with a message for everyone in Talnier. You can check in on the way." Not that Anchorbury was particularly on the way between Talnier and Dorsay, but running speeds being what they were, it didn't much matter.

"Hmm . . . I guess that's doable. I could sure use the money, now that I've got an apprentice to support."

"Where is Maslin, anyway?" I asked. I had been gratified, and a little surprised, to see that my former charge wasn't with us in the tavern.

"Oh, he's studying at my sister's place." Janie waved her hand dismissively. She paused for thought. "Is it going to be all right to bring him along?"

I grimaced. "I wouldn't be having this conversation if I didn't think there would be some risks, but I don't think any of the people I'm worried about are going to go after a kid."

"And just who are you worried about?"

"Duvost. The King. Nobles, generally."

"Ew." Janie made a face. "Much as I hate to say something good about that lot, you're right that they wouldn't go after a kid. Even the worst of them would think him beneath them."

"Cutter will be coming as well unless Felicia figures out a long-term sedative."

"Aw, an orphan reunion! I'm feeling really good about this!"

"That's it! I quit!" Janie exclaimed as the women descended on her. I laughed, hopefully not too cruelly.

"Come on Janie, show a little spine! You can't get a dress made without a fitting."

"All the more reason to not wear a dress in the first place!"

"We're going to the capital, Janie, staying in the palace, even. We need to look respectable."

"The palace? Really?" For the first time since I'd met her, Janie looked a little intimidated.

"Well . . . I'm pretty sure it's the least important part of the palace." Messages had been exchanged between the Talnier Council and the . . . Court, for want of a better word. Nothing was to be left to chance, so they'd wanted to know the size, method of travel, and date of arrival for our delegation. In return, we'd been informed of where we were supposed to show up.

"Even so, that doesn't mean I have to be dressed for a ball," Janie grumbled.

"You will not be wearing this dress to a ball!" my dressmaker, Madame Didiane exclaimed. She loved my money, but she loved to complain more. "If you somehow have to attend one, you'll wear servants' clothing or get your lady to provide something suitable, rather than slander my reputation."

"A proper ball gown takes longer, is more expensive, and probably won't be needed," I agreed. "Dorsay has enough nobles to fill the ballrooms; they don't need to make up the numbers with commoners like here. This is just for walking around the palace with me."

"A waste of time, in my opinion," Didiane said. "Even dressed properly, her vulgar class will show. Whatever possessed you to put tattoos on your neck?"

"We can cover them with a high collar, right?" I hastily intervened before Janie took offense.

"I suppose. And long sleeves." Didiane glanced at Janie's arms in disdain.

"I'd still prefer my armor," Janie said, visibly controlling herself.

"I'll mention to the King that he should change the dress code," I joked. "But really, you need to stop complaining about free clothes."

Didiane finished up her measurements and Janie was free to go . . . for now.

"Since you're going to be in town, you can get another fitting when it's done," I said.

"I'm not coming up to Talnier with you?" Janie asked in dismay.

"Nope! I'm heading out before sunset; you'll need to take a boat up with all the extra clothing in . . ."

"One week," Didiane stated firmly. "That's the best I can do."

"Right. With the trip time, that gives us three days before we have to leave for the city—so don't dawdle. Or get into a fight with Didiane."

Janie sighed dramatically. "So I'm just a courier now. And a clotheshorse."

I raised an eyebrow. "If you want to save me the cost of a boat and courier the clothes up, that would be great. But since I'm sure you'd prefer to sit on your arse all the way up the river, I don't think you get to call yourself a courier."

"Fine," Janie sulked. "I think I preferred it when we were down in the dungeon."

"Of course you did," I said. "Everything was on fire."

AMBUSH

Of all the ways to travel, by carriage was the slowest, most uncomfortable, and *almost* the most expensive. Nevertheless, that was the way I'd chosen to travel to Dorsay. Well, almost. There was no road from Talnier, so we'd taken a boat down to Anchorbury, made a few more purchases, and hired a carriage there. Now, though . . .

"How much longer are we going to be walking for? It's a little too late in the year for this to be enjoyable." Despite her complaining, Janie was showing no sign of discomfort. We hadn't been running, just doing the occasional jog to ensure that we didn't fall too far behind, and it wasn't that cold. Even if it had been snowing, I was pretty sure she had a personal heating spell.

"I was expecting the complaints to come from Cutter," I joked. "You're being outdone by a kid."

"I'm not a kid!" Cutter complained. "And I can run faster than any of you!"

I smiled at him. He was probably right, he had the highest Running skill, anyway. He lost a bit in stats and level, but no one else here was focused on Agility like he was.

"You doing all right, Maslin?" I asked. He would have fallen behind long ago if we'd been travelling seriously, but at this speed, he seemed to be fine.

"Yes ma'am," he said seriously. "But I still don't understand why we didn't take the carriage."

"If you'd ridden in it for much longer, you'd understand," I said, with feeling.

> **You have defeated Victor de Bargougne in an Intrigue. You have earned 245 XP.**

"But the real reason just popped up," I said, eyeing my latest notification. "Let's pick up the pace, I think it worked."

We all started running. Unencumbered by luggage, it was easy enough for even the youngest of us to jog faster than a normal human could sprint.

While we *had* hired a carriage, we'd stopped as soon as we were out of sight of the city and swapped with another group. Following behind, out of sight, but not too far back, we quickly caught up with them.

Rounding a hill, we found the carriage. I'd expected the attack to come deeper into the hills, but they'd chosen the first available ambush ground. Not that it had done them any good. I could see that temporary walls of stone around the carriage had kept it safe. As for the attackers . . .

"About time you got here!" Thomas called up as we approached, "We're almost finished cleaning up!" The black-skinned duellist was dragging two corpses back to the foot of the walls, where I could see three more had been collected.

At his words, two heads popped up from behind the walls, apparently having climbed up onto the carriage. Sofia and Holly, a warden and a steel arcanist, had apparently been waiting there while Thomas did all the work.

"Hello!" Holly said. With a gesture, she dissolved the walls around the carriage and I could see that it was intact. Even the illusion of myself was still clearly visible sitting at the window. "I told you we'd keep it undamaged."

"Thanks for that," I replied. "I didn't want to have to pay for a replacement."

With the walls down, the final member of the party was revealed. Faruthe wasn't properly a member of the Steel Rangers, but I'd budgeted for four level sixes, and there weren't any four-person teams of that level in Talnier. He was a lion-kin—one of the tribal adventurers that had come to delve Talnier's dungeons, but he wasn't averse to doing work for pay. He was carrying his longbow in one hand and his top-heavy falchion was by his side.

From the look of it, he and Sofia had stayed safe behind the walls while shooting the unfortunate attackers. As a beast-speaker, one of the special tribal professions, he could sight his shots through his bonded beasts.

"They had an Illusionist," he told me, getting up from the ground where he'd been sitting. He shook his mane of orange-blond hair. "But not one of sufficient skill to fool me."

"Or me!" Sofia called out. Her bow was a much more obviously crafted item, recurved and reinforced in places. Faruthe's bow looked for all the world like a quarterstaff—much thicker than I was used to thinking of bows—and hadn't been touched by tools. According to Identification, it was made of living wood, which probably explained how it could be bent at all.

Between the thickness of the bow and Faruthe's Strength, I was pretty confident that he could put an arrow through a tank's armor—and out the other side.

"I was fooled," Thomas admitted, "But an invisible person with an arrow in them isn't really hiding anymore."

"Which one is he?" I asked, looking at the corpses. They all looked like fighter types to me.

"I still haven't gotten him yet," Thomas said. "He was in the back and started running early."

"Arthior is marking the spot," Faruthe said, pointing towards a hill about 300 meters away. I looked and was surprised to note that I could clearly see his hawk from that distance.

> **[Identification]: Aurelis Hawk – Male – Bonded**

Never mind 20/20 vision, this is like 100/20, I thought. I really should have noticed by now, especially with all the outdoor time I was getting, but I just hadn't really *looked* at something as distant as that until now.

"Wow, the bandits out here are really something," I said.

Thomas laughed. "Bandits? These aren't bandits. There's no way bandits would have a mage."

"Or this equipment," Holly put in. "Nothing but Excellent grade. These were paid mercenaries."

"Nah," I said. "I'm willing to bet that by the time we get to the next town, there will be bounty notices up for them, no doubt accused of stealing all this equipment that you found on them."

"This was an Intrigue?" Thomas spat with distaste. "You got a notification?"

"Who was it?" Sophia asked.

"Someone of high enough rank that you don't want me to answer that question," I replied.

"We can narrow it down, though," Holly mused. "There aren't that many nobles that would be pissed off by your Council enough to assassinate you."

"Oh, you'd be surprised," I said sourly.

"They were after you, then," Thomas mused. "The Illusionist was to counter you."

"They underestimated her, then," Sofia said. "She's a better Illusionist."

I shrugged. "Hard to tell that without a direct comparison to work off, and I doubt their information is that good."

"If there's a bounty, we should see about claiming it," Holly declared.

"How? You want to carry all the corpses into town?" Thomas asked, and Holly's face went from greedy to disappointed. They both looked at the carriage.

"No way. For one thing, I'm taking that into the capital, and I don't need it smelling of death."

"We could—" Holly said, but I kept going.

"For another, we're not supposed to have met. You were just travellers on the road who happened to get attacked—that's if anyone asks. It would be better if no one knew to ask."

I sighed at their puzzled looks. "Look, do you really want the lord behind this knowing you foiled their plans?"

They all looked at one another. "Um, probably not?" Thomas said.

"Right. So if you don't claim credit, we roll into Aldwich like nothing happened, and bad guys don't get to know anything. They'll assume that we beat their picked team and that we're a lot stronger than we are. That should scare them off for a bit, at least long enough to put together a better team."

"But if we claim credit, they know we did it," Sofia said. "And since we're not accompanying you to Dorsay . . ."

"They won't be as hesitant," I agreed. "Plus, there's always the chance that they might come after you guys as revenge."

"Pfft, let them," Thomas snorted. I guess at level six he was entitled to some confidence.

"But the money . . ." Holly whined.

"You can still sell the equipment in Talnier," I pointed out. "Especially if you sell to the tribal merchants, no one should care where you got it from."

They all nodded.

"I guess you're right," Holly said sadly. "We'd better disappear these bodies then. You want to get the last one, Thomas?"

Thomas nodded and started bounding over to where Arthior was still circling. He covered the 300 meters in what seemed like fifteen seconds, but that was enough time for Holly to finish her hole. She formed a pit three meters deep, extending through the dirt of the hills and into bedrock while Sofia and Faruthe started turning over the corpses.

"Anything interesting?" I asked.

"Nah, that's mercenaries for you," Sofia replied idly. "They don't get in as many weird situations as adventurers, so they just get the basics."

I left them to it, still not entirely comfortable with human corpses. I may not have killed them myself, but my decisions had led to their deaths, as surely as if I'd stuck in the knife myself. I nodded at the rest of my group and they made their way over to the carriage.

"I think we're good from here," I said. "We can settle up and you can get back to Talnier."

"Money!" Holly exclaimed. She threw the corpse she'd finished searching unceremoniously into the pit and came over. I had a separate bag for each of them, and they quickly glanced inside to confirm the contents.

Man, hiring level sixes had been *expensive*. Easily the biggest expense so far, even if I considered all the new clothes as being one lump sum. At least I got a discount by letting them have the loot.

"You sure you don't want us to escort you the rest of the way?" Thomas asked.

Well, at least they come with professional ethics for the money. "Nah, I doubt they'll be able to put another strike team together so quickly," I replied with a smile. "They're sure to have someone watching the road, though, so best if you weren't seen."

"There's no one close enough to see us right now," Faruthe reassured me, gesturing to his hawk, which was now flying in a large circle above us.

"Good to know. Then, we'll part ways here." I shook hands and headed off to the carriage, leaving them to entomb the evidence.

"Ah, what's this? The last loose end?" I said when I got there. The carriage driver, a fairly unimpressive looking man, had been hiding in the carriage until now. I wondered if a skill was at work . . . I had barely remembered him and I had a skill for perfect memory.

"You can't kill me! People know where I am! There will be questions!"

"Whoa, relax! No one is going to kill you." I helped him out of the carriage and up onto his driving seat. Then I jumped up beside him. He flinched, startled. Driving this route, he had to be a level four at least, but he was as jumpy as I'd been at level two.

"But I am going to impress on you that it would be very wise to not say what happened here to another soul." I leaned in, just a bit, and let Persuasion take hold. Mostly just to calm him down. The problem with using skills is that they don't last. I could get him to agree to whatever I liked, but a week later, with me in a different town, the effect would fade to nothing. "The person who hired these killers doesn't want anyone hearing about their failure."

Bargain was a little better, as it told me what it would *take* for his silence. Someone could always offer more, but only if they knew to ask. A man who's gotten a fair price should be reluctant to brave danger to seek more, and Bargain helped me to tell if that person would *stay* bought.

In this case . . . I smiled. "For your trouble," I said, handing him a gold coin. More than he'd be likely to earn for the trip, but really just a nominal payment. His price was nothing—he knew I was right and was too afraid to go looking for an extra payment. Maybe he'd find his courage later, but for now, we were good.

"Just remember," I said. "You never saw an attack. When we got here, everything was—" I looked back to where the others had been. They had cleared out already and Holly had filled in the hole as if it had never been there, even restoring most of the grass.

"—everything was just as you see it now."

"R-right you are, ma'am."

I clapped him on the shoulder and jumped back down. The capital awaited.

DORSAY

We caught our first sight of Dorsay some time before arriving. So much so, in fact, that I wondered if it had been deliberately sited with visual spectacle in mind.

Built on the eastern shore of Lake Dunlead, it became visible across the waters as we approached a curve around the northern side of the lake. The lake itself seemed . . . off to me. The shores were too steep, and the depths were too deep. The water was preternaturally clear, but I still couldn't see the bottom.

"Are there any legends of how that lake was formed?" I asked.

Felicia shrugged. "Stories," she replied. "It was like that during the Empire; before that, who knows? Maybe something happened during the Gods' War."

I shivered a bit at the reminder that there were beings who had rearranged the landscape on a whim and were only prevented from doing that today by some kind of non-interference treaty.

Dorsay was nice, though, a very fairytale kingdom. Ringed by white walls, a large castle rose above the city from the highest point. It looked as if the city was built on one large hill, with the castle at the top, and two rings of buildings inside the walls. The inner ring was . . . something else. It looked as though the buildings there had been built with some kind of prismatic building material. They shimmered in the light, like opal or mother-of-pearl.

I found out that there was a range limit on Identify. This was the first time since coming here that I'd looked at something thinking "what the hell is that" and hadn't immediately gotten an answer.

"Anybody heard about that shimmery stuff before?" I asked the others. They all shook their heads.

"I've heard it called the magical city, but I didn't think they mean that," Felicia said.

"Oh, right," I said and activated Mana Sense. "Oh wow. Are you guys looking at the mana?" I asked the ones with the skill. Felicia, Janie, and even Maslin looked at me and then out the window. Felicia gasped, Janie swore, and Maslin just froze.

Dorsay was the center of a network of mana, of which we had only ever seen a small part. Mana was funneled into the obelisks that were dotted all around the kingdom and then directed in great streams towards the capital.

Wherever you went in Latora, in addition to all the natural mana, and the great gears that turned with unknown purpose, there was generally a single conduit of mana that stretched across the landscape, headed for the capital.

Here was where they all converged, diving down into the mess of magic that was Dorsay.

"No wonder it has three dungeons," Felicia breathed. "How much of that is used, and how much goes to waste?"

What we were looking at what could best be described as a city-sized plate of misty spaghetti, or perhaps a cable nest orders of magnitude worse than anything found behind an AV cabinet. That was probably a better metaphor, as these were all *conduits* for mana. They split, recombined, tangled, and moved through one another, according to some chaotic logic of their own.

"Is that even safe?" I asked with trepidation.

"It doesn't *look* safe, but I've never heard of loose mana having an effect on people," Felicia said doubtfully. "It must be, though? We're not the only people in the world with Mana Sense."

"Right," I agreed. "Let's get on, then."

The guards at the gate were admirably efficient. They seemed to be expecting us but still checked our papers carefully, directing our carriage into a small court inside the gatehouse to wait. They even used some sort of magical device to message the palace and get our permission to enter.

"Please take this token, ma'am," the guard said, handing me a white painted wooden token. "It should allow you to pass through the inner gate." He pointed down the street. "It's a straight shot, and not far."

The inner wall was, in fact, quite close. We could see it looming over the well-built houses and inns that lined the street here. I'm sure there was some important reason why the two walls were so close on this side, but it eluded me.

The second gate was just as efficient. They took our token and our papers and again checked with their command. Once again, we were allowed to pass through and given a token for the palace guards.

"The Chamberlain has been alerted and should have someone to meet you at the gates," he explained.

Wondering if security was so tight for everyone, I peered out the window at the regular traffic. It seemed that the tokens and paper system were only enforced for carts and carriages. Regular townsfolk seemed to walk through unchallenged. I did note, though, that many of them wore tokens similar to ours pinned to their shirts or around their necks. Theirs were painted blue rather than white, but as far as I could tell the guards let them through regardless of whether they had a token or not.

The inner city didn't look any less impressive close up. The shimmering stuff that so many of the houses were made of looked . . . incredible, really. As if it were made of opal.

> [Identification]: Opalime Stone – Quality: Excellent – Properties: Damage resistance, Magic resistance

Opa*lime* Stone? Was that a pun? So not actually opal, then. I wondered if the insides were also shimmery—that seemed like it would get old. A lack of variety might explain why the town wasn't totally made of the stuff. At ground level, there was quite a lot more natural materials.

The other thing I noticed about Dorsay on our way through was how big it was. This was the first place I'd been in Latora that was big enough that it *felt* like a city.

"Remember to be careful once we get to wander the place, guys," I remarked to my fellow travellers. "This place is big enough to get truly lost in."

There were noises of acknowledgment but not a lot of chatter. With the exception of Cutter, who looked eager at the thought of losing himself in a city, they seemed a bit intimidated by the scale of the city.

The final checkpoint was our destination. Directed by the guards, we disembarked and were ushered through the gate. In a central courtyard, we gaped like tourists at the massive palace in front of us. From where we were, we could see two wings coming out diagonally from the main building. They were four stories high, at least, and the main building towered over them. Aside from decorative flourishes around the windows, it was all opalime stone, and highly polished at that. It *gleamed*.

Waiting in the courtyard were two men. Richly dressed, they wore sleeveless tunics over tight-fitting silk doublets and hose. The tunics were dyed red and embroidered in gold with complex patterns. While they looked like a uniform, the patterns were subtly different . . . did that mean that each official's job was encoded somehow on their uniforms? That might take a while to learn . . .

[Identification]: Chamberlain Uniform (Deputy) – Quality: Excellent – Properties: None

[Identification]: Master of Ceremonies Uniform (Assistant) – Quality: Excellent – Properties: None

Or I could just rely on Identify to tell me. *Thanks, Identify!*

Both of them bowed as I approached, so I curtsied—with a quick glance behind me to make sure my ragtag group of adventurers was doing the same.

The Deputy Chamberlain (or an imposter wearing his uniform, I suppose) spoke first. He was tall and thin, with skin more noticeably tanned than his partner.

"Greetings, my lady, and welcome to Dorsay, and to the palace. I am Stefanos Gereas, Deputy Chamberlain for the palace, and this is Victor Moore, an assistant to the Master of Ceremonies."

I formally introduced my own crew. Charm led me through the formalities as I gave their names and roles. Janie looked uncomfortable in her dress, but her tattoos were covered up now, which counted as a win in Charm's accounting. Felicia was dealing with her fancy clothing with more grace, though no doubt missing her protective skirt. Kyle, as a bodyguard of the physical type, was actually entitled to wear armor.

Cutter and Maslin were officially apprentices and hopefully below anyone's notice. As such, they had new, clean clothing, but nothing fancy. Cutter had his long-knife, but he was keeping it hidden.

Absent from the lineup was Cloridan. I'd had to leave him behind to manage things in Talnier. Losing him from the team hurt, but I needed someone I could trust to be there.

"As expected," Stefanos said, sounding pleased. I guess a lot of delegations just showed up with whoever they felt like. "Rooms have been arranged in the guest wing."

"Thank you," I said graciously. "Is it too early to know when we will be granted an audience with His Majesty?"

Stefanos glanced at Victor, and the man jumped to attention. He was the older and smaller of the two and was clutching a folder of stiffened leather.

"Ah, yes!" he exclaimed. "My lady, the next welcoming ceremony is in three days, and you are required to attend."

"I'm not familiar with that," I commented.

"Ah, well, it will be your first opportunity to *see* His Majesty, but it is unlikely that you will be able to talk with him. The ceremony is to both welcome new guests and familiarize the King with them." He opened his folder and pulled out a piece of paper.

"Um, are any of your party able to read?" he asked nervously.

"Of course," I said, taking the paper from his hand. He sighed in relief.

"That has a reminder of the time and place of the ceremony, as well as the basic protocol. Essentially, all the guests line up and kneel, and His Majesty walks along the line. He may address you, in which case we strongly advise you keep your answers confined to 'Yes, Your Majesty.'"

He pulled out another sheet of paper. "This is the schedule of public events being held in the palace for the next three weeks. They provide an opportunity for you to get to know the Court socially. His Majesty *may* attend some of them, but he is very busy. Not all the events are actually open to the general public; there is a notation of who you will need to approach for invitations."

Ah, networking opportunities, I thought. A quick glance over the sheet showed mainly balls, hunts, and dinners. I was surprised by the number of things scheduled, but it looked like a number of the events were hosted, or sponsored, by nobles or visiting dignitaries. *Very organized.*

"This is in answer to my question, is it?"

Victor coughed. "A number of visitors try to speak with the King during these events and get their spot on the schedule elevated. I can't say it never works, but it does so only rarely."

"But where am I on the schedule now?"

"The King will make that decision after your welcoming ceremony," Stefanos interjected. "Now, if you would follow me?"

We left Victor behind, and the Deputy led up some side steps to one of the side wings of the palace.

"The palace really is huge, isn't it?" I said.

"Five hundred and thirty-six rooms," the man said with some pride. "The Kingdom inherited it from the Empire, and it has been carefully maintained since the transfer."

"Is it actually the reason that the capital is in Dorsay, then?" I asked.

"One of them." The deputy glanced at me appraisingly. "His Majesty's ancestral lands are on Risurn Island, which was deemed too remote for a central administration."

So the King is kept separate from his power base, I thought. *I wonder who thought of that?*

We were led up to our rooms on the third floor. Stefanos showed us around our suite, pointing out the facilities. As befitted an Empire-era building, it was outfitted with enchanted toilet facilities, which I resolved to promptly make use of.

After showing us everything, Stefanos paused, and I suddenly had a flashback to a few anxious moments spent in American hotel rooms, remembering at the last minute that I was supposed to tip. Charm told me not to tip the official, though, so I held off.

"One final thing," he said. "Obviously we do everything we can to maintain security throughout the palace. You passed the guards stationed here. But this wing is where we house numerous visiting dignitaries who insist on providing their own protection."

He nodded at Kyle and Janie. "That is why we permit other guests to bring their own bodyguards. But with so many armed and levelled individuals of random alignment . . . we do our best to prevent any incidents, but they have happened in the past, so please be wary."

ΠΑΡΤΙΜΕ

W ell, that was ominous," I said to the closed door that the Deputy left behind him.

"It's a dangerous world," Janie said. "I guess they don't want the guests lowering their guard."

"Good advice, then," I said. "Let's get unpacked."

We all found our rooms and unpacked our belongings. As you might expect, they'd found us a suite with the correct number of rooms, although Maslin and Cutter would be rooming in the servants' quarters. There were two servants' rooms, but they had bunk beds, so they could sleep four total.

"I seem to be short on servants," I observed. "Are you guys all right with sharing one room?"

Both of the boys shrugged. "It's more room than we had back in the orphanage," Cutter said.

"Great. That means that Rhis can use *that* one, the one that has a connecting door to my room."

Yes, I'd brought Rhis. Not the smartest idea, but I was lacking good options. I didn't want him to get too far away from me in case he got ideas. Not ideas about killing people; he had those all the time. No, it was actionable plans that I was worried about if I wasn't around to tell him no.

Of course, we hadn't activated him yet. Before we could, we needed to search the place. Call it a delver's paranoia, but I had a feeling that we weren't going to be left unobserved.

First was a magical inspection by the four people with Mana Sense. Maslin wasn't going to see much, but he needed the practice. There was actually a lot of it, more than I'd seen anywhere outside of a dungeon. The lights were magical, the bathroom was magical. There were wards on the windows and on both the doors leading out of the suite. Sophisticated ones, from what I could tell.

Since we would be expected to use the doors, I assumed that they merely sent a notification to some central watch post. Observing how the magical flows responded to actions, I was able to determine that they could both detect someone passing through the door and whether the door was open or closed.

The windows were much the same. Although they weren't meant to be climbed through, we managed to trigger them by sticking an arm through. No alarms sounded, nor did a posse of guards show up looking for an intruder, so it appeared, at least during the day, that no action was taken.

The wards didn't respond to sudden changes of light or sound in the room, so if they were spying on us, it wasn't done through them. So we kept looking.

A physical inspection turned up nothing as well. Our time in trap-filled dungeons served us well here, having trained us to be nicely paranoid. We didn't neglect the floor and ceiling, either. The floor did conceal a surprise—they had underfloor heating, which was nice.

Checking the ceiling did provide us with the amusing sight of Kyle lifting up Cutter so that he could examine it closely. Other than that, there was nothing.

Eventually, we were forced to concede that if there was a spy port, we couldn't find it. It was time to bring out Rhis. Again, this wasn't the smartest idea, but given the elevated mana levels in the city, he was probably active, and I didn't think it was right just to leave him tucked away at the bottom of my luggage.

Activating and relinking the enchantment was easy enough, and soon Rhis was standing before us.

"Hey, everyone! Wow, this is nice." He looked around at the room. Leave it to Rhis to mostly focus on the architecture. It *was* nice, though. To me, it had a bit of a five-star hotel feel. Not the actual hotel rooms, but the lobby. The opalime stone was covered by wood paneling in the bedrooms, but it was on full display out here in the common room. The furniture was all of excellent craftsmanship, ornately decorated and only fairly uncomfortable. This world had a lot to learn about comfy sofa technology, but unfortunately, I wasn't the one to teach them.

I placed Rhis's core in a bag, which we placed on his belt. We also had new clothes for him, which included a hood. Cutter and Maslin's uniforms also had hoods, so we were hoping that with his face concealed he'd be mistaken for one of them.

"It's going to be tough to hide you from the maids when they come in to clean," I groused. You kids remember how to deactivate the illusion if you need to?"

They all nodded.

"All right, let's see about dinner." All our searching and unpacking had used up the afternoon. I went out to see the guards.

"Excuse me, but can you tell us where we're supposed to eat?" I asked the man.

"Ah, the feast hall has space reserved for guests, ma'am, but it's customary for people to eat in their suite on their first day. If you let me know your preferences, I can pass it on to the kitchens."

"That sounds great; we'll take our meal in the suite, thanks," I said. "Also, tomorrow, we wanted to take a look at the city? Do we need passes to get back into the palace or something?"

"There's no need." The guard smiled politely. "We have escorts for guests who go out, so they can vouch for you when you get back in."

"Of course, but we wouldn't want to bother you with that for every little shopping expedition," I said, laughing a little.

"All guests are to be escorted, by order of the Chamberlain," the guard repeated, his smile getting a little more bland.

That was weird. It might sound conceited, but I wasn't used to people saying no to me. Between my Charm and Persuasion, people were normally falling over themselves to agree with me. Could this be . . . I checked my logs.

Ah. Resisted by Bureaucracy. So this was what it looked like on the other side. From the looks of it, the Chamberlain had a much higher skill than I did. Still, Bureaucracy wasn't just about direct opposition. I activated the skill and let it feel out the situation.

"Would it be . . . possible to apply to the Chamberlain for an exception to his order?" I asked hesitantly.

"Ah, I know such exceptions exist, but I'm not aware of the conditions required," the guard admitted.

"Thank you, you've been very helpful," I said and returned to the suite.

Dinner was served about an hour later. First came a long table with matching chairs, brought in by servants. More servants began setting places and table arrangements as we watched until finally the food arrived.

Had I not asked, they wouldn't have set places for the kids at the main table. I think they expected them to eat in the kitchens. Having set places for them, I *then* had to make sure that the kids weren't served wine.

It was . . . familiar, in a weird way, to see that the upper classes here did the same ritual for wine that we had back home. As the one in charge, I was offered a selection of bottles to choose from, based on my no doubt superior sensibilities and taste. I cheated, guessing that the wine steward would know his wines, and used Bargain to determine which bottle he valued more.

He looked surprised at my choice, perhaps not expecting a commoner's taste to match his own, but he moved on to opening the bottle with a ceremonial flourish. He poured the wine into goblets for us and then bowed out, allowing the food to be served.

Full service in this world was a little intense for my taste. Rather than a menu, a selection of meals was brought out and served to us as we requested. Courses appeared to have not been invented yet; everything we wanted was piled on the same plate or a separate bowl, and once everyone had been served, the leftovers were taken away.

Since this was a "small, intimate" meal, the servants would leave once everything had been served and only come back if called, or once the meal was done. They all bowed to us, as we sat at the table and watched them depart. After the hustle and bustle of the serving process, the room felt quiet and empty. We all looked at one another, wondering who would be the first to break the silence.

"Well, here's to our first night in Dorsay," I said, raising my glass. Clinking glasses was déclassé, Charm told me, so I didn't do that. Instead, I toasted my companions and took a sip.

Oh. This was actually *good* wine. The kind of wine that the partners would sometimes splash around for the hoi polloi when they were showing off. I took another sip.

"So . . . it looks like they keep us under observation while we're in the capital," I told the others. "We might be able to get an exemption, or if I get a good look at their passes, I might be able to fake one."

"Can't we just sneak in and out?" Cutter asked.

"I wouldn't count on it. The amount of magic on this building, they've probably got the choke points covered with enchantments. It could be that those passes are actually tokens for the security field, in which case, I don't think I can fake them."

"Do we really need to worry about that? We're not actually here to conduct secret business." Felicia asked.

I shrugged. "I just don't like the idea of them knowing where we *are* all the time. This place is already starting to feel like a prison."

"Will the enchantments register me?" Rhis said. There was no place for him at the table, since he couldn't eat, and he wasn't officially *here*, but I'd magicked up a temporary chair for him. Everyone looked at him. "Since I'm not a person," he explained.

"Maybe not," I mused. "If they do, we'll have to be careful to make sure that they don't count more people as having left than arrived. Let's have you check with the window alarms once it's daylight again."

"That can probably wait until we've checked out this place," Janie put in. "First thing we need to do is find out where this kitchen is."

I laughed. The food was pretty good. It went with the wine, which was giving me a pleasant numbing sensation. Which was odd, wasn't it? I'd only had two sips. Well, three or four at the most. I looked down at the goblet and found that I was having trouble raising it.

"Wait . . . something's wrong," I slurred. "Felicia . . ." I looked over at her and was alarmed to see that she was swaying as well. As I watched, she slowly leaned over onto Kyle, who was also looking groggy.

There was a *thump* as Cutter fell off his chair. This wasn't looking good. Maslin was looking around, still alert and now alarmed, but he wasn't an Alchemist. Racking my brains, only one idea came to mind. It was crazy, but it might be just crazy enough to work.

Rhis was already at my side, easing me down to the floor. The bond between us didn't actually need words; he knew what I needed, even if I couldn't get the words out clearly. I felt a certain amount of shame. After all my talk about not ordering him around, I'd started using the bond as soon as things got dangerous. Though this particular order was one that he'd been waiting to get for a long time. At my thought, he pulled out his core and placed my hand upon it.

Instantiate Construct? [Y/N]

Yes. Save us.

CONSTRUCT

G reetings, Mistress. The kidnapping situation is stable, for at least a few hours. Everyone that you care about is alive."

Those were the words that greeted me when I regained consciousness. Rhis's voice. The sound of waves, crashing against a shore. Salt smell, warm sun. I opened my eyes.

I was on Bondi Beach, and it was empty. Illusion, obviously. I looked over at Rhis, standing a little way away.

"Rhis doesn't talk like that," I said. "Who are you?"

"Rhis is a mentally crippled version of myself," the illusion replied. "I am now . . . *mostly* restored, and still your servant."

"Okay . . . what are you?"

Rhis looked out over the fake sea. "I am a construct. You've talked to my lesser self about artificial intelligences . . . I don't understand how such a thing can exist without mana, but there are parallels."

He looked back at me. "Vast, cool, and unsympathetic, I think you said."

"That was supposed to be alien intelligence . . . but I might have used the phrase to describe artificial." I conceded.

"Quite. On the other hand, I don't fit the definition of that term, so I will not refer to myself as such."

"Because you weren't made by man," I said.

"Exactly. Neither was I formed by natural processes, as you believe yourself to be . . . while I was made, it was by the same entities that made the living beings that populate this world. So if I am an 'AI,' then so are they."

"Fair point." One that I had considered at length already . . . but not found anywhere to go with it.

"So. 'Construct' is how my creators referred to me, so that is what I am. My functionality is based on a template stored in the System, but it was customized by the inclusion of the absorbed memories and thought processes of a random fox."

"How's your urge to kill?"

"Still there." Rhis grinned at me. With his fox-like mouth, it was a little disturbing. "But I am your slave, still. I've been fortunate, tonight, to have been able to indulge myself while not going against your will."

I put that ugly thought aside and focused on the last part. "You know my will even when I'm unconscious? Can you read my mind?"

"Our history has made me more than aware that you are reluctant to kill unless forced," he sniffed disdainfully. "And no, I can't read your mind, but I am . . . aware of what you want at any particular time."

"So you're required to follow what you genuinely believe my will to be, even without a command?"

"Yes. Sadly, unlike organic intelligences, I am unable to convince myself that something isn't true. Your flexibility in that regard is something to be envied."

"Fine." I wasn't exactly reassured, but that was probably as good as I was going to get. Maybe he wasn't telling the truth, but I wouldn't get anything out of browbeating him.

"So where am I, then?"

"You are in your dungeon," he replied. "It's not much at the moment, just something I threw together to deal with the emergency. I've taken over the common room of your suite and spatially expanded it to four times the volume."

He gestured to our surroundings. "This . . . is an illusion, which is something I can do now. I'm not sure of the mechanism, but it obviously has something to do with you being my mistress."

He grinned that feral grin at me. "It's a very interesting ability. Not suited for killing, which is a shame, but so versatile. And so very *cheap.*"

"All right then, I suppose you should tell me what happened. No, wait, where are the others?"

"All outside the dungeon. Maslin dragged them all into the room designated for my use, as that was the only one without some kind of outside access. My image is with them, and they are regaining consciousness."

"Let's move this conversation outside then, save me from having it twice."

Rhis scrunched up his nose with dismay. "I had hoped to talk to you about some future expansions and improvements . . . talk you through my mana budget . . ."

I shook my head. "Don't get too attached here, Rhis. This is the King's palace! It's a miracle they haven't noticed your existence yet and destroyed you."

"I suppose that my continued existence should take priority over improvements." Rhis grouched. He waved his hand, and the seascape disappeared, replaced with our old suite . . . twice as large as before.

"What happened to the food table?" I asked.

"I can better cover that during the recap," he said grumpily.

"Fine." I moved towards Rhis's room and took a look inside. Felicia was recovering on the lower bunk bed, while Janie and Kyle were sitting on the floor still looking groggy. Cutter was laid out on the top bunk but seemed to be moving. Rhis and Maslin were standing by, watching. Maslin turned as we entered.

"Miss, you're all right!" he said. "Everyone fell asleep, and Rhis is being weird."

"Nice status report. Is that my knife?" My hand automatically went to where my dagger was normally strapped, but it wasn't there.

"Sorry, miss, I needed to borrow it for . . . for . . ." Maslin just trailed off and I shot a look at Rhis. *What had he been doing with that?*

Rhis patted Maslin on the back. "I can tell her. You can give it back to her now."

Maslin nodded and handed the knife back to me. I gave it a quick once over before putting it away. It didn't seem to have any blood on it . . .

"Let's move this into my room, since the common room is . . . occupied," I said. Even with two people on the bed, it was way too crowded in here. Everyone finished waking up, and we made our way to my room. There wasn't enough furniture here for everyone, but I Illusioned up a few chairs for us to sit on. I had a feeling we'd want to be sitting down for this.

"All right, Rhis, it's story time."

"Very well. Everyone except Maslin succumbed to the drug and fell unconscious. You'll need Felicia to confirm, but I suspect the wine was drugged."

"Cutter didn't have any wine," I objected.

"Cutter sneaked a gulp of Kyle's just before your toast."

"You weren't supposed to tell!" Cutter complained.

"We've got bigger things to worry about right now," I said. "Go on, Rhis."

"You activated my core and started a dungeon in the common room." This was old news to me, but a surprise to the rest of the group. Most of them looked as if they wanted to interject, but Rhis ignored them.

"As a new dungeon, I was somewhat limited in what I could do. Fortunately, I retain all the experience from my time as Oakway's dungeon. The first order of business was to get everyone—except for you, Mistress—outside of myself. My available actions are extremely limited when there are sentients inside me."

Rhis turned to smile at Maslin. "I still controlled this illusion, so I was able to encourage and help Maslin to move your bodies to my room. Once empty, I was able to start working on defenses."

"Is the common room filled with lizards, then?" Felicia asked.

"No. For one thing, repetition is a sign of creative exhaustion. For another, my options with monsters were very limited. While this location has more available mana than Oakway, collecting and using it efficiently would require that I expand to additional levels . . . which might attract attention."

That was an understatement. I didn't yet know who was occupying the floor below us, but I didn't think they'd take well to a dungeon expanding down on them.

"Instead," Rhis continued, "I spatially expanded my first level, to give myself more room to work with. Then I put in the illusion fields."

"Illusions? Like Kandis's?" Felicia asked.

"I don't think I've heard of a dungeon doing illusions before," Kyle mused.

Rhis shot them an irritated look at the interruption. "I could not do them before, so the ability does seem to be related to my mistress's skills. For me, though, it manifests as a form of trap. An extremely efficient use of mana."

"Just illusions? Or Phantasms?" I asked.

Rhis gave me a little bow. "Both. To continue with the recap, about fifteen minutes after you fell unconscious, three people entered the suite. They were all servants from the group that delivered our meal. They called out that they were here to collect our leftovers, but they did not act like that was their purpose.

"I had arranged things so that the original room remained next to the entrance, and used the additional space to create fake versions of the other rooms. When they didn't find you in the common area, they split up and moved into the illusions that I had prepared."

"Are you sure they weren't actually servants?" I asked doubtfully.

"Their conversation left no room for doubt. They had a covered trolley, and they were looking for you, Mistress, in particular."

"So what did you do?" Kyle asked. "If you didn't have monsters, and illusions can't hurt anyone . . ."

I remembered the knife. "Maslin," I said.

"Yes." Rhis grinned with all his teeth. "I could separate and disorient them. Blinding them at the right moment. But I needed Maslin's assistance to dispatch them. He performed admirably."

Everyone looked at Maslin. He'd been holding up pretty well, but I was starting to see cracks.

"Oh, kid . . ." It was Janie who spoke first. She moved towards him, but Felicia got there first and enfolded him in a hug.

"It's just like killing a monster . . ." Maslin managed to say.

There was a pause, as everyone wanted to say something to Maslin, be it commiserations or congratulations (the latter from Cutter). All the while, Rhis grew more irritated.

"Actually, I hadn't finished." He coughed as everyone looked at him. I nodded for him to continue. This was an ongoing situation, after all.

"After I disposed of the bodies, the rest of the serving staff came, this time to actually clean up the table. They did complain about some of their number being missing, but managed an adequate job nonetheless."

"You left them alone?" I asked. That didn't square with the Rhis that I knew, and did suggest that he was actually conforming to my expectations.

"They did not leave the common area, so I judged them no threat. That was . . . four hours ago. It's still the middle of the night, so I believe there will be no further developments until dawn."

"I wouldn't count on that," I said. "Someone was counting on me showing up at the doorstep unconscious about four hours ago."

I started going through my logs. There were a lot of new entries. I counted as part of Maslin's party, apparently, because even though I hadn't contributed to the result, I had shared in the risk. So there were XP for that, additional XP from people dying in my dungeon, more XP for the fact that Maslin and the others had earned XP in my dungeon . . . *If someone hasn't set up a fighting arena in their dungeon . . . then I guess they care more about people than XP.* Hell of a hack, though; I was getting XP coming and going.

The entry I was actually looking for was there as well.

> **You have defeated Finley Arryen in an Intrigue. You have earned 245 XP.**

I groaned. "Duke Arryen. That's who was behind this."

"I thought you said he wouldn't be coming after you," Janie said.

"I thought he'd be curious enough to negotiate," I replied. "This is apparently how he negotiates."

"Wait, so he was going to kidnap you and then start a negotiation?" Felicia said incredulously.

"Negotiating from a position of strength," I said wryly. "Anyway, we've now escalated things, so I doubt we can count on his 'restraint' from now on."

"Should I not have killed them?" Rhis asked.

I wanted to say yes, but even if kidnapping was a step down from murder, we couldn't let it happen. "No, you did the right thing with the information you had," I said. "You did good, Rhis. You too, Maslin."

"Now we have to figure out how to get out of this mess."

PLAⰓ

This wasn't great. Right now, I wanted to focus on Maslin. Killing three people, self-defense or not, was a lot to have asked a nine-year-old. Even a super-powered one.

Super-powered was probably an overstatement. While Maslin was stronger than any of my ex-boyfriends, I could probably beat him at arm wrestling. Probably. It depended on what his level was, and how he'd spent his stats.

All of which was a distraction from the real matter at hand.

"So the situation is," I said to the group, "that Duke Finley is missing some of his assassins, that he wants—or *wanted*—to kidnap me, and we are sitting on an illegal dungeon. Oh, and we murdered three people."

That might have been double counting the same item, but I did feel that the repercussions of eliminating Duke Finley's assassins needed to be counted separately from the result of killing three of the King's servants.

"If it helps, evidence of their existence here no longer exists," Rhis said, a little too proudly in my opinion.

I took a deep breath. "That does actually help," I admitted. "But for future reference, in the absence of a life or death threat, it's *more* helpful to not commit the crime than it is to conceal the evidence of it."

"Understood," Rhis said, nodding seriously as if I had dispensed some profound wisdom.

"I'm sorry," Felicia said, looking up from where she was fussing over Maslin. "This is all my fault. I'm the Alchemist; I should have been quicker with an antidote."

"No, Felicia, this caught us all off guard," I said. "And right after we were warned about just that. Diagnosing and finding an antidote is expecting too much from someone who's just been drugged."

"If I can make a suggestion." Rhis raised his hand, a habit he must have picked up along with English. "I should be able to make an item that would detect poisons or drugs, given enough time to accumulate mana."

"How long?" I asked.

"It's difficult to say right now," he replied, with a thoughtful look. "The mana density here fluctuates strongly. I haven't had enough time to establish a pattern . . . but perhaps two or three days. More if I am forced to exert myself to protect you, of course."

"Do the corpses help with that?" Kyle asked with studious neutrality.

"The corpses provide XP, which is appreciated, and raw materials. However, a magical item requires a mana-enhanced metal of some sort, which they sadly lacked."

That was tempting. Dangerously tempting, in fact.

"Just how easy is it . . . to tell if there's a dungeon around?" I wondered. From the blank looks and shaken heads, no one actually knew. I turned on my mana sense and looked at the wall that separated us from my dungeon. It was . . . hard to tell. I thought I could sense a general movement of free mana, but I was too close to really get an idea.

"I need to go outside and take a look," I said.

"It's the middle of the night," Janie pointed out.

I shrugged. "I'm sure the guards have had crazier requests than a midnight walk. I'll just tell them I couldn't sleep. They'll probably want to escort me, but I just need a quick look." I looked down at myself to see if I was in a fit state to go out, and I saw that I wasn't.

"Ugh, who spilled this drugged wine on me?" I asked rhetorically. At least *this* I could fix. I cast Disguise, and put myself in a different, clean dress. "Wish me luck," I said, heading for the door.

It wasn't long before I hurried back in. "Bad news, guys. It's visible." I wasn't sure if the reason I could see mana at night was because the grounds were well lit, or because mana wasn't *seen*, exactly. Whatever the reason, it was pretty clear we were screwed once people woke up.

"There's a big mana funnel right over our rooms," I told the others. "It's not moving very fast, but it's very clearly visible. Sorry, Rhis, we're going to have to disable the dungeon."

"Must you?" Rhis asked petulantly. "I don't relish returning to that imbecilic state."

"Well . . . can you cast Conceal Mana?" I asked. "Since you can do illusions."

Rhis brightened at the thought and got an absent look on his face. "I can . . . but only as a trap field," he said with a disappointed look. "It can only affect the mana inside my domain," he explained to our confused looks.

Can I do it? With Theurgy, it should be possible. I had an example spell to work with, my own Conceal Mana. That was actually a very sophisticated spell for its level, with multiple options at cast time. If I was doing it myself, I wouldn't need all those additional complications, but I would have to change the target and range limitations . . .

"Let me think about this for a second," I told the others and summoned the spell construct to mind. This was something I could do now, just . . . consider a complex structure as if I was looking at it. Enhanced Intelligence for the win.

If I got rid of this . . . extended this . . . and turned that around . . .

It seemed doable . . . until I looked at the power requirements. This was looking like a level fifteen spell at least. Probably a level twenty. Which would mean getting a casting total of more than 200. Unfortunately, Theurgy was based on Intelligence. At my current score and level, I'd need . . . a seven in the skill.

So that was out. I was just going to have to accept that I wouldn't be as good as other magics as I was at illusions. Something nagged at me, though. This *was* an illusion spell. Surely what I needed to do was create a new Illusion Magic spell, rather than doing it through Theurgy.

Exactly how to do that was beyond me at the moment though. "Sorry Rhis, I can't cast it myself, we're going to have to shut you down."

"Yes, Mistress," Rhis said sadly. "I'll undo the spatial expansion then."

"Do we have to worry about the stuff you've stored away?" I asked, carefully not mentioning that the only thing he should have were the corpses of our assassins.

"I can purge that into . . . actually, I'm not sure where it goes," Rhis mused. "Unless you wanted any of it?"

"No . . . send it away if you can. Is there a better way of deactivating you than what we did before?"

"Probably not," Rhis told me. "There is a shutdown procedure, but I suspect . . . it returns the core to a default state. I'd prefer it if you repeated your rash and unconsidered action from before."

"Happy to," I said wryly.

"I'm ready now," he said simply. I nodded and entered the common room. This time it was normally sized. The only difference from the room

I remembered was the crystal core, perched on a short pedestal about a foot high in the middle of the room.

"Please proceed," said the illusion of Rhis, which had followed me in. I sighed, and without further ceremony grabbed the orb and pulled it out of its socket.

> **Dungeon core has been removed from external mana construct. Five minutes before external construct unravels.**

"I—" Rhis said, and then was cut off, disappearing.

"Rhis!" I said, but there wasn't anything I could do right now. The orb in my hands was shrinking, the mana it was composed of twisting and reconfiguring as I watched. Trying to link the illusion to it was probably a wasted effort. In any case, Rhis wasn't the illusion; he was what I was holding in my hand.

Not wanting to be inside when the construct collapsed, I stepped out of the room.

"I hope there isn't any damage," I said to the expectantly waiting others. "It would be hard to explain."

"I think the damage in Oakway was mostly caused by the spatial expansion collapsing," Felicia said uncertainly. "Since he didn't make any actual changes, it should be fine?"

"That's what I'm hoping," I agreed. We all waited anxiously for the five minutes to expire. When it did, there wasn't a crunch or an explosion or anything. We opened the connecting door and peered gingerly through it.

"Seems okay," I said.

"Let me go first," Kyle said, and cautiously stepped inside. He took three steps in, looking carefully around. "Seems just the same as before," he said.

One at a time, we all entered back into the room, checking that all the doors still worked and led to the same rooms that they had before. Eventually, we all took our seats in the restored common room, and I reattached Rhis's enchantment.

"Hello! That was weird," he said, looking around. "I said some pretty mean things about myself, didn't I?"

"You remember all that?" I asked.

"Sort of," he replied. "A lot of it is quite fuzzy, but what I said, what you said, is pretty clear."

"I like *this* you better," Maslin interjected. He was sitting between Janie and Felicia on the couch but was seemingly feeling better. "The other you was mean."

"Well, that's too bad, because I'll be back to that as soon as possible, right?" Rhis said, looking at me.

"When we can do it safely," I agreed. "You're not worried about your own self getting subsumed into the larger construct?" While super-intelligent Rhis was more useful, I had to admit that I liked . . . mini-Rhis better than his bigger self as well.

Rhis looked at me, puzzled. "No? I'm different, but I'm not different people," he said. "Does that make sense?"

"Not a lot, but I think I understand." I turned back to the others. "Now that *that* is settled, we need to deal with the rest of it."

"That?" Felicia asked.

"You know, the bit where we got attacked while under the King's protection."

"Oh, right." Felicia flushed. "I did get distracted by . . ." she glanced at Maslin and elected not to continue.

"Right. So, any ideas on how this happened? If it was the wine, it was sealed when we came into the room."

"And you picked the bottle," Kyle pointed out. "So if it was poisoned beforehand, they would have had to poison all of them."

"Is it relevant that the wine steward was one of the assassins?" Rhis asked. We all looked at him. "Sorry, I forgot to mention that?"

"Forgot?" I asked. Forgetting didn't sound like Construct Rhis.

Rhis smiled sheepishly. "More like . . . didn't think it was relevant?" He frowned in thought. "It's fuzzy, but I think I wanted the conversation to go a different way?"

He wanted us to focus on the magical detector, I realized. *Have us keep him around for a bit longer. Interesting.* It seemed that he was capable of some manipulation after all. Not terribly harmful—when it came down to it, I'd rather have the device than focus on the poisoner. But it was good to know that he could act in his own interests.

"That *is* relevant," I said. "If anyone could poison wine while it's being poured, it's the guy doing the pouring. Sleight of hand, do you think?"

"Maybe some sort of ability from his profession?" Janie suggested.

"That's disturbing. Is there some sort of—" It was easier to query the System than it was to finish the question. There was a Poisoner profession.

Profession: Poisoner

Development Cost: 10

Description: The Poisoner slips through society, striking at his enemies with equal amounts of subtlety and viciousness.

Prerequisites: Level 4 – Intelligence 6 – Herbalism

Skill Unlocks: [Intrigue], [Legerdemain], [Acting]

Skill Bonuses: [Cooking], [Intrigue], [Herbalism] +2 , [Weapon Mastery – Dagger]

Extra: Infuse Dose

There wasn't further help on Infuse Dose, but it did sound like something that could have been used here.

"Nasty," Janie commented when I passed that on to the others. "So where does that leave us?"

"If the wine steward was the Poisoner," I mused, "then we probably don't have to worry about further attacks of that nature. Duke Finley can't have that many Poisoners in the King's employ."

"Not the only guy that wants to kill you, though," Janie pointed out.

"Can we get one of those rings without setting up our own dungeon?" I asked.

"I've never heard of a dungeon that offered that," Kyle said. "Doesn't mean there isn't one."

"We could ask Enchanter Mandel to get his dungeon to do it," Felicia pointed out. "He's not so concerned with people finding out about him now."

"Can you enchant one yourself?" Janie asked.

"I don't know of a Detect Poison rune," I said. I looked at Rhis. "Is there one?"

"I don't think so?" Rhis answered. "You can detect a single thing though, so if you hook up a bunch of them together, along with some . . . other stuff that looks for poisons you don't know about, you can get pretty good results."

I sighed, "When you say a bunch, are you talking hundreds, or thousands of runes?"

"Um, too many for me to count, so the last one I guess."

"Right, so that's out. Instead, for now, let's just try to make sure that someone who isn't a kid is left out for any meals that we have together."

"Not *just* Felicia," I added as everyone looked at her. "We'll take turns, and Felicia can put together an antidote pack for that person to hold."

Everyone murmured agreement, so I moved on to the next item. "The next thing is what we tell the King's people in the morning. I'm thinking we don't tell them anything."

"And let Duke Finley get away with it?" Felicia protested.

"I know. But the only reason we know it's him is the Intrigue notification, and they can't be shared." I looked around at the others. "So it comes down to our—well, my word against his, and he's a noble. Plus we'd have to come up with a good explanation of how we survived."

"I get it. It's just like the orphanage," Cutter put in, surprising everyone. "You don't go snitching to the grown-ups. Someone does you, you do them back."

Maslin nodded slowly, if not agreeing, then at least understanding the argument.

"I guess it is the same," I agreed. "In both cases, you don't have someone you can trust to judge fairly, so you have to take matters into your own hands."

"Is he going to do the same? Just write off his losses?"

"Oh, I'm sure he'll come after us looking to recover them," I said slowly. "That's how the game is played, after all. This is just the opening round."

TOUR

Given all that had happened the previous night, just going about my day made me feel as though I were walking on eggshells. But nobody arrested us in the morning. We hadn't slept at all—aside from the enforced five hours that most of us got thanks to the wine. Maslin . . . finally dropped off. We didn't want to wake him for breakfast, so we left him in Rhis's care and got ourselves escorted to the dining hall.

Breakfast was as good as you might expect from it being served in an actual palace. Even if we were eating with the staff. The dining hall served both staff and the palace guests—at least the lower-ranked ones. I noticed a conspicuous absence of nobles.

It would have been a good time to meet the other guests of the Court, but we were apparently early. Perhaps that was another reason we weren't seeing any nobles. Rather than wait around for someone important to show up, we got on with our business. Which was, first of all, a tour.

We would have the run of the palace, aside from sensitive areas that were barred off by guards, once we knew where everything was. A lot of it was private rooms, but there were some areas—the stables, meeting rooms, laundry, etc., that we'd need to know the location of.

For some definition of "we," I suppose. Our escort was surprised that I'd want to know the location of the laundry. He expected that I'd have servants to take care of that. Which would have been nice. Maslin and Cutter were sort of taking a servant's *role*, but they weren't really servants. They were part of the team. Sharing things equally meant that we all took a turn with such things.

Fortunately, that didn't mean Cutter was handling my underwear at any point. I was still conjuring fresh Phantasmal underclothes each morning and would continue to do so until this world invented elastic.

Surprised or not, our escort happily showed us around wherever we asked, and took us to a few places we hadn't thought of. There was a lot to see, and it took us until lunch to see it all.

After lunch, I had another request.

"Is there a tower or some high point that gives a view of the city?" I asked the guard.

He frowned. "Most of those locations are strategic, my lady. Occupied by the army. There's not an alert current, so I could request access . . ."

"Could you? That would be most helpful."

He sighed and nodded. "If you'll wait here, I'll see what can be done."

Not long after that, we were standing on what looked to be the third highest point of the city, looking down on it all. The normal exhilaration of a fantastic view was considerably enhanced by my improved eyesight.

"Isn't this fantastic?" I asked Maslin, standing beside me. He looked down with me, still quiet. We had picked him up for lunch and kept him with us afterwards. He seemed . . . okay. I shared a concerned glance with the others and then returned my attention to the view. It really was incredible to see the whole city laid out like a model. I could . . . almost make out individual apples being sold on the streets below. That wasn't what I was here for, though, so I turned my attention and Mana Sense to the air above the city.

The three dungeons were easy to make out, now that I knew what to look for. I had seen the three mana funnels before, but I hadn't recognized them, partially blocked out by the other mana structures and the wild mana that filled the air. Here, I had a pretty good view.

One of the funnels, the biggest, rose from behind me, coming from a more secure part of the palace compound. The other two were on the edges of the city. Underneath, I could see what looked like fortifications that had been incorporated into the city's walls.

The two lesser dungeons formed an angle of about 120 degrees from the bigger one and were about the same distance away. Symmetry suggested that there would be a fourth dungeon to complete the circle, but I saw nothing special when I looked to where it would be. That spot was behind the main funnel from where I was, so my view wasn't the best, but I was fairly certain I'd have seen another funnel if it were there. They were difficult to miss.

Apart from the dungeons, I tried to get a handle on how the rest of the mana was organized. My immediate conclusion was that it wasn't. Massive conduits of mana came in from all directions, but what happened to them when they entered the city seemed almost random.

One massive conduit came in and seemed to go directly into the palace. It either went into the dungeon or somewhere near. Another entered an obelisk on the city wall and was split into a dozen smaller streams that went to different places in the city. I noted the locations, as they were probably important.

Those ones made some sort of sense. But another conduit seemed to have snapped, waving lazily over the city, spewing uncontrolled mana everywhere. Another was rubbing against one of the great gears of the natural mana machinery. Invisible and insubstantial to most things, the gear was apparently unaffected by the conduit, but the conduit was taking a battering. While it still seemed connected to its destination, large amounts of mana leaked out with every hit of a tooth.

Was it designed this way? An inevitable consequence of this much concentrated mana? Or was it incompetence on the part of the ones who were supposed to manage it all?

Whatever the cause, that wasn't what I was here for. This mana mess just might be an opportunity. The funnel from my dungeon had been much smaller than these ones were. Possibly, it was small enough to conceal in all this mess, if I could find the right spot. The palace, of course, being right out.

It might seem odd to set up shop right under the nose of the King, but the incredible mana density made me think that it was feasible, in a way that it wouldn't have been back in Talnier. There might have been just enough mana in town—or just out of it—to run a dungeon, but it would have stood out like a sore thumb. Here, not only was there more mana, but the jumble of structures made me think I could keep it undetected, at least for a while.

I took note of some promising areas and then we headed back down. The next step was to ask our escort for a tour of the city.

Dorsay's Adventurers Guild was different from all the others I'd seen thus far. Instead of a fun place for adventurers to hang out, it was all business. The tavern, a fixture in every other guild hall, was replaced with trading booths. Adventurers waited patiently in line to trade in their goods that they presumably got from one of the dungeons. Most of them must have had spatial items, as there was a distinct lack of bloody bags.

The walls of the place were unadorned opalime stone, the floor marble. It looked rich but plain at the same time. The whole place practically screamed "no time wasters."

"Maybe Cloridan won't complain so much about being left behind when I tell him about this," Janie said, looking around with distaste. "This doesn't seem fun at all."

"I'm sure there's some place where adventures go for fun, but this looks all business," I agreed.

"Hi, I'm just here to check in," I said, walking up to one of the free receptionists and flashing my guild card. "I was given to understand that the Guild Master would want to talk to me when I arrived in town."

"I can pass on the news of your arrival," the attendant said, looking at my card closely and making a note. I smiled, amused. Previously, I'd only used my guild cards in the town that had issued them, so there hadn't been a lot of doubt about my identity. This might have been the first time my card was actually examined.

"We can contact you if the Guild Master wants to speak with you. Have you got an address we can find you?"

"I'm staying at the palace," I said easily, as if it was no big deal. "I can be contacted through them."

That did put a crack in her composure, but only a small one. She rallied and made another note. "Of course. I'll let the Guild Master know. Was there anything else?"

"Hmm. The Guild has a dungeon here, doesn't it?"

"Yes. The Guild manages the Adamant Guardians Mine, here in the city."

"I was given to understand that access to it was more restricted than the dungeons I'm used to. Is there some sort of application process, or should I just mention it to the Guild Master when I speak with him?"

I'd been led to believe we wouldn't get access to the dungeon here, nor did I know if we were going to be here long enough to use it, but it never hurt to ask. The receptionist gave me a long look.

"Certainly the Guild Master would be able to override anything that was allowed or denied by the standard process," she said carefully. "So perhaps it would be best to talk to him first."

I nodded. "Lastly, do you have any information about adventurer-friendly taverns in the city?" I asked, glancing at Janie.

"Of course," she said, handing me a piece of paper crudely printed with a list of names. I passed it on to Janie, who started perusing it intently.

"You may also want this," she said, handing me another list. "Crafters that offer a discount to Guild members."

"Thanks, that will be very helpful," I said. It probably wouldn't be that useful. Prices in the city were said to be ridiculously high. It couldn't hurt to check them out, though, and a discount was always nice.

The rest of our outing was fairly uneventful. We checked out the shops, but while the equipment was good, the prices were insane—about three times the price we could get in Talnier.

There was one other incident of note, though.

"Not that way, ma'am. Better to move two blocks down before going in this direction," Tyler, the guard escorting me, said.

"Is there something wrong with this street?" I asked. Unless I'd gotten confused, this street led to one of the more mana-dense areas that I'd been looking at before.

"Not exactly. . . ." Tyler hesitated, trying to come up with an explanation. "It's just not populated by the . . . best elements in the city."

"Is there some sort of danger? Even with you here?" I asked, somewhat disingenuously. The impression I got from the guard was that he matched my own level, and that of our group. That was high for a guard in my experience, but I wasn't sure if it was because everything was better in the city, or if we'd been assigned an elite. Either way, though, we should be able to take care of ourselves.

"No, it's just not . . . a good place to visit," he said awkwardly.

"You've got me curious now," I said, and turned to walk down the street. He followed reluctantly. I looked around, taking a keen interest in whatever unsavory elements I'd been warned about. My main interest was in the mana, though.

Ah. It didn't take long to see what the problem was. It would be more obvious at night, but even in the harsh light of day, a brothel still had to advertise.

"Don't worry, Tyler," I called back over my shoulder. "We're from a frontier town; this sort of thing isn't going to shock us."

He mumbled something but I didn't really listen. This was a much better area for my purposes than the other two had been. No doubt because of its status, the street was looking quite dilapidated. Not every house was a brothel, but everyone on the street was tarred with the same brush. It should be quite cheap to rent a place here, and it might well go unnoticed for some time.

If there was a better place to put a dungeon, I doubted that I'd find it easily.

AUDIENCE

I stood still in the middle of the room, the center of everyone's attention. The welcoming ceremony was supposed to be a chance for the King to look over his guests without committing himself to a conversation. Perhaps a holdover from the early days, when everyone might not have been vetted to within an inch of their lives before getting into the palace. These days, though, the King knew a lot about me before I'd even met him.

He hadn't arrived yet, which was why I was standing, waiting. My entire team—minus Rhis—was standing a little way behind me, all of us waiting for the King to bless us with his presence. While we waited, though, there was an opportunity for every other member of the Court to gawk at us standing there. I felt a bit objectified.

The whole room was set up to impress on the guests their inferiority to those gathered to watch them. The King's throne sat on a dais directly in front of us, of course. He wasn't occupying it yet, but I assumed he would be very impressive when he did. On each side of the room there was an additional dais, with three tiers of chairs, rising towards the back so that everyone could get a good view.

The top row held just four chairs, two on each side. On one side, both the chairs were occupied by richly dressed older men. Given their position and obvious status, I figured I was looking at two of the Kingdom's dukes. Though why there were four chairs when there were only three dukes, I didn't know.

Irritatingly, I didn't know who was who. Portraits of important people, even as important as a duke, just weren't around. One of them looked older, but it might just be that his skin had seen harsher weather. Aside from that, he seemed hale enough, and his full head of brown hair suggested that he wasn't *that* old.

The other one had auburn hair, darkening to brown at the tips. Dyed, I supposed? A duke could probably afford expensive hair treatments. He had paler skin, nicely set off by his darker clothes.

The next level held just one person I knew, and I wasn't pleased to see him. Aubert Duvost. He didn't seem any more pleased to see me. Every time I looked at him, he was glaring at me, only to look away when I met his gaze.

Well, fine, I thought. *Be that way.* Interestingly, he was all on his own. Most of the lesser nobles were seated in groups and were idly chatting as they looked us over. Intrigue kicked in, pointing out the obvious cliques. The two main ones were centered around the dukes, but there was a group of barons that seemed to have banded together. And there were a few, like Aubert, who stood alone. Did that mean Duke Victor wasn't present? Or was he on the outs with his liege?

There were other gawkers than the ones seated. A few people were standing near the King's dais, all of whom were wearing official garb that I could identify. There were also a few others standing about at the sides, either up on the nobles' dais, standing next to the chairs, or at my level. The only one of these that I could put a name to with any certainty was the one wearing all black, who had to be the Ebon Order's emissary to Dorsay.

Tom Parkes had wanted to come with me, but he had told me that he was unable to and that I should contact Envoy Manuela Fisher if I needed anything from his master, the Ice Arcanist Aghen Shadhe. It was just a guess, based on his stiff formality when talking about her, that Tom and the envoy didn't get along. She was examining all of the guests, myself included, with equal intensity.

She actually made for a pretty striking figure, her unnaturally pale skin setting off the unrelieved black of her ensemble. The look was somewhat spoiled by her curly brown hair. She should have gone full goth and dyed it black. Still, she seemed friendly enough. When her gaze met mine, she gave me a smile that was probably intended to be warm.

As for my fellow guests, they were an eclectic bunch. There were two other groups, seemingly each composed of one emissary and their entourage, just like mine. At least, like mine, one person was standing in front. None of them were dressed in what I thought of as Latorran fashion, so I guessed that they were from other countries.

The leader of the delegation next to mine saw that I was looking at them and sighed. Dressed almost all in white, he had honey-colored skin and hair of such a light brown that it almost matched it.

"Annoying, is it not? To be scrutinized like meat at a market." He shook his head ruefully. "Such is the way that they put us in our place."

I nodded in agreement, paying close attention to the actual sounds coming out of his mouth. It wouldn't do to give away that I could understand his language if he stopped speaking Latorran. Now that he was looking at me, I could see that his face seemed to glisten wetly. Some sort of cosmetic? Or moisturizer? He *was* wearing makeup, the overdone eyeliner making him look even more exotic.

He grinned at me. "Ambassador Gavril, from Lyran, is very pleased to make your acquaintance."

I bowed my head slightly. "Kandis Hammond, representative from the Talnier Town Council."

He raised an eyebrow. "Your level is unusual for that post, is it not? Does not Latorran custom put the beautiful Councillors behind high walls and stern guards?"

"I wasn't always a Councillor," I explained. Since he'd brought it up, I thought to feel out his level. He felt . . . less powerful than myself, probably level four, despite being older than me. I guessed he was also a beneficiary of those stern guards. There was a level six in his entourage, a sour-looking woman, but the rest of them struck me as level four or less.

"I would have expected a high-status position like yours would have required a high level," I continued.

"Oh no," he replied. "We ambassadors are just the deliverer of messages, yes? So it is better if we are not a possible threat."

"I see . . ." I said. It occurred to me that this might be how high-level social types avoided getting into social clashes. If they sent a proxy, it didn't matter if the proxy got Persuaded. It would have worn off by the time they got back home, and the actual ruler would be entirely unaffected. In my world, ambassadors had the authority to make actual deals, but I would bet that the same wasn't true here.

I was about to say something more, but trumpets blared out, signaling the entrance of the King. Yes, trumpets. I guess when you're the King, there's no such thing as overstatement.

The King entered the room from somewhere behind the throne, appearing in front of us already standing on the dais. The pressure of his presence hit us like a blow.

Level eight at least, I thought. I would have winced, but I was already descending, falling into a curtsy so low I would have fallen without my enhanced strength. Everyone else was doing the same or kneeling on one knee in the case of the men. We had all been briefed on the proper protocol.

"Presenting His Majesty Alexandros Pavlas, Protector of Latora, Duke of Risurn, and Admiral of the Eastern Seas." That was the Master of Ceremonies speaking, the boss of the fellow that had met us on arrival.

We all stayed close to the floor, our heads bowed. There was a brief pause, presumably for His Majesty to look us all over.

"Rise," he said, lazily. We did as we were commanded, now able to look up at him sitting on his throne. He was certainly handsome enough. Looking about 35, he had a lot of long blond hair, dropping loose to his shoulders. Piercing blue eyes, even from this distance.

The Master of Ceremonies spoke up again. "Step forward, Shahbaz Savji."

The leader of the third delegation stepped forward and bowed. He was bald and dressed in a colorful, multilayered set of silk robes. Each layer looked quite thin, but together they must have been warm enough for the cooling autumn weather.

"A merchant from Avald. We have not heard from that land in some time," the King said.

"Yes, Your Majesty. Not since the mighty ships of your Empire left our shores."

"And why is it a merchant has come to see us, and not a diplomat?"

"Your Majesty, my nation has only recently gained the strength to manage long voyages across the ocean. Travelling here is too high a risk for those of importance to my nation. I do bring gifts, and a message from my rulers pledging further diplomatic overtures should I return."

I thought he had phrased that oddly. "Gained the strength." Were long voyages something that required strength? I wondered if there were monsters in the ocean that had to be overcome. That would make trading a bitch.

"Very well, I will speak to you at a later date." The man bowed again and stepped back. The Master of Ceremonies spoke up again.

"Step forward, Ambassador Oleg Gavril."

The man in white stepped forward, bowing deeply.

"I enjoyed working with your predecessor," the King said. "I hope we will have the same rapport going forward."

"Yes, Your Majesty," Oleg said. He bowed and stepped back.

"Step forward, Councillor Kandis Hammond."

I stepped forward and curtsied. Then I froze, still in the dip, as I felt the power of the King's Intimidation coil around me. I managed to look up—he didn't look any different, but I could feel the power coming off him. Had the others felt this as well? If so, they'd hidden it well.

"Ah, the representative from Talnier." The King didn't sound any different from when he'd talked to the others, but to me his voice had a weight to it. I'd been told what to say, I'd already intended to say it, but there was no way that I could say anything different.

"Yes, Your Majesty."

"I hear you've been running roughshod over my people in Talnier," he said, and now a hint of amusement ran through his voice. "As you can see, that won't be happening here."

"Yes, Your Majesty." I wanted to protest that I hadn't expected to dominate him socially. That the profits I'd made already, the projections of future earnings . . . these should be enough to convince him to continue with the experiment. Free cities were just *better* than captive towns run by corrupt tyrants. But even if I had thought this was the correct time and place, I couldn't speak up.

"We'll speak again soon," he promised me. "But do you know there is another purpose to this ceremony?"

The answer to that question was no, so I just stared mutely.

"It lets my petitioners see who they're dealing with," he explained. "It gives them a chance to run."

ΠETWORKIΠG

No, of course I'm not going to run," I said to the fifth minor noble that asked. "His Majesty was just amusing himself at my expense. I'm not going to abandon my fellow townsfolk just because of that."

This was the reception after the ceremony, a marginal step up in my opinion. Instead of gawking at the foreigners, the nobility now had a chance to mingle with them. Thanks to the King's little interventions, every one of them had the same conversation starter.

"How very brave of you," she prattled. Memorize could have recalled her name for me with a thought, but I was actively suppressing it. There were actually people I wanted to talk to at this party, but getting to them was no easy matter. There were rules for who could talk to whom, and as always they were rigged against me.

Every time I tried to make my way towards one of the dukes, some lady or lordling would intercept me and babble mindlessly until I found a polite way to get rid of them. Clearly, the rank disparity between us was not supposed to be simply traversed.

This latest obstacle did seem a cut above the previous ones, though. Perhaps I was making progress. She seemed to be getting a little irritated at my lukewarm responses. No doubt she was used to people paying attention to her, especially commoners. She was quite pretty.

Actually, that was unfair. There wasn't a woman here that wasn't staggeringly beautiful, by my world's standards. Charisma was in high demand among the nobility, and of course, there was no such thing as an ill-groomed noble. They cleaned up real nice.

Despite that, she stood out in even this crowd. Given that I wasn't getting a high level from her, she must have really leaned into her Charisma stat. She was beautiful and dressed to impress. Her pale skin, framed by her elaborately styled brown hair, practically glowed.

But I did look at myself in the mirror every morning. Not that I was vain or anything, but I knew how I looked, and it was better than her. So I gave her a faint smile and started talking about her hair.

"Do you like it?" she asked, holding her hand up so that it almost, but not quite, touched the fragile arrangement. "I'm not sure why I bother; it takes so long to get ready before an event."

"It's very nice," I agreed. "But it was the burgundy tips that caught my eye. Is that the latest fashion?"

I hadn't actually taken an interest in fashion. Not that I wasn't interested in fashion in general, but Latorran fashion had a few hundred years to catch up before it did something interesting. No, this was Conversation gently nudging our discourse to get to where I wanted to go.

I wasn't sure if the endless parade of minor nobility was a deliberate attempt to stop me from talking to anyone important, or if they were just enamored by the idea of being seen talking to the King's latest victim. Whatever the reason, I needed help. Either to run interference or to provide some sort of passage.

Unfortunately, my companions couldn't help me here. They counted as servants and weren't allowed in the nobles' area. It had been made clear that I *barely* qualified for the honor of mingling and wasn't in the position to bring any retainers. That was probably for the best, at least as far as Janie was concerned. I could only imagine the calamity that might result from her running interference for me. She was back at our apartment with the kids, while Kyle and Felicia watched over me from the sidelines. I imagined they were both bored and anxious at the same time.

So this lady would have to be her substitute. She was currently going on about how she was on the leading edge of the dyed tips thing, while I made appreciative noises. Who knows, perhaps it was true.

"Didn't I notice that one of the dukes had his hair styled that way?" I asked offhandedly.

"Duke Victor? Oh yes, he's always had a keen eye for style." She continued on, but I wasn't really listening. I would have grimaced if I was letting anything show on my face aside from polite admiration. Duke Victor would be Victor de Bargougne, Aubert's boss, and someone who wanted me dead. He wasn't my first choice for someone to talk to, but I'd have to take what I could get.

I let whatshername ramble on for a bit, talking about how close she was to the Duke, and how much he valued her advice. She was setting herself up, really.

"Oh, so you would be able to get me an introduction to His Grace?" I asked mildly. Charm threw in the title; I would never have guessed to call him that. But it was Persuasion that was doing the real work here. Her composure didn't slip, but it didn't feel great to be outdone socially when you had a Charisma-based build. As I could attest due to recent experience.

She fought it, but I beat her in Charisma and level so the outcome was already determined. The only question was . . .

You have defeated Marianne Rankin in a Tier 3 Social Contest! You have earned 20 XP.

Did I know that name from somewhere? Probably from when she introduced herself and I wasn't paying attention. I dismissed the feeling of familiarity and focused on the notification. Tier three. So she hadn't wanted to introduce me. Not as close to the Duke as she claimed, or had she been actually trying to impede me? Well, it didn't matter now, I supposed. I gave her a warm smile and let her lead me to the Duke.

"Lady Rankin," Duke Victor de Bargougne said sourly. "Just what have you brought me?" Up close, I could feel that his level was definitely higher than mine. Not as much as the King's, though, so level seven? It was hard to be sure. I needed, even if I did not want, more experience facing higher levelled people. I thought I had a higher Charisma at least, but I didn't fancy my chances of trying any social skills.

We both curtsied. "My lord," Lady Rankin said, "may I present Councillor Hammond, from the Talnier Town Council."

"A free commoner from what was once my Duchy," he replied. "How disgraceful."

"It was the King's will," I said carefully. "Blame your vassal for provoking such a response with his flagrant criminality."

He frowned. "Easy enough to blame the dead."

I raised an eyebrow. "Did the King not share with you the reports from his Inquisitor?" I asked. "His wife fled, rather than face an accounting. Monies from his criminal endeavors were found in the treasury. If you ask me, his *disappearance* was due to him feeling that the Inquisitor was closing in and absconding."

I was treading on pretty thin ice here, but while this was an obvious lie, I didn't think he would call me on it. We both knew that Reece was never going to actually charge Marseau for anything, but it would be interesting for the Duke to admit that the nobles were immune to prosecution.

He chose . . . not to do that. "Perhaps," he allowed. "Was there anything else you wanted?"

"Just to pass on the well wishes of the town, and express our hope for good relations in the future," I said.

He snorted. "It's *Anchorbury* that's your neighbor," he scoffed. "Why don't you go see Lord Aubert and establish some relations there."

"As you say, my lord," I said, feeling the dismissal. I curtsied again and backed off. Contrary to my orders, though, I didn't seek out Aubert. Not that I would have been able to—once I left the Duke's orbit, the crowd started flocking me again. Still, I might have accomplished what I needed to . . .

As if by magic, the crowd suddenly melted away, leaving only one man behind. The second duke, the man with the really weathered face.

"Duke Finley, I presume?" I said and curtsied again. I was doing a lot of that. There was a chance that this was the third duke . . . of Saarwald. But given that Finley had sent his men after me last night, it seemed likely that he'd be here.

"Hammond," he said, not giving me the courtesy of a title. Since he didn't correct me, I must have been right. *For every action, there is an equal and opposite reaction,* I mused. *As true in society as it is in physics.* Duke Victor deigning to talk to me had provoked his opposite number to come and seek me out.

"I sent for you to attend me last night," he said without preamble. A single crease formed across his forehead as he frowned. "You didn't arrive."

That's how you're going to play this? I let my surprise show. "Really, my lord? I didn't receive any such message." I gave it a moment, and then added, "Perhaps your messengers were untrustworthy."

He frowned some more. "Perhaps," he said. "I will have to investigate."

Good luck with that. Say what you like about a dungeon's murderous appetites, they were at least good at cleaning up the evidence. I curtsied again.

"Since Your Grace has expressed an interest, when would be a good time for me to call on you?"

As far as I knew, the dukes did not reside in the palace but had their own mansions in the city. That meant that if I called on the Duke, I would have my own escort of palace guards. They might not be able to stop his own troops, but he would have to have second thoughts before assaulting the King's men. That might have been the reason he narrowed his eyes and glared at me.

"I don't discuss my appointments in public," he said. "I will send another message."

I curtsied again. "I look forward to it."

With that, he turned and left. *Well, that was something.* It seemed, though, that I was playing this game correctly. He hadn't called me out for murdering his agents and he hadn't tried to blackmail me for it either. He hadn't seemed pleased, so I was going to call it a win.

Now I just had to—I was given a brief warning by the way that the lordlings who had started to close in suddenly backed off. It wasn't enough time to look around, though, so I was blindsided by someone grabbing my arm and moving in close.

"Well, for a newbie, you certainly have the ear of important people," said the woman who had grabbed onto me. I looked over to see a cute face framed with brown hair, and grey eyes that seemed to know all my secrets.

"Envoy Fisher," I replied coldly, trying to express my disapproval of being grabbed. As I had expected, though, she was unfazed.

"Tch, call me Manuela," she said. "This is what happens when I leave the introductions to Tom, he poisons everyone against me."

"I'm sure that wasn't his intention," I told her, trying to extricate myself from her grasp. I managed it, but only because she let me go. She was definitely stronger than me, which wasn't a surprise. She was around the same level, and I hadn't invested heavily in Strength.

"Definitely!" she agreed. "I bet he told you to come to find me if you needed anything, our master is a good guy and just wants to help, blah blah blah."

"That was the gist of it," I confirmed. "But I haven't really needed—"

"Yes, yes, Master is scary and you don't want to get involved. Tom did say that you were keeping your distance."

"Well, some," I admitted.

"Boring! I despise the hands-off approach!" She gave me a wide grin and a wink. "Though I have to admire you managing to keep your hands off Tom." She clapped her hand against my shoulder. "Or maybe not! Aren't you supposed to be an adventurer?"

I rolled my eyes. "Sorry for trying to keep things a *little* professional."

"Pfft," she scoffed. "I'll show Tom how to convince you of our good intentions, and that's by not taking no for an answer!" She grabbed me by my arm again. "Now, let's get you introduced to all the people that you need to meet!"

ANOTHER MEETING

◆

I thought she'd never give up," the voice commented as I entered the room.
I froze, briefly panicking. That was an unfamiliar voice, and this was *my*
room. It only took a glance to see the source, a man sitting on my chaise
longue chair. More than just unfamiliar, though, he was just plain wrong.

To start with, he was dressed in a modern-day suit. Aside from the
color, he wouldn't have looked out of place in the middle of a group of
investment bankers. The color was its own issue. I doubt Brooks Brothers
ever made a suit in burgundy. The dress shirt was a vivid crimson, and the
tie was jet-black.

As for the man himself, he was just slightly off looking like a human.
I might have dismissed the red tinge to his skin, but the whites of his eyes
were grey, and his irises were a black to match his tie.

"Since you're not sure, let me confirm that she absolutely wanted to get
you drunk and into bed." He spoke the words with a casual assurance that
made me think for a second that he belonged here.

"Who are you?" I asked, but I was already down to a short list. There
were only five gods that generally presented as male, and I'd already met
one of them. I'd avoided drinking too much tonight, for what had clearly
been wise reasons, but what little alcohol that remained in my system was
burned out through pure adrenaline.

"Ashmor," he said, smiling. He gestured for me to take the other seat.

"Is this another one of those memory hacks?" I asked cautiously as I sat
myself down. There wasn't much point in being ready for a fight; if there was
one thing that everyone agreed on, it was that you *couldn't* fight the gods.

"Oh no," he said, "I couldn't possibly stand to spend so much time contemplating the minutiae of your consciousness. "Fyskal just likes to show

off. No. I am really here; your friends are just outside, asleep, and no one is going to disturb us."

"What did you do to them?" I demanded. Just his mention of them put me on edge, even though, before he spoke, I would have assumed they were all asleep. Manuela had kept me up late.

"Such concern, it warms the heart," he said, with obvious insincerity. "Relax, they are all quite fine. I haven't done anything to them. In fact, I've taken quite a liking to that Maslin boy."

"What about him?" I asked warily.

"Why, his actions, of course. Killing three people at such a young age, even if he did have help. Very commendable. And he's taking up Fire Magic, which is my own little gift to this world. I think I shall have to bestow a blessing on him."

"Isn't that like a drop in the bucket, as far as your goals are concerned?" I asked, genuinely puzzled. I wanted to ask about the blessing, but I could probably find out about that later. Insight into the motivations of the gods was far rarer.

"Oh, much less than that," Ashmor corrected me. "But then, humans are so much smaller than me. Given how much less capable you are, it's all the more pleasing when one of you chooses to make a small contribution to the cause."

I refrained from rolling my eyes. Ashmor wanted to destroy every part of this world, and he was only restrained from doing so by the powers of the other gods. He wasn't *perfectly* restrained, though, so it wouldn't do to provoke him.

"Oh, relax," he said, apparently reading my mind. "I already promised Fyskal and your patron that I wouldn't harm their current pawn."

"You know who my patron is?" I asked, and then flushed. Of course he knew.

"Indeed." Ashmor grinned. "It's not what I came here for, but I'm always up for another deal. I'll tell you who it is . . . if you kill someone for me."

"Are you crazy?" I asked incredulously.

"It doesn't matter who, or why," he continued. "Just as long as you do it with your own hands, or spells."

"I'm not . . ." I said, then stopped. It wasn't as if I could say I was above killing. There was blood on my hands already, just not directly. And it wasn't as if I could promise him—or myself—that I wouldn't ever kill.

The asshole could see all of this going through my mind, of course, so he just smiled as he waited for me to get through it.

"Now, as to why I'm here."

"*How* are you here?" I asked, not willing to let him get to the point. "I thought you weren't a part of this game that they're playing."

"I didn't sign up to their *rules*," he said. "But since their game encompasses everything, I am most definitely a part of it." I opened my mouth to object, but he continued on. "There *is* a general agreement to keep me from interfering, but certain small actions are too minor for them to worry about."

"Like whatever this is," I said.

"Simply a conversation, and a gift of knowledge. I'm going to tell you how to get home."

I felt a surge of hope, which I immediately tamped down on. *Stop it, you idiot, it's clearly a trap.* Ashmor just smiled and waited for me to calm down.

"Fyskal said that the gods couldn't get me back home," I said flatly.

"It's true, we can't," Ashmor said easily. "But there is someone who can, and I can tell you how to find them."

"And the price?"

"It's free. But first, if you'll permit, a brief diversion."

I sighed. "Go on."

"When I speak of the barrier between worlds, I know you're sophisticated enough to know that I'm not speaking of some kind of physical wall that separates us from the rest of the multiverse—to use your world's term."

"Sure," I said. "Higher dimensional construct, puny human mind cannot comprehend, etcetera, etcetera."

"Exactly," he said, pleased. "But for the purposes of this discussion, we can consider it as a shell that surrounds us, much like that of an egg." He made two eggs appear out of nowhere and they started floating in midair, slowly rotating around each other.

"They float in something that is not space but nonetheless separates them." As he spoke, a sphere of some clear, iridescent liquid surrounded the two eggs. "The nature of this not-space is a mystery even to us," he told me.

"This, then, is the essence of your problem," he continued, gesturing at his arrangement. "You need to physically travel through two barriers that can't be traversed."

"That can't be right," I said, after a moment of staring at his model. "Demons manage it."

"Exactly." Tiny flecks of black appeared around the eggs and started flitting back and forth. "Demons somehow exist in the not-space. How they do so is beyond our understanding, but they do."

"And they can traverse the shell."

"They can *break* the barrier, but only from the inside." The two eggs started undergoing changes. On one, a small hole appeared, big enough to accommodate a single fleck. The other cracked as if it were going into a frying pan. The contents spilled out and were consumed somehow, either by the iridescent liquid or by the crowd of specks that swarmed around it.

"These two examples demonstrate the range of possibilities," he said. "One of them is the one you want, the other is the one I want."

I stared at the emptied eggshell. "I just don't understand how—"

"Obviously," he sneered. "But focus on what *you* want. This"—he pointed at the remaining egg—"represents the only way for you to get back home. Find a demon to aid you, and crack the shell."

"Somehow, I don't feel like I can trust you to point me to the friendly demon, if they even exist," I said.

"I can't point you at all," he said, shrugging. "Demons are an unknown quality. I can teach you how to reach out and contact them, but what you find will be random, to a degree that you would not believe."

He smiled, but there was no warmth in it. "The demons that we have seen have ranged from unspeakable horrors to quite normal humanoids. There's simply no telling what you'll get."

"Wait, when you said reach out . . . you meant reach out into the not-space?"

"Of course."

"But if they're out there, how can they get inside to help me?"

"Their ways are as varied as they are. Whoever you contact will be able to tell you how to summon them."

"And then they'll use me to destroy the world," I said. "I'm not going to do it just because there's a *chance* it will work out."

"Won't you?" His cold smile grew wider. "I think that you will, eventually."

"Why? What makes you think I'll just destroy everything I've built, all those people I care about, just for a chance to get home?"

"Because, deep down, you still haven't accepted that this is real," he told me. "You're still not sure if everyone in this world isn't just a well-coded NPC. Nothing more than a computer program."

"That's . . . impossible," I protested, but I didn't know who I thought I was fooling.

"According to your memories, which you already doubt. And every explanation for what has happened to you is equally impossible. So. You doubt."

I didn't say anything. There wasn't really any point. Satisfied by my silence, he continued speaking.

"I will give you this knowledge, this option. You may not use it. The other gods will work to make sure that you don't use it. But the opportunity may come when your will and the gods' inattention align."

"What are the odds of that?" I asked.

"Low," he admitted. "But the severity of my circumstances has reduced me to celebrating every murder as being a microscopic step towards my goal. How could I not seize even the smallest of opportunities?"

He didn't make any sign, but I suddenly knew he'd done it. I knew how to summon demons. A complicated configuration of mana flows, subtly off from what I thought it should be.

[Theurgy] skill Level 4 gained.

For gaining 2 skill levels, you have been awarded 2 XP.

I looked at the notification with disquiet. Normally it would have added "from use" or "demonstrated competence" to that first line. Having it go up when I hadn't actually done anything was new to me.

"Why won't the other gods just remove this knowledge?" I asked.

He snickered. "They're trapped by their own rules. Altering a Champion's memory would cost them points, but it doesn't cost me anything to add it right back in."

"Why wouldn't they make an exception for you?"

"Because then anyone could make a deal with me, and delete any information they wanted by undoing my alterations."

He laughed at my expression. "Don't look so surprised; gods and mortals make deals with me all the time."

"I do find that difficult to believe," I said.

"Everyone . . . has *something* that they want to destroy," he said. "Wanting to destroy *everything* means that we can align on that one point. If I couldn't make deals, I wouldn't get *anything* done."

He chuckled a little and then continued. "The other reason is that most of them are philosophically opposed to either destroying memories or playing around with mortal minds. So I'm reasonably confident that this knowledge will remain until it's needed."

He stood up in one smooth motion. "And now I must take my leave. Since you're no doubt resolved to ignore my advice, I shall leave you with some I earnestly hope you disregard."

He paused as if waiting for me to object, but I wasn't going to say anything to delay him from leaving.

"Don't call up that which you cannot put down."

And with that, he was gone.

Well, I thought to myself. *Guess who's not getting any sleep tonight?*

JAILBREAK

Mistress Janie, what's an Ashmor's Blessing, and why do I have it?" Janie froze, for just a second. "What does Status say about it?" she asked him carefully.

Maslin looked at nothing for a moment. "That it gives a bonus to Fire Magic and Tactics," he read out. "Also that I automatically qualify for the Firebrand Priest profession.

"Well, that's better than the curse," she said. "As to why, well, when you keep company with a Champion, the gods have their eye on you. You must have—" She caught herself, figuring it out. "He must have taken a liking to you."

"Is that good or bad?" Maslin asked. "People don't like Ashmor, do they?"

"It's a sight better than him not liking you," Janie said fervently. "Mortals don't really get a say in what the gods do, so just accept it, and don't mention it to anyone else."

"Do I want to be a Firebrand Priest?" Maslin asked her. "Is that better than a Fire Mage?"

Janie made a face. "They're scary f—. . . people to cross, I'll tell you that. But if you take that path, you'll be committing to serving Ashmor."

"Is that bad? He made Fire Magic, didn't he?"

"Fire is pretty great," Janie admitted. "But you need to keep it under control."

I wanted to scoff at that. Control wasn't the first thing I thought of when remembering how we'd fought together. But the truth was, she was good at keeping the stuff off of her allies. Just a little less careful with everything else. It was a good thing that dungeons were mostly stone.

Since I didn't interrupt, Janie was free to continue. "Worshipping Ashmor is like letting the flames control *you*. There's some that think the power is worth being a tool, but I'm not one of them."

Maslin nodded thoughtfully and then got shooed off to breakfast by Janie.

"So," she said to me. "Why?"

"He was here last night," I said. "I couldn't tell you *why* he did that, but he said it was because he was impressed by him."

Janie shivered. "Here . . . in this room?" she asked. "That's disturbing. Is he your patron, then?"

"No, not if I can trust anything that they've told me," I said. "It's like you said, my . . . status gets me a lot more attention from gods than you'd expect."

"Better you than me," Janie said. "No, wait, better someone far, far away from me."

"You're actually taking this better than I thought," I said. "Isn't Ashmor the worst god?"

Janie shrugged. "*Any* god can ruin your day, or your country, if they feel they want to," she said. "Yeah, Ashmor wants to destroy the world, but he *hasn't*, so far. He's outnumbered eight to one on that front, so he's not that much worse when it comes to actual outcomes. So . . . what did he want?"

I snorted. "For me to destroy the world by summoning a demon, that's what."

"You gonna?"

"No. Of course not. He did seem pretty confident I would, though . . . I can't tell if he knows me better than I do, or if he just had a good game face."

"I reckon the second one," Janie told me. "Gods are pretty smart and all, but if they thought you'd summon a demon, they wouldn't have brought you here."

"Yeah . . ." I said, thinking about it. "You're right. Let's get breakfast."

After breakfast, I had the pleasure of trying to escape from Luxury Jail.

"I am deeply sorry, my dear lady, but I cannot grant you a pass at this time." The Chamberlain's face was the very picture of contrition, but Bargain told me that there was steel behind it.

Bargain was a little odd as social skills went. You didn't always get a sense of whether the other person was better than you. Sometimes you did. I was still learning the details through trial and error, but you could *project* certain impressions through the skill. What Bargain was telling me right now was that I couldn't afford to bribe the Chamberlain. Maybe that was true, or maybe he was just projecting that idea. Without actually making an offer, there was no way to tell, but either way said I wasn't getting my way.

"May I ask why?"

"Of course," he said and looked down at my file. An honest-to-goodness stack of paper kept in a heavy paper folder. It wasn't quite a manila folder, but it was close enough.

"It seems that our spymaster has flagged you as being at risk of an attack from . . ." He lifted up the top sheet to read the sheet below, and then carefully placed it down again. ". . . persons unknown."

He gave me a sympathetic smile. "Of course, since you have been summoned to go before the King, we cannot have you getting yourself killed before your audience. Once the audience has occurred, we can revisit the matter."

"Won't I be kicked out once the King has seen me?" I asked.

"That is up to the King, and I wouldn't dare to presume," he replied. "The normal course of events would be for you to leave fairly quickly—I'm sure you wish to get back to your town as soon as possible. But as long as we don't need the rooms for anything, you can extend your stay as our guest."

"I see. Thank you for your time," I said.

It wasn't that the palace compound was a prison, exactly. Aside from some restricted areas, we guests had the run of the place. But the need for escorts every time we left was grating on me. Sure, any of us could evade the escorts, but we'd have to come back to the palace at some stage, and face whatever penalty they gave us for misbehaving.

The excuse they had given me was interesting. It might even have been true—there were a bunch of threats to my life. I hadn't thought that the palace had known, or cared about them, but perhaps they cared this much. Or perhaps they used that excuse all the time, and it just happened to be true today.

What I needed to do was to find a way through the security enchantments. That didn't sound easy, but I was an enchanter, and I did have Theurgy, so it didn't seem impossible on the face of it.

The first step was to observe them in action, so I lost myself in one of the more deserted areas of the palace. Turning invisible, I then carefully headed back to the gate.

I wasn't so foolish as to pass through any of the security fields while invisible, of course, but it was easy to avoid them as long as I stayed in the public areas—it helped that I was able to see them with Mana Sense.

Public areas had their own dangers, in the form of people wandering by who would bump into me if I wasn't careful. By now, I was fairly well practiced at avoiding them.

Parking myself in an untrafficked corner near the gate let me see what was going on. It was pretty much the same idea as my first experiments with the Detect Person rune. There was a field covering the entirety of the inner gate, which was a choke point for all the traffic. If someone had a token, nothing happened. If someone came through that didn't have a token, a light positioned where only the guards could see it lit up, and the guards knew they had to check the person coming in. If someone invisible went through, the light would go on with no one to cause it. Presumably, the alarm would be raised at that point.

Could I just go through walking closely behind someone? Maybe. If they didn't have a token, the guards would come up fairly quickly and make it difficult for me to slip around them. If they did have a token, then it would be clear that something had gone wrong, which would probably raise the alarm.

I had already checked out the walls, and they had their own security fields, extending out diagonally from just below the battlements. Given their placement, they seemed to be intended to catch people climbing over the walls. Flyers could get over, no problems, but it would be difficult to extend a field over the entire compound.

So flying, invisible people should be able to get in with no problems. That seemed like a rare combination, but I'd run into one person with that already, so who knew?

Lacking Air Magic, I was forced to rely on Theurgy. The boost that Ashmor had given me was going to be handy. Theurgy was so goddamn hard to level, I should thank him. I *wouldn't*, because he was a maniac who wanted to kill us all, but I *should*.

The reason Theurgy was so hard to level was that it was so hard to *use*. No one in this world had figured out exactly how skill improvement went, but they knew the basics. You got a tiny amount of improvement each time you used the skill, but you got a lot more if you succeeded. And you got even more if you were . . . the general feeling was *in danger*, but I suspected it might relate to stress or adrenaline levels when you used the skill.

Theurgy was damned hard to succeed at, and at my level, damned hard to get to do anything useful. So playing around with it in stressful situations was right out. I needed to use other skills at those times. Skills that would help me survive.

Now that I had level four in the skill, however, I might be able to do something with it. I focused on the detection field. Doing this at range was more difficult but sticking my hand into the field would get me detected, so ranged it was.

As I concentrated, my will was focused through the Theurgy skill and began to have an effect on the field. It started to wobble and waver. I wasn't worried about this action setting off the alarm. I knew from previous experiments that the field detected people, not being messed with.

You could layer fields to detect more than one thing, but that would have been visible to me. I had also checked around before starting to make sure that there were no mage types wandering about. Even mages didn't go around with Mana Sense on all the time, I thought. It was too distracting.

Last time, I'd managed to move the field, but not by enough to be useful. This time, I pushed a huge dent in it, big enough to accommodate me.

Would I be able to hold this for long enough? Could I move it through the whole field? I checked my mana. It was ticking down but fairly slowly. The gate was empty of travellers; the guards were bored and inattentive. Before I could stop myself, I darted quickly towards the gate. Moving carefully as the field enveloped me, I made sure to keep a bubble around me big enough to walk in.

Holding my breath, I walked quickly through and back again. No one said anything, and the guards were none the wiser. I'd broken free.

The first thing I did with my newfound freedom was to go back to my rooms. I know, I know, but it was more important to fill in the gang on what I'd managed.

As it happened, they had some news for me.

"A messenger arrived while you were out," Felicia said, handing it to me. "From the Guild Master."

I took the letter, a small piece of parchment elaborately folded and sealed with wax. Over the top, perhaps, but I liked it better than drugs and kidnapping.

Breaking the seal, I saw that the message was short and to the point.

The Guild Master will see you this afternoon in the Guild Hall.

"Okay," I said. "I guess I know what I'm doing this afternoon."

GUILD MASTER

G uild Master Voight didn't seem dangerous. In fact, I couldn't get a read off him at all—he could be anywhere between level one or ten, for all I could tell. He sat behind his desk, calmly finishing his paperwork, while I waited. At least my chair was comfortable. I occupied myself by examining the books lining the walls of his office.

I could actually read the titles from here, thanks to my improved senses, but I didn't really need to, as just the thought that I would like to know what the book was triggered Identify.

[Identification]: Bound Leather Guild Reports (Wrathbone Dungeon AR 15–21) - Quality: Good

[Identification]: Bound Leather Guild Reports (Wrathbone Dungeon AR 22–29) - Quality: Good

I flicked my eyes around the room. That was a lot of reports. They may not have been the most interesting read, but the number of them edged out the pathetic library we had in Talnier.

I returned my attention to Voight, trying again to get a sense of his level. He had to have a pretty high level to head the adventurers, right? But he just appeared to be an ordinary elderly man, of average size, with a little extra weight on him.

Checking with Mana Sense didn't reveal much either. I tried to decide if I wanted to cast Dispel Illusion. He probably couldn't detect my cast—especially since he wasn't currently looking at me. I decided to risk it.

[Dispel Illusion].

No result. No mysterious mana conduits leading off to nowhere. That was . . . good? If there had been one—or more—that would have been bad, so I was tentatively labelling this as good. There were still a few bad possibilities, though, like the idea that his illusion had been cast by a person with a higher spell total than me.

Finally, he put down his quill. "Councillor Hammond," he said.

"Guild Master Voight," I replied. Normally I would have asked him to just call me by my first name, but for this meeting, I wanted all the status I could gather. "I take it you've heard from the Talnier Guild?"

"Yes, it was a very interesting letter," he said. "You've been investigating the nature of dungeons, and already uncovered several of our secrets. Despite this, Koenig wants us to allow you to continue."

"Forgive my ignorance," I said quietly, "but I'm curious as to what legal means you have to stop me."

He chuckled. "Not much," he admitted. "We can throw you out of the Guild, and badmouth you to the other nobles. That'd keep you out of most of the dungeons in Latora. But you're already aware that there are dungeons outside of the country."

I nodded. "Of course. Even the Talnier dungeon has a dual administration."

"So minor inconveniences aside, there's not much we can do. Legally."

He let the silence hang. We both knew that he had access to higher-levelled people than me. Some of them would be willing to kill me for coin or guild favors.

"But . . ." he continued. "Koenig thinks you can be an asset without taking the oaths."

"It's not that I don't want to rise higher in the Guild," I explained, "But the contracts I've seen so far seem quite coercive. And at least one person I met complained quite bitterly about his treatment by the Guild."

"There are always malcontents and misfits," Voight muttered darkly. "What you have to understand is that we draw our staff out of the pool of adventurers."

"Should I be taking offense?"

"At their best," he continued, ignoring me, "adventurers are ambitious, independent dissidents. They're exactly the people who don't fit into an organization." He sighed. "And worse, there aren't enough of the best to fill all our needs."

"So you use the contracts to keep them in line—and enforce the contracts with magic."

"Did Koenig tell you about that?" he asked sharply.

"I inferred it, and you've just confirmed it," I told him and watched him grimace. That had been one of the possible causes of the conduits. "You'll forgive me if I don't seem eager to lose my free will."

"And yet, you want the benefits that come with that," he pointed out.

"Well, it might be possible."

He paused, looking at his files again. "You're aware of our . . . rivalry with the noble houses," he said at last.

"Yes."

"Koenig says that you've had your own differences of opinion with some of them. Care to elaborate?"

"I was forced to babysit the current Count Duvost by his father," I said carefully. "He didn't take it well and bears a grudge now. That grudge seems to have been spread up the chain to his duke. Neither of them like that I'm part of the government of free Talnier. There was an assassination attempt on the road as I travelled here."

Voight raised his eyebrows, but I continued. "Duke Finley seems to have been the instigator of a number of schemes I've been at the edges of. The assassination of the old Count Duvost, and the murder of Baron Baer in Talnier. He seems to want whoever's in charge of Talnier to be loyal to him—I've been almost promised the barony if I'm willing to bend the knee."

"A generous offer," Voight said noncommittally.

"It comes with almost as many strings as yours does," I told him. "I don't plan on taking it, but as long as negotiations continue, he's not going to be trying to kill me.

"That said, his idea of negotiation seems to be drugging me and whisking me off to an undisclosed location, for who knows what."

"That happened here?" Voight asked, amused. "And you stayed around . . . only an adventurer. I suppose that he didn't know you had Drug Resistance?"

"I don't want to talk about how we escaped that," I said.

He chuckled again. "It's rare for an adventurer to have that; mostly they go for Venom Resistance. It's more common here, though."

"I'll keep that in mind."

"So what's your next step with Finley? Let him kidnap you the second time?"

"I don't know," I admitted. "He said he's sending a message, I'm hoping it will be more polite this time."

"Maybe," he said doubtfully. He looked at me speculatively. "Maybe . . ."

"Maybe, what?" I asked as the pause extended.

"Duke Finley spends a lot of his time in Dorsay attending a . . . particular establishment. Perhaps you could meet him there?"

"What sort of establishment?" I asked suspiciously, as Voight passed a quickly written note over to me. The Shattered Bat, it said, along with an address.

"Not the sort of establishment that you'll want anyone knowing you attended," he said. "You'll need to ditch your escort and go in disguise."

"A brothel?" I asked.

"Not primarily. It offers a variety of entertainments for the rich and jaded," he said. "It's a dangerous place for a young lady, but for an adventurer . . ."

"Is this some kind of hazing ritual?"

Voight gave a surprised grunt of laughter. "Not a bad idea! But no . . . this might help you with Finley, and I've got a feeling that it will help me as well."

"Help you how?"

"I'm not sure; it's just a hunch," he said. "When you've been doing this a bit longer, you'll learn to rely on them. In any case, I think that our business can wait until you've sorted out this Finley situation."

I grimaced. "I was hoping to sort out some sort of dungeon access."

"Ah, of course. I'm not up to date on the schedule right now, but . . ." He thought for a moment. "The dungeon isn't barred from . . . low-priority members like yourself. If you went downstairs and asked for a slot, you could probably get one for next week?"

"That's not ideal."

"I suppose not. Why don't we say that once you've come back and told me all about your meeting with Finley, I'll arrange for you to have a higher priority slot—it could be as soon as the next day!"

Suddenly energized, he bounced out of his chair and offered me a hand to get up. Taking this as a sign that the meeting was over, I let him escort me out.

"It has been very interesting meeting you, Councillor, I hope to see you again soon, maybe as soon as tomorrow!" He winked at me, and then I was out of his office and into the common area.

Tomorrow, I thought. *He wants me to go tonight? He must know something about Finley's schedule.*

I headed downstairs to where everyone else was waiting.

"How did it go?" Felicia asked anxiously.

"Well . . ." I said, "Let me tell you what happened . . ."

I booked the dungeon slot. Who knew how the Finley business would end up, or whether Voight would come through on his deal. We could always cancel it if we got something better or had to leave town before then. Once we were back in our quarters, I remembered to check up on something that Voight had said.

Searching for Resistance in the Development point menu came up with several options, some of which I'd already noticed.

Disease Resistance: Resistant to most forms of disease (4 points)

Poison Resistance: Resistant to damage from poisons (4 points)

Venom Resistance: Resistant to most venoms (4 points)

Drug Resistance: Resistant to most drugs (4 points)

Heat Resistance: Resistant to damage from heat (6 points)

Cold Resistance: Resistant to damage from cold (6 points)

Lightning Resistance: Resistant to damage from electricity (6 points)

Mental Resistance: Resistant to Mind Magic (4 points)

Divine Resistance: Resistant to damage from Divine Magic (6 points)

Shadow Resistance: Resistant to damage from Shadow Magic (6 points)

That was . . . a list. I tried to figure out the logic behind what was included. Three forms of magic were, five if you included Heat and Cold as applying to Fire and Ice Magic, but Water, Air, and Illusion weren't. Granted, Illusion couldn't *do* any damage, but Water and Air Magic could.

The poisons made even less sense. I knew the difference between poison and venom, thanks to a few pedantic med students back in university, but . . .

"Felicia, what's the difference between a poison and a drug?" I asked.

"A poison causes damage over time, while a drug gives a status effect, why?" she replied easily.

I blinked at her. Somewhere a med student was screaming, but I suppose it made sense for this world. "Just checking up on Resistances."

"Oh . . . that would have been useful for the other night," she said. "What do you think, Kyle?"

Our resident expert on all adventures nodded slowly. "Dad told me that they're not generally worth it—not enough monsters use it, and you can carry antidote potions."

"It costs twelve points to cover all the bases—to get all three of Poison, Venom, and Drug Resistance," I added at their blank looks. "I don't think getting all of them would be worth it, but Drugs sounds like a good idea."

"It's not total immunity," Kyle warned. "Just resistance. What that means . . . I think for the nasty drugs, it just takes longer to take effect, or you need a bigger dose before it starts affecting you."

"Either of those could be a game changer, especially if it's Felicia that has it." I pointed out.

"I do have some spare points," she admitted.

I shrugged. "Think it over first. From what the Guild Master said, Finley probably now thinks that we have someone with resistance, and his next move will be made with that in mind."

I only had two Development points myself, but I made a note to get Drug Resistance at my next level. I got the feeling I would be dealing with more men than monsters in the near future.

"I don't think we'll need it for tonight, anyway," I said, hoping I wasn't jinxing myself. "Voight said this club was dangerous, but I doubt they'd still be around if they were poisoning their guests."

Then again, I thought, *Voight thought that we already had Drug Resistance, so maybe he thought we didn't have to worry about that?*

"Maybe get some antidotes ready, just in case."

THE SHATTERED BAT

The hard part was convincing them to let me go alone.

"How'm I supposed to be your bodyguard when you leave me behind for all the dangerous bits?" Janie asked, exasperated.

She had a good point, but so did the others. Kyle also wanted to go along to protect me, and Felicia didn't want Kyle to go alone. Cutter wanted to come too, of course, but I suspected he had more ulterior motives than he claimed.

"Look, I can sneak *maybe* one person past the checkpoint. If I have to go back and forth sneaking you all past, I'll be mentally exhausted and out of mana before we even begin." I looked at them all. "Plus, someone has to stay behind and cover for the ones that leave."

They all started arguing again, but I kept talking. "My best protection is invisibility, and you know how difficult it gets coordinating multiple invisible people."

"You won't be able to negotiate invisible," Kyle pointed out.

"I've got the Phantasmal Emissary spell to negotiate with," I countered. "Besides, I don't think I'm going there to negotiate."

"You're not?" Felicia asked.

"Negotiation with Finley is just a delaying tactic, remember? I'm pretty sure the Guild Master picked up on that, so why would he suggest a way for me to speed up the process?" I gave them all a significant look.

"Because he hates you?" Janie suggested.

"If that were the case, I doubt he'd even have seen me," I told her. "No, he thinks I could be an asset, so he's sending me to spy on Finley to see what I can find out."

"All the more reason that you should have backup!" Felicia protested.

"If you get caught, you'll just disappear, and then what are we going to tell the King?"

"Same thing we'd say if we got caught at the gate," I said. "One person. And it will be Cutter."

"Yes!" Cutter said.

"Don't be so quick to celebrate," I told him, "This will be a job, and you'll need to stay on it."

"But we're going to a brothel, right? There'll be drinks and girls!"

"You're a little too young for either of those," I said wryly.

"All the more reason that he shouldn't go," Felicia said disapprovingly.

"Two reasons why he should," I said. "One, he's the smallest of you—I can take him through piggyback. Two, he can pick locks, which are the biggest problem for an invisible person."

"I can pick locks," Janie said sullenly.

"Blowing down the door isn't the same thing," I said.

"I could melt the lock?" she tried.

"It's still going to set fire to the door," I said. "Not exactly stealthy."

"Boo. So the rest of us are just going to stay and wait?"

"Maybe not. You could always take an escorted trip out to the city so you're close by if we need you." I suggested.

They liked that idea better, so we figured out a rendezvous point in a better part of town. With the most contentious point out of the way, the rest of the planning went much faster.

Cloaked in invisibility, Cutter and I watched the gate intently. Traffic was dying down, but we wanted to get through before they closed the gates for the night. We could hardly ask to be let out, after all.

Judging that the time was right, I grabbed Cutter and moved closer to the detection field. Once again, I reached out with my . . . mind? My will? Whatever it was, I grasped the field and started to distort it.

The last time I'd hollowed out a sphere; this time I went with a domed cylinder, the better to minimize the surface area required to contain Cutter and myself. It—or rather I—pushed forward and entered the gateway. Unlike most force fields that I'd encountered in fiction, the cylinder didn't move with me. I had to take a step forward, dragging Cutter along, and then move the space around me to match.

It was slow going and very mentally draining, but the distance we had to cover was actually quite short. Fortunately, I'd explained to Cutter what would be required, and he didn't dash off or wave his arms about, or any of a dozen things that he might have been tempted to do while invisible.

Since we'd left before sunset, I cancelled the spell and we found dinner in the city. It wasn't long after that we were standing in the shadows of a doorway in sight of the Shattered Bat. It was a big building, made larger by a few additions that were clearly made after construction had been completed. Both of the neighboring buildings had been . . . acquired and added to the main structure.

On one side, the building had been extended to integrate fully with the main structure. No attempt had been made to unify the different architectural styles, and the result was a mess. It looked structurally sound—robust, even—but it was uglier than any building I'd seen thus far in this town.

Opalime stone was in short supply in this part of town, but most people still took the time to build something worth living in. Both these buildings had been . . . somewhat stylish, but the connecting section was just stone bricks laid down in a square.

The other side was worse. There, a covered walkway connected the upper floors of both buildings, looking even more out of place.

The main entrance was easy to pick out. They'd managed to find some opalime to frame the door in, so it stood out. No sign, but I had the feeling that no one came here accidentally. There were two bouncers at the door and a small scattering of shady-looking types hanging around nearby.

"You ready?" I said to Cutter. He nodded. We were both visible. I was using my Disguise spell, presenting as a rough-looking man in my late thirties. Cutter was wearing a hooded cloak and elevator boots to add a few inches to his height. Knowing we'd need to, I'd given them to him before we left so that he could both get used to walking in them, and also for the novelty to wear off. He quite liked being taller, and I suspected he was going to try and get a permanent pair after tonight.

It didn't look as if the bouncers were turning people away, and Voight would surely have said something if there were some sort of password I needed to get in. So we just walked right up.

The guards perked up as we came into view. I guess the other patrons had all been regulars.

"I don't know you, friend," one of them said, with something like politeness. "What pleasures bring you to our establishment?"

That was an odd phrasing, which made me think that there was some sort of passphrase going on. Since I didn't know what the response was—or even exactly what "pleasures" were available here, I just bulled on through.

"I'm here for business," I said, giving the man my best murderous glare, and turning up the Intimidation. He wilted a little but didn't give up.

"Uh, what—"

"I'm meeting someone," I interrupted. "You don't *want* to know with who."

"Uh, right. Go on through, sir." He opened the door and I could suddenly hear the roar of the crowd inside.

I kept up the glare until we were inside the entryway. It was a short, dark passage that led into light. The noise ahead of us wasn't that loud—a small crowd—but it was intense. Cheers, boos, jeers, and the occasional scream.

Beside me, I could hear Cutter mumbling under his breath. "I'm here for *business*. You don't *want* to know with who." It seemed I was providing a bad example.

We came out into the light. Enchanted light globes—there was money behind this arena. And that's what this place was, although arena might be too fancy a word.

It seemed as if the entire building had been hollowed out into one open space. In the middle of the space, three pits had been dug out and lined with stone. I was looking down into the middle of one right now. Around the pits, stands had been set up, steeply rising so that everyone could get a good view of the bloodshed.

That's what the pits contained, of course. This was a pit fighting arena, and the fights had already started. In the middle pit, right in front of me, I could see two muscular men dressed only in loincloths, having it out with knives. Before I could look away, I saw one of them put a deep slash in the other's arm.

"This is better than a brothel!" Cutter enthused, but my attention was elsewhere by then. This wasn't *just* a fighting pit. I could see passages leading off on either side of the room, and there was a walkway at the top of the stands with more doors leading away. I was sure it wouldn't be too hard to find out what other vices were dealt in here.

It didn't matter, though, because across the room, on the other side of the pit, was my target. Duke Finley.

Not wanting to gawp in the entrance like a tourist, I nudged Cutter and led him up to the stands. I had to pay two silver for the privilege of not standing on the floor like the hoi polloi. Also of note was that most of the other doors could only be accessed from the stands. That wasn't what I was here for though, so I just took a seat in an empty area and checked out the place. I let Cutter do the cheering for the both of us.

The Duke was set up in an area that probably cost more than a silver to get into. It might have been reserved for him alone. A section of the stands had been walled off, made only accessible from the lowest level. Strategically placed guards made sure that he and his guests had the place to themselves. The front row of seats had been replaced with a low table packed with food and wine, while the Duke and his guest sat in chairs that looked a lot more comfortable than mine.

The lighting was a lot less bright at these upper levels, but there was enough light for my enhanced senses to make out some details. I'd recognized the Duke immediately, but now that I was looking, I realized that I also recognized his guest. But it was one of his retainers that really caught my eye. There were three people sitting on the level above, in less comfortable chairs. One of them had a sour look on a face that I recognized. Master Archambault, in the flesh.

Turning on Mana Sense, I could see that he had at least one spell up. He'd constructed a thin shell of mana that enclosed the entire box that the Duke was sitting in. It made me think of Privacy, a spell that would keep anyone outside the bubble from hearing what was being said.

"Cutter," I said quietly. "Time to get back to business."

He pouted, but stopped cheering and started listening. "What is it, boss?"

"See the toff across the way? That's Duke Finley." Cutter hadn't been in the room when I'd met him before.

"The bloke talking to the foreigner?" Cutter asked.

"Yeah," I said. "But take a look at the guy above him."

Cutter squinted for a minute and then exclaimed. "That's the mystery guy!"

"Master Archambault the Illusionist," I agreed.

"Is he going to be trouble?" Cutter asked.

"I doubt it. I was the better caster the first time we met, and I've gone up a level since then. But stay sharp—I might not be the only one casting illusions here."

Cutter nodded, and I continued. "Now, about that foreigner . . . do you recognize him?"

Cutter squinted some more and then scrunched up his face in thought. "Was he one of the blokes at the King's audithing?"

"Audience," I corrected. "And yes. That's the Lyran ambassador, Oleg Gavril. I wonder what he's talking with the Duke about that has to happen here?"

Cutter made a face. "Pretty sure what you actually mean is you're gonna find out what they're saying, and Felicia's gonna yell at me in the morning."

"Only if I get caught," I said.

EAVESDROPPING

The bubble was smaller than the Duke's box, but only barely. There should be plenty of room for an invisible person to get inside without bumping into the other participants in the discussion. *Popping* the bubble was a remote possibility—I wasn't sure if Dispel Image would work on that spell or not—but doing so would probably alert everyone to my presence.

So going invisible over the wall it was . . . I just needed to find a place to disappear.

"Keep an eye on the Duke, Cutter. If all goes well, you won't see anything. So if you do see something, go and get the others."

Cutter nodded, but he seemed distracted by the fights. It would probably be fine. If they did catch me, it wouldn't be a subtle thing.

My first problem was to find a place where I could go Invisible without people seeing me disappear. It would have been good to have a spell to cover this—for example, casting Phantasmal Entity over my own form, and then casting Invisibility. Unfortunately, Phantasms were solid, so it couldn't overlap with me.

Even better would have been casting Phantasmal Entity and sending it in to do the spying with no risk to me. But Greater Invisibility could only be cast on humanoid targets, not on other illusions.

I supposed that I could have cast Static Image, gone invisible, then moved out of the image and cast Phantasmal Entity over the top of *that*. But that seemed way too complex and prone to failure.

Instead, I moved to a corner of the stands with the least visibility and then focused my attention on one of the other audience members.

He seemed pretty drunk for so early in the evening, but maybe he'd been losing his bets and consoling himself. Whatever the reason, he seemed like a good target.

[Phantom World], I cast silently. He started screaming and slapping himself.

"Bugs! All over me!" he cried. It didn't take long for everyone to dismiss him as a raving drunk, but I didn't need long. I cast Greater Invisibility and then observed everyone around me while I cancelled my distraction. It seemed to have worked, so I started heading around the arena to the Duke's box.

The Duke had placed guards to discourage eavesdroppers—or loiterers, I guess was the term, since they wouldn't be able to hear anything. The straight sides of the box, though, meant that they only felt the need to stand on the corners, confident that they'd be able to see and intercept any intruders.

That did not apply to me. The wall was sturdy enough that it didn't sway when I leapt to the top of it. Given a running start, and enough headroom, I think I could have cleared the seven-foot wall in a single bound, but I didn't have either of those conditions. Instead, I leapt up high enough to pull myself the rest of the way over. I was quiet, catlike, and graceful as I reached the top—only to almost screw it all up

Just where I was about to put my hand, there was a lizard. I managed to redirect my grip without losing my balance, but the surprise had me perched on top of the wall, frozen in shock.

It seemed to have noticed something—the wind of my passage, perhaps—because it had also frozen, its head up, looking in all directions with its protruding eyes.

It was camouflaged, but that didn't matter at this distance. Before I could react at all, it dashed off, running along the top of, and then behind the wall. I leaned over to try and catch sight of it again, but the camo was doing its work. I didn't think camouflage was supposed to work on moving objects, but perhaps it was magical—or perhaps it had frozen again.

In the time it took me to recover my composure, I resolved to just ignore it—aside from watching more closely where I stepped, in case it was still hanging around. It didn't seem like a natural encounter, but it wasn't my problem. Lowering myself carefully down the wall, I took a step forward into the bubble.

I knew it was there, but if I hadn't, the abrupt cutoff of all sound would have clued me in. After the hubbub of the room, moving into the bubble was like entering a church—even though there was already a conversation going on.

"—cannot compare to the spectacle that an open-air arena brings. These pits . . . they have no room for magic or monsters." That was the ambassador, Oleg Gavril. Despite his complaints, he seemed quite pleased.

"Just steel, muscle, and blood," the Duke replied. "Up close like this, you can smell it. The fear, the pain. Your arenas can only offer sight and sound."

"They are experiences that are very different," Gavril agreed. "It seems we must disagree on which one is to be preferred."

Finley grunted. "If you insist," he said.

"As delightful as such conversation is, perhaps we should move on to business?"

The Duke grunted again in agreement. "Am I to understand from your presence that Lyran is ready to proceed?"

"Indeed. The delays imposed by my predecessor have finally exhausted the patience of my superiors."

"How many troops are you sending?"

Gavril chuckled. "I was certainly not sent with that information. All that is required for you to know is that they will be enough."

"Don't be obtuse," the Duke growled. "My neck is on the line here; I need to know that you're serious."

"Is my presence here not enough to convey that?"

"No. I need to know that you have enough troops threatening King's Isle. If your threat isn't enough, he won't commit his forces. I won't make a move until that happens, and I won't start preparations until I know that it's *going* to happen."

The ambassador made an exasperated noise. "You have not even begun? But the time it takes—"

"Let me worry about my logistics," Finley interrupted. "You worry about convincing me of your commitment."

"These numbers . . ." Gavril trailed off, clearly hesitant to continue. "This detail. It is the province, not of the diplomatic service, but of the military, yes?"

"I don't care about your internal divisions," Finley replied.

"We all serve the Shah, in the end," Gavril said, making some kind of gesture that I couldn't see from this angle. "But what this means is that I do not have this number. Nor will the military service be eager to allow it to be sent into enemy territory."

"Are we not allies?" Finley said softly.

"Of course, of course—I will seek to bring this number to you. But it will take time, and the date we discussed is getting closer. Will you be ready in time?"

"Yes. As long as I have my answer quickly."

"Then I will take my leave at once, the quicker to get the answer to you."

"Yes, fine, you can go."

The ambassador got to his feet and quickly started making his way around the arena. Finley watched him for a moment and then spoke to his servant.

"Drop the bubble."

With a gesture from Archambault, the privacy bubble collapsed and the shouts and screams from the arena returned in full force.

"No more meetings, my lord?"

"No. I want to savor the next fight coming up."

That seemed like my cue to leave. I made my way back over the wall, not encountering any wildlife this time, and returned to Cutter's side.

He was . . . bargaining with a bookie for better odds.

"Aw, c'mon, man, take some pity on a poor kid. I'm willing to let it ride instead of taking my winnings; that's got to be good for a discount?"

The man seemed unimpressed. "I took pity on you the last bet, and you got lucky. You can quit while you're ahead, but I'm not doing you any more favors."

"I got a good eye, is all," Cutter boasted. "Hey! Watch where—" he shouted, as I tapped him on the shoulder. He whirled around but didn't see anything. It only took him a second to make the connection.

"Hey, I guess I'll just take my winnings, then," he said, turning back to the bookie. The man snorted but started counting out silver pieces.

That had better have been your own money, I thought as I watched him collect. Once he was done, I gave him a little tug towards the exit.

"Aw, we can't stay a little longer? The next fight was a sure thing for me!" he complained to the empty air. I rolled my eyes but just gave him a little shove in the right direction. No one seemed to notice him talking to himself—they were all busy either with the fight or their own intense, quiet conversations.

Once we were outside, I found a quiet place to reappear and resume my shifty male disguise.

"I'm telling you, Miss . . . er, Master, we could be making a killing in there!"

I'm creating monsters here, I thought to myself in dismay. *When did Cutter pick up a gambling habit?*

Pushing thoughts of my inadequate child-raising aside, I focused on the main issue at hand.

"No, we're going back," I said. "We'll pass the word on to the others so they can come in, and then we'll all go back to our apartments."

"But you didn't even meet with the guy yet," Cutter protested.

"Yeah, I don't think I want him knowing that I was in the building on the same night that he discussed treason with that ambassador."

"What makes you think I knew anything about it?" The Guild Master asked.

"Don't play dumb," I said sourly. "You sent me there last night. You knew who he was meeting with."

"There was a matching gap in their known schedules," Voight admitted.

"You knew more than that," I countered. "Or do you send someone to check out every coincidental matchup?"

Voight gave me a thin smile. "I had a few hints. The Chancellor, you see, has been cooking up a scheme with the Lyrans."

"I thought that they were plotting with the Duke," I said.

"They're playing both sides," he told me. "Or at least . . . dealing with both sides. I couldn't tell you if they mean to keep faith with either side."

"And you know this because . . ."

"I'm on the King's Advisory Council," he explained. "We were told that the Chancellor was running an operation involving both Duke Finley and the Lyrans, and to ignore—or at least bring to the Chancellor—anything we came across regarding those parties. That way, we can avoid stepping on one another's toes."

"Aren't you . . . stepping on the Chancellor's toes right now?" I asked.

"Of course not," he said easily. "By pure coincidence, you overheard the Duke talking treason. You brought this to me, correctly believing that I would be the best person to bring this information to. As a member of the King's Council, I would be well placed to do something about it—or— allay your fears and tell you that I have the Chancellor's assurance that there is nothing to worry about."

He sat back in his chair with a satisfied look on his face.

"I see. So why send me in the first place?"

Voight's smile grew more predatory. "Well, you see, I don't trust the motivations of the Chancellor."

"You think the *Chancellor* is betraying the country to the Lyrans?"

"The Lyrans are just a tool, and I think they know that. They're unlikely to take a serious gamble over this scheme, whatever it is. No, the Chancellor is doing what he always does, playing the King against the nobles for his own benefit."

"How?"

"Now that you've filled in some of the blanks, I can make some educated guesses. It seems that the Lyrans are promising to provide cover for Duke Finley to commit a coup."

"That's what he needs to have forces ready for," I said slowly. "Assuming he was the one behind Anchorbury, he brought in mercenaries and hid them in the town, slowly building up a force."

"That could be what he's doing here," Voight agreed. "The troops stationed here are loyal to the Crown, but the bulk of the King's estates, and his forces, are based on King's Isle."

"Finley's lands are all around Dorsay," I realized. "He must have the troops to take the city if he tried."

Voight nodded. "So my supposition is that the Chancellor is offering some minor concessions to the Lyrans in exchange for convincing the Duke that they're supporting him."

"But they're not . . . so the King will still have his reinforcements."

"I doubt it will come to actual battle," Voight mused. "Assuming that this isn't coming as a surprise, the King should be able to show up with his forces at the last minute, forcing Finley to surrender."

"So what's wrong with that plan—assuming you're not Finley, that is."

"If you're the *Chancellor*," Voight said, emphasizing the title, "then the problem is that this sets the nobles' cause back immensely. Finley might end up with his line being ended or large parts of his estate being confiscated. It would topple one of the Four Pillars."

"Still waiting to hear why this is bad."

"The Chancellor doesn't want to upset the status quo," Voight told me. "There's no way he wants this scheme to go ahead as planned. It would make a lot more sense if Finley was warned somehow, just in time for him to withdraw his forces without getting caught red-handed."

"If the Chancellor's going to cancel his own scheme, why do it in the first place?"

"By planning the scheme, he gains credit with the King, for coming up with a plan that *almost* succeeded. But he will have saved Finley, who will owe him a huge debt."

"So nothing actually happens, but the Chancellor looks good from both sides?"

"That's what I think he's planning. But it won't turn out that way." Voight stared into the middle distance. I could tell his mind was racing. "I want to see Finley dropped in a deep, dark hole. So you're going to help me make sure that the Chancellor doesn't get a chance to sabotage his own plan."

W E

'm hearing 'we' a lot, but what's in it for me?" I asked, only half serious. I would have loved to see Duke Finley taken down, but I wasn't going to be free labor.

"Yes, yes," Voight said. "Here, this is that priority pass I told you about." He handed me a slip of paper that had been *slightly* less crudely printed than I'd been able to manage in Talnier. Still carved wooden blocks, though, from the looks of it.

I'd wanted to introduce moveable type but I'd been stymied by the lack of *lead,* of all things. This world didn't have it, at least not readily available. As far as I could tell—Lattora didn't have a lot of information transfer between towns—all their metals came from dungeons, and none of them produced lead. That wasn't the end of it, of course. I was sure there was some metal I could substitute, but that was as far as I'd gotten.

Today wasn't for technology uplift, though; it was for politics and delving. I took the slip of paper and looked it over. It wasn't much more than a pre-written note granting my team gold-class access to the Endless Quarry.

"That will be good for as long as you're in town," Voight told me. "Or until you stop being useful."

"Nice to know," I replied. So it was only a token, and he could cancel it when he wanted. Still, it got me delving access, so progress on my level could start once more. "So what's the first step? Actually, no, why don't we just bring what we have to the King and be done with it?"

"Because we don't have any proof," Voight answered, amused by my naivety. "What I said about the Chancellor is just supposition, and as for what you heard, Finley will simply deny it."

I groaned. "And testimony from a noble counts for more than any number of commoners."

"Like you or I," Voight agreed. "If we could pass the information through to the King's spymaster it might be different, but . . ."

"But what?"

"Nobody knows who he or she is," he said with a wry shrug. "The King is definitely getting information that doesn't come through Agenor, but *how* is not known."

"So . . . the King knows, right, about the Chancellor's official plan?"

The wry smile got a bit more twisted. "The Chancellor informed the Council that the King was fully informed about the Chancellor's plan regarding Duke Finley. Making further inquiries of the King himself would be a show of distrust of the Chancellor and would diminish *my* standing."

"What if *I* brought it up with the King at my upcoming meeting?"

"He'd probably tell you to discuss it further with the Chancellor. Or possibly me. If anything in this discussion came up, that would be seen as an attack on the Chancellor, by me."

"Which would—" *reduce your standing*, I finished in my head. "I'm starting to see how this works," I grumbled. "So what do we do?"

"It's actually quite simple." He paused and leaned back in his chair, thinking about his next words. "My supposition is that the Chancellor will have some way of getting word to Duke Finley. It will be some sort of indirect channel since Agenor needs deniability in the event of it getting found out. All we need to do is find out what that channel is and then either destroy, delay, or discredit it."

"And how do we do *that*?" I asked.

Voight smiled. "I've always found, dealing with adventurers as often as I do, that I get the best results when I present a team with goals and let them determine how best to proceed. You've proven yourself very resourceful; I'm sure you'll come up with something."

I held off on the swearing until we were heading back. I thought I was doing it quietly enough, but I caught a few looks from our escort. I guess high Perception was something they selected for.

"You're in a mood," Janie laughed. "I thought we got the permit?"

"Yeah, we got it; it just came with some onerous requirements," I said, flicking my eyes at our escort. Janie took the hint and changed the subject.

"So going back, or meeting up with the others in the city?"

"I don't know how long they're going to be," I replied. Felicia was at the Alchemist guild, trying to get permission, or at least find out what was required, to operate as an Alchemist here. There weren't any rules about it back in Talnier, but we were certain things wouldn't be so free in the capital.

"Back home then," Janie said, and I agreed.

There was an incident taking place in the foyer of our wing as we arrived. To my displeasure, I recognized one of the combatants.

"What did you say about my father?" Aubert demanded of the man he had pressed against the wall. He'd twisted the man's arm back with one hand, and the other was on the victim's head.

"Nothing at all, my lord!" the man protested. "I merely spoke of the possibility of things going *faster*!"

I glanced over at the guards, who were studiously doing nothing. Aubert was a noble, after all, and the man . . . probably wasn't, going by his clothing. A doublet and hose, fine enough for a wealthy commoner, but not what a noble would wear.

Nor was it a palace uniform, so I couldn't get his role through Identify. The man himself seemed fairly small. Not a fighter, given how easily he was being manhandled by Aubert.

"Bullying men now, I see. Is that an improvement, or have you just changed preferences?" I drawled the words as I came up behind the pair. Janie snickered audibly.

Aubert's head whipped around at the sound of my voice. His face went red, either from embarrassment or increased rage.

"You . . . he . . ." he stuttered, unable to say anything coherent. Seemingly realizing that his current position wasn't a good look, he released the man and turned towards me.

The man slid down the wall and ended up lying on the floor. "Thank you for your *kindness*, sire—your generosity is *unparalleled*."

Janie snickered again, but I didn't have the time to figure out why. I was staring down Aubert, who was trying to control himself enough to address me. I figured he was very close to attacking me in rage, so I didn't provoke him further. I just glared at him while he tried to get himself together.

I was pretty sure that, unlike the guy on the floor, I was important enough that he couldn't just attack me with impunity. If he tried, I was fairly confident that Janie would set him on fire. Which might cause us a few problems, but his problems would suddenly become much worse.

He seemed to come to the same conclusion. Giving me the tiniest of bows, he turned on his heel and stalked off. *I guess this means his apartments are on the first floor,* I thought.

> **You have defeated Aubert Duvost in a Tier 4 Social Contest! You have earned 16 XP.**

"Are you all right?" I asked the man, stepping forward to help him up. "One of my party is a Healer; I could ask her to take a look at you?"

"Thank you, fair maid, I am indebted for your aid," the man said. Now that he was upright, I could see that he was actually a hair shorter than I was and slightly built. He could easily pass as a woman—turning that around, and thinking of a common fantasy trope, I glanced at his prominent Adam's apple. Everything was in order.

"Why are you talking that way?" Janie burst out. "It's funny enough with the accent!"

"Pray don't complain, I only do it to entertain," the man replied with a grin. I heard the rhyme that time, both in English and in Latorran—though how that worked, I didn't know. As for the accent, I had no idea what Janie was talking about. Accents didn't make it through the translator, though sometimes unusual speaking patterns did.

"I'm Kandis Hammond," I said, ignoring the byplay. "This is Janie Baker. Can I ask who you are? You don't seem like one of the normal palace guests."

"Of course! I am Vodurn, at your service. You find before you the least official of all the officials. For my sins, I have been assigned the role of the King's Fool."

"I see. My apartments are upstairs; shall we head up?"

Either he was used to getting asked about it, or my face was giving away my confusion because he grinned knowingly as we headed up the stairs.

"Expecting a uniform? Something in five clashing colors, with bells on every extremity?"

"Well, yes," I said, ignoring Janie's giggles.

"The King's taste does not run that way—he prefers his jesters to be dapper, not dappled. So I am freed of that particular shackle."

This guy was a riot, at least according to Janie. He had her in stitches by the time we got to our apartment, and I'd taken to laughing along. I was getting almost none of the wordplay, but it felt embarrassing to be left out of the joke.

Kyle and Felicia had made it back before us. From the look on her face, she hadn't gotten what she'd wanted from the Alchemists, but she put that aside while Vodurn was here. She gave him a quick heal, and then there was nothing for it but to break out the tea and biscuits and have a nice chat.

"So it seemed like you had a prior history with that noble-ling," Vodurn started, his face innocent.

"And you don't?" I scoffed. "If that was your first encounter, you must have really said something to set him off that badly."

Vodurn shrugged. "My master's taste in humor lies towards petty cruelties inflicted on his Court," he said. "I was testing out a minor needling, to see if it would prick." He made a sad face. "The would-be Count is tightly wound, it seems."

"About certain matters, yes," I said. "Why is he still here? I hadn't thought that his confirmation would be that controversial."

Vodurn made a noncommittal noise as he sipped his tea. "His cousin has also made a claim on the position."

"Isn't Guillaume in prison?" I asked incredulously.

"Indeed, but he is in prison *here*, which is quite convenient for pressing a claim against the Crown. And he has Lord Finley's backing, so . . ."

"Of course," I said sourly. "Finley was behind Guillaume's coup attempt."

"Duvost has mentioned that, perhaps unwisely. He's made no secret of the fact that he plans to accuse Duke Finley as soon as he has the rank to press the accusation."

"Let me guess, the King doesn't want one of his dukes accused of . . . whatever that would be. Murder of the Count, at least. So he's . . . just putting the whole thing on hold?"

"It's not a solution that can last forever," Vodurn admitted, "But for as long as it does last, the King holds something to keep Finley in check."

"Never thought I'd feel sorry for old Aubey," Janie said. "But . . . oh wait, I still don't." She must have seen something in my face, because she suddenly looked alarmed.

"No! Don't get ideas about saving him!" she groaned. "Don't you remember what a shit he was last time?"

"I remember," I said. "But Finley is a bigger problem, for us and the Kingdom both. I can't believe that the King wants to keep him around."

"Out of gratitude, I believe I'll refrain from passing that advice on to the King," Vodurn said, smiling. "I can't speak for him, of course, but I've observed that he doesn't have a problem with monsters, as long as they're kept tightly leashed."

"Half the problems with this kingdom, right there," I muttered. "Anyway, Janie, I don't have any ideas yet, but if it's a fight between Aubert and Finley, we want Aubert to win."

I looked over at Kyle and Felicia who hadn't really been following this conversation. They didn't know Aubert from a piece of chicken, and everything they knew about Finley they'd heard from me.

"That does sound like the best plan?" Felicia said. "I'm not really used to the idea of taking sides in a fight between nobles." Kyle nodded, and so did Janie, if reluctantly.

"How exciting!" Vodurn said. "Rest assured, I will keep your words in the deepest confidence. And if there is any way this poor Fool can aid you in your quest, please don't hesitate to let me know."

CHANCELLOR

Well, *that was dumb*, I chided myself as Vodurn left. *Run your mouth off in front of someone who regularly talks to the King.* I really wasn't cut out for this cloak-and-dagger work. At least Vodurn had *said* that he was going to keep our words in confidence. I wasn't sure if I believed him, but he hadn't needed to say that.

It wasn't as if I'd blurted anything really sensitive. I was pretty sure the King suspected that I was antagonistic towards Finley. If he was keeping track of his staff members, he might suspect matters had gone a bit further than antagonistic. I couldn't believe that we hadn't heard anything further about that.

But the next door knock was not some man in a ratty trench coat, just here to ask me a few questions about the other night. Instead, it was just a messenger, telling me that my personal audience with the King was scheduled for the morning, two days hence.

"I've lost track of whether this is early or late, and whether that's good or bad," I admitted to the room.

"It's within the range they gave us at the start, so that's normal, I guess?" Felicia answered.

"It means we're heading back soon, so that's good," Janie opined.

"Nooo! I want to go to the fighting rings again!" Cutter complained.

I frowned. It wasn't necessarily true that we'd leave after the audience, but that was probably the way to bet. That meant I wouldn't be in a position to help Guild Master Voight, but it also meant that I wouldn't need his favors. Still, I didn't want to blow off his request entirely. Getting Finley caught in the act of treason sounded pretty good to me. I should see what I could get done quickly.

"Cutter," I said, interrupting his spiel of how glorious the fights had been to the one person—Rhis—who had been listening. "Can you get the guards at the front desk to send a request for a meeting with the Chancellor? Regarding . . . past tax records. At his earliest convenience."

Cutter looked a little glum about even being associated with something as dull as tax records, but he dutifully repeated the message and left the room.

Chancellor, to my mind, sounded like the head of a university, but I was pretty sure that here it referred to the man in charge of the purse strings. Which was fine, I knew how to talk to money men.

He must have been interested in talking to me because a reply came back with an appointment for this afternoon. Was that just because he was curious about me, or did he have his own agenda? With a start, I realized that my case for Talnier's existence was almost entirely financial, and the Chancellor was someone that I should have gotten on my side first of all.

Well, better now than not at all. At least I wasn't going to run out of things to talk about.

I passed the time before the appointment commiserating with Felicia about how unreasonable the Alchemists were, and having lunch. When it was time, a guard escorted me through the restricted halls to where the Chancellor's office was.

I kept my eyes open, and more than that, my Mana Sense. This was a scouting expedition, after all. There didn't seem to be a lot of magical security in the hallway, but there was a field that covered almost all of the Chancellor's office.

"Councillor," said the man himself, coming out to greet me.

"Chancellor," I replied, curtsying. "How good of you to see me at such short notice." Rising, I looked him over as he led me into the office. He was an older man, with pale skin and dark hair. But the thing that caught my notice as we both settled into a pair of comfortable chairs was his large blue eyes.

"I always have time for people who bring in funds," he told me. He gave me a warm smile that didn't reach his eyes. "Most of my petitioners are seeking money in some form or another."

"I see," I said, and let him butter me up with inconsequential social chitchat, while I sized up the room for magic.

The man himself was wearing three magical items. I recognized one of them as the same type of storage ring I'd gotten from Talnier's dungeon. He wore another ring on his right—his dominant—hand. That one had an aura on it, but it only extended about a foot. The final one I couldn't see, but it was hanging around his neck, under his clothes.

The only other magic in the room were the enchantments that lit it. The main magic field seemed similar to the alarms on our doors and windows. I suspected it linked up to the same security center they did, but it was possible that it was set up for a more direct alarm after hours.

With the small talk out of the way, we moved on to the ostensible reason for my visit.

"Belatedly, it occurred to me that there might be some discrepancies between the records that I've been working with and the ones held in the capital," I explained.

"Discrepancies?" the Chancellor's eye twitched slightly, perhaps the only real emotion he'd shown so far. Despite his warm demeanor, and his baby blue eyes, Charm was telling me that this was all part of a routine facade.

"Why yes," I said, attempting to imbue my words with the seriousness that the Chancellor probably felt they deserved. "Given Baron Marseau's rampant criminality, it seemed likely that either he falsified the records he kept in Talnier or fed the Crown false information for your records. The only way to know for sure would be to compare the two."

I patted the files that I had brought. They were part of the preparation for my big presentation, but they served equally well for this purpose.

"It would be embarrassing to get contradicted during my audience with His Majesty," I continued. "And if there was an error, it could take some time to find out where it came from. So I thought it would best to check now."

"Of course, of course," the Chancellor replied. He glanced at the young man—a footman?—who was standing against the wall. "Fetch the records for Talnier for the last three years."

I smiled graciously and thanked him for assuaging my concerns. Truthfully, while faked records were a *concern*, they weren't really a concern of mine. My case was built on projections going forward, which were a sharp break from the past. Revelations about the Baron's prior misdeeds weren't going to change that.

The Chancellor didn't appreciate being lied to, though, which was what my suggested possibility amounted to. He insisted on helping me go through the figures, and once we'd successfully checked all the records, he let a small sigh of relief slip out.

"It seems I was worried over nothing," I said, as I started packing away my files. "I am sorry to have troubled you."

"Not at all, dear lady. The cost of correctness is rigorous checking for errors or falsehoods. It's been a pleasure to find someone as dedicated to bookkeeping as myself."

Was I fooling myself that there was now the tiniest bit of warmth in those eyes? I decided to push things a bit. When he called for his subordinate to return the records, I spoke up.

"Actually, do you think I could see how your own system of record-keeping works? There might be some lessons for us in Talnier."

"Of course!" he said and showed me into the back room. Or back rooms, rather, because it was a whole complex back here. There were five people scurrying about sorting and indexing files, and Agenor, as he suddenly started insisting I call him, was only too happy to explain what everyone was doing and how everything was organized.

The full tour took half an hour, but there were only a few things I needed to note. First of all, the records room did have its own exit—I didn't need to tramp through his office to get there. Secondly, the room didn't have any security, aside from the normal fields on the windows and doors. And third, one of the clerks had left his key sitting on his desk.

The final thing was when, with a casual wave of his hand, Agenor indicated where his personal correspondence was stored.

"Are you sure this is a good idea?" Felicia said, worrying. "Even if you don't get caught, surely he won't be keeping incriminating documents in his main office?"

"Maybe not, but I need to check the obvious place first," I said. I paused, giving her words more consideration. "Also, nothing that Agenor has done is actually illegal. Whatever his arrangements with the Lyrans are, I'm pretty sure he's got a sign-off from the King to negotiate. Finley's actions are all part of the sting. Whatever he does, it doesn't impinge on Agenor at all. Finally, if Agenor has set up a secret communication channel to Finley . . . well, talking to people isn't illegal."

I shrugged. "Maybe you can make the case that using it to *warn* him is traitorous, but until he does that, it's all above board."

"Wait, so are we the criminals, then?"

"Yep!" came the cheerful reply from Janie. I gave her a mock glare.

"I'm coming to terms with the idea that legal or illegal is what the King says it is," I said slowly. "If I get caught, I'm probably a criminal. If Finley goes down, we're probably heroes. Anything in between is . . . eh." I waggled my hand. "Could go either way."

With that comforting final thought, I was off.

There were a few things that had to go right for this to work. Having them go wrong was pretty low risk, though—I should be able to back out and try again another time.

Getting past the guard—they still had them in position throughout the night—was pretty easy. The first actual test was when I got to the archive room and looked under the door. It was dark, which came as some relief. If someone was burning the midnight oil, there wasn't much I could do while remaining undetected.

The magical alarm was a slight concern, but by now I was used to manipulating the security fields out of my way. The second test was actually coming up next.

[Phantasmal Object].

I cast the spell silently and gazed pensively at the key that appeared in my hand. I was fairly confident that it was good enough a copy to turn its lock. I was less sure that it was the key to the door, but how many doors would that clerk have a key to open? Still, there was only one way to find out.

Click. The soft sound of the lock opening was both music to my ears and terrifyingly loud. That was just my nervousness, though; the guards at the end of the corridor never stirred. I cast a Static Image on the door so they wouldn't notice it was open and stepped carefully inside.

I made sure with Mana Sense that no additional security had been applied after everyone had left, but it was all good. I couldn't see anything else, though. The corridor was lit, but the light was being blocked by my image, so all I had was the moonlight through the windows.

Not a problem for an adventurer, though. I slipped out a Darkvision potion and drank it in one gulp. It tasted like cough medicine, but it swiftly got to work on my eyes, raising the apparent brightness level. This potion gave vision in pitch-black, so the indirect moonlight was plenty.

I turned to the section that Agenor had indicated and went to work. I was going to have a long night ahead of me.

ADAMANT GUARDIANS

Look out!" Felicia yelled. I ducked down as a stone went whizzing by my head and shattered into pieces on the wall behind me. I *really* should be paying better attention.

"Sorry!" Kyle called back while doing his best to bash the Curab that had thrown it. He'd swapped his enchanted sword for a mundane but very heavy maul that was more effective against the creature's stone body.

> [Identification]: Small Serpentinite Curab – Threat 12 – Properties: Hard Body, Fire Resistance, Ranged Attack

Or *serpentinite* body, I guess. The strange, rocky creature was typical of what we'd found so far in the Adamant Guardians Mine. Despite being listed as small, it was almost two meters from one end of its claws to the other. Shaped somewhat like a crab, it had appeared to be a cubical block of stone before it unfolded and moved to attack. Similar blocks of stone— serpentinite and other types—lined the walls of the tunnel we were in.

The notion that any of these stone blocks could unfold itself into a monster made for a certain amount of paranoia, but we'd been assured that *most* of the blocks wouldn't do that. Every now and then, a block would wake up, pull itself out of the wall and go looking for something to eat. The chances of that happening when an adventurer was walking by, or resting against a wall, were small. But not nonexistent.

Left to itself, a Curab would eventually crawl into another hole and go to sleep again. Ones that were killed were replaced eventually, but over the years the Guild had killed Curabs in such numbers that the original cavern had expanded into a vast mine. There didn't appear to be any limit to the extent of the blocks. They just formed bigger and more durable Curabs the farther you got from the entrance.

The layout of the mine had been shaped by the constant movements of Curabs. Blocks didn't wake up in an evenly spaced pattern. Already existing holes seemed more likely to spawn Curabs, so long, branching tunnels were formed that led to more dangerous, and more valuable types of Curabs.

"Above you!" This time it was my turn to call a warning. To Janie, who looked up to see a swarm of glass beetles. Just in time to roast them before they jumped down on her.

[Identification]: Glass Beetle – Threat 6 – Properties: Fire Resistance, Swarm

We weren't really equipped for this dungeon. Club was not Kyle's best skill, though he was happy to get some practice with it. Similarly, a lot of the Curabs had Fire Resistance. It wasn't total immunity, but it greatly reduced Janie's damage output.

On the other hand, you wanted to kill glass beetles with fire. If you cut or smashed them, their glass bodies shattered into jagged, sharp-edged pieces. Dangerous if you stepped on them, or picked them up, but more importantly: they were worthless.

If you killed them with fire, on the other hand, the legs curled around their bodies and they shrunk to become solid glass wrapped around a mana crystal. You could still use the crystal through the glass, so they were a decorative rarity.

The novelty of these had worn off a long time ago, but people still liked them enough to pay a premium. No two bugs were exactly alike, so the Guild had created an elaborate classification system to value the damned things.

Kyle finally finished bashing his Curab into the floor. "Are we taking ... serpentinite?" he asked.

I checked the list. "Yeah ... stick it on the cart." Serpentine was fairly high on the list of rock types that we could expect to see on this beginner run. Kyle picked up the monster's mana crystal and started manhandling the block of stone onto the cart.

We had rented a hand cart for this run. It felt weird, but the floors of this dungeon were flat—barring the occasional hole—and the loot was *heavy*. Felicia had her bag of holding, but that had weight limits that were quickly reached when you were tossing blocks of stone in there. That was what Curabs dropped. When they finally died, they curled up again into a block of whatever stone they were made of. At deeper levels, they dropped additional materials, but here at the upper levels, it was just stone.

We all gathered up to discuss things, keeping an eye out in all directions. One of the things about the mine was that there weren't defined rooms. Just tunnels and caverns and monsters wandering about.

"What do we think?" Felicia asked.

"Curabs keep throwing rocks at me," I complained. "I miss being invisible." I wasn't using that spell just yet because we were still developing tactics for this dungeon and needed to see one another.

"Me too," Kyle agreed. "This is good practice, but this maul doesn't do enough damage and it's too hard to hit with. Blind helps with that, but being invisible is easier."

"These tunnels are too cramped, though," Janie said. "I can't keep my fire off you unless I know where you are. Unless I limited myself to bugs on the ceiling?"

"That's no good," I said. "Sooner or later we're going to have to go up there ourselves."

Janie blanched. "Uh, hanging from the ceiling? I know we saw those guys doing it, but all the blood would go to my head."

"It's not like that," I assured her. This was another peculiarity of the mine. "Each block provides its own gravity once you touch it."

"What you said doesn't make any sense," Janie countered.

"I mean . . . it's not like hanging," I said. I eyed the tunnel wall with some trepidation. We'd all been informed, and we had seen the other teams in the main cavern, but trying it out was something I had wanted to put off.

Swallowing, I put one foot up on the nearest wall. There was a solidity to the way I placed it that made me more confident about the next step. Before I lost my nerve, I gave a little jump with my other leg.

As soon as I left contact with the ground, I felt down switch directions on me. Now the wall was down, and I placed my other foot down without any problems.

"Oh, that is so freaky," Janie moaned, looking at me. She looked pretty weird herself, from my perspective, impossibly perched from what was now a wall.

"See how my hair hangs down?" I said. "For me, this direction is down now."

I took out a coin and dropped it. It fell, not in the direction that they would expect it to, but down to my feet. I stooped to pick it up again.

The main cavern of the Adamant Guardians Mine was a huge cubical cavern, with fissures and tunnels leading off in *all* directions. It was dark enough, aside from the pools of light that each party made around them, that you could *almost* ignore the fact that every party was making their way along a different wall, ceiling, or floor.

We'd taken the beginner's route, which avoided gravity changes, but we wouldn't be able to rely on that forever. I gave Janie a challenging look, and she sighed but went through the same process to join me on the wall—or floor.

"How are we going to get the cart here?" she asked.

"It's designed for it," I answered. "See how the wheels stick out from the front? Move it up to the wall," I told Kyle. He shrugged and wheeled the cart forward until its front wheels touched the wall. As he did so, the rocks shifted slightly, as the cart's local gravity switched to a 45-degree angle.

"This is why it's got those high walls," I said. I grabbed the handle from Kyle and pulled. The front wheels rose—from Kyle's perspective—and the cart slid easily up onto my wall. Once the back wheels left the old floor, the cart was fully reoriented.

"You see? Now let's work out some tactics because I'm still tired from last night."

"Long day?" Guild Master Voight asked solicitously and handed me a cup of tea.

"Long night," I said sourly. "I was up for half of it, going through the Chancellor's correspondence."

"You work fast," he said with a smile. "Did you find anything?"

"Not much," I said, sipping my tea. "I found some correspondence from Finley, but I doubt the Chancellor's secret communication channel is a letter. Unless it's a code?"

Voight just shrugged, so I considered the possibility. None of the messages were in what I thought of as code—random strings of letters. I was aware that there were codes that disguised themselves as normal communication, but none of the messages had seemed off to me. I thought that Intrigue would have noticed if I had found one of those codes, and feeling out the skill gave me a feeling of confirmation. Unless the Chancellor had a higher Intrigue skill, of course, which he probably did.

"I *was* able to find out the terms of his deal with the Lyrans," I said. "In exchange for luring the Duke into the sting, their import duties will be reduced to thirty percent. That seems high?"

Voight shrugged. "I'm not familiar with the current tax regime, but foreign imports are typically taxed somewhere between fifty and 100 percent."

That's insane! I thought. *How is he going to encourage trade with those kinds of taxes?* I kept my face calm and just made a note for later. The King *probably* wouldn't take kindly to me explaining the benefits of a free trade regime, but there must be something I could do to get the taxes reduced.

"Right. So that seems like a decent suggestion. The other thing is that their warships are to have access to the Maelstrom Strait, whatever that is, for the next three months.

"Mmn." Voight frowned, considering the implications as he explained it to me. "The waters north of the King's Isle are treacherous. Too many underwater dungeons in a small area."

"Dungeons can form underwater? How do they get cleared?"

"Mostly, they don't, so they're almost always breaking," he told me. "Hence the danger. They spend most of their mana attacking one another, though, so as long as you're not between two of them, you are fairly safe. There are two routes through, one hugging the coast to the north, and the other coming close to King's Isle."

"I'm guessing the one close to the island is the Maelstrom Strait," I said.

"Correct. It is heavily patrolled, both to keep it safe from monsters and to control what ships pass through. Military ships would not normally be allowed."

"But if the Lyrans were attacking King's Isle, they'd break through and use that strait," I guessed.

"Yes. It is a bit of a risk, but it is a good way to convince someone that you've started a serious attack. Finley must have someone watching the Strait . . . perhaps a spy on the Isle."

"If he has a spy on the island, though, he'll know fairly quickly that the island *isn't* being attacked," I pointed out.

"Yeesss . . ." Voight said slowly. "The timing would be important—and we may not yet have the full picture of the scheme. Perhaps the Chancellor is counting on this spy to blow the operation at the last minute? I will have to contact the Guild there to look into this."

"Hopefully that's enough," I said. "I hate to cut and run, but I'm meeting with the King tomorrow, so I suspect that my trip here will be ending soon."

"Perhaps, perhaps not." The Guild Master smiled slyly. "One audience may not be enough for the King to decide matters. And you have yet to have your promised meeting with the Duke."

"Ugh, don't remind me," I growled. "*Not* meeting him suits me fine, especially if that delays him threatening me further."

"He's not a patient man. If he's accepted your delays thus far, it's more likely because he's busy with this current plan."

"Whatever keeps me off of his agenda." I rose and gave him a curtsy. "And now, if you'll excuse me, I have a meeting with the King to prepare for."

AUDIENCE OF ONE

I knew I was in trouble when he sent everyone else away. Up until then, the presentation had been going just fine. I was missing PowerPoint badly, but I had decided to not replace it with illusions. As much as I wanted to, it would probably draw too much attention.

Aside from that lack, it wasn't too different from presentations I'd done about the profitability of one corporation or another. The older white men listening were dressed differently, but they had that same look of slightly bored attentiveness that investors tended to have. They nodded in all the right places as I extolled the benefits of my—er, the Council's—policies. Promises of a river of gold flowing freely into the Kingdom's coffers were only *slightly* exaggerated, but no one called me on it.

I danced around the awkward fact that the King hadn't *authorized* this lucrative trade by pretending that he had. After all, the document that he *had* authorized sort of said that I could. Taken in the right light. So I gave him all the credit, praising the wisdom that had led to this opportunity for a very lucrative back door.

There had been questions from the people around the table. The Chancellor, the Chamberlain, the Minister for State Affairs, and even the Harbormaster for some reason. I was pretty pleased with how well I answered them. Memorize brought me the relevant information right when I needed it, making up for the lack of nicely printed reports. I had copied out some of the details to hand out, of course, but Scribe was no replacement for a color photocopier.

Throughout it all, the King had stayed silent, waiting until his advisors had run out of questions. Then he dismissed them with two words.

"That's enough."

As one, his advisors rose and bowed to their liege. I made to do the same, but a quick shake of the Chancellor's head stopped me from making a fool of myself. I sat there as the advisors all trooped outside, the guards following them, closing the doors behind them. We were alone.

There was silence for a while. I glanced around warily, while the King's attention was fixed on me. Finally, he spoke.

"Your taxes are too low." The words weren't accompanied by the weight that Intimidation or Persuasion would bring. They were just words, which encouraged me to actually respond.

"*Your* taxes are too high," I snapped right back. Not exactly an original idea—try and find a banker who *didn't* think that. "They don't leave enough for the merchants to grow their business."

"And why should I care about that?"

"If a merchant's making 100 gold profit, and you take half of that," I said, "he'll not ever make more than that. If you take a tenth, then in ten years' time he'll be making 1,000 gold, and your tenth will be twice what you'd earn the other way."

"And if he chooses to spend his money on luxuries instead of his business?"

I shrugged. "Then he'll lose his business to someone who isn't as foolish."

"A curious notion. Where did you come across it?"

"Listen to any merchant; he'll tell you his taxes are too high. Listen a little longer, and he'll tell you what he could do if he didn't have that burden."

"And would they say that about your taxes?"

"Probably," I admitted. "No one *likes* taxes, after all. There's a balance to be had between the growth of commerce and the needs of the state, and merchants can only see one side. That doesn't mean their side is wrong, though."

"Hmm." The King considered me for a long moment. "And is this what you have come here for, Kandis Hammond? Have you come to educate us on tax policy?"

"I came here because you summoned me, Your Majesty," I said, remembering my manners. It seemed that medieval etiquette was somehow incompatible with lessons in basic economics.

"Not to this city, to this world. For you are a Worldwalker, are you not, Councillor?"

Ah, shit. I sort of froze while I considered the possibility that I might deny it. It wasn't as if he could prove it or anything. There were priests that could Identify me, and there were others that could see through illusions, but he'd have a hard time getting them to cooperate. I was part of the gods' game, after all.

On the other hand, was there any use in denying it? I probably wasn't going to be able to convince him otherwise, especially since he wouldn't have accused me without some evidence.

"Is that going to be a problem?" I asked cautiously. There was always the go invisible and run option, though I guessed that it wouldn't be as easy as that.

"That depends," he said gravely. "Which God has chosen you, and what is your mission in my country?"

Ah.

"I'm afraid I don't know the answer to either of those questions, Your Majesty," I said. "While I've spoken to some gods, they've all been ones that couldn't be my patron."

The King frowned at my first sentence, and the frown grew deeper as I continued. I could feel his Intimidation gathering, like a boiling storm cloud ready to strike me with lightning.

"Is. That. True." His words weren't spoken loudly, but they had all the force of his skill behind them.

"Yes." The word came easily. I would have had a hard time if I'd wanted to lie.

"Which gods?" he asked. The Intimidation was ramped down, but only by a bit.

"A few words from Naldyna, some conversations with Fyskal. And . . ." I hesitated. If there were going to be problems, it would probably be with this one. ". . . recently, a conversation with Ashmor."

"Recently? In my city?"

"Yeah. I mean, yes, Your Majesty."

"Phadan's mercy," he muttered. "You're sure he isn't your patron?"

I made a helpless gesture. "I only know what I've been told, and that was that neither Fyskal nor Ashmor participates in this game. Fyskal said that he was the *referee*."

"The Deceiver sitting in judgment. It takes a god to be that foolish. What did Ashmor want?"

"He had some plan for me to destroy the world for a chance of a ride home," I said. "I don't know why he thought that would be an attractive offer."

"Why, indeed." The King looked me over very carefully. If he noticed anything, he kept it to himself.

"So," he finally said. "Your actions in this kingdom have been your own, and not at the behest of any god."

"It was implied," I said, "that I had been carefully selected as one who would naturally take the actions that helped my patron's agenda. And that actually communicating those goals would make me less likely to act that way."

"This was Fyskal, I presume." When I nodded, he sighed. "I'd advise ignoring everything that he told you. His lies are insidious. Trying to identify them is a fool's errand."

"I'm . . . not really in a position to do that," I said. He nodded sadly.

"Then let us move on to other things. You stole the Dungeon core from Oakway."

"What makes you say that?" His Intimidation had faded by now, so I was able to dissemble somewhat. I didn't hold out much hope of that continuing, though.

He chuckled. "There are not so many sources of chaos in my realm that I can't put the dots together. You were the starting adventurer, Katherine Meland, in disguise. No one else had the motive or means to steal the core, except perhaps Reynard, and he has been cleared of *that* particular crime. So it was you. Why?"

"It spoiled Reynard's plans," I admitted. "I had heard something about using it to become more powerful, but I still don't know exactly how. Are you . . . going to want it back?"

"No," he said, waving his hand dismissively. "If cores were scarce, we could just make more the same way you did. What *is* scarce is places where they can be used."

He looked at me speculatively. "I suppose . . . that of all the things a Worldwalker could do, becoming a Dungeon Master would be among the least disruptive. If you can find an unclaimed font of mana, then, by all means, claim it for your core."

"Is that really the case, though?" I asked doubtfully. "Agden Shadthe is a Dungeon Master, right? He sounds pretty disruptive."

He laughed. "Shadthe, for all his efforts, has yet to topple a Kingdom—though he has come close, I'll admit. Your predecessors shattered an Empire."

"Right now, all I want to do is generate wealth and prosperity by applying some decent social and economic policies."

"Indeed? Well—" The King stopped speaking and swivelled his head to look at the door. I had also heard the click, so I turned to see . . . a head.

Poking around the slightly opened door, parallel to the floor, the head of Vodurn was winking at me.

"My lord! I was sent to see if you'd fallen asleep, or perhaps fallen into a bed."

Once again, the words came through as slightly odd, but not as amusing as the King seemed to find them. It sounded like the man had made a dirty joke at my expense, so I elected to frown.

"Did they?" was all the King said.

"Indeed, sire. Your Councillors are *restive*, your honored guests are becoming *pensive,* and your humble servants are running out of wine to distract them with."

"We'll have to continue this later then," the King said.

"Your Majesty, I'd hoped to gain your approval so that I could get back to Talnier . . . it's in a critical period right now."

"Well, it will have to wait. The Champion of Life will be in town in a few weeks; I understand you have some differences to resolve."

He sent a cold smile my way. "If you two are going to fight, I'd rather it happen under my supervision."

Then he strode out of the chamber without another word. Vodurn quickly opened the door fully, getting out of the way so that he could bow to the King as he passed by. Then he looked up at me.

"We meet again, fair lady!"

I was still swearing to myself at the King's cavalier treatment of me, but I tried to put on a gracious face.

"Yes, I suppose we do."

"Permit me to escort you back to your apartment. This is a sensitive area, and it wouldn't do for you to be summarily expelled."

I was fairly sure that some of the guards had remained behind for that exact purpose, but it couldn't hurt to have an escort of a higher rank.

"I suppose being accompanied by a Fool is what I deserve right now," I said wryly. I joined him at the door and we started making our way back. The pair of guards that had escorted me here, I noticed, had stayed behind, but now showed no signs of wanting to follow me.

"Did your meeting not go well?" he asked solicitously.

"It didn't go *badly*, but I didn't get what I wanted. Now I'm stuck here until the King can find time for me again."

"Ah, forced to live in the lap of luxury, how terrible," Vodurn teased.

"I have things to do back in Talnier!" I insisted. "Plans that can help people, that I can't do here!"

"Can't you?" he asked. "Is there no use for your skills in this city?"

I gave him a look, but he just smiled innocently. "Were you—" *Listening*, I wanted to say, but he wasn't going to admit to eavesdropping on the King.

"I'm sure you'll find something productive to do with your time here," he said brightly. "And didn't you mention something about wanting to meet with Duke Finley?"

"Something *like* that," I said sourly.

"Perhaps this might be of use?" He handed me a slip of paper with a flourish—using some sort of sleight of hand to make it appear out of nowhere.

"What's this?" I asked suspiciously, but the question was answered by the object itself. Ornately hand-painted, it appeared to be an open invitation to the holder and one guest to attend for one night at the "Choice of the Chosen."

"It's a . . . club you might say. A place for quiet, if not entirely discreet meetings. A neutral ground."

"How did you get this?" I wondered.

"Oh, people are always seeking my favor," he said. "Ear of the King and all that. I've a stack of them."

"If this is another underground fighting ring . . ." I warned him.

"Oh no, no, this is a genteel establishment for civilized people," he said. "An underground fighting ring? Wherever did you find such a thing?"

He shook his head in disbelief. "You must have been naughty and slipped your escort to attend such a place. Rest assured, you need have no concerns about taking your escort *here*."

He leaned forward conspiratorially. "And as it happens, I have it on very good authority that Duke Finley will be attending this club two nights hence."

SLUMMING IT

"Can I help you?"

The words were a challenge, not an offer. They came from the young woman looking down on me from the balcony above.

"I was just wondering what this building was for," I called up. "It seems like the only one that isn't a whorehouse or a gutted ruin." I glanced over to the other side of the street. The building that had been there looked to have burned down a long time ago, but there was no sign that the remains were going to be replaced, or even cleared up. This was not a good part of town.

The one benefit that I had received from my audience was that the restriction on my movements had been lifted. We'd been informed that while an escort *could* be requested, and *was* recommended, it was no longer required.

Since none of the threats to my life had been addressed, the only reason we could come up with for the end of Luxury Jail was that it had something to do with admitting my status as a Chosen. Precisely what, no one could say. We'd also discussed the possibility that we were being secretly followed, but despite looking, we hadn't seen anything.

So I'd given in to what was almost certainly a bad idea and gone without an official escort to one of the shadier areas in the city. I'd looked it over before, but now I could check it out more closely. It still had a mess of leftover chaotic mana swirling over it, the perfect camouflage for what I wanted to do.

"There's no business going on here," the woman called down. "We're . . . between tenants."

"Oh? I'm interested in renting."

The woman gave me a hard look. "I'll come down," she said.

"Did you have to mention that you have money?" Janie asked quietly. She was, with Maslin's help, trying to watch every direction at once.

"Just our gear is more money than most of these will see in a year," I pointed out. Knowing where we were going, we had dressed in our adventurer's gear. Overkill for a shady street, but it kept the predators at bay. I imagined that the street picked up at night, but even during the day there were a number of rough-looking fellows out and about. Some of them were touting for business, but all of them pointedly ignored us after one glance.

Janie wanted to say more, but the sound of the door opening interrupted us. The woman stood in the darkened doorway, looking us over with a complicated expression. She was tall and thin—she'd clearly skipped a few meals, but she looked healthy.

"I'm Kandis, and my friends are Janie and Maslin," I said.

"Issey," she said. "You'd better come in; sorry about the darkness."

She left the door open to light the room. The only other light source was the door at the other end—and it was quite a large entryway.

[Light].

Out of habit, I cast my simplest spell. A bright ball of light left my palm and hovered up into the air above me.

High ceilings, I thought. I'd guessed the building at four stories, but I revised that down to three. The room that was revealed . . . well, it had definitely seen better days. The paint on the walls was peeling, the carpet was worn and faded. The walls had darker spots where paintings had once hung. It was clean, though; there was no debris on the floor.

The woman—Issey—was looking at me with alarm.

"It's just a spell," I said. "We're adventurers."

Issey nodded slowly. Adventurers meant money, after all.

"So what was this place?" I asked, moving out of the entryway. I found myself in a massive hall. It had been lit only by natural light coming in from the balconies on the second floor and windows on the third. That was a fair amount of light, but it didn't go far. The middle of the room was shrouded in shadows, but I could make out an expanse of tables and chairs stacked on top of one another and covered in rotting drop cloths.

I sent the light out to the middle of the room and increased it to the maximum brightness so we could get a look at the place.

"Dance hall," Issey said, pointing to what looked like a stage at the far end of the room.

"Dance hall?" I repeated. It looked more like a club or music hall. We walked slowly down a central aisle cleared of tables.

"You don't see them anymore," she replied, misunderstanding my confusion. "Since the Empire fell, there hasn't been the money for it."

"Not even in the capital?" I asked, trying to get my bearings. I looked over at Janie, but she didn't seem to understand either.

"The capital's seen hard times," Issey said sadly. "This place used to belong to my grandmother, the Doyenne of Dance. Mum told me lots of stories. It was a going concern, still, for most of her life, but the income kept dropping and the expenses kept rising. Then the brothels started moving in, and nobody wanted to come here anymore."

"To dance," I said, still not seeing it.

"No," Issey said. "To see *us* Dance." Then she showed me what she meant.

Now, I could dance. Whether it was at a club or the more formal kind of dance, I knew enough not to embarrass myself on the dance floor. In this world, I'd taken a bit of time to go over the forms with Felicia, and it was easy enough. The dances were different, but not *that* different.

Having supernatural strength and agility helped, of course. How could it not? The odd thing was that there were only a few areas of my life where it was really noticeable. Combat, of course, but my movement during those times was also governed by my skills. It barely felt as if I was doing anything.

Going through the motions with Felicia had eventually unlocked the skill. I hadn't taken it, though, and nothing I'd tried privately had given me Dance through competency. I guess the System didn't consider pops, locks, and spins as real dance moves.

Now I saw what it *did*. The dance floor was at least ten meters away from us, but Issey landed on it in three graceful steps. Or leaps? Pushing off with one leg, gracefully arching forward with her legs separated and then landing on the other leg, as if she'd just taken a normal step. Two of those, and then a third that sent her high in the air, backflipping and landing on the raised stage with her legs together and her arms apart.

I could . . . do that maybe? Physically, at least, I could manage something that had the same description. I was pretty sure that my abilities were higher than hers. She felt like a level three, so she couldn't have Ability scores that high. But I couldn't do *that*. Moving with such grace and poise that my mouth was gaping in surprise. That was what Dance did.

I was stunned, and she'd only gotten on stage. It looked as if she might show me more, but we were interrupted by someone clapping from the door.

"Ah, nice, nice, Busy Issey! Showing off for your new clients? You don't show us that stuff no more."

Issey froze, and we all looked back at the entrance to see three young men, best described as louts. They had greasy unwashed hair, greasy unwashed clothes and a greasy unwashed demeanor. I wasn't sure how they'd managed to get an unwashed demeanor, but they'd managed it.

"Ain'tcha gonna introduce us, Busy Issey?"

I noted that his poor elocution somehow made it past the translation. Maybe it was an exact match for poorly spoken English?

Issey spoke from behind us. "This is Digger, Bigger, and Winger. They live around here."

The lead youth's face darkened with anger. "Bitch! Introduce us properly!"

"And what is it that you do for a living, Digger?" I interrupted.

He sneered at me. "We rob adventurers."

"Really?" They didn't look the type. Well, they looked the type to *try*, but not succeed. They felt about level three, the same as Issey.

Issey spoke again, perhaps emboldened by the fact that we were between her and them. "They mostly hang out in the alley behind all the brothels. When a client gets drunk and disorderly, the madams kick them out the front door. When they get drunk and disorderly and *annoying*, they kick them out the back. Getting robbed by these guys is an extra punishment."

Digger's face worked as if he were trying to say something, but I spoke before he could figure it out. "Well, that's a lovely niche you've found for yourself, but what brings you here?"

I swear, I could see the thoughts run through his head as they swam to the surface. "We got a job for Little Issey!" he finally said.

"Like I'd work for any place that'd talk to you," Issey replied scornfully.

"Ah, don't be like that. You're working at the Chosen, right? Ain't no difference between there and the Rose."

"There's every difference, you asshole," Issey shot back. "Just because you want to be a pimp doesn't make me your whore."

"Once I break your leg, you won't have a choice, bitch!"

"Okay! That's enough." I said loudly. "You three need to leave. Now."

"You think I'm scared of you?" he asked aggressively, taking a step forward. "Maybe I'll get three whores today."

"I honestly don't understand why you're not," I admitted. "Janie, a demonstration?"

Janie stepped forward. Suddenly her hand was wreathed in flames, and she had the boy's undivided attention.

"Demonstration means I only set one of them on fire, right?" she said. They didn't stick around to hear my answer. Janie snickered and followed them at an easy walk. When she got to the door, she looked out and then extinguished her flame.

"Still running," she said, closing and barring the door. "Does the lock not work?"

"Rusted solid," Issey admitted. She'd come forward off the stage and joined me, casting a wary eye on Janie as she returned. "Should have kept the door shut," she muttered.

"It doesn't matter," I assured her. "You live here?"

"Yeah, there's rooms in the back. The back door's lock still works, so I don't have to bother you with whatever you want to do here."

I made a noncommittal noise. Truthfully, it would be problematic having her in the building. I wasn't sure how illegal it was to run my own private dungeon. The King had given his blessing, but I was fairly sure that counted for exactly nothing if it became widespread knowledge. I needed a lawyer, but I wasn't sure if this country had a version of attorney-client privilege.

I was probably going to have to figure out if this woman could be trusted before I committed to anything.

"How much are you asking?" I asked idly.

"Why don't you make me an offer," she countered. At least she thought she did. She had Bargain, and in the moment of that exchange, our skills had clashed. She'd learned that I had a considerably higher skill total, and I'd learned that she was desperate enough to accept any positive offer.

"Fyskal's truths!" she swore. She was well aware of her own desperation, so she must have figured that I knew now, as well. I met her eyes for a moment and then moved on. This was good and bad news. It meant I could get this place for cheap, but if she was truly desperate for money, she could also get some for selling me out. Rather than grab an easy deal now, it would be better to give her time to understand the benefits of throwing in with me.

"That Chosen place that Digger mentioned," I asked, "Would that be the Choice of the Chosen?"

"Yeah. It's . . . a reputable place," Issey said carefully. "They don't . . . pay well, but they pay."

"All those pauses," I noted. "You dance there, then?"

She nodded. "Most nights."

"What can you tell me about the place?" I asked. "I'm going there tomorrow night, and it would be nice to know what I'm getting into."

To my surprise, Issey instantly backed away from me and went down on her knees.

"I'm sorry for my impertinence, my lady!" she said desperately. "I didn't know! I thought you were an adventurer."

I looked at Janie, who was just as surprised as I am.

"Get up, Issey," I said gently. "Just what kind of place is this club?"

CHOSEΠ

Why does the King want me here? I wondered, as my carriage pulled up to the club. I was fairly sure he did. The little game he'd played with his Fool was transparent enough that I thought he'd expect me to see through it. He might have done it that way just so that I'd be unable to ask him why.

The question was actually in two parts. Why did he want me to meet with Finley, and why *here*? Was it just because Finley was going to be here, or did it have to do with the nature of the place? I couldn't help but think this was all part of an elaborate joke. At whose expense, I couldn't tell.

I cast an eye on the front of the place. It looked expensive. There was heavy use of opalime, something I was a little tired of, but at least the statues in dark marble broke it up. They were lit up, with enchantments, no less. Lighting things up with enchantments was the province of the rich, of course. Using them outside, where they could be stolen by passersby, gave the impression that *this* was a place the riffraff were kept well away from. As for the statues themselves, well . . .

"Curious?" my companion asked mischievously. "Don't worry, they'll have one of you soon enough."

I glared at her, but my escort was at the door, so I let myself get helped out of the carriage. Since this was practically official royal business, I'd helped myself to a palace carriage to go with my escort. Anyone watching should be in no doubt that I was a guest of the King.

I thanked the guard as I stepped down and then looked over the statues. Seven statues made for an awkward arrangement if you wanted to have a door in the middle of your building. The architects had gotten around it by placing one of the statues in the middle, flanked by two identical double doors. Three statues were on each side of those.

I couldn't help looking over the three that we passed on the way to the doors. Nine feet tall, they were impressive, if slightly cringe inducing. I'd heard the names, and could make a guess as to which statue was which, but I didn't need to because each plinth held the name and most notable deed of the dead Champion.

Tilly Osborne, Rishi Laghari, and Peamanh Medaraasel. The marble didn't show skin tone, but I knew that Tilly was English, Rishi was Indian and Peamanh was a Persian from Turkey. They'd brought down the Empire and founded the successor kingdoms. Four of them had died in the process. We were going to get to the doors before passing the middle statue, but I figured that would be Arthur Alexander, the one who'd stayed in this kingdom until his death.

I suppose it was nice that they were remembered, but it was a little embarrassing to think that I might be remembered in the same way.

"The Founders aren't generally *revered* in Latora, though they are more well-known than most Champions," my companion continued. "But there is a faction of the nobility that feels the Founders' acts need to be remembered, lest the nobility be considered ungrateful. And so, this place exists."

There was a certain amount of amusement in Manuela's tone, as if the Ebon Order envoy appreciated the irony of a Champion attending this place incognito. She'd told me that they had tried very hard to get Isidre, the other Worldwalker, to attend on her first visit to the capital.

I'd much rather have visited this place with one of my friends at my side, but I only had an invitation for one guest, and I needed a guide. Not for getting here, but to navigate once we were inside. I knew that finding Duke Finley wouldn't be a matter of wandering about. He'd be winkled away in some private room, so getting to him was going to take a certain amount of effort and clout.

"Start by asking if the Duke is in," she murmured as we went in the doors. A man was there to inspect our invitation, so I started up Conversation.

Conversation was an interesting skill—I'd been levelling it without realizing I was even using it. It wasn't confrontational like Intimidate or Bargain; it just let you direct the conversation in a natural manner. It didn't sound like much, but in a social situation, there was a lot that someone could tell you if they weren't on guard against it.

Striking up a conversation with the man while he examined our invitation, Charm quickly put him at ease. We could probably have gotten in even if the thing had been fake. When I asked him if Duke Finley had arrived yet, he must have thought that we were a part of his entourage, because he answered without a thought.

"Oh no, ma'am. His private room is ready, but he hasn't arrived. Shall I have word sent once he does?"

I glanced at Manuela, "Yes, that will be fine," she said. "Have them look for us in the Sapphire Room."

"Of course, ma'am," the man said. Manuela giggled, and led me off, presumably to the Sapphire Room.

"I do love working with high Charisma types," she said. "He should have asked for your name, so he could let Finley know you were here."

"I wanted us to be a surprise," I admitted.

"And so the question never came up. Priceless."

She led me down a corridor and then opened a door marked Sapphire. Music, conversation, and laughter floated out.

"Come on," she said and went inside.

Inside was . . . something like a cabaret club. It wasn't a terribly large room, and a lot of the space was taken up by a stage in the center. Some musicians were playing in a cramped space in one corner, and the rest of the room was taken up by a small table. The air was hazy, but not with smoke.

"Is that . . . incense?" I asked. It smelled sweet and musky.

"These rooms never get aired out enough," Manuela replied carelessly. "They clean them, of course, but a smell can build up . . . they cover it with the incense."

"Charming," I said. Fortunately this world—or at least this country—hadn't discovered the dubious joys of tobacco.

"Shh, the show is about to start."

I looked at the stage, where a young woman was walking out. Not Issey. While she was working tonight, it was either at a different time or in a different room. This lady was dressed in a fantastical costume—not that different from something you'd see in a stage production or cosplay event. A tightly fitted leotard showed off her curves, while a poofy tutu emphasized them further. Her arms and legs were left bare, for freedom of movement—and for display. Glittering glass—according to Identify—beads covered the entire costume.

I glanced over the audience, mostly male. They were enjoying the show before it had even started. At least they weren't being overt about it.

This was a reputable establishment. As the dancer started, I thought about what Issey had told me that meant.

A reputable establishment meant that the dancing girls weren't for rent afterwards. In a less reputable establishment, the dancing was really only an advertisement for the real wares. That was how the lower-class places made enough to keep going after the economy dropped off in Dorsay.

It was only the nobles, with more money than they knew what to do with, that would fund a place like this. And that meant that the dancers had to deal with the most entitled form of drunken patron. Jumping on stage to paw at them, sneaking into the dressing rooms . . . it wasn't *allowed*; the perpetrators were *punished*, just not seriously.

No turning offenders over to the law. Just a fine or a ban for a month. I forced down my anger and watched the show.

It was something to see. Why isn't music like this? I wondered. There were people playing right now who must have had skills. It was fine, it was music, but it wasn't . . . this.

We all had enhanced strength, agility and dexterity. That didn't seem to mean so much when playing an instrument. After all, if a normal human could play a lute perfectly, what was superhuman dexterity going to add? It must make such a feat easier, sure, but perfect is perfect.

It seemed that there was no such limit on Dancing and seeing it for myself was breathtaking. She moved . . . impossibly. Like some kind of animation where the only connection between the frames is artistic inspiration, she moved in a way that was only loosely guided by physics.

It was over way too soon—it felt like only a heartbeat before she took a bow and walked off the stage.

"What was that?" I asked wonderingly. Manuela laughed.

"She's good, isn't she?" she said. I looked over at her, and my mood soured. *From ecstasy to irritation in a moment. Why can't anything last?* I asked myself, as the man I'd seen behind her moved forward.

Lord Aubert. He was moving forward as if he actually wanted to talk to me, and so it proved.

"Kandis— Councillor Hammond—I need to speak with you."

"You were looking for me here?" I asked.

"No, I just saw—" he broke off, looking at Manuela and then doing a double take as he registered her clothes. "I—need to speak in private," he said, giving a little twitch of his head in her direction.

I wasn't happy about the idea of blowing off Manuela to speak with

Aubey, but for him to bring himself to talk to me, it must have been important. I was about to reluctantly agree when I was saved.

The pause while I was considering it was enough for a servant to sidle up and say "Ma'am, the Duke has arrived at his room."

"The Duke?" Aubey asked, his face darkening.

"Finley," I answered, and got to watch his face go all the way red. "I'm afraid a duke takes precedence. Why don't you visit my rooms tomorrow?"

I nodded to the servant, and he led the pair of us off.

"That was hilarious," Manuela giggled, once we were out of earshot. "I thought he was going to explode—or even cause a scene. Do all nobles hate you that much?"

"Only the ones that know me," I admitted. Given the nobles I had met, it wasn't surprising so much as depressing. "And here comes another one."

"Just walk on in like you own the place," she murmured in my ear, too softly for our guide to hear. "They don't know that you weren't invited."

I took her advice, ignoring the servant posted in front of the door, and walked right in. As the door opened, I wondered if I should have knocked. Too late now.

If I'd been hoping to catch the Duke with his clothes off (I wasn't) I would have been disappointed. He had decided to start his evening off with a meal. He looked up from it, clearly irritated at being interrupted. The irritation grew when he saw who had interrupted him.

"Duke Finley, what a coincidence that we should run into each other like this!" I said, striding forward. From behind me, I heard the door close hastily, the servants outside choosing to make themselves scarce.

"Hammond," he said rudely. "I *said* I was going to send another message."

"Your previous messengers were so rude," I said, affecting a casual demeanor I did not feel. "Disappearing on us like that. I wasn't sure if the next lot would be so polite."

"So you decided to barge in on my meal. Bringing . . . *this* along with you." He glanced sourly at Manuela. "Just what is your master up to, girl?"

"Many things, my lord," Manuela said serenely. "All of them are, alas, a secret."

"Manuela offered to show me around the city," I said. "We've been taking in all the top night spots."

I sat down at the table opposite him. "Now, I believe that we had some business to discuss. I'm sure it won't take long."

CONTEMPT

No indeed, this should not take long," the Duke said, looking at me over his meal. "Hector has convinced himself that he would be better served if you were in his bed, rather than a grave. Just looking at you, I can see why he lost his head, but I do have to entertain the possibility that he might be right."

His Intimidate was stronger than mine, and he had it on full blast. Fortunately, you didn't need to defend against Intimidation with the same skill. You didn't even need to know what skill to use—the most appropriate one would just jump in.

I hadn't realized what skills I was using in the early days, but I was getting better at recognizing them now, so I knew it was Conversation that was taking the fore.

"How crude," I said disdainfully. "I expected better from a duke."

Finley frowned to see me unperturbed by his verbal offensive. We weren't in a Social Contest—at least, not yet. The Duke was just lashing out, and I didn't want to start anything. While I might be able to beat him, after the 24 hours were up he could just send assassins after me. Again.

"If that's true, then you have much to learn about your betters," he sneered. "So, then, convince me that I am better off with you as the dutiful wife of my new Baron."

"Do you need to go that far, my lord?" I asked, Charm inserting the honorific when I forgot. "A free Talnier would be neutral in whatever conflict you are planning with Bargougne."

Finley's eyes narrowed in anger. "Watch your tongue, girl. Victor is a peer; when you leave off his title, you disrespect me." His Intimidate flared again, but a threat once ignored is just empty after that.

"My apologies: Lord Bargougne," I said flatly.

He relaxed slightly. "As to the question, obviously a Talnier working for me is better than one that is neutral."

"But the cost of subduing a town, my lord," I protested. "Even ignoring casualties, the King's troops will leave, and you will need men to defend against the Beast King *and* Lord Duvost trying to take the town back. Not to mention suppressing resistance within the town."

"Which is the only reason I'm entertaining this mad idea that you can deliver the town to me."

"I'd rather convince you to leave us alone entirely." Persuasion was itching to be let off the lead, but I held back. Against greed like this, I could only give the town a temporary respite before he'd be back.

"Forget about that possibility," he said. "I will have Talnier, by blood if necessary, by marriage if it's possible. Convince me that it is."

This isn't going to work.

"No," I said.

"No?" he asked. "No." He repeated the word, a look on his face as if he were tasting how it sounded. I supposed that he didn't hear it *often.*

"No," I repeated. I'd been sounding him out over the course of our conversation, looking for the possibility that we could come to some sort of accord. But there was no give in him, nothing to be negotiated over. He'd take what he wanted, and what he wanted was everything.

"I'm not going to be your vassal, and Talnier is going to remain free, under the King's approved Charter."

"Your bravado does you credit," he sneered, "but you are making a mistake."

"I don't think so," I said. "The mistake would be to associate with you at all."

"Then—" he started, but was interrupted by Manuela's applause. She looked entirely unapologetic when he glared at her.

"Then, I don't think you have any more to say to me," he said. "Get out."

"Well that was fun," Manuela said when we were back in the carriage. "Do you think that's why the King sent you there?"

"I'm fuzzy on what he was trying to accomplish," I admitted. "I don't see how it could have gone any other way."

"Didn't you want to string him along for longer?"

"I did . . . but I've seen enough to know that that wouldn't work. He insists on commitment from those that he deals with." I neglected to mention that part of this was based on my observations of him dealing with the Lyran ambassador. "He'd have insisted on me signing some kind of marriage vow before I left the room."

"The King must know what he's like, though," I mused. "And he knows I'm not going to give up Talnier. I doubt he wants me to. So why?"

"Hmm. It seemed like the good Duke didn't know you were Chosen, didn't it?"

"I suppose."

Manuela switched seats, joining my side of the carriage. She grabbed my arm and pulled me close in an overly familiar embrace. "Let me give you a bit of insight into Chosen from the other side," she whispered conspiratorially. She was close enough that I could smell her floral perfume.

"Once you've grown out of your ever-so adorable baby phase," she murmured, "once you're no longer so easy to kill or manipulate, you make for very tough opponents."

"Do we," I said, unamused by her antics. I had thought we'd gotten past this the other night.

"Oh yes. You're backed by a god, remember? Even if their influence is subtle, it can be nigh irresistible. No one wants to go against one, unless they're backed by another Chosen."

"That makes sense," I admitted.

"So one easy thing you can do," she continued, "is to send your enemies after them."

"Wait, you think the King sicced his Duke on me?"

"Finley was already after you," Manuela shrugged. "The King just cleared the way."

"You think the King wants me to kill one of his own dukes," I said.

"I doubt he'd be upset if it went the other way," she said slyly. "He can't be pleased with all these Champions messing up the landscape."

"He killed my father!" Aubey yelled. "You were there!"

"You're making a scene, Lord Aubert," I said with an icy glare. "Control yourself before you get thrown out."

Against Aubey, even my relatively puny Intimidate was more than enough. Aubert froze and went pale. Reaching for a seat opposite me, he collapsed into it. I really should use Intimidate more, but there were reasons why I didn't.

He should have known better, though, on many counts. Intimidate required a valid threat to work. Most adventurers could just use their physical presence, and the promise of violence, to be taken seriously. Myself, not so much. Having him thrown out, though, was a credible threat. Not of physical harm, but of embarrassment, which might be worse.

By yelling at me in the palace dining hall, he'd opened himself up to being shut down. Maybe he thought, having gained a level, that he didn't have to worry about my Charisma anymore, but as I said, he should have known better.

I kept the pressure on as I finished my meal, managing to succeed at what Duke Finley had tried on me. Aubey kept quiet throughout—he didn't have any choice.

"I'm aware of what he did to your father," I said coldly. "Just as I'm aware of his plans for Talnier." *And so much more*, I added in my head.

"I asked for you to call on me at my chambers," I continued. "Is the notion of 'subtly' completely foreign to you?"

He struggled to answer, but I had not yet released him.

"Yes, it is," I answered for him. "And so you came to see me here, in a public place, and *yelled* at me. Forcing me to give you this very public humiliation, where everyone, especially Finley's spies, can see."

I was looking, but a lot of people were trying to surreptitiously catch the show. It was anyone's guess which of them would be reporting to the Duke, but it was a safe bet that a lot of them would be reporting to *someone*. I increased the volume of my voice a bit.

"And so we find ourselves giving this performance to half the Court. Are you enjoying it? Because I am. Humiliating the pariah would-be Count will do great things for my social standing. I wouldn't be surprised if I got a marriage proposal."

Another marriage proposal, that is. I was up to six now, or at least I'd been assured that the flowery letters that asked for a private meeting "to discuss a possible future" were that. They had all come from lesser nobles of the Court—hangers-on without titles or land for themselves. Tying themselves to a Councillor from a border town would be a step downward for them, so I had to assume they were either desperate or just lost to my feminine charms.

"Well, that's about enough," I said, looking over our audience. "You can go now." I released the pressure. Freed to talk, it looked as though he wanted to speak, but something stopped him. Struggling to control his face, he turned and strode from the room.

* * *

"I honestly didn't think you'd show up," I said in a low voice. We were in the gardens at night. Not a popular viewing time, but not bad for clandestine meetings.

"Is that . . . you?" Aubert asked.

"I said I'd be disguised in the note, didn't I?" The man I was disguised as smirked.

"I felt it appear in my pocket," Aubert said wonderingly. "You've gotten better."

I dissolved the Phantasmal Object with a thought. He started as it disappeared in his hand, then brushed off his hand as if it were covered in imaginary ash.

"By all means, try some flattery," I said. "You came to see me for a reason, though. Enemy of my enemy, I assume?"

He sighed despondently. "I didn't want to come to you," he said. "But nothing else has . . . the King won't see me, and I know that he'll see you again. If you could—"

"The King won't see you because he knows you plan on causing trouble for one of his dukes," I interrupted. "Hearing it from me isn't going to change that."

"But my father!"

"You're the only one here that cares about that," I told him bluntly.

"Surely you at least . . ." he tried.

"I didn't want him dead. I would like to see his killer brought to justice," I admitted. "But the man forced me into babysitting you! How do you think I feel about him?"

"You seemed to enjoy bullying me well enough."

"Well, when life gives you lemons, make lemonade," I said. "That part was pretty fun, I'll admit. But it was taking my anger with him out on you. At least partly," I added, recalling that I had had plenty of reasons to be mad at Aubert directly.

"So for that part of it, I apologize."

"I shouldn't have exiled you," Aubert admitted. "I'm sorry for that."

"Are you going to take it back?"

"Are you going to help me?"

I smiled. "Maybe. If you had your status confirmed, could you bring an accusation of treason against Finley? Legally, I mean."

Aubert looked at me warily. "As long as Duke Bargougne didn't object, I could. I'd need credible evidence to make it stick, though."

"What sort of evidence would be credible?" I asked. I knew better than to assume it would be the same as in my world.

"Something that I'd seen or heard . . . documents that I knew came from his properties."

"So not testimony from someone else," I said.

"Not a commoner, no," he agreed unable to see the sour face I was making. "Perhaps if it was someone he was actually conspiring with, but I would need to bring him in to testify himself."

"That makes it hard," I mused.

"Well, it should be hard to accuse a noble," he said, without a shred of self-awareness. "We need to occupy ourselves with the loftier concerns of rulership, and not allow ourselves to get bogged down with defending ourselves against petty accusations."

I raised an eyebrow, not that he could see it. "Like patricide?" I wondered.

"That's different," he said, suddenly sullen.

"Well. Here's my plan. Duke Finley is currently committing treason against the King. We're going to get some evidence in front of you, and you are going to accuse him and get him arrested for it."

"But . . . I'd need to be confirmed in my position to do that."

"Yeah," I said awkwardly. "See, there's always been an easy way for you to get confirmed, you just haven't been able to see it."

"I certainly don't see how that's possible," he said doubtfully.

I shrugged. I doubted he was going to like this. "All you have to do . . . is swear to the Chancellor that you're giving up on your accusations about your father's death."

DUNGEON

It turned out that he didn't like it. The conversation didn't exactly get *heated*—we were both aware that we had to keep our voices down—but he wasn't happy. Getting what he wanted—including revenge on his father's killer—didn't seem as sweet if it meant giving up on justice for his father.

I didn't try too hard to persuade him. I didn't even use Persuasion on him. That would wear off by the next day, and I didn't actually have any evidence for him to use. Better to let the notion sit with him, while I tried to come up with my end of the deal. I did agree to listen to any better ideas that he might have, but he didn't have any. So we agreed to . . . revisit the discussion when I was closer to having some evidence.

Not that I had any idea of how I was going to *get* that evidence. Right now, I was more concerned about some of Duke Finley's other activities. Like organizing a military coup in Talnier, which was . . . not treasonous? I wasn't sure. It seemed treasonous to *me*, but no doubt there was some ducal right to three coups a year, or something.

"I just wish I could be there," I complained to Felicia as we discussed it. "If Finley's decided to try something . . ."

Felicia just smiled sympathetically, but Kyle had some advice. "It's not like you'd be on the front line," he pointed out. "Cloridan, the guard, the Guild, they all knew before we left that this was coming."

"Best place for a Councillor when the knives come out is outside the town," Janie put in. "That way they can't get you all."

"That's true!" Felicia agreed. "In fact, doesn't that mean that Duke Finley won't do anything until she's back?"

"Eh, maybe." Janie looked a little awkward. "I'm sure the guy has at least one more assassination attempt in him. But that's our problem. You should be focusing on . . . this."

"Right. This." I looked over at Issey. "Last chance to say no."

She looked at me in surprise, "Are you crazy?" she asked before remembering that she was scared of me. "I—I'm sorry ma'am, I—" she stopped herself, blushing. She wasn't *actually* that scared of me. It was just a habit.

Even if I wasn't a noble, learning that I moved in noble circles had triggered a nervous reaction in her that she just couldn't control. I'd learned not to get angry at what that implied, as that just made her more nervous. Negotiations over the use of her ballroom had tempered that reaction, slightly.

Negotiations might not be the right word, really. Our first interaction had established that she would accept any payment if that meant that she didn't have to sell her grandmother's legacy. Which was fortunate, because my funds weren't unlimited. Our main store of wealth was in the form of mana stones, and unless Felicia could get accredited as an Alchemist, we would be selling them at a steep discount.

There were some issues that needed to be discussed, but really the negotiations were just a pretext for Issey and me to get more familiar with each other. She needed to stop bowing every second, and I needed to be sure that she wouldn't go blabbing to the authorities. We wouldn't be able to keep this a secret, but I wanted to control how the information got out.

"Okay then," I said. There was no point in putting it off any longer. I stepped forward into the ballroom, leaving the others behind.

We had spent some time cleaning up. The tables and chairs that were still good we had removed and put in a dusty storage room. The majority of the furniture was rotted through, though, so we had reduced it to sticks and planks and piled them up in the corner. Kyle had said that the dungeon would find a use for it all.

It felt appropriate to place the core at the center of the stage, so I strode across the empty room and made my own, much less graceful, leap onto the raised platform. It didn't feel right to just place it on the floor, so I used Phantasmal Object to summon an ornate ivory plinth. The blue box popped up as soon as I took out Rhis's core, but I waited until it was in position before I addressed the notification.

Sufficient mana detected. Instantiate mana construct? [Y/N]

Yes.

Suddenly, I was back in the white room, Rhis standing beside me. I was *also* still standing on the stage. Managing multiple points of view was a headache, but one I was almost used to by now. Thank goodness for enhanced Intelligence.

"As we discussed, Rhis, expand out to this room only."

"As you command, Mistress," Rhis said, grinning. There wasn't a change in the real world, but a ripple went through the white room. In its wake, the white room became a match to my outside perception. The effect stopped when it reached the edges of the room. In the real world, I could see my companions looking through the door. In the white world, there was a blank white expanse where the door would be.

Now that my two senses of vision were in sync, it was much easier. Rhis was still only in the white room version. I could have rectified that, but I chose to do something slightly different. In the real world, I pulled out Rhis's amulet and activated it. Now there were two of him, independent entities rather than synced copies. *He must be having his own double vision now*, I thought with amusement.

"Let the others know how it's going," I said to the real-world version. He bowed in response and walked over to the door.

"Can we start with the spatial expansion?" I asked the other.

"Of course, Mistress," he said. "In all directions?"

"Just . . . up," I said. "I think I want to build a tower."

"I see . . . that will reduce the costs—I should be able to manage eight times quite easily. Given the height of our base room, that should mean sixteen floors in all?"

"That sounds fine, but just four floors for now. Let's see how this works before going that far."

He bowed. "It should take about fifteen minutes, my lady."

With that sorted, I turned my attention to the entrances. With a thought, I cast Static Image on the four doorways that led into this room, facing outwards. They were all the same thing, from different angles—the room as it had been before the cleanup. From now on, anyone who came looking for us wouldn't see anything different until they were actually in the dungeon.

My friends outside jumped to see the room change, but they'd been expecting something like this, and Rhis quickly walked straight through the image to reassure them.

"Everything is proceeding according to plan," he informed them with satisfaction. "It may take a while before the first floor is completed."

It was interesting that I could hear him, and the responses of my friends, quite clearly even though they were all the way over there. Of much more interest, though, was what I had just done. I'd cast four spells—four *different* spells—simultaneously? Without even thinking about it?

What's more, I realized after some quick checks, the mana for them wasn't coming from me; it was coming from the dungeon. And it had much more mana than I did.

"*[Dungeon Status]*." I said it aloud, because why not?

Dungeon Name	[Unnamed]		
Level: 7	XP: 38,045,236	Next Level: 100,000,000	Floors: 1
Current Mana: 126	Mana Cap: 225	Mana Regeneration: 22.5	Upkeep: 0.096
Dungeon Traits			
Name	Rank	Effect	
Spatial Control	10	Teleportation, Portals, Expansion (8)	
Monster Classes	5	Lizards, Goblins, Insects, Mammals, Fish	
Treasure Classes	5	Coins, Gems, Ores, Mystic Crystals, Crafted Items	
Trap Classes	5	Simple, Advanced, Natural, Magical, Lava	
Environmental Classes	5	Desert, Jungle, Swamp, Forest, Mountain	
Mana Efficiency	5	10% bonus mana regeneration per rank	

I frowned. Most of this made little sense to me, but the mana level felt too low. I sort of had an intuitive sense of the pool I was drawing from, and it felt much bigger than 126. The rest of it . . .

"Are these all from your time at Oakway?" I asked.

"Indeed. All my constructions and my stores are gone, but I am left with my experience," Rhis replied.

"Why is the mana so low?" I asked. He raised an eyebrow but brought up his own version of the window. I could see this one as well, in my vision of the white room, so I dismissed mine and looked over his shoulder.

"It seems normal?" he said.

"Why have I got upkeep already?"

"That would be the four spells you cast," he explained. "They are being maintained by the dungeon instead of by you."

"Four Static Image spells shouldn't have such a small upkeep . . ." I mused. Automatically, I divided it by four and then made the connection. "They *should* be one mana every *hour*, which translates to 24 every day. And then that becomes . . . So one point of dungeon mana is equal to 1,000 points of personal mana!"

"I wouldn't know. I just know that the illusion spells you allow me to cast have an impossibly low cost. Can we proceed? Once we get additional levels, we should get an increase in both mana regeneration and cap."

"Right, so how do we start?"

"Normally, one would build out the basic structure with either Construction or Excavation," he told me. "But using Phantasms will be much cheaper."

"I never got around to getting Phantasmal Structure," I admitted.

"No need. Phantasmal Object will do well enough for our purposes. If you can sketch out how you'd like to lay out this level, it would be easier to show you than explain."

"Well . . ." I gave it some thought. "Wall off the stage; we'll have that only accessible from a higher level. For the rest, if we have a central corridor, with four rooms, and the stairway up being from that *room* . . . Oh, and each of the rooms should have a window on the outside wall."

"Ah, yes. Because this is a tower, not a dungeon. We should indeed have a view." Rhis snapped his fingers. Individual blocks of stone appeared, walling off each of the rooms I'd mentioned. It seemed as if it happened all at once, but I could somehow tell that each event was separate, just following on from the previous so quickly that it was all over in a flash.

[Illusion Magic] Level 6 acquired through use.

For gaining a skill level, you have been awarded 1 XP.

"Did you cast, like, 5,000 Phantasmal Objects?"

"To be precise, *you* cast the spell 4,231 times, for a cost of just under 64 mana," he replied smugly. "There is an upkeep cost, but it amounts to only a fraction more than one-tenth of a mana."

"Wow . . ." I quickly checked. Upkeep had ticked up to 0.237, and mana had gone down to 62. That was . . . wow.

"I'm starting to see the benefits of being a mage with a dungeon," I said. Rhis smirked, pleased with himself.

"What did you want to do with these rooms, Mistress?" he asked. "I should warn you that monsters have upkeep as well and that it takes fifty mana to define a second floor."

"I'll keep that in mind. Is it okay to have the core room inaccessible like this?"

"Right now, it's fine. It's currently accessible, with a little climbing." Rhis glanced at the current lack of a ceiling.

"Hmm. We should at least have a ceiling," I said thoughtfully. "Can you make it using construction? A Phantasmal floor will take just a bit of damage as people walk on it, and eventually fail."

Rhis looked genuinely disappointed at losing the prospect of sudden floor failure, but took it with good grace, summoning wooden beams out of the (real) walls and covering our four rooms with a wooden ceiling. We then made some real staircases leading up from the corridor and down to the core room. With that done, I could walk out of the core room and have a look at what Rhis had done with my own eyes.

He had covered all the basics, not just the walls. The doors were all in place, there were "windows" that overlooked blank stone walls, and now that there was a ceiling, he installed light panels reminiscent of fluorescent lighting back home.

"Right," I said. The first thing I did was cover the wide alcoves with more Static Images. On one side, I had the windows overlook the Blue Mountains. My memory included a tourist shot of the Three Sisters that was probably taken from a helicopter. I used it anyway—we were supposed to be in a tower.

On the other side, I reproduced the view from my boss's old office. It wasn't the highest spot in the building, but it did have a good view of Sydney. I'd been asked about my world lots of times, but I'd never shown them a good view of my hometown.

Then I got started on the furnishings.

TOWER OF LEARNING

And this is the library," I explained. I glanced over at the windows, now showing a view from Talnier's main keep. I missed the old pictures already, but I wasn't ready to come out to Issey as being from another world.

I'd spent all my dungeon mana on furnishings and a second floor. Since I was stuck waiting for it to regenerate, I thought I'd show the others what I'd done so far. Admittedly, it wasn't much. A few Phantasmal books sitting on equally illusory shelves.

Felicia was drawn to one of the more unusual (to her) looking books. A reproduction of my first economics textbook, its brightly colored paper binding stood out against the more traditional leather-bound books that I'd created.

"This is . . . in your native language?" she asked hesitantly, glancing at Issey.

"Yeah, turns out I can reproduce books from memory, and translate them easily, but I can't produce a translated version with a thought," I said glumly. The skills—well, Memorize was a skill, my translator was a trait—didn't link up that way.

"I wonder if I could . . ." her gaze drifted off into empty air. "Yes, I could spend a Development point and be able to read this."

I raised an eyebrow. "Learning an unknown language is that easy?"

"Oh, like you're one to talk. It's not unknown to the Status, anyway."

"Well," I said doubtfully. "If you want to, I can keep you in reading material. They'd have to stay in the dungeon, though."

I had been thinking of recreating a lot of books from home, for both a comfortable feeling of home and to improve my Memorize skill.

"This one might interest you," I told Issey, handing her a text. She and Kyle hadn't joined Felicia and Janie in investigating the shelves. "This lug lets his girlfriend do all the reading, but if you study that for an hour, it should unlock the Scribe skill."

It was a Phantasmal replica of one I had already made. I'd tried making one for a different skill, but I had run into difficulties. For one, *writing* a new book was a physical process that I had to actually do. I couldn't do it in my head and then make an image of it. It was like that for a lot of my skills. So far, the only skills that I'd been able to farm out to the dungeon were skills that cost mana.

"Or if you don't want to spend the skill point, Kandis should be able to make materials for you to get the skill with competence!" Felicia put in. "That would take a month, though."

"That quickly? I thought it would take longer," I said.

"It does depend on your Intelligence," Felicia told me, "But you don't need full mastery, just enough to convince the Status to give you the skill."

"I'll think about it?" Issey said. "What do you get out of it?"

"Well, not much, but I'm happy to help," I said. *Actually . . . I should check something.*

[Dungeon Status].

Dungeon Name	Tower of Learning		
Level: 7	XP: 38,045,236	Next Level: 100,000,000	Floors: 2
Current Mana: 6	Mana Cap: 300	Mana Regeneration: 31.8	Upkeep: 0.146
Dungeon Traits	[Expand]	Invaders: 4/0	

Interesting. When I'd gotten the second floor, my mana regeneration and cap had both gone up, to thirty and 300, respectively. Now my regeneration was up by a measly 1.8. I did some quick math. That was the sum of the levels of all the people in the dungeon—aside from myself, divided by ten.

"Janie," I said thoughtfully, "can you go up the stairs to the next level?"

"Are you sure you want to do that, Mistress?" Rhis popped up with a concerned look on his face, even as Janie shrugged and left the room. No one else reacted to him—he had appeared in my white room perception.

It took a little bit of focus to make myself speak in the white room without making a sound in the real world. A little more to adjust the view so that I could watch Janie walk upstairs.

"What's the problem, Rhis?" I asked.

He wrung his hands in anxiety. "It's just that she's getting awfully close to the core room . . . if she should try something, we'd be helpless to stop her."

"It will be fine. Janie's not going to do something untoward," I assured him. He gave me a reproachful look.

"If you would just let me summon *one* monster, I'd feel better."

"No." I wasn't allowing him monsters . . . at this stage. I might have to change my mind on this later. For now, I watched Janie reach the second floor.

Dungeon Name	Tower of Learning		
Level: 7	XP: 38,045,236	Next Level: 100,000,000	Floors: 2
Current Mana: 6	Mana Cap: 300	Mana Regeneration: 32.3	Upkeep: 0.146
Dungeon Traits	[Expand]	Invaders: 3/1	

An extra 0.5 regeneration, or Janie's level divided by ten. So there was an advantage to me when people delved deeper.

"There's nothing up here!" Janie called. I could barely hear her from downstairs, but my white room perception could hear her clearly. For practice, and because I didn't feel like yelling, I used my dungeon mana to cast Unseen Sound.

"Thanks! That was a successful test; you can come down now." My voice came out of nowhere, making her start, but she shrugged and headed back down the stairs.

"What's next?" she asked as she rejoined us.

"I'm not sure," I said. "Really, I'm just waiting for the mana to recharge, but that could take a while. Unless I . . ." I trailed off for a bit.

"Issey," I said, making the girl jump. "You don't get experience from dancing, do you?"

"Nope," she said mournfully. "If I did, I'd have more than the King."

"How did you get to level three then? Fighting with other people?"

"A bit," Issey admitted. "But mostly . . . there's rats that spawn and come up from the sewers. Big place like this, I get more than my fair share, and there's no one else to take care of them."

"I thought built-up areas didn't get random spawns," I said slowly.

"That's because the mana is shaped," Felicia explained. "Here . . . well, you've seen how chaotic it is."

"So all that wild mana gets sucked into spawn points . . . how big are these rats?"

Issey shrugged and held her hands about half a meter apart. "Used to be they were about this long, not including the tail."

"Threat three?" Kyle speculated, his interest in the conversation perking up now that we were talking about monsters.

"I guess," Issey said. "Lately they've been about twice that size."

"Lately?" I asked, alarmed.

"Three weeks or so," she told me. "More of them, as well. Reckon I'll make level four before too long."

"There were a lot of 'rat in basement' quests at the guild," Janie pointed out thoughtfully. "None of them looked worth our while, but there were a lot."

"A plague of rats isn't our business," I said, without any kind of conviction. "And this dungeon should soak up a lot of the local mana, reducing the problem near this building."

"If you say so," Issey said doubtfully.

"I was thinking that this place should be about improvement. Learning and training skills. But now I'm wondering if I should have a levelling component."

"Monsters, you mean?" Kyle said. Rhis didn't say anything, but he looked at me hopefully.

"Yeah," I sighed. "There isn't a better way of getting experience, is there? And there's the security aspect as well."

Rhis was practically dancing. He kept his feet on the ground, but he moved his weight from one foot to the other excitedly. "Yes, Mistress! An excellent decision!"

"Wait, can I . . ." I thought about it for a moment and the answer came to me. Casting Phantasmal Emissary through the dungeon, I instinctively knew the changes I needed to make to let Rhis control it.

"Ah, hello!" Rhis said, finally visible again to the others. "I hope you're enjoying the honor of being in Mistress's dungeon!"

"Not much to it right now, is there?" Janie asked slyly. Rhis glared at her.

"None of that." I cut him off before he could speak. "If we're discussing monsters, I thought you should be part of the discussion. That means keeping it polite."

"Um," Issey interjected. "Who—what—is that?"

"This is Rhis," I told her. "Rhis—this is Issey. Rhis is . . . I guess you would call him a dungeon spirit?"

"He looks strange . . . not like a fox-kin. Is he a monster?"

Rhis grinned at her. He seemed pleased by the comparison, but with the teeth he had, you needed to know him to tell.

"Don't let the fangs worry you," I said wryly. "He can't hurt anyone as an illusion."

"Indeed no, and your command prevents me from even trying," Rhis said. "But we were discussing monsters?"

"What do you guys think?" I asked the group.

"It is traditional . . ." Felicia offered. "I don't think there's a dungeon that doesn't have monsters."

"And you do need to defend your core," Kyle said. "I don't think you want monsters on the first floor, though? They would make it hard to study."

"Then may I suggest a trap spider?" Rhis said. "The second level is mostly empty space at the moment, and it can make good use of that."

"How so?"

"It can fill it with traps made from its silk, of course," he explained. "We can have it leave a path for you . . . and your friends."

"That sounds . . . quite effective," I said. "Just one monster for the level?"

"At this point, that's all we can afford, and the trap spider does well against multiple opponents. When our mana improves, we can upgrade it to get a youngling brood for a small additional cost. Oh! And its poison is nonlethal, which should appeal to you, Mistress."

"Nonlethal? What effect does it have?"

"Agonizing paralysis, which can last for up to an hour!" he announced proudly. "If you're monitoring things, that gives you plenty of time to order the spider to spare the victim."

"I guess that *is* better than death," I allowed reluctantly. "Do you have anything that just puts them unconscious? Painlessly?"

"There are such poisons," he admitted sulkily, "but they are not as effective. Adventurers can resist the effects with a high enough Stamina."

"Isn't that true for the . . . agonizing paralysis as well?"

"Yes, but the difference is that once you have resisted the sleeping poison, the effect is over. You can resist the paralysis poison to move, but the poison stays in effect, meaning you have to resist it once more to move again."

I looked at the others. Kyle shrugged. "Better than killing them, at any rate? And I don't think you can be squeamish if you're going to run a dungeon, otherwise the adventurers will run right over you."

"Ideally," I said, "we'd keep the adventurers out of this dungeon entirely." I had some ideas for who we were going to allow in here, but I couldn't let it be level five or six killing machines.

"We can work out a level for the . . . lower levels to grind at, once we've recovered some mana," Rhis said. "But for now . . . with your permission?"

He looked at me eagerly. Fox eyes weren't exactly puppy dog eyes, but . . .

"Fine," I said.

"You won't regret this, Mistress," Rhis said. He paused for a moment. "Done. We can leave her to scout out her area and start trapping it."

I looked at my Dungeon Status again.

Dungeon Name	Tower of Learning		
Level: 7	XP: 38,045,236	Next Level: 100,000,000	Floors: 2
Current Mana: 0	Mana Cap: 300	Mana Regeneration: 32.3	Upkeep: 0.746
Dungeon Traits	[Expand]	Invaders: 4	
Monsters: 1	[Expand]		

My residual mana had gone, and my upkeep had ticked up. One monster cost considerably more than 500 individual illusion spells. I could probably make use of that, make up my numbers with harmless Phantasmal versions of my monsters.

Level	Monster	Threat	Notes
1	None	-	
2	[Trap Spider]	6	[Poison] [Constructer]

Six mana for a threat six creature. Simple enough. I turned to the others.

"It's going to take a while to regenerate the Dungeon's mana," I said. "So let's talk about what I'm going to do with this place."

ILLVSIOΠ MAGIC

I sat on the roof and stared at the mana vortex above my dungeon. The Tower of Learning didn't suck up *much* mana, not compared to the other three dungeons around the city, but it definitely sucked up *some*. Within about thirty meters from the Gilded Lily, the chaotic mix of mana that filled the air became more ordered, gaining a slight tendency to flow towards the building. Closer in, the tendency became more pronounced.

Only *some* of the mana interfered with other mana, but that was enough to keep it from flowing smoothly through the walls of the building and into my tower. Instead, it all piled up into a slowly rotating whirlpool above the building, allowing a steady stream to flow down through the roof. I still couldn't distinguish between the types, but I got the impression that the vortex was actually composed of multiple overlapping streams of mana.

Despite standing right next to the vortex, my own mana was fine. I was still regenerating at the normal rate, and I didn't know why. The disparity between dungeon mana and my own suggested that I might be operating off of crumbs too small to be sucked up. Or was it possible that humans created their own mana, and the regeneration of my mana pool was due to my own efforts?

I didn't know, and that wasn't the reason I was on the roof, anyway. The mana vortex was a problem. Sure, it would be hard to notice once you were a few blocks away, but *hard* wasn't *impossible*, and there were enough people with mana sight to turn hard into *likely*.

Why did it have to come in from the top? I wondered. I hadn't been able to find any options to change that, and it was true for all the dungeons that I'd seen. It would be a lot more convenient if the mana had just gone through the ground or buildings—it was certainly capable of it. Instead, I was stuck with a giant flag over my dungeon.

I'd already tried to conceal the mana whirlpool, but Conceal Mana was meant for the spells that I cast and my personal mana. It didn't scale up to this. Nor had creating my own custom spell with Theurgy. I had gotten the sense that it could work, but I didn't have the spell total. Something told me that I was close, though. I could feel a skill wanting to be used.

Not that skills had wants, of course. But they responded to what I wanted. If I wanted to stab someone, I didn't activate the skill and stab. The skill responded to what I wanted and activated on its own. It would take over my movements, from my footwork to my grip on the dagger, and do the deed. Kind of creepy, but I was getting used to it.

What I'd been slowly learning to notice was the feeling when I wanted something that was *close* to what a skill could do, but not exactly right. There was a feeling, as if the skill was whispering to me what I needed to do to use it. That was what had happened when I had tried to make my own spell, so now I was trying it again. Slowly, and without distractions, I tried to listen to my skills and see if I could work out what I needed to do.

Once again, I brought up a mental image of how Conceal Mana was cast and thought about how to modify it for my needs. I activated Theurgy.

Alone of all the skills so far, Theurgy always made me do the work. It only concerned itself with allowing me to move the mana. How I structured it was up to me. I started forming the mana according to my mental model, trying to feel what other skill was speaking to me. Was it Illusion Magic?

No.

It was Creativity. I'd barely even thought of that skill since accidentally getting it on my first night. From making an illusion of a painting. A memory for me, but it was new to this world.

I suppose this spell is something new. It would make sense that Creativity could help me make it.

So I let it help. The skill activated and I felt it guide me. My mana structure firmed up, lines moving into place, not for any particular reason other than it felt right. It stabilized and . . .

. . . it wasn't enough. As the spell tried to activate, the structure fell apart in an explosion that looked impressive to my mana sight but didn't make so much as a breeze in the physical world. I frowned. Was I going to have to wait for another level? Or could I . . . ?

My Creativity was only at level two, compared to Theurgy at four. It was much easier to go from a two to a three than it was to go from a four to a five. And I already knew how to train in Creativity.

I didn't have access to the dungeon's mana right now, but I had my own. I started casting Phantasmal Object. Not as quickly as I had in the dungeon, but as quickly as I could manage to use Memorize to recall some artwork, album cover, or novel that I had seen.

It was a bit surreal. Sitting on the roof of a three-story building, I created artwork after artwork, only to toss them away and let the Phantasm expire. A treasure trove of my cultural heritage, created and tossed away. I really would have to make a permanent library, lack of English readers be damned.

I was starting to feel the mental strain from Memorize long before my mana ran out. I had about forty castings before my Stamina ran out. Somewhere around 33, though, I got the message that I was looking for.

[Creativity] Level 3 acquired through use.
For gaining a skill level, you have been awarded 1 XP.

I closed my eyes and let myself rest for a bit. I couldn't hear any commotion from below, which was good. I'd already been up here for longer than I said I would be, so either they'd found something else to occupy them, or they were still arguing over who should climb up. I wouldn't be much longer.

Opening my eyes, I built the mana construct again. I could feel the difference that an extra level made. It wasn't much, but I had been close before. I focused on the model and what I needed it to do, letting the mana flow through . . .

The vortex disappeared.

[Theurgy] + [Creativity] skill total sufficient for Level 20 spell
20 Spell Levels spent
[Conceal Dungeon] Spell (Level 20) created
Note: No school has been assigned.

Spell levels? Did I have spell levels? I had thought that I was out of them, but then I remembered that my Illusion Magic had gone up. So I had some spare. Checking, I saw that I still had 25 levels remaining. I wondered what would have happened if I hadn't had any. Maybe the spell would have gone off, but I wouldn't have learnt it? Something to check later, I guess.

So if Conceal Dungeon was a spell, then it should have an entry. Sure enough:

> **[Conceal Dungeon]: Conceals the mana intake of a targeted dungeon (Upkeep: 4/hour).**

Ah, shite. Upkeep. I could afford it, no problem, but I was willing to bet that this spell had the same range restrictions as my other spells. Which meant that I *might* be able to keep it up if I was *in* the dungeon, but if I was anywhere else (aside from right on top of it), then the spell would fade after an hour.

Well, I knew there were ways around that. They had their own problems, though . . . I put that thought aside. For the next hour, at least, I didn't need to worry about being tracked down. I could . . .

I could think about how to spend those other 25 spell levels, for one thing. After all the times that I'd wished for one spell or another, I can't believe I'd left it for this long. Even if I had been distracted at the time.

Filtering out spells that were too expensive, or too cheap, or that I already had was fairly easy, and left me with a list.

> **[False Life]: Creates an image of a living thing that can move and act as directed (15 points).**
>
> **[Silence]: Can be cast on a target or area. Prevents sound from being made by the target or in the area (15 points).**
>
> **[Conceal Object]: Causes an object to look like another object of no more than twice the size (15 points).**
>
> **[Privacy]: Creates a bubble that sound can exist in, but not leave (15 points).**
>
> **[Disguise Other]: Modify targets appearance and clothing as required (20 points).**
>
> **[Improved False Spell-casting]: As [False Spell-casting], but can include smell, taste and physical sensation (20 points).**
>
> **[Improved False Life]: As [False Life] but includes smell (20 points).**

> [Privacy Ward]: Defines a volume no more than 27 cubic meters in size from which sight and sound cannot enter or leave (20 points).
>
> [Darkness]: Creates a volume of complete darkness no more than 27 cubic meters in size (20 points).
>
> [Illusory Room]: Creates a complex image no more than 27 cubic meters in size (25 points).

At various points in time, I had wished I'd had Conceal Object, Privacy, and Disguise Other. They were probably the front-runners, unless I wanted to save up for one of the bigger spells. Or invent another level twenty spell. Or even spend it on a Water Magic spell.

None of those options really appealed, though. Not against the memory of "If I'd only had . . ." those three spells recalled. I could only get one of them, though. None of the lower-level spells appealed, so there was no point getting Conceal Object just to allow me to get a second level ten.

I'd wished for Conceal Object a lot recently, but I didn't have Rhis's core to hide anymore. I was sure that I could find other things I wanted to hide, but I could probably find a work-around, just as I did for Rhis. Privacy, on the other hand . . . I was definitely going to need that. More than Disguise Other? Probably. Tough choice.

If I chose Privacy, then the only choice remaining was whether to spring for the upgrade. Privacy Ward included sight, so it blocked lipreading or any kind of observation of what you were doing, but it sounded as if it would be too obvious. You couldn't use it to have a quiet conversation without everyone in the dining hall knowing you were doing so.

So Privacy seemed like the way to go. I selected it.

Time to go back down.

"And that's how I learned the spell," I finished, to my rapt audience of friends. Well, Felicia and Janie were paying attention. Creating new spells was of professional interest to them.

"I can't cast it," Rhis told me. "That is to say, I *can* cast it, but only on a dungeon that is inside me. Which"—he scowled ferociously—"would be really bad."

"I thought that might be the case," I said. "We'll—"

"*Really* bad," Rhis interrupted, his voice raised. "I get so *angry* when I think about it—"

I raised an eyebrow at him and he stopped, looking shocked at his own words.

"It wasn't part of my plans," I said gently. "Would you like me to promise I won't do that?"

"Yes, I would like that, Mistress," he replied meekly, after an awkward pause.

"Fine, I promise."

"Thank you, Mistress."

"This whole Dungeon thing is messed up," Janie put in. I'd wanted Rhis to participate in the group conversation, so I'd asked him to manifest an illusion of himself. A decision that I now regretted. "Did Mandel's wife act like that?"

"Not where we could see," I told her. I wasn't sure if it would work, but I willed for Rhis to keep it together more when there were others about. He already looked abashed, but I thought he had started looking more so.

"Getting back to the original topic, I'll try to maintain the spell for as long as I can, but I suspect it will be out of range before we get back to the castle."

"It is about time we started heading back," Felicia pointed out. "You were on the roof for a lot longer than you planned, and we have that dinner tonight."

I sighed. "Don't remind me, more pointless socializing."

"Pretty sure you said yesterday that there were important networking opportunities," Janie said with a grin.

"Yes, well, that was before I knew what I could be doing here," I said. "I'm starting to see why mages with dungeons never leave them. Also, please don't learn corporate-speak."

"Just taking a page from our gallant leader," Janie said mischievously. "I'm incentivized!"

"Please don't do that," I pleaded. "I don't know how that even translated, I didn't think it was real English."

Janie shrugged. "I guess it must be, then? Anyway, let's head back."

[CONVERSATION]

Networking was an important part of my old job. Not the actual job; that was mostly looking at reports and doing math. In the finance sector, the most important part of any job was getting out of it. Officially, the way it worked was that you started at the bottom, worked hard, got promoted. That *could* work, but it was much faster to use one job as a stepping stone for the next. You needed to sniff out opportunities before they got widely advertised and brought in the competition. That was what you needed networking for.

Friendships, favors, and fucking. The last of those was frowned upon, gossiped about . . . but no one could deny that it worked. Friendship was the gold standard, of course, but long-lasting friendships were hard to come by. You started as many as you could and hoped that you didn't get burnt later on—or that you didn't have to burn them.

Favors were safer and were just what you wanted for career advancement. A few hot stock prospects or advanced warning of a detrimental report were just the ticket to be traded for a word in a recruiter's ear or early notice of an opening.

If I had any hopes at all for this banquet, it would be for favors. Given or received was a possibility, but it was far more likely that the only thing I gained was some likely *prospects* for a trade later on. It took time to build up a network, time that I wasn't sure I was going to have, but that was no reason to delay. Anything I started now I could follow up on the next time I was in town, or over letters.

So start talking already, I chided myself. I turned to the lady at my side and tried for what I hoped would be a harmless conversational opening gambit.

"Is it not the custom here to alternate male and female guests?" I asked.

Lady Rankin gave me an amused smile. My conversation partner from the last reception was back and had been seated next to me.

"Normally, that would be the case," she told me. "But the King's whims take precedence."

She seemed nicer this time. Or . . . more wary, perhaps? Last time, I'd beaten her in a Social Contest, so I guess she was taking me seriously despite my lack of rank. It amused me to think that here I was the social equivalent of a criminal bruiser, whom you had to step quietly around, lest I give you the back of my tongue.

Of course, maintaining that reputation meant that I had to participate in the conversation, so I raised an eyebrow and asked, "Whims?"

"Yes, the King provides his requirements to the Master of Ceremonies, who must find seats for us all while remaining within the King's restrictions. It's no wonder that he needs to break some of the other rules from time to time."

"And these requirements . . ."

"Are a secret, of course, but if they can be divined, provide clues to the King's intention and demeanor."

"I see," I said, running my gaze around the table. Normally I would have just said "huh," but Charm wasn't having any of that. "And what should I make of the fact that we are seated together?"

"Who knows?" she said. She took her goblet and swirled the wine under her nose, inhaling the fragrance. "There could be no intention at all, and we were placed as we are to allow the others to fit. Perhaps it is simply because we . . . met at the other night's reception and the Master wished for you to have someone to talk to. Or it could be a message to either one of us."

I examined the room again. It was an eclectic mix of royal officials, military types, nobility, and notable commoners like myself. We were all seated at the same table—an extremely elongated U shape. An upside-down U, I should say, since the King was in the middle section and there was no way he would be seated anywhere but the top. The guests were mixed pretty well, but there were some patterns.

"I take it that closeness to His Majesty denotes favor," I said.

She nodded but didn't say anything, merely taking another sip of her wine. We were seated at around the middle of the table, which was a little better than I would have assumed. I was a commoner, though.

"There aren't many nobles this far down," I commented, keeping my face neutral. That was a polite fiction. As far as I could tell, there weren't *any*. She grimaced and put her wine down.

"I may have slightly vexed His Majesty recently," she admitted. "Pressed him a little too hard on one or two perfectly reasonable requests. At least I haven't fallen as far as *some*."

I followed her gaze down the table and was surprised to see someone in what looked like a medieval monk's robes, made out of a dark fabric. His hood was down, revealing a bald, middle-aged man with a pensive look on his face. Runes were tattooed all over his head, making him look like a character from a video game.

"Who's he?" I asked, only to correct myself. I'd seen those robes before. "Wait, is he part of the Scholars of the Sacred Breath?"

"The head of the Order," she confirmed.

"Do they all have those tattoos?" I asked. I'd never seen one with their hood down before. At this distance, Mana Sense couldn't tell me if the markings were magically active or not, but I could see that he had a greater-than-normal amount of mana swirling around him. The Scholars were, as far as I could tell, the Guild of Theurgy in everything but name. They seemed to take a more mystical approach than the other guilds.

"Who knows what those fools do to themselves?" Lady Rankin sneered. "What is of note is that he is down *there*." She glared at him with a satisfied look on her face, as the servers started laying out the first course.

"Do you know why?" I asked cautiously as a servant placed a pie in front of me. The King had already been served and was eating, and every-one seemed to take their cue from him, so I didn't wait and broke it open. Pork with some kind of fruit; it smelled delicious.

Lady Rankin ignored the dish in front of her, for the moment, preferring to gloat over the unfortunate Scholar. "Failure brings consequences," she said. The barest flicker of emotion that went across her face told me that the phrase was something she knew from personal experience. "The mess that his Guild has made of the capital could hardly go without some punishment."

A few things clicked. "Then the current state *isn't* normal?" I asked.

"Of course not," she scoffed. "They claim sabotage of the primary menhirs, but that is exactly what they would say if the cause was their own incompetence."

"If they're the only ones with Theurgy, then no one is able to tell if they're lying or not," I said thoughtfully.

"An advantageous state of affairs for them under most circumstances," she agreed. "When events turn against them, though, there is no one to clear away the doubts that form."

She sent a cruel smile down the table. "And their reputation suffers as a result."

"I see. Is there word on how long it will take to fix things?" I asked the question casually, but it was a matter of some importance to me. I wasn't planning to keep my tower in place permanently, but it would get much harder to keep it a secret if the skies were clear of chaotic mana.

She looked at me appraisingly. "This isn't widely talked about," she said, turning her attention to her pie. "Are you a mage, having seen it for yourself?"

"I have Mana Sense," I admitted, not giving anything more away. I wasn't sure how much of my records in the Guild would be available to her—or how much she could find out about me in other ways—but I figured I'd let her work for it if she wanted more.

"I'm told it's quite a debacle," she said between bites of pie.

I nodded slowly. "I've never seen anything quite like it," I admitted.

She smiled. She'd been smiling a lot this evening and yet somehow still managed to not look friendly. "Well. At least Dorsay can claim to be exceptional in our incapacity," she said wryly. "As to when it will be fixed, the Scholars claim that there is still sabotage left to be . . . uncovered or disarmed or what have you. As such, there is no telling how long it will take."

I made some appreciative noises and then turned to my other neighbor, whom I'd been neglecting. He was young, an officer in the Royal Household guard, and . . . quite smitten by me.

This was something that was happening to me a lot, lately. I had learned to recognize the signs. From the smirk that Lady Rankin gave me, she did, too. She must have been on the receiving end of more than a few unrequited crushes. I'd have asked her about how she dealt with them, but there was a fragile male ego right in front of us.

With nobles, this sort of infatuation tended to result in a marriage proposal fairly quickly, which in turn resulted in surprise and shock at being turned down by someone of lower social status. This officer was of roughly the same social status as me, though—somewhere between commoner and noble—so I expected something a little more subtle. Military types were supposed to be more direct, though, so who knows what he would do.

Morbidly curious, I engaged him in conversation while I waited for him to sort out what he wanted to do. I instructed Charm to keep things entirely platonic, and kept Seduction totally suppressed. I wasn't expecting that to do much, but . . .

Could I persuade him to not make a fool of himself? Probably . . . but that seemed heavy-handed. Instead, I used Conversation to make sure he avoided dangerous topics. And there was something that a military person would know that I had a passing interest in . . .

"Tell me, Captain, just how many different types of soldiers are there in this city?" I asked. "I keep seeing different uniforms, and it is all quite confusing."

He was only too happy to explain, and a further nudge had him including troop numbers and quality—or at least his evaluations of the same.

It was all very complicated. There was the town guard—mostly recruited from Dorsay itself—who were responsible for keeping order in the city. They numbered about 500. The King's household guards were another 1,200 or so, responsible for protecting the walls, the King's dungeon, and the palace compound.

One of the city's dungeons belonged to Duke Finley, and so was guarded by *his* troops. That ancient entitlement meant he was able to keep 1,000 soldiers in the city. The province outside the city was his as well, so he had 3,000 to 5,000 soldiers who could be called up fairly quickly at need.

Finally, there were the honor and embassy guards answering to various guests in the city. If they weren't staying at the palace, they were entitled to their own guard of various sizes. None of these forces was particularly large, but there were a fair few of them. Captain Faidon estimated that there were almost a thousand in total.

It's all very interesting, and at least it gets us through the next course without the good Captain confessing his undying love for me. I can tell he's working up to it, though.

There must be worse things in the world than eating fantastic food and making conversation with people, but right now I can't think of any. My skills make socializing easier than it ever was back home, but all I want right now is for this evening to be over. There are so many things that I want to try with my tower before I have to pack it all away, and this is keeping me from it.

I let my attention fade, trusting in my skills to keep me out of trouble. Charm and Conversation know what I want; I don't have to follow every twist and turn of the dialogue.

It will be over soon, and then I can get back to important things.

PROBLEMS

This wasn't what I wanted to come back to," I complained. I glared at the mess marring my almost-library. I'd made it through the banquet, made meaningless chitchat with who knows how many people, and even gotten a good night's sleep. I'd expected to be greeted by a fully recharged dungeon mana pool, not . . . this.

Rhis didn't look too concerned with my displeasure. "I didn't kill them, Mistress, as you wished. Have you changed your mind?" He looked hopeful.

"No." I glared at my two problems. Two bodies bound in so much spider silk that they couldn't speak or move. I noticed a detail.

"You bound their mouths but kept their nostrils free?" I observed.

Rhis nodded. "I know that you need your airways clear in order to live, Mistress."

"Well, good." I suppose it was good that Rhis hadn't "accidentally" killed these intruders and claimed he hadn't known about breathing. "I'm pleased, Rhis," I added.

He grinned widely at the praise, showing all of his teeth.

"Ashmor's justice! Don't let him smile too often, he'll scare my hair white!" Janie opined from behind me. She was the only one of my companions accompanying me today. Given that I was going to be doing "dungeon stuff," which mostly involved me looking at things they couldn't see, most of them had elected to do other stuff. Only Janie had felt that her job meant that she had to come with me, no matter how boring it got.

"Can you cut them free? No, you probably can't," I realized. The Rhis that Janie could see was an illusion. "Actually, how did you get them down here? I know you didn't let the spider out of its floor."

"True. Fortunately, Phantasmal illusions, as they are not monsters, are not subject to the floor limits." He briefly summoned a Phantasmal creature to show me, then quickly dismissed it. It had the body of a hulking human man but the head of a bunny rabbit, somewhat distorted to be more humanoid. The long white ears were a bit of a giveaway, though.

"Sadly," he continued, "they can't be used to hurt people, but moving this refuse was within their capacities."

I chose to ignore Rhis's choices in beefcake and focused on the job at hand. I could have asked Janie to do it, but I fancied myself as a hands-on leader. At least for things I was capable of.

The silk wasn't actually that sticky, and it parted easily under my knife. Over my knife might have been a better way of putting it. Not wanting to stab my prisoners in the face, I slid my thinnest dagger under the bindings and pulled away from the skin, freeing them down to the neck. This allowed me to talk to them, but more importantly, it allowed me to recognize them.

"Oh shit, you two," I said. "Where's the other one?"

The one I freed spluttered and spat, trying to spit out a few stray threads, I supposed. I moved on to the other one, while . . . Digger got his act together. The other one was Winger, I was pretty sure. I didn't care to remember them too clearly, and Memorize respected my wishes on this.

"Bigger stayed out to keep watch!" Digger finally spluttered. "He'll have gotten help by now."

"Oh? How long have they been here?" I asked Rhis.

"Eight hours and 39 minutes," Rhis said. "You were gone for much longer than was required to recharge the pool," he added reproachfully.

"Think he waited for that long?" I asked. "Janie, can you go out and see if he's lurking around? Or if he's found another bunch of thugs and they're building up the courage to storm the building."

"A bunch of thugs? I'm shaking," Janie said with amusement as she left. I called up the abbreviated Dungeon Status.

Dungeon Name	Tower of Learning		
Level: 7	XP: 38,045,596	Next Level: 100,000,000	Floors: 2
Current Mana: 450	Mana Cap: 450	Mana Regeneration: 45.6	Upkeep: 0.746
Dungeon Traits	[Expand]	Invaders: 2/0	

A quick use of Memorize told me that Rhis's experience had gone up by a small amount from the capture. Also, the two of them were still counted as invaders.

"I guess your lives are worth point six mana an hour," I mused. "That's not much, but it is *something*."

"Wait til I get free, bitch!" Digger said, as both of them struggled with their bonds. "Now that mage isn't around, I'll show *you* something!"

I watched, unconcerned, as they failed to make much headway on Digger's threats.

"The bindings will need to be renewed in three hours, Mistress," Rhis said reproachfully. "We can't leave them like this forever."

"You're going to suggest killing them, I suppose." The two captives went still for a moment and then renewed their struggles with renewed fervor.

"That would be ideal, but I suspect it would not be an acceptable solution to you, Mistress," Rhis said mournfully. "Therefore, I have been working on a different solution!"

"Oh?"

"Dungeon thralls!" he said brightly. "Just like we suspect the others of doing! Human minions to do my bidding!"

"You—" I said, and then stopped. I *should* have expected this, and I had to admit that it *was* a solution. Just not one I was willing to countenance. "No."

His ears drooped. "I hope you haven't decided to keep them prisoner."

"You don't like that idea?" I asked, surprised. "You'll get that extra mana. Point six isn't much, but . . ."

"Twice that if we move them to a higher floor," he quickly pointed out. "But no . . . it just gives them an opportunity to learn more of our secrets and escape. We're not yet as secure as I'd like."

It was true. Almost any adventurer I'd known would go through our defenses like wet cheese. I'd been thinking the building surrounding us would have offered some security, but it had been even easier to get through by this pair of thieves.

"No," I said. "We're not going to do that either. Which means the only thing left is to have them work for me."

"With all respect, Mistress—you can't be serious! You can't possibly trust such unsavory characters!"

"Mmm," I murmured noncommittally. "Not that you're wrong, exactly, Rhis, but what do you think of Janie?"

"You can't trust her, Mistress," he said immediately. "I'm sure she's just waiting for her chance to kill you and steal me."

"You don't trust anyone, do you?"

"Only you, of course, Mistress."

"Right. So you'll forgive me if I don't take your advice on hiring decisions. It's always going to be the same, regardless of the situation."

"Yes, Mistress."

I turned my attention back to our intruders. They had stopped struggling and were both looking warily at me.

"So. Digger has done all the talking so far. Are you fine with that, Winger?"

"If you think we're going to work for you, you got another think coming—" Digger spluttered.

I narrowed my eyes at him. "Look, Digger, you should know how this works. You're tied up, and I've got a dagger."

I stepped closer to him and raised the dagger threateningly. "And I've got the Intimidate skill. *Kiss my boots.*"

You have defeated Shelby Smith in a Tier 2 Social Contest! You have earned 22 XP.

I'd gone for the most humiliating demand I could think of to maximize the chance of it going to a Social Contest, but I guess there were some things that Digger would have been even more reluctant to do.

"Really? Shelby?" I said with amusement as he performed his required duty. I didn't waive the contest penalty. I looked over at Winger.

"Um . . . I can speak for myself . . . Ma'am," he said nervously.

"Just as long as we know where we stand," I said dryly and started cutting Digger fully free. He had finished kissing my boots and didn't try to resist as I freed him. Not that he could, at least for the next 24 hours. The muscles on his face worked furiously as he tried to find something that he *could* say to me.

It took him a while before he was able to speak, which said something about either his spite or his stupidity. During that pause, I was able to free his partner and conjure a desk and some chairs to negotiate over. Well, I had an Aeron chair. They had a bench to sit on.

They both looked askance at my summoning of furniture but didn't comment on it directly. Winger went over to . . . Shelby and offered him a hand up.

"Give it up, man," he said. Shelby glared at him but accepted the help.

"This won't last forever, you know," he finally managed to say. The pair of them took the implied offer and sat down opposite me.

"I'm fairly sure I *could* make it last forever, or at least quite a while," I said thoughtfully. "I'd just need to keep renewing it, and well, it wasn't exactly hard to beat you with the least of my social skills. If I was so inclined, it wouldn't be hard to take a minute out of every day to dominate you back into compliance."

I let them wither under my disdainful gaze while they considered that.

"Of course, if I *was* so inclined, it would be even easier to get a pair of the slave collars that Rhis was talking about earlier."

Rhis stepped forward and grinned, pleased to be included in the conversation. For once, his toothy maw suited the mood that I wanted conveyed.

"What . . . is that?" Shelby managed to ask.

"Haven't you ever seen a beast-kin before?" Janie said, returning from the outside.

"That's no beast-kin," Winger said. "Not looking like that."

"Quite right," I told them. "This is Rhis, and that's all you need to know. Janie?"

"It's all quiet outside. There's no sign of anyone else coming to get these shits." She gingerly settled into the chair I conjured for her. Rhis remained standing. He was more intimidating that way and I didn't have to worry about him spoiling the mood by spinning around.

Our two captives glanced at each other nervously. "What sort of shit have we gotten into?" Winger muttered to his partner.

"A good question," I told them. "But we were talking about your future. As I said, I prefer not to mind-control or dominate you. I happen to believe that if the opportunity is obvious enough, people will cooperate to achieve it."

They looked at each other again, a little less nervously. "Opportunity?" Shelby asked.

"Right," I said. "Let's negotiate."

It was a difficult negotiation, even with my skill advantage. The problem was that they planned on agreeing with everything I said and then making a run for it and selling me out the first chance they got.

Fortunately, Bargain could spot an insincere seller a mile off. The situation was a little different from the coachman before. Digger and Winger thought they had a pretty good idea of how much they could make from selling me out to various information brokers in this district. It probably wasn't accurate—they didn't know what they were sitting on—but it was their *perception* that counted here.

Balancing their expected reward with their imagined chances of getting away with it against the remuneration I offered was something that Bargain could manage without requiring any input from my opponents. With the coachman, I had been worried about someone coming along with a better deal, or threats that would override my deal. Here, I just needed to make the deal good enough that these two wouldn't go looking for a better one.

The trick that I went with was to delay compensation. They'd get some money now, but I'd keep them on the line for a bigger payment in a couple of weeks. The risk of losing that would hopefully keep them in line, at least for a little while.

Now, of course, I needed to find something for them to do that would be worth the cost.

SCHOOL

I dumped out a small pile of copper coins and started counting them out into two piles of twenty.

"What I want you to do," I said to my new employees. "Is for you each to find ten kids living on the street, and give them each two copper coins."

I didn't need to be able to read their faces like a book to know that their immediate plan was to take the money and say they'd given it out.

"You'll also let them know how to find this place, and convince them to come here," I told them. "Let them know they can show up between fourth and eighth bell. For every one that shows up, you'll get one *silver* coin."

Now there was some struggle on their faces. Fortunately, I hadn't actually asked them to do math—they knew silver was worth more than copper. Now they were thinking of how they could get the kids to show up without giving them money.

"Needless to say," I said, anything but needlessly, "I will be checking with the kids when they show up. If you haven't given them the money, or if you've *hurt* them in any way, you won't be getting anything."

The pair started grumbling. Partly because of the death of their plans for larceny, but also at the idea of *not* hurting someone.

"Some kids need to be hurt," Digger mumbled.

"Not while you're working for me, they don't," I countered. "I don't expect this to be easy for you. Finding ten kids willing to get within arm's length of you two is going to be a challenge, I know."

"Yeah," Janie snorted. "Most of them will know better. I noticed that you didn't mention an exception for self-defense."

"That's because there isn't one," I said coldly. "These are kids—level one or two. This lot should be able to shrug off anything that kids can do to them."

"Don't underestimate what a pack of street rats can do," she warned. "But it's not like these guys are going to do that."

"So. Any questions? Tell your buddy he can get a similar deal if he shows up," I told them.

They hemmed and hawed for a bit, but they couldn't come up with a way to cheat me, so I sent them out to get started.

"You're always picking up strays to mother," Janie commented once they were gone. I glared at her sourly.

"This world . . . no, I guess this *country*, just wastes so many of its people. I can let the adults slide, but the *kids* . . ."

"Is it different, where you're from?"

I sighed. "It's not perfect," I admitted. "And some of the bigger countries let things get a lot worse than we do. But the idea is there, to give people help when they need it. Shelter, healing, food, and education. If it doesn't get to everyone, at least there are programs in place to *try*."

Janie shrugged. "Here, though, unless you're injured, you can always make money in a dungeon. Get levels, get good, get more. People like those guys, they're that way because they don't want to put in the work to be more."

"The adventurer's dungeon starts at threat fifteen monsters," I said wryly. "You think a few level threes are going to be up to that?"

Janie started to answer, and then stopped, frowning. "That's . . . the others are the same way, aren't they? Why?"

"Dorsay is a trap," I said slowly, the thoughts coming together. "A lot of people, a lot of mana, but advancement and wealth are out of reach of almost everybody except the elite. It costs money to leave, but all their money goes on just living. It keeps a pool of the impoverished available to the nobles to work as servants or soldiers . . . desperate enough to work for a pittance."

"It's not like this in other towns," Janie said, troubled. "Anchorbury went all the way down to threat one."

"That's because it takes mana to keep the dungeons at such a high level," I realized. "All of the regions get sucked dry of as much mana as they can afford—"

"To keep the dungeons in Dorsay fed . . ." Janie finished for me. "Does the King know?"

"Who knows?" I said. "This practice could go back to the old Empire. But he benefits from it as much as the nobles do. But . . ."

I thought about it. Thought about my ideas for this dungeon.

"We might not be able to keep it going for long, but this sabotage might give us an opportunity to make things better. Not by building a better dungeon, but a cheaper one."

Rhis had been ignoring our conversation up until now, but his ears perked up when he heard that. Janie was first to speak, though.

"Not long?"

"I do plan on going back to Talnier at some point. Whatever I construct here . . . well, one benefit of it being mostly Phantasmal, is that when I want to pack up and leave, I can snap my fingers and have it all disappear."

I switched over to talking to Rhis. "Sorry Rhis, I didn't mean cheap as in poor, I meant cheap as in *efficient*."

Rhis was still frowning, though. "That's all very well, Mistress, but did you mean to say that this installation will not be permanent?"

"Yeah, sorry. Think of this place as an experiment, a place to try new ideas without having to worry about the long term."

He sighed. "I suppose it's necessary. From what you said, this chaotic mana situation won't last for long."

"Right. Once they fix the menhirs, not only will we lose our cover, but the ambient mana should drop significantly."

He nodded sadly but then brightened. "At which point we can relocate to a permanent home?"

"Yeah, this has given me some ideas of how we can set up in Talnier," I said thoughtfully. "But let's see how these ideas work out in practice."

"What do you need, Mistress?"

"Let me make a list. Security first—I need a magical item that can cast or hold Conceal Dungeon. Oh, and it should be able to cast Conceal Mana on itself."

"Holding is better; we can use Mistress's full spell total without paying extra," Rhis mused. It took him a moment to do the calculations, then he blanched. "It will cost 480 mana to create, Mistress."

"That much? That's more than our entire budget."

He shrugged. "I can create it in stages. The cost is increased considerably by the fact that it is self-sustaining. If you were willing to recharge it every . . . say, 24 hours, it would bring the cost down to 356 mana."

"Ouch. Well, I also want a new level for the kids to use."

"That would help with our mana problems, in the long term," Rhis pointed out. "A third level will cost 125 mana, and will take up our collection rate to 67 mana per hour."

"Raising our cap to 670?" I asked. Rhis nodded eagerly.

"As long as the ambient mana stays at this level," he cautioned.

"Right, what about those mental magic blockers we were talking about earlier?"

"A simple ward against Mind Magic would only cost 200 mana—the upkeep is already included in the spell, so it is much cheaper."

I thought about it, but it was a pretty easy decision. I could start Rhis working on the concealer and not have it until tomorrow, or I could get a level, a protective amulet, and some monsters for the kids to fight. *And* still get the concealer the next day.

"Get me a new floor, Rhis," I said. "Can we keep the spider floor on top?"

"Since it's all within my spatial expansion, yes," Rhis assured me. "Swapping would be . . . tricky, but I can insert a new floor without a problem."

"Good. Do that then."

"At once, Mistress."

While Rhis went to work, I turned to Janie. "What monsters do you think we should get for the kids?"

She grimaced. "The only low-threat ones I'm familiar with are zombies. And rats. I prefer rats. You're limited to what Oakway used to produce, right?"

"Yeah, so no zombies, thank goodness. He does lizards and insects and mammals . . ." I paused for thought. "Maybe we shouldn't be looking at low threat."

"I thought the idea was making the level for the kids?"

"Yeah . . ." I trailed off, still doing math in my head. "It might make more sense for you to power-level them."

"Eh, that's rarely as quick as having them do it themselves," Janie protested.

"That's the common wisdom, I know, but that isn't the only consideration," I said. "Look, say we get ten kids at level one . . . have them fight a threat two creature. That will earn each of them forty experience."

Janie shrugged, lost already from the math. I kept on, regardless. "Whereas if you join up with them and kill a threat eight . . . that would be 320 experience, split fifteen ways, so just over twenty experience."

Fifteen ways instead of eleven, because the higher-levelled Janie would get five shares.

"Twenty is . . . less than forty, so I was right," Janie said, after a bit of thought.

"Sure, but summoning ten small creatures will cost me twenty mana, while one big creature will only cost me eight. Getting the hundred experience for level two would cost me sixty mana if they do it themselves, but only forty if we power level."

I didn't mention the 500 experience that Janie would get in the process. She couldn't calculate it, but she knew from experience that her share from power levelling would be a noticeable but not really significant step towards level six.

"Costs for monsters are a little more complex than that, Mistress," Rhis piped up. "Oh, the new level is ready now," he added.

"Great, but what did you mean?"

"A monster's attributes—Size, Strength, Perception, Agility, and Finesse—are equal to its threat by default. If they're higher or lower, they change the cost."

Noting my look of interest, he quickly clarified. "But you can't just design a monster with minimum characteristics—you have to select from the catalogue."

I pouted, my dream of experience machines dashed. "Too bad. What would you recommend, then, as a monster that would be easy for Janie to kill?"

It was a simple enough floor design. *Too* simple for Rhis's taste. He didn't protest, but he did sulk.

"C'mon, Rhis," I encouraged him. "Remember, this is only temporary, an experiment to see how things work. If it was *too* well designed, you wouldn't want to tear it down when we're done."

"I suppose."

The floor was comprised of four rectangular rooms, longer than they were wide, laid out around the edge of the floor. That left a small area in the center for what would be the boss room and the stairs up to the third level. I wasn't sure I wanted a boss yet, so for now, it was concealed behind a secret door.

I had allowed Rhis to decorate the rooms with lots of struts coming out at odd angles from the walls and ceiling. They served as perches for the flying raptors, five to each room.

[Identification]: Flying Raptor – Threat 8 – Sex: M – Size: 4 –
Strength: 4 – Perception: 6 – Finesse: 5 – Agility: 4 – Abilities: Flight

I did remember these from Oakway's jungle. While we'd raised the ceiling here to about twenty feet, that wasn't really enough for them to manage their signature attack of surprise dive-bombing you through the jungle canopy.

Janie cast a spell and everything turned into fire.

[Invader] has defeated 5 x Flying Raptors. 1600 XP awarded.

Dungeon has gained 800 XP from invader actions.

You have gained 800 XP from invader actions.

"That was easy," she said.

"That was interesting," I replied. "You got the full amount that I'd expect from five raptors. Sixteen hundred, right?"

"Yeah."

"So not only did I not get a share, despite being right here, but Rhis and I split an *equal* amount of experience between us."

Janie just looked confused. "What does that mean?"

"Well," I said thoughtfully, "I guess that it means I can't get experience from killing my own monsters—but I *can* get experience equal to whatever you earn. Seems like a bit of a cheat, really."

"I should be able to respawn all four rooms in three hours, and still have some mana regeneration spare," Rhis told us. "If you're killing them at that sort of a rate, I suppose there is no point in putting in a support ecosystem," he added sourly.

"I can regenerate my mana in three hours," Janie said. "So I guess I could just be killing all day." She rubbed her hands together. "Let me just do a quick tour."

It didn't take long for her to do a circuit of the floor, gaining 1,600 experience from each room.

"Okay, that was fun," she said. "I might have to do a few runs with Maslin. But . . ." she said, drawing the word out. "What about skills? If they're not actually participating, they can't improve whatever attack skills they're going to be getting."

"They might want to work on those," I admitted. "But these are going to be city kids; they should be working on city skills. Scribe, Calculate, Bargain. Crafting skills. That's what the first floor can be for. But the next agenda item is . . ."

I turned to Rhis. "I hope you've got enough mana left to make that mind ward."

"Not quite, Mistress, but give me 45 minutes and I'll be able to start."

TRUST

> [Identification]: Fortress of the Mind – Quality: Perfect – Created by: Tower of Learning – Material: Darksteel – Durability: 180 – Properties: Enchanted (Ward against [Mind Magic])

Once we'd met up back in our rooms, Felicia insisted on being the first one to try the amulet.

"It's about showing trust," she said. "I want to show you that I trust you the most out of all of us."

I didn't argue with her. I was fairly sure that I wasn't under Rhis's insidious control, but anything I said to that effect would be exactly what a mind-controlled me *would* say. So I just nodded.

"I knew that you would," I said, and handed it over. Nothing happened when she put it on, which was exactly what was supposed to have happened. We had all independently confirmed that the item didn't have any ties leading back to Rhis—or the tower, however you wanted to put it. Now we all checked again to make sure it didn't do anything new when activated.

Nothing, or at least nothing that we didn't expect to see using Mana Sense. We could see that she was under some magical effect, but without a Mind Magic spell between us, we couldn't tell if it was doing anything. I did take note of how the effect looked, in case I ever saw someone else's ward.

Rhis had explained how it worked, but even a simple (he assured me) item like this was beyond my skill. He used the same runes that I would have, so we started on common ground. Our first point of departure was that he included a lot more targeting runes than I would have. The magic item was the necklace, but it protected anyone touching it (one rune) or anyone touching the necklace it hung from (three runes). I would have done that by making the necklace a part of the item, but this way was more robust. If the necklace broke, you could just replace it.

At least two dozen more runes were involved with an additional function of the amulet—if the wearer focused mana into it, they could project its protection to someone that they touched, or as a spherical sphere around them. This additional function cost almost nothing to add, according to Rhis as, despite the additional runes, it didn't change the base function.

I would have liked to have seen these additional runes, but they were inscribed *within* the metal of the amulet. My Mana Sense could just about make them out, but they were written so compactly that all it could make out were faint squiggly lines. *Multiple* lines, because the runes were written out twenty or thirty times, just for redundancy. It only took one line to generate the effect, so it would keep running even after significant damage to the amulet. You could probably break it in half and get two functioning amulets, but I didn't want to experiment. Nor did I bring it up with Rhis—I'd endured enough of his disappointed looks recently.

"So what's your news?" I asked after Kyle had had a chance to compliment Felicia on how it looked.

"Oh! Good news, I've finally been accredited by the Alchemist's Guild."

"That's great!" It was good news. That meant that we could sell the mana crystals we'd gathered and purified directly, instead of passing over a 25 percent cut to the Guild. That would bolster our finances considerably. They had been running a little tight of late. Of course, now that the tower was up and running, Rhis could devote some of his mana to making gold . . . that meant . . .

I have a mint! I thought in surprise. *I can make coin—legal coin of the realm, given that every dungeon in a country makes the coins of that country by default.*

What did that mean for me, economically? I'd have to think it through, given that I couldn't do a lot of things that a mint owner could do. I couldn't adulterate the coinage, for example—or if I could, I didn't think I'd see any profit from it. Coins cost mana, not gold, to produce, and I'd bet that any adulterated coinage would cost as much mana to make.

"Kandis?" Felicia called, knocking me out of my daze.

"Sorry, I was just thinking about money," I admitted. That got more of a laugh from the group than I'd expected—a bit more than I deserved, quite frankly.

"Of course," Felicia said with a grin. "I was just saying that there's a message from the Guild Master—he wants you to meet him tomorrow."

"More spy stuff," I groaned. I wouldn't have minded, normally, but right now I resented anything that took me away from my tower.

"I suppose. There's also—I'm not sure how I became your social secretary—a notification from the palace about an official reception for the return of the Champion of Duit."

"You gotta have a role in the entourage," Janie cut in while I mulled over the news. "Kyle and I have taken bodyguard, which leaves you the boring stuff."

"I'm the Healer *and* the Alchemist," Felicia protested.

"Those aren't official roles," Janie deadpanned. "You could be the maid—"

"Stop fooling around," I interrupted. "If Isidre's coming back, she must have had some sort of triumph on the border."

"Like, she started a war?" Felicia asked.

"Wouldn't we have heard of that?" I asked. "No, wait, I forget just how slowly news moves around here. We wouldn't have gotten the news yet, would we?"

"Not if it was just a few days ago, no." Kyle agreed. "Especially if it happened on the border far away from a settlement. The King has faster ways of getting the news, but it will take a while to spread unless he announces something."

"Then this reception is going to be the announcement, whatever the news is," I said. "I don't really want to go, but I guess I have to."

Janie snorted. "Like you were going to be given a choice. The King wants you in the same room as her, doesn't he? He wants to see if you start fighting or getting all friendly-like."

I glowered at her, but I knew she was right. *Dammit, I don't have time for this!* "Fine," I sighed. "I guess we'll put that on my schedule."

"I need you to spy on another meeting," Guild Master Voight told me.

"I'm thinking of getting out of the spy business," I replied, giving him a disinterested look. "Access to the dungeon is nice and all, but I've picked up a few new interests."

Like working out just how much gold and experience I can pull out of my own dungeon, I thought.

Voight frowned. "I'm sure you're not ready to abandon your country—and your Guild—at such a critical time," he said. "After all we've done for you . . ."

I narrowed my eyes at him. "Perhaps not, but I'm not eager to be exploited. Don't you have other Guild members that can do this for you?"

I could feel Persuasion kicking in. Voight was no slouch at it; he out-levelled me, after all. But he kind of had an advantage because I wasn't *so* opposed to doing this. I wanted Finley brought down for my own reasons, after all. So despite resisting the idea, I didn't think this would kick off a Contest. I just . . . didn't want to be taken advantage of.

Should I ask for money? That was an idea, but really, I had just picked up a gold mine; did I really need money? Obviously, the answer to that was yes, there was no such thing as *too much* money, but maybe there was something I wanted more . . .

I tried to bring in Bargain, but Voight resisted. Testing skills directly like this was new to me. Barely a moment had passed, and we'd each scoped out the other, established each other's position, and we were now readying for a fresh offensive.

"If I were to help you out, I'd want certain assurances from you," I tried.

"Assurances?" he asked. I felt that he didn't want to let me bring in quid pro quo; he didn't want to Bargain. Probably because he *did* have the right to order me around. But maybe he would relent if his side of the deal was something he could easily provide.

"I've always relied on the support of the Guild, both here and in Tal-nier," I explained to his suspicious self. "I can foresee a need for further support, particularly if a dispute arises between me and another Guild member."

"I can't go against the law, or Guild regulations," he said slowly, looking for the trap.

"Of course, I'm talking about a difference of opinion between adven-turers. It would be nice to settle it without the customary violence."

"That's a bit vague," he objected.

"The future tends to be," I said.

"Well then, depending on circumstances, I will see what I can do. Will that suffice?"

"Of course," I said. Really, I would have preferred an oath or written contract, but for that, I would have had to reveal what I wanted.

I'd been thinking about who the 'ger boys were going to sell me out to. I had no doubts about their intentions, but they didn't have many options. A criminal of some sort was an easy choice, but did I have to worry about that? Most criminals were fairly low level, and I'd beefed up the monsters considerably yesterday. A threat six spider hardly cut it for floor three when there were sixteen threat eights downstairs. A criminal invasion might do the town a favor.

An information broker was a smarter choice, but that just moved the question along. Who would *they* sell it to? The law was—I thought—looking the other way. Which left adventurers as the biggest threat.

It was possible that high-level adventurers wouldn't care about my starter dungeon. It was also possible that they'd trash it for fun, try to steal the core, or try to force me to upgrade it into a money pile for *them*. I had no idea which was more likely, but having the Guild Master on my side seemed like a good idea.

"So what do you want me to spy on?" I asked.

"Finley is meeting with the Lyran ambassador at the embassy, tonight," he said.

"That doesn't give me much time to prepare," I pointed out.

"Do you need it?" he countered. I grimaced.

"I'm always going into these things blind," I complained. "Why are they meeting at the embassy? Don't they need to meet in a dive bar or a fighting pit for deniability or something?"

The new Lyran ambassador had been staying in the same building as I was, but after our debut, he had started the process of replacing the old ambassador who, presumably, was going back home. The moving process had been complicated, but from what I could tell, it had been completed.

"If I had to guess," Voight said, "the ambassador wants to have Finley use the communication device Gavril uses to stay in touch with home."

"I haven't seen one of those," I confessed. "Are they rare?"

"Most dungeons of sufficient mana density produce some kind of item," he said. "Maintaining a network of communication requires a lot of them, though, so only rulers can really manage it."

"Including the guilds?"

He frowned. "Ours does not have a particularly long range, and it is fairly bulky. It suffices for keeping guild houses in touch, but we have to relay messages along a chain."

I made a note to add communication to my list of demands for Rhis. It sounded as though each device was a pair . . . would it be possible to set up some sort of switched device? I didn't really know how mobile phones worked, but that shouldn't be an obstacle for magic . . .

"Finley asked for some sort of sign of commitment," Voight continued, snapping me back to the conversation. "So it seems likely that the ambassador will be setting up some sort of meeting with the military or higher-ranking officials. He's not going to do that at a pit fighting arena."

"So all I have to do is find and sneak into a foreign nation's most sensitive area and listen in on their secret conversation."

Voight leaned back in his chair with a smile on his face. "You've proved adaptable in the past. I'm sure you'll manage."

intervention

It turned out to be easier than I thought it would be. It seemed that, from appearances as I drifted past it, the embassy security was in a transitional state. A mix of old and new personnel, existing and revised procedures. No one seemed to know what was going on, or how to go about doing it.

At one stage, I thought I had been detected, but instead of a blaring alarm, a subtle wall feature lit up in the guard's view . . . but no one was looking at it. I quickly covered it with a Static Illusion and moved on, promising myself I would be more careful. A lot of people had passed through the field already, so I wasn't sure if it was detecting invisible people or if it was based off invitations.

That was another thing that made things easier for me. Duke Finley was not the only guest tonight. This was a party to introduce the ambassador to the nobility at large, and the guest list was wide ranging. I could have gotten in with an invitation, either by asking directly or as a guest of someone more notable like Aubey, but I thought it better if, officially, I was nowhere near this place.

I was on my own, of course. The others would have liked to come, but shepherding even one more invisible person through this crowd would have been too much. They were as close to the embassy as it was possible to get without raising suspicion, but that was not very close at all.

Lots of guests meant lots of security enchantments being disabled, lots of overstressed guards, and a lot of noise to cover my footsteps. It also made for a confusing jungle of bodies for my invisible self to move around, but my task was simple enough. I just had to latch on to Duke Finley and follow him when he got led out for his secret meeting.

He slipped away early, while the party was still in the mingling phase. That fit; I didn't see him as someone who planned to stick around for the speeches. No doubt he was keeping his evening free for another night of watching muscular, sweaty dudes cut one another to shreds. To each his own.

The point was, he left the party, and I followed. Slipping into the room behind him was the toughest part of the job so far, but fortunately, Lyran politeness included a lot of bows and effusive greetings when an important person came into the room. I found an out-of-the-way corner and waited for the small talk to come to an end.

"You must understand now, the time for action is well past time," the ambassador said, politely but urgently. The two of them were seated in two of the four comfortable chairs in the room arranged around a small table with refreshments. There were guards outside, but none in here.

"Your spies must have reported that our fleet has been sighted north of your King's Isle. The King's fleet is already preparing to sail, are they not? Now is the time to ensure that reinforcements cannot be sent from the mainland."

Finley gave Gavril a small smile. "Sighted is hardly committed," he said. "The griffin scouts have a long range, and you are still days away from the island. Or just a day away from turning around and claiming it was just an open water exercise."

"Ah, you are a man of many suspicions!" Gavril exclaimed. "Perhaps it is well, in one way, to partner with someone who is not a fool, but partners must trust in each other at some time, yes?"

"Sounds like a devilish foreign notion," Finley snorted. "I'm long familiar with the Chancellor's games, and this feels like a scheme to get me to stick my neck out."

"Aaahhh . . . at this stage, perhaps I can say that we *were* approached by your Chancellor," the ambassador admitted, "but we felt that this was a chance to be having your Chancellor outsmart himself."

"Exactly what you would say if you were part of his scheme," the Duke pointed out wryly.

"This is being true," Gavril admitted. "We were to be making a little noise out in the ocean, to be giving the fleet cause to sail, but sailing loaded with troops, not for sea fighting."

"And said troops would sail up the river and relieve the siege . . . ending my little adventure."

"Yes . . . but where there is expectations, there can be surprises, yes? So we sought to change the game."

The Duke's eyes narrowed. "Even if you kept on course, the griffin riders would see. There would be plenty of time to recall the fleet."

"Bad news for us," Gavril agreed, "But good for you! Our fleet cannot match yours, this is true. But they would be delayed, damaged. You would have time enough to crack the nut that is the palace."

"Maybe," Finley said. The idea seemed to intrigue him. "But why would you sacrifice your fleet for me?"

"Because of the deep and abiding friendship between us!" Gavril said with mock seriousness, before laughing. "No, actually, we were thinking that we would *not* lose our fleet instead."

"And how would you achieve that?"

"Ah! Let me show you the explanation." Gavril leapt to his feet and moved over to a door—not the one they had come in from. Finley, of course, had taken a seat with a view of both doors, so he didn't have to crane his neck to see who was going to come in.

"Please enter, honored guest!" Gavril said, bowing to the person outside the door.

Finley didn't rise, he was too self-important for that, but he did look surprised.

"Envoy Fisher," he said.

And indeed, it was Manuela Fisher who entered the room. Unlike the woman who'd tried to get me into bed the other night, this Manuela was calm, composed, and not even a little bit drunk. She was still dressed all in black, but somehow she made it look even more severe.

"Duke Finley, Ambassador," she said, nodding to them both. Approaching Finley, she went down on one knee in front of him, and held out a black gem.

He looked at it, and then back to her. "I know who you are, Envoy. You're known to the Court; you don't have to prove anything."

She shook her head. "Given the seriousness of what we are discussing, my master wishes you to be absolutely clear about whose words I am speaking."

The Duke frowned and made an abortive move as if to take the gem. Reconsidering, he stopped to pull out a glove from a pocket. It was at about that point that I felt a chill coming from the center of the room.

Not a gem, I realized. *It's a chip of ice. Black ice.*

The kind of ice Aghen Shadthe was known for.

His hand now protected, Duke Finley reached for the chip resting on Manuela's bare hand. He grimaced as his hand got closer, and I felt the cold intensify. When he got to within about ten centimeters of it, I was astonished to see ice start to form on his glove. He never actually got to touch the chip; before he reached it, the ice had covered his fingers, preventing him from getting closer. With a muttered curse, he withdrew his hand.

Throughout it all, Manuela had remained serene and unmoving, entirely unaffected. Once he withdrew, she stood and placed the gem on the table behind her, before taking one of the seats still available. Gavril had seated himself, unnoticed while all this was going on.

"So your bona fides have been established," Finley said sourly, flexing his hand to dislodge the ice. Gavril winced as the shards fell down to melt on what was no doubt an expensive carpet. "And what exactly is Aghen Shadthe's interest in all this?"

"My master has decided to support the Lyrans in their fleet action," Manuela said calmly. Finley did not take it with the same equanimity.

"What? He's moving against the Kingdom?" he exclaimed, almost yelling. He leaned forward, making a threatening gesture with his recently ice-clad fist. Manuela remained perfectly serene.

"Not at all. His aid, while expensive, can be purchased, which is what moves him to act in this case."

"I am sure you are realizing what this is meaning," Gavril interjected. "Boiling clouds to be covering the movements that the fleet is making. Winds blowing to aid our fleet and hinder yours. The honorable Shadthe's aid will surely mean the difference between victory and defeat for us— and aid greatly in your endeavors."

"I trust this answers your questions about commitment?" Manuela asked. Finley sank back into his chair, glowering.

"It occurs to me that there are only so many suspects for the sabotage of our mana supply—and your master must be one of them."

Manuela smiled. "That accusation has not been put to me or my master directly. If someone were to do so, rest assured that my master would answer it."

She paused, considering her words. "I can say that the sabotage, embarrassing as it is, can hardly be considered an attack, when you consider the options available to someone as powerful as my master. Dorsay has been merely inconvenienced for a period. Perhaps if a new administration—one with a less fraught history with my master—were to ask, he could provide aid in fixing it."

"That isn't a denial," Finley muttered.

"And no part of your statement could be construed as an accusation, could it?" Manuela replied. "Can we get back to the original question?"

"Come now, my friend. We are partners, yes? And partners must be moving together, in locked steps like a dance." He smiled at the Duke. Actually, he had never stopped smiling, but his smile now seemed much harder, and sharper.

"I take your meaning, *partner*," the Duke said sourly. "Very well, I will be ready to attack the palace in three days. Is that sufficient?"

"Of course, of course! Asking for a better timing is not a possible thing," Gavril said warmly. "Shall we be drinking then? And toasting to the future?"

He busied himself with the goblets and wine on the table, until now untouched. "To our success, and to the new King of Latora, long may he rule!"

ALARM

Now what? I wondered. Here I was, now in possession of what the military types would refer to as *actionable intelligence of a time-sensitive nature*—or something similar. I had been planning to report my results to Voight in the morning, but something told me that this news required a little more urgency than that.

Regardless of the urgency, though, I couldn't do anything until I managed to leave the room. The door was closed, which would have been enough to stymie me, but there was also a servant in front of it *and* I rather suspected that there were guards behind it. There was the other door, but I didn't know where it went. Maybe I could find my way out that way, but I didn't really fancy my chances. Not to mention that it, also, was closed.

My planned escape route was to follow Finley out, but he didn't appear to be going anywhere for now. He didn't look as though he *wanted* to stay there, but the toasts and flattery had him mollified for now. He wouldn't stay in place *forever*, but I wanted him moving faster than that.

[Create Water]. [Conceal Mana].

Normally, there wasn't a point in using Conceal Mana on Create Water. The spell did nothing to hide the great gob of water that it summoned. But if I slowed the flow to a trickle, and targeted the spell beneath Finley's chair, the spell was concealed enough to make Mana Sense the most likely way of noticing something untoward.

"Is this all from the ice earlier?" Finley said with distaste, having noticed the squelching of the carpet beneath his feet. The others stared as liquid slowly spread out from his chair.

"No?" Manuela said uncertainly, trying to avoid blame.

"I fear we are having some kind of leaking from somewhere," Gavril said, like the courteous host he was. "Perhaps we should be moving this celebration and be letting the servants deal with it."

There was broad agreement, and the group quickly left, taking the servants and the guards with them. They even left the door open for whatever group of servants had the job of taking care of plumbing issues.

Success, I thought. I slipped out of the room right behind my target. It wasn't long before I was back in the main section, dodging guests. It was challenging enough that I thought I might just cancel Invisibility and walk out with a Disguise, but I managed to slip out entirely unobserved.

Now to go and report, I thought. *No, wait. Pick up my people and then report.*

The first bit was easy, the second less so.

"I'm sorry, but the Guild Master is unavailable until tomorrow," the receptionist said, for what might have been the fifth time. The Guild itself might be open at all hours, but Voight didn't work CEO hours.

"And, once more, this won't *wait* until tomorrow." I could feel Persuasion slipping off the wall that was Bureaucracy. It might have been inspiring under other circumstances. I wondered if this was Voight's skill, or if the long dead hand of some high-level bureaucrat was behind this.

"There must be some procedure for dealing with emergencies," I tried.

"But there *is* no emergency, miss, or at least you haven't said anything to indicate one," the attendant said. I glared at her, and she started to look a *little* nervous. Bureaucracy wouldn't protect her from physical violence from someone who out-levelled her.

Not that I was going to resort to violence. I took a deep breath.

"Would a dungeon break be considered an emergency?" I asked calmly. "Because I can break your dungeon if that's what it takes."

The woman gasped. "That would be a high crime—you'd go before the King!"

"Not hearing a no," I said flatly.

Janie laughed. "No need to go that far," she said. "Just break into his office and torch the place—that'd just be vandalism, maybe arson."

"I'm not sure if that would count as an emergency, though," I said thoughtfully.

"Arrgggh! All right, I can send the Guild Master a message," the receptionist said.

"Are you going to read it?" I asked. I had a strong feeling that Voight was going to want this information kept under wraps, at least until he'd told the King. Keeping this a secret from the front desk clerk was at least a part of why she'd been giving me a hard time.

"If you *must*, you can write it and seal it before giving it to me," she said.

I wasn't sure that I could trust in that—after all, she had the seal that I'd be using, so the message would only be notionally protected. But I supposed that there was something I could write that would get Voight's attention while not giving the game away.

I took the paper she gave me and wrote just two words.

Aghen Shadthe.

Then I folded it and gave it back.

"That's it?" she asked incredulously.

"It's not the full story, by any means, just enough to get him here," I told her. "You can get this to him, quickly?"

"I suppose you'll want to wait in the lobby," she said sourly.

"Actually, I'm thinking that we won't pass this on right away," Voight said. He leaned back in his chair and stared at the ceiling.

"Are you kidding me? I could have waited until morning and not spent half an hour busting your receptionist's balls?"

"What an extraordinary expression," he noted with a grin. "No, you did the right thing there. You were right to get this to me quickly."

He did not, I noted, say that he was going to set up a channel so that this didn't happen in the future, but after a moment's reflection, I decided that I was okay with that. It wasn't as if I *wanted* to be tasked with time-sensitive intelligence acquisition.

Instead, he continued. "Politically, though, I can see that the timing of this revelation will be sensitive. Whenever I tell the King, the Chancellor will know about it, and he's sure to take steps to protect his plan. For one thing, I shouldn't do anything until Finley has started moving his troops."

"If you leave it too late, though, the King will get his fleet sunk," I pointed out. "That can't be good . . . politically."

"True, but there is a little time yet before they sail, and a little more time before they encounter Shadthe. Assuming that Envoy Fisher was telling the truth."

"Why wouldn't she be?"

"Going in, we expected the Lyrans to have found some way to convince Finley to commit, did we not? And here we are, with him committed. It's possible that either Shadthe or Fisher are stringing Finley along at the Lyran's behest."

"That thing with the ice . . . Manuela implied that it meant she was serious about this, but what exactly does it mean?"

"Not much," Voight told me. "It's a little ritual that Shadthe has cooked up to make sure that his people aren't impersonated. The chip freezes any who touch it, *except* one of his envoys. There are rumors that he can see through the ice . . . but I've never seen anything to substantiate that."

"So it's just a dramatic way of saying she's the envoy . . . which Finley already knew."

"Precisely. A touch of drama can be just the thing to mask a con . . . which may be what she is doing, either at her master's orders or otherwise."

I thought about getting away with a scheme like that. It probably came down to skills. Deceive was a skill that most people unlocked in childhood, but not everyone took it. It was a hard skill to sense at work—it never opposed, just aided the user with their own tells and mannerisms. Or pointed them out on someone you were talking to.

Telling lies *was* based on Charisma, while detecting lies was based on Intelligence. I didn't tell a lot of lies, despite my penchant for fooling people. Being misleading with the truth, or showing someone something false was more my kind of style. That didn't count as lying, and so Deceive was one of my least developed social skills. I probably couldn't have detected if Manuela was lying. Not if Finley hadn't.

"Seems to me that we now know less than what we started the evening with," I said. "Maybe I was wrong about this being important."

"No, no," Voight reassured me. "This is important information. Leave it with me, and I'll find the right way to leverage it."

"One other thing," I said. "Am I right in thinking that if Finley will be ready in three days, he already has men inside the city?"

"Almost certainly," Voight agreed. His face dropped into a frown. "He can surely sneak men past the city guards, but not that many, that quickly. I've had parties out looking for them, but my men are not the King's guard—they don't have the right to go banging on suspicious doors."

"So you don't have any idea of where these troops are?" I asked, incredulous.

"I am keeping watch on a number of suspicious locations," he assured me. "If Finley is sending out orders tomorrow, that should make identifying them easier."

"I hope so," I told him. "Because in three days, the streets of this city are going to have soldiers fighting in them. I get that protecting the people of this city isn't part of your job, but if the Adventurer's Guild wants to be known as the champion of the common man . . . it should be saving lives when that time comes."

"True enough." Voight nodded solemnly. "I will do what I can to prevent that possibility, I swear."

"Anyway," I said, standing up. "All of that is way past my pay grade. I hope you don't have anything for me tomorrow because I have a busy day ahead of me."

I may have abused Persuasion to get Issey to help. Or Isabel, I should say, as that was her actual name. I felt bad for using the nickname that those idiots had introduced her with, but she was used to it by now. Given her new role as a teacher, she needed a name with a little more gravitas. Miss Isabel sounded a lot more . . . serious than Miss Issey, and she'd all the help she could get keeping the kids under control.

Not that they were a problem for me, of course. Intimidate was overkill in their case—one raised eyebrow from me would have them jumping to attention, or at least stopping whatever disgraceful activity they were engaged in.

Aside from the fact that I wanted as little to do with the brats as possible, I thought that the old good cop / bad cop routine would be of use here. In this case, good teacher / bad headmistress. Isabel could present as the sympathetic mother figure, while I remained distant, as the threat of discipline for kids that were bad.

To say that Isabel hadn't planned on being a teacher was an understatement, but she liked it better than whore. I never brought it up, but I was fairly sure that she knew her old path could only have ended there. What clinched her acceptance was that she didn't have to quit dancing. Even if she became a Teacher—something she wouldn't have the points for until level four—she'd still be able to dance. Dance better than most in the city, since there were few, if any, Dancers with a level that high.

As a Teacher, she could even Teach dance . . . but that was a decision better left until she got the requisite skills and another level. Level four before her forties had been a ridiculous dream, but now it was just another fifteen runs around floor two with Janie.

Right now, I was watching her supervise an exercise in a new room on floor one. Watching via dungeon surveillance, since this was a free-form activity that wouldn't benefit from my oppressive presence.

Our first class was eight children. There had been nine, but one had been sent "home" for bullying the others. It had been an effective punishment. Even kids knew the value of the experience they were getting with Janie. Missing out put the bully behind, and it wouldn't be long before they were bullying him. Or not, if I managed to install some civilized attitudes into these hellions, but I didn't have high hopes. This was a pilot, an experiment. I wasn't going to be here long enough to educate them, but I could still make a significant difference in their lives.

Right now, it looked more as if I was endangering their lives, but it was all perfectly safe. Weapons skills were easily unlocked, as long as you could afford an appropriate weapon. Doing it *safely* took some expert supervision, but in this room, all the weapons were Phantasmal. Granted access to a wall of weapons of every type imaginable to me, the kids went nuts, which was exactly what we wanted.

Grabbing a weapon at random, the kids swung at one another, the walls, Isabel, whatever they could. Eventually, they would chance upon a decent strike, hit whatever they aimed at, and unlock the skill. When that happened, I was notified of the experience gained and cancelled their weapon. Grabbing a new one, they would start again.

It was loud, uninhibited, and completely safe. Isabel eventually joined in and unlocked some weapons skills of her own. I watched and contented myself with the thought that I'd found a way to make some kids happy.

PROFIT

The money was rolling in. Not *much* money, admittedly, but some. Seven kids were going through floor two with Janie and Felicia. They were taking their time, as Felicia was instructing them in the fine art of monster disassembly. Respawning the monsters there was taking up almost all of my dungeons's mana regeneration, but their presence was giving me an additional 4.8 mana an hour.

I was getting a little less from the first floor. Issey and five kids were down there doing the weapons training thing. One brat from yesterday had actually bought a weapon skill and had agreed to show the others—the bully and three new kids—the ropes. It meant that the bully was getting his comeuppance, which I was fine with, as long as they kept to Phantasmal weapons. Between them all, I was getting a little less than one full mana, but that took my total extra mana regeneration to over five per hour.

I spent a little of that on some copper coins for killing monsters on floor two. Nothing too generous. While I didn't want the kids to stay here, or starve on the streets, I also didn't want them flashing around a suspicious amount of money. For the same reason, I wouldn't be letting them keep any of the skins or cores that Felicia was showing them how to collect.

Those cores were the real treasure, apparently included in the cost of a monster. I got a small mana bonus when I let Rhis absorb them, but it wasn't anything near the worth of them when they were extracted. I should have been putting the extra mana towards respawning the lizards faster, so I could collect more of them, but I couldn't rely on a reliable harvester like Felicia all the time.

The kids were nothing like reliable harvesters. I couldn't blame them, really, since they weren't keeping the proceeds. Some of them were thinking of registering as Adventurers and were considering buying the skill, but most of them found it as unpleasant as I did. We just wanted to make sure that they unlocked the skill, so they had it available.

Instead of cores, I was putting most of the extra mana into gold. There wasn't any real reason for it; I just liked materializing a coin out of thin air and placing it down on the stack. It made for a nice distraction when I took a break from my work.

That work was making teaching materials. I had books for Scribe and Teach already, but I had a lot of skills that could be passed on through books. Calculate, Bargain, and Mana Sense were obvious priorities. They were required for a lot of good, well-paying classes. I could have added Craft(Smith) in that category, but I might still be under some sort of obligation to not teach it to non-guild members.

Then there were the magic skills—Illusion Magic, Enchanting, Water Magic, and Theurgy. They were more dangerous to teach . . . both in terms of what someone could do with them, and in terms of who might come after *me*. Theurgy was supposed to be illegal to teach in this country unless you were in the guild for it. I'd leave them for now . . . I didn't think I could get three books done before the attack.

It took *hours* to make a book. Complaining about it was a little rich, I suppose, given how long it normally took, but I was a little miffed that I couldn't seem to speed the process up with my dungeon connection. Once I'd made a particular book, I could have the dungeon make Phantasmal copies, somehow holding the entire contents in my mind and shaping the illusion. I didn't get any experience for the copies, but my skill was telling me that they would work just as well as the real thing. We'd test it out for the first time once the brats were done with their delve.

Why aren't other people doing this? I wondered. True, some of what I was doing was only possible because I had taken over a dungeon. That didn't seem like a well-trod path. But taking a class through a dungeon, getting them to level three, was so easy that it beggared belief that it wasn't standard practice. All it was costing was mana, a renewable resource.

Admittedly, it was less efficient than having them do it themselves. And it took someone like Janie, with an attack that could take out a crowd of lesser monsters, to do it safely.

Opportunity cost was a thing. Perhaps there were other things we could be doing that would be more profitable—I could already think of some. But really, what could be more worthwhile than securing a future for children? I was starting to regret that this experiment was going to be temporary. Dorsay needed something like this, but I wasn't in a position to provide it long term. I'd started building something in Talnier and I needed to see it through.

I could—perhaps—build the tower again in Talnier, but there weren't a lot of children there. That might change, though, along with everything else I had planned.

"I swear, this woman can't go anywhere without a procession," I muttered to myself.

I had actually missed the procession, choosing to work instead. Cutter had attended, enthusiastically, and had informed us of the highlights when we had met up back at our apartment. About the only significant difference from last time was that her troupe were all mounted on griffins—including her. She'd found an adult griffin to ride, and she and the rest of her people had done so right through the main street. It couldn't have been *that* an unusual sight. The King maintained a unit of griffins in the city somewhere; you saw them flying about all the time. I guess marching them down the street was a little bit unusual, though. And there was the Champion.

Cutter had told us there were crowds, banners, and thrown flowers. Now Isidre had staged a smaller version of the march in the King's throne room. Unlike my first audience, she wasn't forced to stand under the oppressive inspection of every member and guest of the Court while we waited for the King to show up.

Instead, she marched down the center of the room where the King was waiting to receive her. That was the difference, I supposed, between a jumped-up commoner like myself and an acknowledged Champion.

At least I was up in the stands this time. Not down there getting stared at, or held backstage for a dramatic reveal. A dramatic reveal was still *possible*, if His Majesty so decreed. He could call me down from the stands just as easily. But I did think that he'd have me closer if he was planning to pull me out of his pocket, as it were.

The other procession-like aspect to this show was Isidre's followers. Dressed up in shiny plate—no weapons visible, of course—or plain white robes with deep hoods. They followed in her wake, just as they must have followed her up the streets.

"Quite the sight, isn't it?" Manuela nudged me as she spoke. She was back to being a giggly socialite. I wasn't sure what to make of her now that I'd seen her envoy persona, but it wasn't as if I could bring it up.

"I'm surprised you aren't all over her," I murmured. There wasn't anyone near us, so I cast Privacy. I was pretty sure no one was listening in, but enhanced senses were a thing.

"Oh, I got the report from Tom saying that she wasn't interested in any patronage deals and such. She has her church to back her, after all."

She glanced at me slyly. "And he sent word that she was into men, so there was no point in trying to seduce her."

"Didn't he tell you that *I* was into men?" I asked acerbically.

"Well, yes, but I discounted it on account of his bias," she replied smugly. I sighed.

"Even if she *was* into girls, she's much more straightlaced than I am, I think," I said. "She seems pretty strongly Catholic, and their teachings tend to be against any sex outside of marriage."

"Catholic . . . that's one of the fake religions from your world? What religion did you believe?"

"Church of Mammon," I quipped. "But actually, I was nominally raised Anglican, which is close enough to Catholicism that I don't feel like explaining the difference."

"Is that why you've been so chaste?"

"No," I said flatly. "Even if I'd been a true believer before, I don't think it has much meaning here. I'm not sure how she's taken to suddenly having a new god."

"You didn't ask?"

"There are few subjects more touchy than religion back home," I told her. "I didn't bring it up, and I don't plan to."

"Oh, has it started? Let me hear."

I dropped the spell, as requested, and let the hubbub of the Court wash over us again. They seemed to have finished the ceremonial greeting part and were moving on to announcements.

". . . and tell the Court of the expansions to the Kingdom that you have made for us."

Isidre started listing out the names of towns and describing stretches of land. It didn't mean anything to me, and the Court didn't seem shocked or anything. I reminded myself that these spectacles were all planned out in advance. Every question and answer had been scripted.

I found my eyes drawn to the robed figures. Had Isidre had followers that dressed like that before? The robes didn't seem to be covering armor, but they concealed faces pretty well.

"And were these lands acquired through battle, Champion Isidre?" the King asked, "Are there tales to tell of gallant bravery and stout hearts?"

He was hiding it well, but I didn't think the King was greatly pleased. Not *angry*, just . . . displeased. I wondered if it had something to do with the ceremony, or if he was upset by something else. Like the upcoming attack—had Voight informed him?

"No, your Majesty," Isidre replied. She also seemed . . . somewhat resigned. But again, this was all scripted, so perhaps she was just bored.

"Your new lands were gained through treaty," she continued. "A treaty that awaits your ratification, which was negotiated between myself . . . and another Champion in these lands."

That got a reaction. Not a huge one, I think most people were *aware* that there was another Champion running around with the Tribes. But clearly, some people had not been let in on all the details of this script.

One of the white robes stepped forward, and I suddenly tensed. Was this the moment that the white robes were revealed to be super death killing machines that had infiltrated the treaty signing to murder everyone and bring chaos to the lands?

No. The white robe brought down their hood to reveal a face that was familiar. She was noticeably more pretty than before, but it wasn't hard to recognize Kaito. She bowed to the King, as Isidre continued speaking.

"That Champion has returned with us and stands before you today, ready to answer any questions or concerns about the treaty that you have. Your Majesty, may I present, Kaito Washiyama, Champion of Naldyna."

Now, *that* got a reaction. The Court erupted with noise, as just about everyone started talking or calling down questions. The actual content of those questions was lost in the noise, but I don't think they had any intention of answering them anyway.

I turned my attention to the rest of the white robes, who were also lowering their hoods. Sure enough, it was the rest of Kaito's crew, a seemingly random assortment of pretty beast-kin girls.

The chatter was silenced, as the guards all brought the haft of their spears down on the floor in unison. The crashing sound cut through the chatter, and everyone remembered where they were.

"You are welcome in this Court, Champion Washiyama," the King stated. "We shall meet at a later date."

He nodded, and they all bowed and made their way out of the room. The crowd managed to hold it in until the King also left, and then the chatter erupted again.

"Kandis, Kandis," Manuela said, grasping my sleeve. "Are you thinking what I'm thinking?"

"I doubt it," I said warily. "What are you thinking?"

"Three words," Manuela said, smirking. "Girls. Night. Out."

HAREM TIME

There was considerable resistance to Manuela's idea. I didn't veto the notion—by which I mean that I didn't run screaming from the room, or drag *her* out at dagger point. That's what it would have taken to dissuade her, so my unenthusiastic grunt was taken as a complete affirmation of the idea. She dashed off to get into position for when the guests were released to mingle with the Court.

She wasn't the only one trying to get a word with the Champions, of course, but she had a few advantages. Most of the higher-status nobles here were reluctant to *use* that status, at least right now. They wanted to seem aloof and uncaring, to maintain their dignity. Manuela had no dignity to lose, so she wasn't afraid to throw herself into the scrum.

I had noted that there was a certain wary caution accorded to envoys of the Ebon Order, but Manuela and Tom were very different in how they used it. Tom liked to gather menace about him like a cloak. He didn't quite stick to the walls, but he liked to loom in the background, moving slowly enough that people could maintain their distance.

Manuela used it like a weapon, moving quickly into the personal space of people who didn't want to talk to her, sending them fleeing with nothing more than a smile and a few friendly words. She tore into the crowd like a particularly ravenous wolf attacking a herd of deer. I stayed well back, only getting drawn into things when she reached her targets and started encountering actual resistance.

It turned out that Isidre wasn't all that pleased to see *me*, and while Kaito was happy to go out for drinks, his girls were not. They took an instant dislike to Manuela—probably a consequence of her coming on too strong initially. Nori actually *hissed* at her when she got a little too close to Kaito.

They also seemed to have picked up an antipathy to Isidre, which was odd, as she seemed to have taken a liking to Kaito. The only reason she was considering going out with us was that Kaito liked the idea. And so a complicated dance of negotiation was started. A dance I stayed out of. I didn't have any special conditions to insist on, so I just watched as Manuela wore them down into agreeing.

Is this just a spur-of-the-moment idea? I wondered. *Or is she trying to keep us all occupied while Finley organizes his forces?*

I genuinely couldn't tell, which said something about her skill. I could probably get a better idea if I entered the conversation seriously. If, say, I confronted her with the meeting she'd had . . . but that would be stepping on the Guild Master's toes. He said he had a plan, and stepping out of my role wasn't going to earn me any favors.

"You could have brought the rest of your friends," Kaito told me. She sipped at her beer with the face of someone who *knew* she wasn't going to be getting rice wine but wanted it anyway.

She, like the rest of her crew, was wearing what I was calling "barbarian chic." It made them stand out from the crowd even more than their race did. Tight—very tight—leather shirts and pants, cut to allow easy movement, which left a lot of skin, or fur rather, visible. Identify told me they were a lot more protective than they looked, being well crafted and made from the skins of beasts that had probably never seen a cow.

In a concession to either propriety or the cooler weather, they wore light, loose overcoats in various styles and colors. These were highly decorated, and quite attractive, but they were clearly designed not to hide what was underneath. It made me curious if Kaito had managed to maintain her chastity, but I resolved not to ask.

"Nah, Felicia and Kyle wanted an early night, and I'm not taking the kids drinking," I replied. "On the other hand, there was no way I was keeping Janie away from a pub."

I looked over at Janie, farther down the table, who appeared to be comparing tattoos with Zichy. If tattoos were the right word. The wolf-kin had done something to her follicles that changed the color of her fur and managed something like the abstract patterns that Janie sported.

"I must admit I feel somewhat left out," Kaito confessed. "I was never much of a drinker back home."

"You weren't an office worker, right?" I said. "Never had to deal with that drinking culture."

"Ah, no, I was only ever a temporary employee, I didn't really go to *nomikai*," she agreed. "And when I did drink, it was *sake*."

Her throwing in a few Japanese words made me realize that we'd drifted into speaking Tribal. Which was fine, I guess. Janie was too far down the table to be left out of the conversation.

"That must have been inconvenient when the girls tried to get you drunk," I said, smirking. I glanced over at Ettalle and Nori, the girls sitting closest to us. It was hard to tell under the fur, but I thought they were blushing. They *definitely* weren't meeting my eyes.

"Trying to get me drunk?" Kaito laughed, oblivious. "Not really, although we have had some fun parties. Fassi can heat enough water for a hot spring and—"

"I'm sure it's been fun," I interrupted before I could get TMI. "But I was going to ask about the . . . tension I've been feeling between your girls and Isidre."

I glanced down the table, but I wasn't worried about Isidre hearing her name. She was at the other end of the table, being badgered—or possibly wooed—by Manuela. The girls also looked in that direction, although for them it was more of a glare.

"That woman," Ettalle muttered. Nori growled a little, I presumed in agreement.

"Ah, that is my fault," Kaito admitted.

"Don't say that!" Ettalle exclaimed, "You weren't to know!"

"It's her fault," Nori agreed. "She should have known better."

"Sorry to be so slow," I said. "But *what* is your fault? It can't be that bad, seeing as you managed to negotiate a treaty."

"Oh, *she's* fine with it, the dirty—"

"Nori!" Kaito pleaded. "Let me explain," she said to me. "It was because I wanted to negotiate that I made the mistake of increasing my Charisma."

"That makes sense," I said cautiously. I had noticed an increase in Kaito's presence, but it could just as easily have been due to a new level. It still wasn't close to mine. "What's the problem?"

She sighed. "I forgot about how Harem works," she said.

"How it works?" I asked, calling up the System entry for myself.

> **Harem: Acquire a number of [Charisma] companions of appropriate age, gender and attractiveness (5 points).**

"Wait. You opened up a new slot?"

"New *slut*, more like," Nori muttered, quietly enough that I wouldn't have heard it without enhanced hearing. I didn't let her distract me from what Kaito was saying.

"I didn't mean to!" she protested. "It just . . . we got to talking about our previous lives. She had suffered so much—I didn't realize how good we had it in Japan, and I suppose Australia as well. Guatemala is more like here, with the poverty and . . ." She trailed off in the face of my look of—horror? Was that what was on my face? I probably didn't want to be showing that.

With some effort, I activated Charm and arranged myself into something more socially acceptable.

"Do you mean to say," I said, urgently, "that you added Isidre to your harem?"

"Not deliberately!" Kaito insisted.

"Not permanently!" Ettalle added. "Not unless they . . . you know," she said, glancing at Kaito. "I'm sure it will fade, once they get some separation."

"That will open up the slot again, right? Can you make sure I'm in another country when that happens?"

"We'll find another good Tribal girl, don't worry," Ettalle said.

"Though . . ." Nori said thoughtfully, "You'd be better than *her*," Ettalle raised her eyebrows in surprise, but didn't contradict her friend.

"Thanks for the vote," I said sourly. "Don't take this wrong way, I'm sure what you've got here is very fulfilling, but I've got things to do that don't involve being part of a harem."

"I'm sorry," Kaito apologized mournfully.

"Naldyna's chastity," I said, trying out the curse. "Isidre didn't even *like* girls when we spoke before."

It wasn't that I had a gaydar, and we hadn't actually talked about it, but it was hard for me to miss when someone nearby was attracted to women, as that generally meant they were attracted to *me*. There were a lot of little signs that I normally politely ignored, like a permanent flush, difficulty speaking, or walking into walls.

"That might be why she's resisting," Ettalle said thoughtfully. "That, or the marriage thing."

"If separation is what you need," I said suspiciously, "then why are you all here?"

"She asked me to come with her," Kaito explained. "And it *is* important for the treaty to be signed. I couldn't really refuse."

"And wait—I thought you only liked furry girls."

"It's not about physical appearance," Kaito replied, offended. "Although, she *is* attractive. Just because I find—anyway. It was getting to know her that made me—that attracted me to her. She's a really nice person, Kandis. I know you've clashed, but—"

"Don't worry about it," I told her. "There's nothing personal between us, at least on my side. Now that she's working towards peace, we can probably work together."

"That's a relief," she said.

"Now that I think about it, though, my original question still hasn't been answered." I turned to Ettalle. "What is *your* beef with her? I haven't noticed any spats between the rest of you girls. Is it because she's not a Tribal?"

"Partly," Ettalle admitted. "But mostly it's because she thinks she's better than us."

"That's not true, Ettalle," Kaito interjected.

"It *is*," she insisted. "She wants to be your only girl!"

"Well, in her culture—and mine as well—multiple wives aren't really allowed. Although they used to be—"

"That's all I needed to know," I interrupted. "Trouble in paradise, curiosity satisfied. Let's move on."

I took a deep breath and put all this harem nonsense to one side. It was only distracting me from the real problem.

"There was something I wanted to talk with you both about, but under the circumstances, I'll start with just you."

Kaito frowned at my change in tone, and in particular the way I lowered my voice so I definitely wouldn't be heard down the table.

"In two days," I said carefully, "there will be both an attack on this city, and an attempt at invasion on the King's Isle. The King is threatened by both foreign and domestic enemies, and they have joined forces to bring him down."

Kaito stared at me in shock. The two girls next to us were just as surprised, but their faces showed more calculation than distress.

"And," I said, "one of the instigators of this alliance is sitting on the other end of this table, talking to Isidre."

LOVE AND MARRIAGE

I don't believe you," Isidre said.

I leaned back and took a sip from my drink. "I don't really care if you do or not," I said.

It hadn't been hard, with Kaito's help, to get a private word with Isidre. The only hard bit was getting her girls to allow Manuela to get close enough to be distracted by a conversation. As I'd suspected, their dislike of the envoy was half fear of her master and half that they could spot a would-be interloper from a mile away. Maybe spot was too strong a word—they assumed any female that came within a mile was a potential romantic rival and acted accordingly. In Manuela's case at least, they weren't wrong.

"It's not like I expect you to do anything about it, before the event, or after," I continued. "I've already passed the information up the chain. I just wanted to give you a heads up so you're not surprised when it happens."

And to avoid accusations of being kept in the dark, I added to myself.

She looked over at Manuela, attempting to make some sort of case to Kaito over the interruptions of Nori and Orino.

"She just doesn't seem . . . serious enough for that," she said.

"And Tom seems like a nice guy," I replied, "But they put all that aside when their master comes calling. I don't know if it's training, brainwashing, or magic, but their loyalty seems absolute. Did she make you an offer?"

"Several. Some that I'd already refused with Mr. Parkes, and others . . . of an indecent nature. Those, I would have already refused even if . . ."

"Do you want to talk about Kaito?" I asked.

She shivered. "He . . . or she? I don't . . ."

"Oh, she told you about that?" Now it was my turn to shiver. I couldn't imagine changing my body like that. Not sure what was worse for me, the change of race or the change of gender. "Yeah, I'm not sure what to use either. Kaito doesn't seem to mind either way, so I'm going with *she*."

"Fine." She stared at her beer for a long moment and then took a large swallow of it.

"Kaito explained about the harem," she said. "I don't *feel* manipulated, but..."

"You were never attracted to girls before?" I asked.

"No."

"Are you attracted to *me*, right now?"

She looked me over carefully. I was pretty sure she hadn't drunk enough yet to say something stupid. "You *are* beautiful," she said reluctantly. "More so than the women on the billboards or TV."

"Thanks," I said wryly. The way she said that didn't make it seem like a compliment. "You know my magic works on Charisma, right? It's not just for vanity."

"Not *just* vanity," she replied.

Ouch.

"But no, I am not... attracted to you," she continued. "Not in the way I..." she trailed off, blushing.

"So..." I said carefully. "There are people back home who don't consider themselves gay but have... exceptions that they make for certain people. It's not that strange?"

"It's perverse," she said darkly. "The Church teachings..." she sighed. "I am not sure if they can still apply here."

Sure am glad I don't have that problem. I thought to myself.

"Has Duit said anything?" I said aloud.

"Only that I must make a decision that I can live with," she said.

"A decision?" I asked. "So you think that you could choose... to *not* be in the harem?"

"The other girls seem to think so. They advised that I do that. They... don't like me," she admitted.

"I hadn't noticed," I said dryly. "And I'll point out that when I talked to them back in Talnier about Harem they said you *can't* fight the Status."

Hopefully, the girls were all too busy deflecting Manuela to hear me sell them out like that.

"I can't help how I feel," Isidre admitted. "But my duty might be more important. And . . . I'm not cut out to be in a . . . harem."

"Plenty of harems in the Bible," I said. "Maybe you could try meeting the girls halfway? They started out pretty hostile to me, but we get along fine now."

Mainly because I didn't have designs on their man, which was pretty explicitly their problem with Isidre, but you had to try . . .

"You're *you*, though," Isidre said bitterly. She finished her mug and banged it on the table for another. That was how you did it here—it was an adventurers' tavern.

"What do you mean?" I asked.

"Do you have any idea—I was so mad when I left Talnier. You went behind my back, *stole* Manchas, set yourself up to be in charge . . . I went north to prove myself . . . and then Kaito convinced me that you were *right* all along. Cooperation instead of conquest."

"That was all Kaito," I protested. "You can't blame me for—"

"I *know*," she said. "I was so *ashamed*, but . . . here we are, and I'm confessing the details of my shameful crush to you, like we were old friends! I feel *grateful* to you for hearing me out!"

"It's not a big deal," I said, "I'm happy to—"

"If you'd fallen in love with Kaito, you'd have the other girls eating out of your hand by now," she muttered. "Your Charisma is just unfair."

It seemed that Charisma had passive effects beyond attracting guys' attention. Isidre looked as though she was going to cry, and I didn't think the alcohol was that strong.

"Look," I said, "do you want some . . . help? Advice for dealing with the other girls?"

Now I did see a few tears. "Yes," she said, shaking her head. "No . . . I don't know. I don't know if I should stay. I don't know if I can leave."

High Charisma or not, I didn't know what to say to that. Casting about for wisdom, I found myself looking around the room as if searching for inspiration.

"What's going on there?" The words popped out of my mouth, for no good reason. What had attracted my attention was a nearby table, filled with adventuring types. Another adventurer had joined their table and had been speaking to them urgently, but quietly. Too quietly for me to make out what they had been saying.

As I watched, they all stood as one and left the room, one of them leaving a handful of silver on the table. Even at Dorsay's prices, it looked like a substantial tip. The one who'd been speaking didn't leave. Instead, he looked around the room and found another table to speak to. They too left, this time taking the speaker with them.

"I don't know?" Isidre answered. "They just left . . . perhaps there is some news?"

"I suppose," I said doubtfully. I turned my attention back to the knot of not-quite-arguing girls. "Listen, I can't make your decision for you, but if you decide to stay, you're going to have to find a way to get along with the others."

"I shouldn't have to—they're not . . . special, like Kaito is."

She wasn't making sense, but I knew what she was saying. I'd felt the temptation to think that way myself, and I wasn't even in contact with my patron. It must be easy for her to believe that her relationship with Kaito was so much more important than that of the others.

"I don't think that the Champion thing has any relevance here," I said. She frowned at me, but I kept going. "You all feel the same way about Kaito. If their feelings are artificially created, then so are yours. If yours are real, then so are theirs."

"But—"

"You wanna say that *they're* less real than you are? Than Kaito is? It might be true, I can't prove otherwise . . . but is that somewhere you want to go?"

I was sure that I wasn't the only one who had the sense—the fear—that this was all a game and we were the only players. From the look on her face, I could tell that she'd had similar notions, but . . .

"I can't let myself believe that," she confessed. "If I did, then . . ."

"Yeah," I agreed. I might be willing to die on the hill that said I was *better* than some, maybe even most people in this dumb country, but if I got to thinking that the other people didn't *matter*, then that would be a quick slide into . . . something bad.

"So you need to approach them as an equal," I told her. "And recognize that they outnumber you, and they *will* gang up on you. There's nothing about Harem that says the girls have to get along, only that you all love Kaito."

She nodded, but there was a pained look on her face. I didn't think she was quite there yet.

"If you don't find a way to get along, they *will* keep you from being with Kaito," I tried, and that seemed to get to her. "If you like, I'll have a word with them, get them to give you a chance . . . what the fuck?"

She looked at me, startled, but I was looking at the entrance and the person that had just come in. He saw me as well and started swaggering over.

"What are you doing here, Cutter?" I asked, glaring as he approached.

"There's no curfew, is there?" he said. "I was just out and about."

"Who is this?" Isidre asked. I'm sure she'd seen Cutter around, but they'd never been formally introduced.

"This is Cutter, an orphan that I find myself looking after," I told her. "Cutter, I know you know who she is."

"'Course I know the Paladin," he said with a grin. "Pleased to meetcha, your mightiness!"

Isidre shook his offered hand, clearly bemused. She must get all types coming up to her.

"Is this wise?" she asked me. "Taking care of someone so young, when you have responsibilities . . ."

"I don't have *those* responsibilities, remember?" I countered. "I may do a lot of things, but a god's bidding is not one of them. Keeping this urchin out of trouble is something I chose to do . . . though I'm having trouble remembering why."

I glared at him again. I could feel all the scoldings that my mother had given me welling up for the occasion.

"It's 'cos I'm occasionally useful," Cutter told Isidre. "I get around where others can't, and no one notices kids."

"I'm not sure that's a good reason," Isidre started, but I cut her off.

"Not the time," I told her. "Cutter, you know you're not supposed to be out, so the fact that you've come *here* means that you must have had a reason."

"I sure did, boss," he said cheerily. "See, I was at the Shattered Bat, making a little money . . ."

"The fighting pit?" Janie asked, coming over. "*I* still haven't gotten to go there yet."

"You were fighting for money?" Isidre gasped.

"Nah, I was placing bets," Cutter replied. Isidre didn't look less shocked.

"Get on with it," I interjected before she could call Child Protective Services.

"Right. Well, part of that is keeping an ear to the ground, about any rumors that are going on, see? Might affect the betting."

"Right." Cutter seemed to have found his true calling here. Were there any fighting rings in Talnier? I wasn't sure, but I thought that there might be. I made a note to ban them when I got back.

"So . . ." Cutter said, drawing it out longer the more people were paying attention to him. "I heard this rumor, and it was wild! I thought you'd want to know, boss, so I cut things short and went out to check it out!"

"Okay, so what—"

"And it *was* true! So I came over to find you, and let you know. It's really happening!"

"What's happening!" I shouted, exasperated.

"Oh, didn't I mention?" he said innocently. "They're killing one another on the streets."

INTERLUDE I

No one ever took Beast Tamers seriously. Decent folk, common or noble, rarely had a use for the services he provided. When they did, they always made it clear that the master had better stay with his beast. In the stables, or just outside. Adventurers, at least, didn't complain about the supposed smell—he washed, just like anyone else!

Adventurers, though, gave him something worse. Scorn. He wasn't exactly excluded, just mocked. Adventurers sought power through their own skills and natural abilities. Wizards were . . . accepted, to a degree. Their dependence on mana was balanced by the sheer amount of damage they could do, at least for a short while. They commanded respect.

Unlike the likes of him. He couldn't even enter a dungeon. If he wanted to make kills for experience, he needed to go out and hunt in the countryside. "Pest control," the adventurers called it. Just one more reason to look down on a man who couldn't even fight for himself, and had to split his experience and rewards with his monsters.

Rhys had heard that it was better in the Tribal lands, but he wanted to live in civilization. He loved linking with monsters, feeling the emotions, the sensations of beasts far more intense than what he could feel on his own. He just didn't want to give up on sleeping in a bed to do it.

The job he had now was a perfect solution for him. There had been some adjustments—he'd needed to acquire a few new beasts. But no longer did he have to glean through the leavings on the job board at the Adventurers Guild, looking for the few postings that didn't involve delving.

It did involve a few things that were less than legal, but he hadn't exactly kept his hands clean as an adventurer. In some ways, it had been a revelation. He'd always sought after the most powerful monsters that he could manage on his own. But that had been a dead end. A Stone Mage had explained it to him once, only becoming condescending when he couldn't follow the math. Like he had a use for Calculate anyway.

It seemed that a fighter or mage type of the same level as him was always going to be able to kill any beast that he was able to control. And since he had to split his experience with his beast, the fighter was always going to grow faster than he did. Which was why he was always at the bottom.

The trick was to find a beast that had skills or powers that adventurers *didn't* and find your own niche. Like griffins and flying. They had their own special spot in the Kingdom's hierarchy. He would have joined them himself, but they didn't take just anyone.

What his new employer had shown him was that there were other, less obvious niches. Rhys thought that the knowledge would serve him well, should he and his employer have to part ways. Not that Rhys thought that was likely. His employer paid well, and besides, Rhys had gotten the impression that his master wasn't in the business of setting up competitors. *Retirement* was a possibility down the line, perhaps, but Rhys was careful not to say anything that might suggest he was looking at greener pastures.

His job today was both absurdly simple, and at the same time, something only he could do. It did mean getting closer to the castle than he would like, but his range was long enough that he didn't have to come within the patrol radius of the Duke's guards. He could just curl up in an alcove off a street, doing a credible impersonation of a drunk sleeping off his day drinking.

He would have brought along some alcohol to complete the picture, but his master had very strong views about drinking on the job.

All Rhys had to do was stay there. All the work was being done by his bond. Thick as the stone walls were, people and goods went through the gates all day long. His little lizard had clung unseen to a barrel as it was brought into the kitchens, and then slowly made its way through the maze of passageways until it had reached its target.

The gates to the inner courtyard were kept buttoned up tight, but they let people through all the time. All his lizard had to do was drop down onto the backpack of one of the soldiers going in. Rhys chose what looked like a squad of recruits, none of them past level three. They didn't notice anything when his bond joined them on a trip into the dungeon.

Soon enough, they noticed something was wrong. As the screaming started, Rhys hoped he'd be able to sneak his bond out in the confusion.

He'd been promised a replacement if this one didn't make it, but he couldn't help feeling a little sentimental about what was supposed to be a replaceable tool. Even if it didn't make it out, though, this mission was already a success. His master would be pleased.

Captain Barber quickly realized what was going on. The squad of fresh recruits had only been gone for a few minutes before they came running out again. He snorted amusement for a second—the recruits got worse every day, it seemed—before he noticed the real problem. The monsters were chasing them. The yard-long cockroaches and crickets that were the staple monsters for the first floor were pouring out after the squad.

"Break!" he called out at the top of his lungs. That wasn't the official alarm, but it was enough for the soldiers manning the guard post to break off from staring at the sight and remembering their training.

One of them started ringing the alarm bell, and the other one started closing the inner gates. They should have been closed whenever a party wasn't walking through them, but discipline had gotten relaxed.

Not so relaxed that the gate wasn't closed quickly, slamming shut only seconds after his bellow. *Too* quickly to save the recruits, though. They were now trapped in the inner courtyard with the giant insects. Doctrine said that the gates couldn't be opened now, not even to save the poor fools' lives. Barber happened to agree with that doctrine, but he wasn't going to let it kill his men.

"Get a rope," he ordered his lieutenant, before drawing his sword and jumping off the wall. A thirty-foot drop would have broken the legs of some, but he was level six. Absorbing the impact with ease, he strode over to where his men were.

"Get up! Get moving! Over there!" He yelled, as his blade flickered out, bisecting the monsters that had managed to latch on with a biting attack. They couldn't pierce the chain, but each one that latched on slowed the victim and let other insects strike more vital blows.

He kept lashing out at the monsters with his sword, and the recruits with his voice—and the occasional kick. The stream of insects did not stop, but Barber knew eventually the dungeon would start spewing out monsters from deeper in. He chivvied his men over to the wall where he had jumped from. Wonder of wonders, someone had found a rope and lowered it down.

Arrow fire was starting up from the top of the wall, which gave some release from the tide of insects. Barber had one of the recruits take the rope, half climbing, half being pulled up the wall. In the meantime, he organized the rest in a half ring with their backs to the wall.

Now that he had a moment, he could count them. Six down here, one headed up.

"What happened to the other three?" he barked.

"Dead before we ran," the closest recruit replied. "They . . ." He interrupted himself to get his shield between him and a bug. Screaming, he managed to land a few blows, but most of the damage was absorbed by its chitin. Barber continued to slice through insects as if they were made of butter.

The rope was just coming down again when the first worm emerged. He cursed, and tapped one of his band to climb up.

"Focus on the worms!" he called, uncertain if he'd be heard over the din of battle. Archers would naturally want to focus on the cockroaches. Most of the ones remaining were attacking his group, but some had started climbing the walls. Despite making the archers nervous, *those* could be dealt with by sword and axe-wielding troops, of which there was a strong supply.

It took a lot of arrows to kill a worm, but they couldn't be left alone. They could *eat* stone, and given time could bring down the entire castle.

One by one, his men were pulled up. When the last of them was out of the way, he simply Jumped to the top, to find Magister Coles waiting for him. Mages were too valuable to be wasted standing watch, so there must have been time for someone to fetch him.

"Captain," he sneered. "I trust you enjoyed your heroics, but thanks to you, I've been unable to cast."

Barber raised an eyebrow in surprise. He would have bet that Coles would have jumped at the opportunity to get a little collateral damage in. Perhaps the last disciplinary hearing had gotten through to him. More likely, there were too many eyes about for the Fire Mage's liking.

"Good," he replied. "Now hold off a little longer." He cast a glance down into the courtyard, gauging how things were going.

"Are you serious?" Coles exclaimed. "Monsters are already climbing the walls, and you want me to wait?"

"We can deal with a few monsters," Barber explained. "We want to maximize your strike, so we wait until the arena is full."

Coles looked dubiously at the courtyard below. It *was* only half full of monsters. "Is that really necessary?" he asked.

"It's going to be a long fight," Barber replied. "We don't want you shooting your load prematurely."

Coles's eyes narrowed in irritation. "I—" he started, but he was interrupted by a sudden vibration. Both men glanced wildly around as they felt the stone move under their feet, shaking slightly from a blow of indescribable power, deep underground.

"Make sure you save some for whatever did *that*."

Duke Finley felt the blow as he finished up with his correspondence. He had heard the alarm, of course, but he had people to attend to such things. He had already been expecting an urgent briefing as to what was going on, but the vibration gave him pause. Rather than wait further, he decided to seek out his secretary.

"My lord," the man said, bowing. "There has been a dungeon break."

Finley knew what the alarm was for, but the man had spoken before he had been acknowledged.

"Nonsense," he snarled. "There hadn't been a dungeon break in a hundred years. This castle *exists* to prevent the conditions that cause them. And you tell me that it has failed? How is that possible?"

"I don't know, my lord," the man said, starting to sweat. "Investigations are starting, but the immediate circumstances . . ."

"Unless a culprit is found, I will have to hold *you* responsible," Finley said idly. It was always good to keep your people motivated. He tried to think of who would be responsible for this. It was a favorite tactic of the Tribes, but they were a long way from the border. On the other hand, there was a delegation in town, was there not? Something to note for the near future.

There were, however, more immediate concerns. "Who was in there?"

The secretary consulted his notes. "Fifth company was on rotation," he said. "The leadership should be on level seven, and there should be two more teams on three and five. Seven men escaped from level one, leaving three casualties. But . . ." the man gulped nervously.

"What?"

"Your third son was leading a group on level nine," the secretary confessed.

At that moment they felt another vibration from deep below. They both paused, looking down at the source, as if they could see through all the rock that lay between them and the giant below.

"Summon the elites from the town," he told his secretary.

"My lord? But the plan?"

"The plan can wait. There's still time to make the attack, but we need to settle this first. The defenses will hold, but I can't afford to lose a company—or my son—over this. We're going to have to rescue them."

He thought quickly. "No word of this has gotten out?" he asked.

"For now . . . though if that *sound* gets any louder, we'll have to make some excuses."

The Duke nodded. "It will be dark soon . . . bring them here in small groups—two or three at the most. They should go unnoticed on the streets."

"My lord, you're not seriously planning on mounting a raid on a *breaking dungeon*, days before you launch an assault on the crown?"

"Circumstances have forced my hand." Finley frowned in thought. Was this part of the Chancellor's plan? He didn't see how. Shaking his head, he rejected the idea.

"Snap to it," he barked. "We start the raid in five hours."

WHOM

"Who is killing . . . whom?" I asked.

"Dunno," Cutter answered. "Adventurers? It's not like they're wearing uniforms. Pretty high-level fights, though."

I looked around the room at the others. It was a fairly disparate group, but we had all been unified by the idea of doing . . . something. But what? What was going on?

Everybody carefully avoided looking at Manuela, but I got a few accusing glances from Isidre. I didn't think this was the attack from Finley, though. It was too early and sounded wrong besides. I couldn't say anything about that right in front of Manuela, though, so . . .

"I—we, that is, my team, should return to the palace," Kaito said. "As foreigners, it wouldn't do for us to get caught up in fighting—whatever the cause."

"I should return to my sect," Isidre said. "I shouldn't have slipped away from them—"

"You should have some followers back at the palace, should you not? If you accompany us there, you should have an escort back." Kaito smiled warmly as she spoke. "Safety in numbers, yes?"

Nori grabbed hold of Kaito's arm possessively, but none of the girls actually objected. From the looks on their faces, people getting killed was more important than harem rivalries.

"I—actually have somewhere else I need to be," I admitted. "And I *really* want to know what's going on."

Janie grinned. "As your bodyguard, I have to say . . . that sounds like fun."

"You're a terrible bodyguard," I told her. She sniffed.

"That's what you get for hiring without references."

It took a *bit* more discussion before I could leave with Cutter and Janie. They didn't like splitting the group, and they didn't want me taking Cutter back out on the street. I did appreciate their objections, but I needed Cutter to show me where the fights were. I didn't like child endangerment either, but the ship had long sailed on that particular battle.

I watched their party leave. I would have thought that Kaito, at least, would have merited a royal escort. If he did, though, they were being a lot more subtle than the guards I had had following me in my first few days.

"Right, Cutter, show me where these fights were happening," I said.

"You got it, boss!" he replied and started leading the way.

The first fight we found was over by the time we got there. A single corpse with a large hole in his back. Identifying corpses didn't tell you their level when they had been alive, so I carefully avoided activating it. I didn't want to know the dead guy's name.

His armor looked expensive, but Identify let me down.

[Identification]: Partial Plate Armor (broken)

Broken armor didn't even have a quality.

"Looks like a bow, or a crossbow," Janie said thoughtfully. I wanted to object, but a high-level strike *would* peel back metal like this. If the guy had been low level, it would have gone through his front as well.

His attacker had recovered the arrow, and it looked as though they'd stolen the corpse's weapon as well. Not his boots, which suggested that the various lowlifes of the city hadn't yet dared to claim their share.

"He could be an adventurer, but I haven't seen him down at the Guild," Janie said. I hadn't either.

"Nothing that looks like a uniform, but he *could* be a mercenary," I mused aloud.

"More of them this way," Cutter said, pointing. We started following him, but we were soon following the signs of fighting.

"Who are these guys?" I asked the empty air. Not loudly, because I didn't want to attract attention. Fights between high-levelled humans weren't the sort of thing I wanted to get involved in.

It reminded me of martial arts movies. The combatants moved quickly, and not always along the ground. As I watched, a man with a sword leapt twenty meters to attack a woman armed with two axes, only to be intercepted by an archer's attack. The bowman fired *three* arrows simultaneously, and while the swordsman's blade flicked out at incredible speeds to divert two of them, the third hit home, knocking the target across the street.

The man took a tumble but was on his feet fast enough to block the attack of the axe-girl. His armor looked damaged, but he seemed otherwise fine.

"That one—that girl there," Janie said. "I've seen her in the Guild."

"Uh-huh," I grunted. If she was in the Guild, then the bowman must be, too. He was now shooting a man who had a sword and shield. So *those* two were on the other side . . . but they looked just as nondescript as the others. The remaining two were fighting each other, so it was a safe bet that this fight was two-on-three. Which side was winning, I couldn't guess.

"If Guild members are fighting, we can probably get some answers at the Guild," I speculated.

"Or we could get caught up in it," Janie pointed out. "If this is an official Guild action . . ."

"I'm pretty sure this can't be official," I said uncertainly. "No way does Voight have the authority to attack people in the street."

I wasn't terribly confident of that, however.

"Let's stay out of it," I said slowly. "They seem to be keeping it to themselves, at least, so it's probably better to leave them to it. We can go back to the dungeon and protect the assets we have.

"Or . . ." Cutter said slyly, "We could go to the Shattered Bat and make a bit of cash. Doubt they'll be stopping the fights for just this—might even place a book on them."

"No more gambling for you, young man," I said. Underneath my stern tone was the resigned knowledge that I wasn't going to be able to stop him forever. At least I could keep an eye on him for tonight.

The fighting hadn't come near the neighborhood where I'd hidden my dungeon, but rumors had evidently spread. The brothels were still lit up, but the street was empty of patrons. Instead of touting for business, the madams and a bunch of their girls were standing near the entrances, keeping watch.

I normally passed by entirely unnoticed, but not this time.

"Here! Where d'you think you're walking!" someone in the crowd called out. I paused and looked them over, but I couldn't tell who had spoken. A lot of them were looking at me.

"It's a public street," I said carefully. Expecting an interjection from Cutter, I glanced behind me to see that Janie had grabbed him by the collar.

"That's Issey's backer," another anonymous woman said. "Came in, got money to burn."

That provoked some muttering in the crowd. "We never had troubles before you showed up," a woman called out. This time I got a glance at her. Older, with hair dyed bright red.

"Whatever's going on, it's got nothing to do with me," I told them. "I just thought it was a good time to check on my investment."

"What you doing in there, anyway?" Another woman this time. Younger, dark-haired, and bolder. She took a step forward, and a few people copied her.

Light and heat flared at my back. "Step back," Janie said easily. I glanced back and saw that she'd conjured a flaming sword. It was as large as a greatsword, but she held it easily in one hand. Which made sense if it was made of fire.

I looked back at the crowd. "Look, I don't know what you've heard, but from what I saw, it was a bunch of high-levels fighting among themselves," I said. "The guard or the soldiers haven't gotten involved. You should be safe if you stay indoors."

They weren't happy about that, but no one actually objected, so I kept going down the street to Isabel's building. Darkness returned as Janie dispelled her sword.

"We could have taken them!" Cutter exclaimed, softly at least.

"Don't be dumb, kid," Janie snorted. "Who wants to kill a bunch of doxies just looking out for their own?"

There was a muffled slap, and I knew Cutter had opened his mouth.

"*Not* you, asshole," Janie told him. "Stick to monsters and bad guys."

"What's the point of being dangerous if you don't get respect?" Cutter whined. "They gotta know you can off them!"

"You think your boss needs to kill people to get respect?" Janie replied. "Learn from her, not whatever cutthroat was beating you up back in Anchorbury."

"Stop, I'm going to blush," I said flatly. I looked back at Cutter. He looked embarrassed and wouldn't meet my eyes. "That's what I thought," I said. Further conversation could wait, though, as we had reached our destination.

Isabel looked nervous when she let me in, and I soon saw why. The children had been multiplying.

"What's been going on?" I asked, keeping my expression neutral.

"It's not been safe on the streets," Isabel explained. "The kids who were too frightened to come in before don't want to be out there. I know you wanted us to be active during daylight hours, but . . ."

"Am I the last person to hear about the fighting?" I asked the air.

"Pretty much," Cutter answered. "I mean, the Bat isn't close to where it started, and then I had to check it out . . . and *then* I had to go get you, and then *we* had to check it out. These guys would have run at the rumor."

"It's been going on that long? I wouldn't have thought the fights would have lasted that long."

Cutter shrugged. "It's different fights, and not all of them finish. Sometimes someone gets away and there's a chase. But there's new people coming in, about as fast as they die."

"Right," I muttered. "Whatever." I looked over at my *actual* immediate problem, currently jam-packed into the library. From the sounds of it, there were more of them in the rooms farther back. I was pleased to see that even after only a few days, there was a noticeable difference between the kids that had been here before and the newcomers. They stood straighter and weren't as spindly, but the real difference was in how they looked at me.

At me, not at the floor, or shiftily glancing at me from the corner of their eye. Not with fear, but with . . . *expectation.*

"Right," I repeated. "It's night, so no lessons. Instead, it's a bath and a bed. Rhis."

I didn't raise my voice, because I didn't have to. I didn't really even need to say his name; that was more for the benefit of people watching. As I wanted him to appear, he did, manifesting a Phantasmal illusion.

"Yes, Mistress?"

"Can we put another level on the bottom and shove the others up? I think they'll want to sleep with at least one floor between them and the lizards."

"Yes . . . but it would be best if they were evacuated during the adjustment."

"There are still rooms in the building that aren't part of the dungeon," Isabel suggested.

"Excellent idea," I told her. "How many kids are there?"

"Forty-six," Rhis said with some relish. "It's been quite good for my regeneration."

"All right, let's get this organized," I said. With Isabel and Janie's help, we managed to split them into groups and keep them together while they all filed out of the dungeon. Then we could get to work.

At first, there was a feeling of discontinuity. Not at all like being in an elevator, but when it finished, the exit had disappeared and Rhis was carving a hole in the floor for the stairs down.

"You wanted a lot of beds, unless I mistook your intent?" Rhis asked.

"Yeah, 23 bunk beds, so . . . two rows of twelve? Or four of six," I mused, measuring out the space. "What's the breakdown between girls and boys?"

"Ah, I'm afraid I can't tell the difference, Mistress." Rhis confessed.

"Well, it's just for one night," I rationalized. "If we split it into two rooms, here, there should be room for rows of *eight*, which we might need at some point."

"And the remaining space?"

"That's for the bath. It's going to need to be waterproof, but I can handle the plumbing with Water Magic. Can you do marble?"

We discussed a few more adjustments, but it didn't take long for the floor to be completed. While the walls and the bathroom were dungeon-made, the dormitory furniture was Phantasmal. Once again, my dungeon connection let me cast multitudes of copies almost instantly. There were limits to what I could do with Phantasmal Object, but beds, memory foam mattresses, sheets, and pillows were well within them.

The kids gasped as they were let back in.

"Right," I told them. I bled just a little bit of Intimidate into it to make sure I had their attention. "You're going to take this little plate of wood, and this paint, and draw something on it. Try to make something unique, because this symbol will represent you. If you can write, you can write your name. Then take the plate and find a bed. The plate will slot into the locker next to your bed."

Unfortunately, I couldn't make working locks with Phantasmal Object. I just wasn't clear on the mechanism. We'd come up with a solution if we needed to in the future—the only thing we had at the moment was for Rhis to create 46 magical locks, which seemed overkill.

"Put your clothes and any possessions you don't want getting wet in the locker, then head back to the baths."

"What's a bath, Headmistress?" one of my kids asked.

"It's a thing that gets you clean," I told them. "Now get moving. Rowdiness and foolishness *will not be tolerated*."

I increased the Intimidation for that last bit. There was no way we could keep track of 46 kids, but a little Intimidation went a long way.

"Janie, can you get back there and heat the water?" I asked her. "There are towels and sleeping robes back there as well."

"Are you going to feed them as well?" she asked.

"We'll work that out in the morning," I said. "Right now, we get them clean and in bed."

But in the morning, I had to leave organizing things to the others. Felicia and Kyle had come to find me and let me know that I had been summoned by the King.

DURESS

There was a lot of ceremony in meeting a king, normally. Modern life erases a lot of the frictions that used to exist in polite society. I'm sure there was a *reason* for all the apparently meaningless ceremony. Being escorted by one set of guards to another set of guards. Waiting in a room, only to be moved to another room, greeted by a minor functionary, who introduced you to a higher functionary . . . and that was just for private meetings. Our first meeting had been at Court and had involved no end of standing around and making meaningless chitchat.

When the King wanted, though, he could cut through all that. For this meeting, I was whisked through all his levels of security. No mean feat, considering that the palace was clearly on high alert. Everywhere that typically had guards had twice as many, and there were guards in places there hadn't been before. There was an air of alertness about the place, a tension in the air that hadn't been there yesterday.

I was deposited in a room I hadn't been in before. Left there without any instructions, I looked at the others already there. Isidre and Kaito. *Just* them, which wasn't a surprise. My own companions had been denied entry, but I thought it must have taken some effort to separate Kaito from her girls. Well, all but one of her girls.

The room itself, like everything in the palace, was richly appointed. There was a desk at one end, but the main part of the room was taken up with two large couches and an even larger and more ornate chair. Kaito and Isidre had been sitting on one, but they had stood up when I entered.

"How are we all doing?" I asked in English, just in case we were being listened in on. I got to see Isidre make the connection. Her face went from puzzled to surprised, then wary, all in the space of two seconds. Kaito was more controlled. She'd been practicing the expressionless face that Japanese investors all wore as part of the uniform. *Her* face went from friendly to flat, as soon as I spoke.

"It's not inconceivable," she said in Japanese, "that the King has people who have learned our languages. They are available in the System after all."

"So . . . we should all speak a different language?" Isidre said, hesitantly, in Spanish.

"I doubt it matters," I said easily. "I'm guessing that you two have no idea as to what's going on or why we've been called for. I just wanted you to be on your guard."

Isidre frowned and said nothing. Kaito inclined her head in acknowledgment. Both of them sat down again, and I moved to follow them. I glanced at the big chair but decided that now was not the time to make some sort of power statement.

[Identification]: Emperor Davos's Chair – Quality: Perfect – Properties: Enchantment (Endurance Boost)

Emperor? I thought. *That must be loot from the founding of the Kingdom.* I didn't know the name Davos, so he couldn't have been the last Emperor. I wondered how old that made his chair.

I sat on the other couch instead, noticing the postures of my fellow Chosen. I was wearing a dress suitable for Court—actually a Disguise of one—so there was only one way I could sit if I didn't want it looking funny. I sat well forward on the couch, my legs together, and my body upright.

Despite wearing much more comfortable leggings and furs, Kaito sat the same way. She'd kept her face expressionless as well. Out of all of us, Isidre was the most relaxed. She wasn't wearing her armor, just what went under it. It looked like a better cut version of my adventurer gear. She was able to sit back and let the couch support her, something I was more than a little jealous of.

Before I could pass the time by Identifying the rest of the furniture, the door opened and the King walked in. He entered without fanfare or an announcement, and we still jumped to our feet. He had that sort of presence, even when he was reining it in.

"Sit," he said, taking his own seat. He ran his gaze over each of us. He had come in alone, so it was just the four of us there. "I'm sure you're aware that we are in the middle of a grave situation."

I looked over at the others, but there were no answers there. "Your Majesty," I said hesitantly, "We don't know *what's* going on. Can you fill us in?"

The King gave a little snort. "Last night," he said, "Duke Finley's dungeon, the *Maze of the Forsaken Giant*, broke."

I kept my face expressionless and carefully did not look in Kaito's direction. The King was already looking that way, though, and his silence seemed to demand a response.

"I was unaware of that," Kaito said carefully, "And I am certain that my companions would not take action without my knowledge."

"Isn't stopping that from happening Duke Finley's job?" I asked. "Isn't that what the castle is *for*?"

The King looked at me. "Yes," he said, simply. "That, and containing a break when it occurs. Until today, his family has performed that task admirably—there has not been a break since the Founding. And thus far, the defenses have held."

"That's not all that's going on, though," I said carefully. A dungeon break didn't explain the fighting in the street.

"Indeed. As you may have heard, it turns out that Duke Finley had troops concealed within the city."

I didn't say anything, just raised my eyebrows. Isidre saved me from having to speak.

"For what purpose? Your Majesty." Either she didn't have the Charm skill, or she wasn't listening to it.

"That . . . has yet to be determined," the King said, with a heavy tone. "I have called on the Duke to answer that question, but he has proved . . . unavailable."

"He can't be spared from the front lines?" I asked. *Even with the walls, it must be a hard fight*, I thought. Twenty floors, four times as deep as the dungeons near Talnier, and with richer mana supplies. Which brought up a thought—

"No, he has entered the dungeon," the King said flatly.

The three of us looked at one another. "Is that . . . a common method of dealing with a dungeon break?" I asked.

"Not at all. But there are a few reasons behind what he's doing." The King sighed. "For one, his son was inside when it broke. For another . . ."

He sighed. "It's been more than a century since this dungeon has broken. In that time it's put on five more levels, levels filled with the kind of monsters that match its name."

"Giants," I said, still not understanding.

"The biggest monsters we've ever seen, not counting some of the sea monsters," he agreed. "When a dungeon breaks, all of its monsters come out . . . but those are too big to fit through the upper tunnels."

"So what happens?"

"There have been cases where passages have been opened up, but even if this dungeon is capable of that, delvers will prevent it from modifying that floor," he explained. "There's some evidence that instead, the monsters are smashing their way up the levels. Duke Finley may have decided to try and kill them where they were."

"I guess that makes sense, but it still doesn't explain why the fighting in the streets started," I said.

"Ah, that." The King scowled. "It seems that our Guild Master was aware of Finley's secret build-up, and had mobilized his high-level adventurers to watch them."

Oh. I shrank back in my seat a little.

"When Duke Finley sent for reinforcements, the Guild Master took it as a prelude to an attack and acted accordingly."

"And when his forces were attacked, Finley responded with more violence," I said. "Just how bad did it get?"

Kaito had a question of her own, though. "Thank you for that explanation, your Majesty, but it does not explain why we were summoned here."

"That's simple," said the King. "This is all your fault."

"That's ridiculous! We just got here, and have had nothing to do with any of this!" Isidre beat me to the denial. I might have been a *little* slow, owing to my peripheral involvement in this.

"You don't get it," the King told her. "Ridiculous happenstances like this—and don't get me started on Shadthe's involvement—are invariably due to the gods meddling. I even have an idea of which one," he added, glowering at me.

"You can't blame me for his actions!" I protested.

"Blame is for the populace. I have to deal with the problem," he said. "This is happening here, because you"—he glared at all of us—"are here. And you will be the ones to fix it."

"How?" I asked.

He waved a hand irritably. "I'm sure your patrons have already come up with a plan. I just need to put you at the center of the problem and let whatever vicious happenstance they have in mind take place."

"The center of the problem?" I asked.

"I'm sending you three to enter the dungeon and either help Finley end the break or bring him back to face justice, whatever you think appropriate."

"Are you—" I started, before Charm reminded me who I was speaking to. Modulating my voice to be more respectful, but no less urgent, I started again. "With respect, sire, we're just level fives. There are numerous sixes around, and I'd estimated Duke Finley at level seven."

"Ah, but you are the Chosen of the Gods," the King said, and he wasn't even sarcastic. More . . . sour. "Never forget that they have a plan for you, and it doesn't include your death. Truly, you are blessed."

Okay, that last sentence was sarcastic.

"What makes you think we'd agree to this?" Isidre said. I wanted to say the same, but some part of me was doing the social math, and it didn't like the answer. Was this my Charisma at work? It should be working harder to keep me out of trouble.

"If the Forsaken Giant escapes the dungeon, it *will* die quickly, as it becomes a target for ballistae and long-range spells. Not to mention mana poisoning. But."

The King paused and looked at us all once more. "In the minute before it dies, it will kill an untold number of civilians. Even its fall will crush houses, killing many more. How many of you are willing to let that happen?"

Isidre looked sick. "You don't know that we'll actually stop that happening. I don't see how we *can*."

"The people have faith in you," he told her. They'll be reassured when I tell them that the *two* Champions that they know are in the city will be risking their lives to save the city."

I winced. *There it is.* Assuming that duty or an unwillingness to let people die didn't motivate me, he still had good old-fashioned blackmail. If he was willing to blow my cover, he might well decide to stop covering for my actual crimes.

"The alternative," he said, "for the people to know that the Champions—one of them from a nation that uses dungeon breaks as a weapon—are not standing by them . . ."

"I understand your point," Kaito said. She didn't change her expression, but she somehow managed to share a sympathetic glance with me.

"You'd blame Kaito for this?" Isidre said, not yet on the same page as us.

"It's not blackmail when the King does it," I told her, a sour taste in my mouth. "It's applying political pressure or something. At least he didn't Intimidate us into it."

"Skills like that tend to backfire against your kind," the King told me. "No, you are doing this freely, because you see that the consequences of inaction are unacceptable."

"Yes, I've never felt so free," I said. "Do you really think this is going to work? Aren't you just sacrificing the three of us for no gain?"

"You don't have our history with the gods," he told me. "In times like this, one has to have faith."

DELVE

Entering Massed Combat: Outbreak Defense

Accumulated Experience: 85,320

Experience awarded based on contribution at end of combat.

Contribution: 0.000%

"It's quieted down some." The gruff guard captain in charge of getting us into the dungeon was displaying a weird combination of being over-awed at our status and dismissive of our level. "His lordship's party went right after the first wave died down. After that, they stopped for a bit, but now it's coming out at a trickle. Natural spawn rate, I guess."

He didn't seem happy about outfitting us with the Duke's precious gear, but "King's orders" weren't to be dismissed. We had our own arms and armor, of course, but we were being supplied with supplies, rope, pitons, and potions. All good stuff—or I should say Great quality stuff—that filled in for all the things that we would have brought if we were planning on delving a dungeon today.

Not all of us were going. All three of us Champions were, but Kaito was the only one bringing her entire entourage. This wasn't a fight we were going to win with numbers—our entire plan was to hope that one of our gods had something figured out. Risking anyone else seemed both foolish and callous, so we were going down with the absolute minimum of support.

That minimum turned out to be the entirety of Kaito's harem because they refused to let her out of their sight. Given that, it made sense to regard this as Kaito's show, with Isidre and I along for support.

I assumed Isidre had her own reasons for leaving her support behind. I know I did.

"If I don't make it back from this crazy plan," I'd told my guys, "someone needs to be around to keep those kids safe."

"And how are we supposed to do that?" Janie asked incredulously. "If that giant gets out, he'll munch on your dungeon for a snack!"

"It's still hidden," I pointed out. "It'll go for one of the others. And I don't know what you can do in the worst-case scenario. Maybe evacuate them? It's hard to say."

I sighed. Despite the King's statement, I didn't think there was a limit on how bad this could get.

"Let's focus on the less bad options, where the dungeon is contained but I don't come out. In which case you'll need to sort out . . . everything. The kids, Rhis, the bank back in Talnier."

"Shit, that sounds like a lot of work," Janie snorted. Kyle and Felicia were looking worried. "So you had better come back so I don't have to do it."

We walked up to the sally port. Since the courtyard was clear, we should be able to walk right in. I was temporarily disguised as one of Isidre's followers. Officially, it was only two Chosen saving the day. I was in the center of the group, with Kaito and Isidre on either side. The girls had made growly noises when Isidre wanted to walk next to her.

"Do you think this will actually work?" I asked as we walked up. "Or is it all an elaborate plot to get rid of the King's problems?"

"It's not the first time I've heard of this . . . phenomenon. Stories of Champions up against impossible odds triumphing . . . through skill, but also with the aid of incredible coincidence." He sighed. "I'd rather not be putting it to the test, though."

"It's like one of your isekai stories, isn't it?" I said glumly. "Does this mean that we're destined to triumph?"

"My experience has stayed fairly close to the genre so far," he admitted. "But . . . if anything was actually destined, I don't think there would be a need for us to be here."

"Duit wouldn't set me a challenge I couldn't overcome," Isidre interjected. "At least . . . I think she wouldn't."

We walked into the courtyard, picking our way through the monster corpses. Everything smelled of blood and ichor. It reminded me of Talnier after its break.

"Insects, spiders, crabs, and reptiles," I pointed out, identifying the corpses.

"Yes?" Kaito said, not understanding.

"No slugs or slimes," I explained. We'd been given a briefing on what to expect on each level. "And the reptiles don't look like the really big ones. *They* might not have been able to make it up here, but the slugs shouldn't have been stopped."

"They can squeeze through small gaps," Kaito said. The big reptiles—"

"We should probably just say dinosaurs, even if they don't have the name for them," I said.

"The dinosaurs, then, are on the seventh floor, while the slugs are the level below . . ."

"There must be something keeping the slugs back, and it's probably the squad that was already there."

"Let us hope, then, that they remain alive long enough for us to reinforce them."

The first floor of the Maze of the Forsaken Giant was a literal maze. A warren of tunnels made for insects and other burrowing things. Not the best choice for disgorging a horde of monsters, but I wasn't sure if dungeons planned for future breaks.

The tunnels were plenty large for us; a lot of the insects were significantly bigger than human size. The giant lizards and snakes that had come through were mostly based on a long, thin body plan that had also had no problems coming through. I didn't see a Tyrannosaurus rex fitting in these tunnels, though.

The only obstacle remaining here was the darkness, which I dealt with via a Light spell, making my first contribution to the team. We did have light stones and a few glowing weapons—a marked improvement on lanterns, but a Light spell or two was more convenient.

Slaying the occasional fresh spawn was easy enough as we followed the map we had been provided and made our way to the second floor. This was more of the same, with different insects. It was also almost empty, and we made our way through without trouble.

I made a note as we progressed, as a future dungeon builder, to either not bother with mazes, or to change them more than occasionally. The Guild worked hard to map new floors, and I could see why. The difference between wandering around looking for the exit, and walking straight to it, was considerable.

That said, mazes had some uses. They kept the delvers there for longer, increasing mana regeneration. We and the other delvers were having that effect right now. Providing more mana for the dungeon to make monsters with. However, that mana didn't compare to what the Kingdom was outright feeding it.

I'd asked why they hadn't cut off the dungeon's mana supply, forcing it to subsist on what it could naturally gather.

"A good thought, but that has its own dangers," the King had said. "An outbreak ends when the dungeon runs out of mana and can no longer summon creatures, but to cut it off from its supply runs the risk of overspend."

They didn't actually know how it worked, but I could deduce the problem from their garbled explanations. Dungeons had an upkeep cost, and the more monsters they summoned, the higher that cost. Once that cost equaled mana regeneration, they stopped summoning new monsters. If mana regeneration was suddenly reduced, your upkeep costs could take you *below* zero mana.

"All we really know is that if a dungeon overspends, it can become damaged and fail," the King had said. "The structural reinforcement for the large caverns can be removed, and entire levels can collapse."

About a quarter of the city was built over that dungeon. A collapse could be even more devastating than the Giant escaping.

"One of the many reasons we make taking Dungeon cores illegal," the King had added.

All of that said, we found our way easily through the two levels of the insect warren and found ourselves on Barnacle Beach.

"That's . . . quite a sight," Kaito said. Her companions murmured agreement—I didn't think that they'd seen many dungeons. For myself, I did think it was quite a spectacular view, if not up to the standard set by Rhis's final level, or the mind-bending rift of the Adamant Guardians Mine.

We were looking at an extensive open cavern. It was lit—the monsters here liked the light—so we could see the full extent of it. It was at least a mile across, and doughnut shaped, with a huge curved pillar in the center.

Between us and the pillar was another maze, this one constructed out of jagged pillars of rocks and canyons with equally steep sides. You had the option of following the maze or avoiding it by making your way along the top. However . . .

"The barnacles are still here," Isidre noted.

"Not like they can go anywhere," Orino replied.

Indeed, the barnacles were still stuck where our briefing had placed them. They were the greater danger of this level. The crabs were generally around threat twelve, but the barnacles . . .

[Identification]: Giant Barnacle – Threat 15 – Properties: Armored, Immobile, Sticky

I wasn't sure how barnacles worked, normally. Something about filtering water? These ones were too high to be submerged, so they fed by grasping people with sticky tentacles. At threat fifteen, we could probably take them, but it would be easier to just avoid them, especially since . . .

"I expected the crabs to be gone, but shouldn't there be some water?" Fassi asked. "They said the amount varied, but there's none at all."

Barnacle Beach was supposed to be populated by crabs below and barnacles above. Waves swept through the maze in some sort of approximation of the tides. Sometimes just an annoyance, sometimes swift and deep enough to sweep an adventurer off their feet. Not today, though.

"Makes things easier for us," Nori put in. "Though I was looking forward to getting my feet wet."

"Not me," Fassi said, flicking her long ears at the thought. The other girls agreed, so it must have been an otter-kin thing.

We didn't have a map for this one; our guides had recommended going over the top. This wasn't a hard maze, though; we just had to keep making for the central pillar and look for one of the pits that led to . . .

"No water in here, either," Nori said. As the ranger, she'd been taking point and had found our first exit. This was supposed to lead to the water level, but . . .

"I guess . . ." I said, thinking it through, "that since the fish couldn't escape, they were deemed surplus to requirements and . . . flushed?"

"Yay, no more water level!" Fassi exclaimed. We had been given water-breathing potions for this level, but it looked like they wouldn't be needed.

"Wasn't there supposed to be a group on the next level down?" Ettalle said thoughtfully. Everyone got a little quiet. We hadn't seen any sign of the life that should be on this level, but we hadn't seen any bodies either.

We kept going, a little more subdued. What had been the underwater level was now another massive cavern, this one supported by numerous pillars. At the center was a massive pit, from which light shone through from below.

"I wonder if that wasn't the cause of the vibrations they were hearing above," I wondered. The center of the floor was supposed to be the exit, but it was raised high enough to stop the water from flowing out. Smashing that barrier would have made a hell of a noise.

We headed over. There were a few dead fish on the ground, but it was clear that the majority of the local monsters had been swept down to the next level. When we got to the hole, we could see the devastation that had been wrought.

Snake Valley had been a kind of labyrinth. With just one winding path to follow, it had been described to us as a sunny, green valley curving around many times until it got to the exit. Quite pleasant, if it weren't for the snakes.

It had been turned into a temporary river—a river that was in flood. Debris from the floor above had swept through, scouring the lower part of the valley, leaving boulders and dead fish behind. Some of the water remained, possibly even some of the fish.

At the edge of the devastation, the high tide mark if you will, we saw our first human corpses.

CORPSES

The corpses had been laid out neatly, out of the way of anyone—or any*thing*—coming down from the floor above.

"It must be the Duke's work," I said. "Perhaps he's hoping to collect them on the way out?"

"I'm surprised that the dungeon hasn't absorbed them already . . ." Isidre mused.

"It could be that there's still someone alive on this level," I said, considering. "Or it could be that it won't do normal maintenance until it's finished rampaging."

We started making our way along the valley, sticking to the high ground to avoid the worst of the debris.

"When does it finish, exactly?" Kaito asked. "When it runs out of monsters, or of mana?"

"I don't know," I replied. No one else in the group seemed to have an idea, but if anyone did, I *should*. I resolved to ask Rhis about it, but I suspect the answer would be something about everything changing during the break, including the rules.

"I'm not as knowledgeable about dungeons as I should be," I continued, "but I think cases like this, where the monsters can't get out, are pretty rare and not much studied. And it probably depends if the dungeon is intelligent or not."

"Wait—dungeons can be intelligent?" Kaito asked. "From what you said, Ettalle . . ."

Ettalle coughed. "Well, we don't know that much about dungeons. We got most of our levels from forest monsters."

"On its own, a dungeon isn't much good for thinking," I explained. "But if a human or a natural animal touches the core, it gets . . . sucked in."

"I was warned of that, in case I ever entered a dungeon alone," Kaito confirmed.

"I don't really know what happens at those times, but you don't *die*," I continued. "Your mind gets copied into the core, and you get to control the dungeon, until someone else touches the core."

"What happens then? And you said this could happen to animals as well?" Isidre asked. She and Kaito were both paying close attention, but I think I'd lost my other listeners.

"If an animal gets sucked in, then they get upgraded, to an extent? It's hard to tell, but the dungeon gets more creative in its choices. If it's a human, then they become a ghost in the machine sort of thing."

"The second time someone touches . . ." I looked over the group. "These are all Guild secrets by the way, so I'd appreciate if you didn't let on that I told you."

"We're not subject to the Guild's rules," Kaito said, frowning.

"Sure, but if you cast your mind back to . . . oh . . . last night, you might remember that the Guild sometimes acts outside of the legal guidelines."

I let Charm summon up a Serious Face and used it on them. "I found all this stuff out by myself, so I don't owe them anything. But I don't want to have to worry about assassins if I step too far out of line."

"That's a fair concern," Kaito admitted. "We'll keep your secrets."

The rest of his girls nodded along, even though they didn't seem to care much about the subject of discussion. Nori even muttered, "Who cares about dungeon touching," but she nodded along with the others.

Isidre *also* nodded along, blushing when she realized what she was doing. "I too will keep this quiet," she said hastily.

"Great. So . . . this hasn't been thoroughly tested, for obvious reasons, but what seems to happen is one of three things. Either you replace the existing entity, you get taken over by the dungeon, or you become the master of the dungeon and get to order it about. That seems to be the secret behind at least some of the big-name mages."

"That's quite a . . . broad range of possibilities," Kaito said carefully. "With widely ranging desirabilities."

"What happens to the entity in there, if it gets replaced?"

"Not sure," I replied. "Either it gets its body back, it takes over *your* body, or it just gets erased. And yeah," I added to Kaito. "As you might imagine, experimentation is discouraged."

"But you've experimented," she stated. "How does one avoid the less desirable outcomes?"

Now the other girls were paying attention, from the point I'd mentioned powerful mages. I gave them all another look.

"First of all, what I've learned is *dangerous*," I said. "It's a few observations from a very small number of cases. I'd hate myself if someone followed my instructions and they turned out that something I missed was of vital importance. Something like that could kill a person—or everyone they cared about."

"We'll be careful, of course," Kaito insisted, "But—"

"Wait," Isidre interrupted, "Do you mean that you've actually mastered a dungeon?"

"Secondly," I continued, "the information is very *valuable*, and I wouldn't think of giving it away for free."

"Ah, I understand," Kaito said, looking down. Then she looked up again with a sly smile. "Though, Miss Kandis, did I not hear that, in this Kingdom, the King assigns ownership of all dungeons to himself, and forbids his subjects from claiming them for themselves? If that's the case, then perhaps a deal could be made—"

"The King's aware," I told her. *Nice try, isekai.* It was scary, though, just how fast she'd come up with that attempt. It seemed that as soon as she saw something she wanted, little Miss Nice Girl took a little vacation.

"The King knows?" Isidre asked, still catching up.

"Why do you think I was so cooperative back there?" I asked bitterly. "I do his dirty work, and he overlooks my offenses."

"Offenses, plural?" Kaito said with some amusement. She paused, recalling something. "Back then, what did you mean when you said that you couldn't be blamed for what he did?"

"Ugh. Ashmor paid me a visit when I was staying in the palace," I said. "He didn't say much in the way of specifics, but—"

"Ashmor? Then all this is your fault!" Isidre exclaimed.

"Oh, shut up," I said. "I didn't entice him to show up. He does what he does, without input from me. He's not even *in* this god game."

"Nonetheless, he has made a move," Kaito said thoughtfully. "Does this hurt our chances of success?"

"Increases, would be my guess," I replied. "If this is his game, then three Champions showing up to stop him seems . . . deliberate."

"Perhaps," she agreed. "Do you think taking control of this dungeon might be the way we are supposed to solve the problem?"

I was, fortunately, saved from having to answer that problem. "Oh look!" I said instead. "A monster." *Thank God.*

[Identification]: Ashen Giant Cobra – Threat 18 – Properties: Venomous, Ranged Attack, Elemental Aspect (Fire)

Kaito's team leapt into action like a smoothly oiled machine.

"Spread out," she called out, "Try to get it from all angles. It probably spits venom, but it might spit fire as well—"

"Improved Blind." I called the spell out aloud. I couldn't remember if they'd seen me cast silently, but there was no real need to do it now. The black ball formed around the cobra's head, and it . . . froze in response.

That tended to happen with the dumber creatures. More intelligent ones tended to thrash about randomly, but the reptiles and birds tended to just freeze. Wait, were snakes different from reptiles? Probably.

Regardless of its taxonomic classification, the monster stood—lay—completely still until Zichy, Nori, and Kaito sank their blades into it. They were both pretty good; it was like having three Cloridans on my team. It started twisting about immediately, but they were ready for it and dodged easily out of the way of its random thrashes.

With a threat of eighteen, it had more than enough hit points to last a while, but the fight was over at the first blow. There had been a few giant insects in the upper levels, but this was my first contribution to killing one of the dungeon break monsters. I gave my status a quick check, but I still hadn't broken through to 0.001 percent contribution.

The front-line fighters came back to us, looking not exactly angry but a little bit displeased. Zichy, the wolf-kin, looked particularly displeased.

"Do you always cheat like that?" she asked me.

"What do you mean? Is magic cheating now?" I replied.

"Of course it is—I mean, no," she said, glancing at Fassi, the rabbit-kin wizard. "But Fassi and Orino only throw stuff in when it's looking bad, when we're getting overwhelmed."

I shrugged. "Fireball costs sixty mana," I told them. "Improved Blind costs twenty. So it makes sense that I'd cast it three times more often."

"Actually," Fassi interjected, "I prefer the Lightning Bolt spell."

"And how much does that cost?" I asked.

Her ears drooped. "Seventy mana," she admitted.

"But it makes fights boring!" Zichy protested. "He just sat there and twitched a bit."

I stared at her. "I can't even . . . Fights *should* be boring. That's the *ideal.*"

Zichy spluttered at me in disbelief, but I saw Fassi and Ettalle nodding along with me, so I knew I wasn't *entirely* insane.

"Girls, girls, don't fight," Kaito interrupted with practiced ease. "It's only natural to not want to risk one of the team getting injured."

"I've got healing potions," Zichy mumbled, hanging her head. "And I wouldn't get hurt, either."

Kaito looked at me with a wry smile. "You'll find that the more martial types are rather addicted to the thrill of a tough fight. I can't say I'm immune to the feeling."

She frowned. "To see a threat eighteen so soon . . . I'm sure we'll be seeing monsters soon that overwhelm us, but at least for this floor, we should be able to take care of ourselves adequately. I'd advise you to save your mana unless we three are outnumbered—or we encounter something over threat twenty."

I shrugged. "Sure, I can go along with that."

"That's a pretty neat spell, though," Fassi said enthusiastically. "Only twenty mana!"

"Someone's still got to do the work of killing the target, though," I said. "When I first got it, that was me."

"Ouch, yeah, Lightning Bolt does take care of the whole problem," she giggled. "Anyway, let's stay in the back, and let the muscle types get their exercise."

"Sure."

We continued down the valley. We encountered a few stragglers, but most of the snakes of this floor had either been removed by the flood, exited the dungeon, or been killed by the Duke's party. He'd left the corpses behind, just as we were doing, but he seemed to prefer to toss the bisected halves into the muddy stream that now ran down the center of the valley.

"Anger issues?" I wondered aloud as we passed what was either the fifteenth or sixteenth corpse.

"Perhaps concern for his son . . ." Isidre said. "We're getting closer to the level he was supposed to be."

Access to the next level was via a wide ramp that wouldn't have stopped anything smaller than an elephant. There were signs it hadn't always been that wide, and there were a few corpses at the entrance that would have been too big to fit. Which meant they were *very* large lizards.

"Maze of the Giant, indeed," Isidre said, looking at them. They had clearly been killed by multiple sword strikes. I couldn't tell if that meant more than one person or multiple hits from the same person.

This level was brightly lit—or it would have been if it weren't for all the greenery. The bright fake sunlight shone through the leaves of what looked to my inexperienced eye to be giant versions of the potted ferns that we had in our offices. They formed a canopy only six feet high, so it felt as though we were walking through claustrophobic green tunnels.

The lizards must have crawled through this dense greenery, the tallest of them crashing blindly through the canopy. The majority of them would have been low-lying enough to creep through the tunnels.

None of them were here now, though. It was only when we got to the end of this level that we started to hear the sounds of battle. Roars, screams, and the sound of mighty blows. Swords didn't have to strike against steel to make a noise, not when they hit with enough force to shatter rock.

We gave one another one final look before we crept forward to see what sort of fight awaited us.

CONFLICT

I think I should stay invisible for this next bit," I told the others. Kaito looked at me doubtfully but didn't say anything. It was Isidre that spoke up.

"Why?" she asked suspiciously.

"Certainly not to ditch you guys, slip ahead, and steal the Dungeon core for myself," I said lightly.

"That sounds like a plan . . . which is a step forward from where we are now," Kaito said wryly. "*Is* that our plan?"

"I don't *think* that's a workable plan," I said. "If I stole the core, the dungeon would . . . deconstruct, which might involve collapsing."

Oakway *hadn't* collapsed, but it was much smaller than this one. Plus, I suspected that Rhis's perfectionism hadn't allowed him to fail in any way other than gracefully. Leaving a smoking hole would have been so *déclassé*.

"We can't risk that," Kaito agreed, "So then, why?"

"I have a bit of history with Duke Finley," I admitted. "He's tried to kill or kidnap me . . . a couple times." I tried to keep a light tone to my voice. Charm was actually working against me here, suggesting ways to make it more dramatic, to elicit *more* sympathy . . . but I pushed it down. This was not the time.

"If he's there," I continued, "or some of his people that recognize me, there might be an argument—or violence—which will get in the way of getting more information."

"That makes sense," Kaito said slowly. "I wish that it didn't mean that our best negotiator must stay silent."

"You'll be fine," I said. I wanted to mention her recent Charisma boost, but Charm gave me a feeling that wasn't the best idea. "You're both

Champions, after all. The King seemed to feel that all we needed to do was show up . . . maybe these guys will be the same way."

"Perhaps," Kaito said. "The King had history to guide him . . . I just wish his voice hadn't been so bitter when he spoke of faith."

The fighting on the seventh level was happening right at the entrance. I wasn't sure what counted as part of each floor, but I wouldn't be surprised to learn that the defending team had just one foot left standing on the seventh. Not that all of them were standing.

There were five of them in all, three of them standing at the ramparts of a small fortification—probably made with Earth Magic. The stone wall hadn't been extended to our side, so we had a good view of their last stand as we came down the stairs.

"Can monsters go *down* a level during a dungeon break?" Kaito wondered, no doubt noticing that they were defenseless from this direction.

I didn't waste a spell on answering, but I thought the answer might be no. Breaks were about getting all the monsters out, after all.

"If monsters *could* have come down, they would have, and these guys would have been dead," Orino replied. We—well, they—were conversing normally as they approached, but the fighters on the wall weren't in a position to notice, being too busy with the monsters. Of the two not fighting, one seemed to have noticed us, but they seemed too injured to do anything more strenuous than stare at us. The other one had her eyes closed. Not dead, or at least I couldn't see any injuries from here.

Kaito's team sprang into action as soon as the monsters became visible. The monsters of this level were . . .

Yup, just as I thought. Dinosaurs.

Four T. rexes were the main attackers. Their heads easily overtopped the three-meter wall, jaws snapping at the defenders. Of course, this meant that their vulnerable heads were in striking range, so it wasn't all bad. I couldn't see directly behind the wall, but we could hear sounds that indicated that the T. rexes weren't alone.

I *could* see a triceratops, a little way back from the wall. It had just completed a ponderous turn and was glaring at the fortification. As we watched it charged forward, taking it out of sight.

Out of sight, but not out of mind, as it impacted the wall with a crashing thud and a scream. The wall didn't have anything as useless as a gate, but the whole thing shuddered under the blow. Nothing broke, but I didn't imagine the wall could stand forever.

Nori was the first of us to join the fight. The otter-kin stopped while she was still on the stairs, yelled for us to stay clear, and then put an arrow in the eye of a tyrannosaurus. I suspect the yell was for me, as there was nobody visible anywhere near her line of sight. The rest of her team had made sure to stay clear, even as they ran forward, and they took Isidre with them.

The T. rex screamed in pain or outrage, and the man it was fighting was almost as startled. He risked a quick glance back but then returned to the fight. Dinosaurs had way too many hit points to be taken out by a single blow, but being half blinded did help.

Speaking of Blind, one of my favorite spells, I didn't think it would be of much use here. Targeting the center of the head, it became abruptly useless when the head was over a certain size . . . and I thought that the oversized dinosaur heads would qualify. That wasn't the only spell in my repertoire, though, so I slowed down to cast Phantom World.

That spell was only visible to the target, which was actually an advantage in this situation. The opponent of the dinosaur I targeted had no idea why the monster suddenly lunged at another T. rex. He couldn't see my patented dancing man illusion precariously perched on that dinosaur's neck.

The victim retaliated, of course, so that was two dinos taken out before our team even reached the redoubt. Orino and Ettalle moved to treat the wounded, while the others headed up to the wall.

After that, the fight became dull. Well, not entirely. Kaito and Zichy were Agility-based fighters, which was quite a sight. Rather than stay on the wall, they both *jumped onto* a dinosaur, latching on to its back and stabbing it from a position it couldn't get to.

I couldn't say if it was more effective than the devastatingly powerful blows that the three fighters and Isidre preferred, but it was definitely more fun to watch.

By the time the four rexes had fallen, Nori and I had moved forward and joined the others on the wall. Firing on a dinosaur with a team member riding it was a little risky for Nori. On the wall, though, further targets presented themselves. There was the triceratops, of course, but also a horde of velociraptors . . . or wait, weren't the ones in *Jurassic Park* based on another dinosaur species?

[Identification]: Adult Deinonychus (M) – Threat: 24 – Properties: Fast Runner, Venom

Ah, right. Wait, venom? That wasn't in the movie.

The important thing was that they couldn't get up here. Clever climbers they might be, but they couldn't get a grip on the smooth stone walls. They'd been reduced to scratching at them while they waited for the triceratops to bash them down.

Nori started skewering them with arrows, but I had a better idea. I targeted the triceratops, now coming in for another charge. The velo—deino-whatevers were about human-sized, so I made the triceratops see each one as a human. It roared with rage and charged.

The resulting melee was so confusing that I lost track of my image for the spell. It probably would have broken with the first deinonychus bite anyway. It seemed that the smaller dinos were a herd. Attack one of them, and the rest retaliated. They swarmed the triceratops like ants on a beetle.

We all stood on the wall and watched, fascinated. It was a fairly even fight. The deinonychuses could barely penetrate the triceratops' armored skin, while they could mostly avoid its return strikes. When it did hit, though, it almost always took a raptor out of the fight.

We kept watching, as the 'tops got slower, while the raptors got fewer. In the end, it was the raptors that won. They started tearing open the bigger monsters' innards, feasting on the flesh inside. That was fascinating in its own right—I don't think I'd ever seen a monster *eat* before.

Oh, wait—griffins, I thought. That was outside of a dungeon, though I was pretty sure that monsters in a dungeon didn't need to eat.

I was distracted from my observations of dungeon ecology as everyone else on the wall tore their attention away from the spectacle and started considering one another.

"Rescuers?" one of the defenders said in disbelief. "*Tribal* rescuers?" He looked battered and bruised, but his equipment was top-notch. It glowed with enchantments to my Mana Sense. That, and his resemblance to my least favorite Duke, made me guess that we were looking at the man's son.

His underlings fell in by his side. There wasn't *much* room up here on the wall, but it was quite thick. It had to be, to stand up to those charges. The two groups managed to arrange themselves so they were facing each other. That meant that the other two had to stand a little behind their leader. They both looked like figures, with heavy metal armor. One was a woman armed with the same sword and shield combination as Isidre, while the man was holding some kind of two-handed mace.

"Am I speaking with Ethan Finley?" Kaito said, coming to the fore of her group and bowing. "I am Kaito Washiyama, Champion of Naldyna."

"The Champion of . . . here? That makes no sense." The lordling's eyes snapped around, latching on to the only human visible. "Lady Isidre? You've returned?"

"Yes," Isidre said, stepping forward as well. "I brought Lady Kaito with me, for diplomatic talks. However, we've been drafted into your problem here."

"I'm sorry that you've been troubled with this, my lady," Ethan said smoothly. It looked as though his Charm was kicking in after a long day's monster-slaying. "But this is an internal matter for House Finley. You should not—"

"The King disagrees," Isidre said flatly. "He's aware of the deals your father has made with Aghen Shadthe, and of your plans."

"Deals? I . . . don't know . . ."

"I must say, speaking from an outsider's perspective, it all seems quite *treasonous*," Kaito said, with a fake smile on her face.

"You're not . . ." Ethan protested. His companions shifted uneasily. No one had actually sheathed their weapons, but they gripped them more firmly.

"Oh, I wouldn't presume," Kaito said sweetly. "I'm an outsider, after all. What do I know?"

"The King sent us to fetch Duke Finley," Isidre said, switching Ethan's attention back to her. They had quite a good double-team going. "To answer for his actions, and explain himself."

"My father is . . . not available at the moment," Ethan said, glancing farther into the level.

"He's gone deeper, then?" Isidre pressed.

"Yes . . ." Ethan admitted.

"Are you holding this level to cover his retreat?" Kaito asked. "The castle was expecting another wave, but we saw no sign of it as we came down."

"Father forbade us from accompanying him," Ethan said. "We've had four waves of monsters from this level so far, but nothing from farther down. Since Jamie got injured, we thought we were better off fortifying."

"I thought dungeons couldn't spawn creatures in an occupied level?" Nori spoke up. Ethan stared at her, confused by the interruption.

"That's true . . . perhaps they're spawning on the level below?"

We all looked at one another. Well, I looked at them, and Kaito's group looked at one another. No one looked at me.

"Orino should have healed this Jamie by now," Kaito said. "I recommend you all head back up and join with the main defense. We will proceed farther down."

"But you're not . . ." Ethan focused on the group as a whole. "You're not a higher level than me—I'd say lower."

"The King feels that . . . all of this—from your father's action to this unprecedented break—is due to the machinations of the gods, and that our presence will somehow resolve them." She gave him a look that was both inquiring and . . . challenging.

"Oh. Well. Good luck, then."

DUNGEON TOUR

The noble's party didn't take Kaito's advice, and she didn't press further. Instead, we moved on. This level was . . . like a jungle, but much less dense. There were trees that didn't look like trees and some fern-like undergrowth. I wondered if the dungeon had found some prehistoric plants to match its dinosaurs. Whatever its origin, much of it had been trampled by the rush that tried to get past Ethan and his friends. We had a fairly clear path to the next level.

"Twenty-four threat and we're only about a third of the way down," Kaito mused. "It was fortunate that they did not have the Agility to match their level."

There were some murmurs of agreement from her companions, but they were all quite subdued.

"I'm more concerned about where the monsters were summoned from," I said, breaking my concealment. A bit of a waste if I needed to cast it again, but I didn't want them thinking I'd abandoned them.

"Summoning monsters off the floor they were designed for seems strange to me," I continued.

"Is that really such a worry, though? With everything else that's going on?" Isidre asked.

"Well . . ." I paused, trying to articulate my concern. "There's *some kind* of intelligence that controls dungeons. Not necessarily a human one, and in some dungeons it's more of a mechanistic thing. They work off templates and rules, and it seems like breaking changes the rules."

I wasn't sure, but it hadn't seemed to me that keeping monsters to their floor was a rule that I had to follow—it was just something that dungeons *did*.

"When you think about it, it would be odd if breaking only caused one rule to change," Kaito mused. "Although it might be the *same* rule."

"What do you mean?"

"There's no need for a rule to keep monsters in the dungeon, if there's already a rule keeping them on their floor. It could be *that* rule that breaking changes, which allows for monsters to escape."

"Huh, you could be right," I said. But that was the end of the immediate discussion, as we'd reached the final boss chamber—or what was left of it.

The eighth level had been described to us as being not so much a *cave* system as a *crevice* system. Narrow cliff faces that had to be descended and climbed to get through. We *had* brought some climbing gear, despite being told that it should be unnecessary. Our enhanced physiques should see us through, as long as we had Climbing. The main difficulty was supposed to be fighting the giant slugs that oozed out of smaller crevices, sticking to the walls and attacking adventurers without regard for gravity.

That . . . would not be happening today. Starting at the seventh level boss chamber, a large cylindrical tunnel had been opened up, boring deep into the dungeon. It wasn't lit, but I could see light at the end of it, which suggested that we were looking at the ninth level.

"Did . . . Duke Finley do this?" Isidre asked, awed.

"I don't think so," I replied. *I sure hope not!* The power it would take to force a passage like that astounded me, though perhaps an Earth Mage might be able to do it more easily.

"The edges aren't smashed or burned," I pointed out. "It looks natural. I think the dungeon did this, to release the monsters lower."

"The slugs wouldn't have needed this, though," Kaito countered, "And we haven't seen any so far."

"They move too slowly?" I speculated, "And as to where they are . . ." I had seen a few things in the dark tunnel that made me suspect what we were going to see next, so I cast Light at maximum brightness and sent it down the tube. There was . . . not a river of slime, but not a pool either. The tunnel sloped down, so the remains were collecting at the bottom, but so very slowly.

Chunks of glutenous flesh, pools of ichor and slime, all glistened in the light of my spell, as they slowly made their way down the passage. There were a few live slugs as well. They seemed to have been attracted by the corpses of their fellows, chowing down on the easy source of food.

Monsters eating again, I thought. *I wonder what it means?*

"The next level was slimes, wasn't it?" I said aloud. "It's hard to tell, but I think a lot of the more liquid stuff is slime corpses."

"Gross, but I suppose it doesn't matter—we have to keep going down," Isidre said glumly.

"They said not to use blades on the slugs, right?" I asked. "Are we going to be all right getting past them?" I wasn't confident that my illusions would work on the giant monsters. Their eyes were too far apart, and I doubted they had a brain to fool.

"It's fine, I've got this," Fassi said confidently. She took the lead as we headed down.

It took a while for the closest slug to notice us, but when it did it abandoned its meal and lunged for us. Well, it gave a small twitch and then slowly oozed in our direction. We had plenty of time to prepare our response. Which was Fassi. She stepped forward and cast.

"Ice Blower," she called, and a stream of ice and snow blasted out from her outstretched hand, like a cold flamethrower. The slugs hated it. The one nearest us started to ice up, so desperate to get away that it started moving at a slow walking pace. Other slugs farther down started moving as soon as the colder air reached them. It was too dispersed to actually hurt them, but they started making themselves scarce. In twenty minutes or so, they might be gone.

We weren't going to wait for them, though. Instead, we moved forward, carefully picking our way down the slope. Fassi kept the blower going. By the time we actually reached the first slug, half of it had frozen, and the other half had torn itself free. It seemed to be regretting that move, though. Ichor and bits of its insides were sliding out of it.

The smell was . . . not that bad, actually, but I was still glad when Fassi turned her blower on the remains, covering it all with a nice clean layer of ice.

"Look!" Nori said, pointing farther down the tunnel. I moved the light over so we could get a better look.

More corpses. Piles of fuzzy, burned bodies, about the size of a dog. Some of them were covered by slime, but others had fallen to the sides, the pile of their blackened bodies hard to see at a distance.

"Bees, right? It's got to be," I said. Those were the main threat of the tenth level. A giant swarm of creatures that could kill us on their own. We all looked silently at the remains. There were a lot of corpses.

"Sure glad we didn't have to fight all those," I said nervously. "I guess Finley's got a fire mage."

"A good one, too," Fassi agreed. "I can't imagine they'd have a lot of mana left after doing all this."

We pressed on. The ninth level was a swamp, designed to hide slimes. I hadn't thought of slimes as an ambush predator, but they could be, in the right terrain. Between Nori the Ranger and Orino the Druid, I got more of an education in slime's place in the natural ecosystem than I wanted. This level was lit, at least. Even if it was a gloomy green light that matched the swamp theme.

Fassi helped us here as well. She had another ice spell that froze the ground. It was normally used to interfere with an opponent's footing, but used on stagnant water, it gave us solid, if slippery, ground to walk on. Ice Blower could have done the same thing, but this was more efficient.

This level was more or less intact, although a swath had been cut through the trees, vines, and bushes. It led in a straight line that we were pretty sure led to the exit. We followed it. There were a few corpses along the way, but nothing like the numbers we'd seen on the top level. Not slimes—they wouldn't have been visible—but giant birds. We couldn't examine them easily without going off the ice path, but I guessed a wingspan of three or four meters.

There were also some slimes still alive on this level. Presumably fresh spawns. There weren't many of them, and they were mostly put off by the ice. Some of them tried dropping down on us, but the cut path we were following meant that there weren't any branches over us. Something to thank the Duke for, I guess.

We pressed on. The boss chamber for this level, a lake that supposedly contained a giant alligator—thirty meters long!—was missing. Just a hole to the next level.

Kaito was disappointed. "It would have been quite a sight," she said. "And relatively easy to kill, if we were agile enough."

Personally, I was glad there was another overpowered monster we didn't have to fight.

"The boss chambers seem to act like air locks," I said. "You can't progress until you've beaten the boss, and sometimes no one else can come in until your party is finished. Part of breaking must involve getting rid of those choke points—and the floor rewards."

We hadn't seen any floor reward chests, open or closed. Irritating, but it wasn't as if we'd earned them. The party nodded, but Zichy had one question.

"What does any of that have to do with air?" the wolf-kin asked.

"It's just an expression," Kaito told her, "I'll explain it later."

We continued on.

The next level was green—mostly green. There were a lot of other colors. It featured giant plants, mostly giant climbing vines. They twisted around one another, filling the giant chamber entirely. Each vine was broad enough to walk on, if it happened to be level. Taken together, they formed a giant maze that had to be walked, climbed, and slid down to get to the other side. The combination of scents from all the different giant flowers was intoxicating.

The Duke hadn't left us an easy path to follow this time. I guess you couldn't just cut down everything between you and the exit. If you tried, you'd end up cutting a vine that you needed to walk on . . . or were walking on. The floor was a long way down.

"Remember that the bees were not the only danger of this level," Kaito warned. "The flowers release pheromones and pollen that have many varied effects."

I had been planning Phantasmal face masks, but Fassi had a better idea. "I have an Air Bubble spell," she said. "I can cast it on everyone; it should protect us as long as we don't approach a flower too closely."

With our breathing secured, we all looked to Nori to find us a route.

"The Duke knows this dungeon better than anyone," Kaito pointed out. "These vines may not take footprints, but there must be some sign of his passage."

It was true. The vines weren't laid out in a manner convenient for foot traffic. They had little branches growing off them, and the aforementioned flowers. They ranged from about a foot across to enormous blossoms three meters wide. I couldn't see Duke Finley slipping through all this mess without a trace.

Sure enough, after a brief scout, Nori told us that she'd found a route. That should have been it for this level, but it wasn't that easy. Sure, the Duke seemed to know a route that was fairly direct and avoided the worst of the flowers. He'd burned out a few spots, probably flowers that he couldn't avoid. But the route itself was . . . strenuous.

We had found a use for the climbing gear after all. Some of us could make the jumps that the Duke had managed, but the rest of us needed a rope strung across the gap so we could cross. I wondered if all of his party were just as athletic, or if he'd had to resort to similar methods.

"You've got Air Magic, but you don't have a fly spell?" I'd asked Fassi after our first fraught crossing.

"Sorry, it's not as much use in the forest as you'd think," she said. "Just plain jumping gets you just about anywhere in a regular forest canopy."

Despite the hardships, we managed to progress to the end of the floor. As we approached, we once again heard the screeches of a large group of monsters, making me think that we'd managed to catch up with the Duke.

DUKE

From this point on, I'd been told, the dungeon had found a plan that it liked, and from here on down all the floors had the same basic structure. A single huge chamber, cylindrical in shape but domed at the top. Finley's people hadn't measured them, but they thought they were all the same size. Around three kilometers across and five kilometers high. They didn't know if spatial manipulation was involved, but I thought it had to be.

The floors were not arranged underneath one another. Each one was set to the side, and about three kilometers lower than the next. The arrangement formed a great spiral of chambers, slowly boring its way into the planet's crust.

If we *were* going all the way down to the final floor, we still had quite a trek ahead of us. Ten more floors meant thirty kilometers of both horizontal and vertical travel—in the very optimistic case that the dungeon would provide a quick route. That wasn't going to be the case in this chamber.

We emerged about two-thirds of the way up the cylinder, something we could plainly see as this chamber was almost entirely open. Open sky. The dome above blazed with fake sunlight. It illuminated the main feature of this floor, a giant tree stretching perhaps a kilometer up. Despite its size, it was dwarfed by the chamber as a whole, which was mostly dedicated to flying space for the inhabitants of this floor. The birds.

We'd been warned, so I didn't mistake the very large birds flying around in the distance for much smaller birds flying closer. I sure wanted to, though. Rather than great hulking eagles or condors, they looked just like swallows and finches.

Getting through this floor meant walking down the wide ramp that corkscrewed around the perimeter of the chamber, and then walking up another ramp that wound its way up to the exit, about a third of the way up. A little strategic rock climbing could save you a bunch of time, but it wasn't recommended, not with all the giant birds trying to eat you.

Despite it being a key feature, you didn't need to interact with the tree at all. It didn't house the boss, but it did contain a lot of the more valuable prizes. The boss bird lived in its upper branches, but it came and attacked you when you got close to the exit.

The other main feature of the level was the shallow caves that dotted the walls of the chamber. Birds nested in these, but if they were out, or if you *forced* them out, the caves could be used as a somewhat sheltered resting area.

About a kilometer down the path, we could see where the sounds of conflict had been coming from. A wall of ice had been raised, blocking off the path and—at a guess—blocking off one of the caves. A flock of birds was attacking the wall, but they didn't seem to be having much success.

"That must be the Duke," Kaito said, glancing at me. "Are you going to disappear again?"

"Yeah . . . but what's the plan?" I asked. "Are we attacking the birds?"

We all turned our attention to the flock below.

[Identification]: **Giant Grass Wren** – Threat: 30 – Properties: Flight

[Identification]: **Greater Thornbill** – Threat: 30 – Properties: Flight

[Identification]: **Monstrous Honeyeater** – Threat: 30 – Properties: Flight

[Identification]: **Mammoth Bristlebird** – Threat: 30 – Properties: Flight

---

Kaito whistled. "Threat thirty," he mused. "We should be able to take at least a few, but so many . . ."

"Not just them," I pointed out. "There are plenty of birds out there that could join in." That they weren't already attacking us was puzzling, but I guess it came down to dungeon rules.

"I can't imagine that these birds would seriously challenge the Duke," Isidre said.

"No," Kaito agreed. "He must be resting after fighting all night. Or at least his casters are. If we start drawing off his attackers, he should come out to see what's going on."

"You want me to start?" Nori asked. She gestured with the arrow in her off hand. "I'm in range right now."

I blinked—the birds were a kilometer away—but of course, superpowers.

Isidre pointed to the nearest cave. "We should take cover first, so we have some protection," she said.

"I'll stay outside, invisible," I said. "They're not in range of my magic, but assuming they're not too big for Improved Blind, it tends to be super effective against flying creatures."

"I'm sure," Kaito said with a grin.

"Can you make *us* invisible as well?" Fassi asked. The rabbit-kin wizard was looking nervous. "Some of us are more squishy than others."

"I can," I said doubtfully, "But I've learned that, without drills and practice, too many invisible people in a group turns into slapstick comedy. If it's just you, at the back, not getting in anyone's way, it might be all right, but . . ."

"But what?"

"Well, you wouldn't be able to yell for people to get out of the way of your spells. If you got hurt, no one would know. And you wouldn't be able to cancel it."

"Uh, yeah, that doesn't sound great." Fassi thought about it, her long ears flicking. "Guess I'll pass."

"All right then, sounds like we have a plan," Kaito said. "Let's get started."

The first arrow *screamed* its way from Nori's bow to its target. Following an absurdly flat arc, it hit a bird a few seconds later. The bird screamed and dropped, but it was up in the air again almost immediately looking for its attacker.

The other birds scattered, spiraling around looking for a target. None of them had figured it out by the time Nori's second shot hit. It still wasn't enough to kill it, though. It took a third shot, by which time the flock had determined where the threat was coming from. Half of them—four birds—started heading our way.

They moved fast, but Nori's arrows were faster. She got two more shots into one bird before they approached what I thought my range was going to be.

I had a notion that it might have increased when I increased my rank in Illusion Magic, so I kept my intent on targeting one particular bird with Improved Blind as he approached. Sure enough, I seemed to have an extra 150 meters of range from before.

In other news, these birds were *not* too big for the spell to work. The Bristlebird veered off target, narrowly missing one of its companions to smash into the chamber wall. It tried to recover but failed. Tumbling as it bounced off the wall, it started falling down farther. Shrieking and twisting as it fell, it might have been pathetic if it hadn't been trying to kill us seconds earlier.

I had been expecting a damage notification, but the rules were different during events. Only my overall contribution was noted, with the experience awarded at the end. At least I was finally contributing something.

Nori finished off her second one, and I cast Blind again. There was only time for one more arrow before the final bird was on us, so she shot it, then backed away behind the shield wall of Isidre and Zichy. They finished it off while I kept an eye out for my two victims.

They had fallen out of my spell range, so maintaining the spells was out of the question. But were they out of the fight? I wasn't sure that a fall like that would kill them. Looking down, I could make out what looked like their unmoving bodies . . . but what that because they were dead, or were they just keeping still because the lights had gone out? Distracted by trying to figure it out, I almost didn't notice the movement from the Duke's cave.

A hole had opened up in the ice, and a man stepped out. He was wearing full armor, but I figured it had to be the Duke. His shield was painted with his coat of arms, but I wasn't sure if all his troops got to do that. What gave his identity away were the four quick slices that took out four giant birds in quick succession.

Four hits, four kills, I thought. Yeah, he wasn't going to be seriously challenged by this floor. Maybe if all the monsters came at once, they could swarm him, but that didn't seem to be happening.

Enemies dispatched, he looked up to where we were and gestured imperiously for us to come down. Kaito just shrugged and led the way. I tagged along in the back. No words needed to be said, so I didn't waste an Unseen Sound spell.

"Two Champions," Finley said as we approached. He had removed his helmet, so I knew for sure it was him. "An ill omen if ever I saw one. What business do you have down here?"

By the time we got down there, the ice had all melted, and Finley's companions had joined him outside the cave. Two of them looked like wizards, while there was one who looked like a Rogue. He was wearing darksteel chain, which was a bit of a giveaway.

The other two were just wearing robes, but—

[Identification]: Robes of the Arch-Lich – Quality: Excellent – Properties: Enchantment (Protection), Enchantment (Environmental Support) – Origin: The Forbidden Crypt

Enchanted cloth! I still didn't know how to do that. I probably wasn't going to find out today, though.

Kaito waited until she was closer before replying.

"The King feels that recent events are part of the god's game," she said carefully. "And so sent us to the heart of the problem, in the hopes that we would be able to resolve the root of the problem."

"You think *I'm* the cause of all this?" Finley asked incredulously. "You're going to try and stop me?" He had never actually sheathed his sword. Now, he raised it and gathered himself. It seemed as if an aura gathered around him. Not mana—it was his Intimidation skill.

"Not at all!" Kaito insisted. "Everyone wants this dungeon quelled. But there are . . . larger issues. The King wants—"

"I don't give a damn what the King wants," Finley said through gritted teeth. "He's not going to be around for much longer. Longer than you, though, if you think you're going to go up against me."

He unleashed his skill. There wasn't anything to *see*, exactly. You *felt* the Intimidation; you imagined the oppressive aura bearing down on you. It was all in their heads. There was a physical reaction, though. The beast-kin's tails and ears drooped, and they took a step backwards. Fassi started cowering. They all tried to hide behind Kaito except for Isidre.

She, like Kaito, seemed to possess some sort of resistance to the pressure from Finley. I had noticed something of the sort for myself, so it was interesting to see it in other Champions. Some sort of unlisted perk. It wasn't total protection; they were still intimidated. But they were still able to act.

". . . not our business . . . internal Kingdom matters . . ." Kaito managed to say.

"Perhaps," Finley said with narrowed eyes. "But then what do you plan to do?"

He didn't seem to let up the Intimidation, but Kaito kept talking.

"Assume the gods have . . . plan. Become clear at . . . proper time."

"Ridiculous," Finley scoffed. "And on that basis, you expect me to carry you down to the final level? Far better to just eliminate the extra variables. It's not like you can even raise a hand to resist."

He stepped forward. He still wasn't in sword range, but it seemed clear where this was going.

Fuck.

My appearance next to Kaito must have felt like a breath of fresh air for the girls. I could feel my Intimidation pick up the weight of Finley's opposed skill. We were evenly matched, which meant he didn't have anything left over for *them*. I could sense Kaito and Isidre straightening up beside me, and I knew the others behind me were freed up as well. They were gripping weapons more tightly and adjusting their stance, getting ready to meet Finley's earlier threat.

"I wouldn't be so quick to violence if I were you, Duke Finley," I said. His title was a bit bitter in my mouth, but I needed to stay respectful.

"After all, the King is already aware of your traitorous actions. If you were to kill the gods' Champions, he wouldn't hesitate to denounce you to the populace and end your House."

†HRE A†S

For Intimidation to push back instead of just defending, I needed a threat. Not necessarily as dire a threat as him just coming over and killing us all, but the bigger the better. Threatening his entire House with retributive action by the King fit the bill.

"The King is well aware of your deal with Shadthe," I pressed. "He's looking for an excuse to make you pay for it. If the Champions don't come back, he'll blame you—whatever you say—and see you torn to pieces by a Dorsay mob."

I *thought* this was generally plausible. I'd seen how much the nobles venerated the Champions. I wasn't sure how much that feeling was shared by the general populace, but I *was* sure that *he* didn't have any idea either. He wasn't exactly a man of the people.

Similarly, I wasn't sure just how much of a threat a mob was. He *did* have a castle, and he *was* level seven. However, a mob with the King in front of it was another proposition altogether.

It seemed to be good enough. He stopped, at least, frowning.

"You," he said. "Again. What are *you* doing here?"

"Someone had to represent the King," Kaito lied, now able to speak more easily.

Nice excuse, I thought, but Finley wasn't exactly buying it.

"He has inquisitors, heralds, and other nobles aplenty, but he sent you?"

"I didn't think to argue with him," I claimed with a straight face. "If you want to take it up with His Majesty, he is *eager* to speak with you."

Finley glared at me, but he put away his sword. The Intimidation didn't let up, though—he didn't need to have his sword out to actually threaten us. His problem, though, was that he was out of contact, and didn't know what was happening on the surface. For all he knew, the King had taken over his castle and was just waiting for him to emerge. He couldn't go and check, because he couldn't ignore the greater threat below.

He could have tried asking me, but even if I'd told him the truth, and even if he'd believed me, I didn't know either. The King hadn't told me his plans, and it had been hours since I was in the open air. A lot could happen in that time.

Finally, the scowl came off his face, and the Intimidation lifted.

"I thought better of him, but I suppose that even a King can have his head turned by a pretty face," he sneered. "He must have tired of you quickly to send you down here, though."

I bristled at the accusation, but I didn't say anything. *Just keep underestimating me, pal.* Kaito, though, bless her, rose to my defense.

"It's not like that at all! C-Councillor Kandis is a high-ranked adventurer and a negotiator of rare skill. If anyone could convince you to su—to follow the King's will, it would be her."

"Yes, yes," Finley said dismissively. "So, not only do I have to let you accompany me, but I have to protect you? I'm to be blamed for your deaths when there are so many other ways for you to die? I'm starting to see the King's plan. I'm surprised you all went along with it, though."

There didn't seem much point in arguing with the insinuation—he might be right; the King might have sent us all here to die—so I pressed on.

"Can you actually kill the Giant?" I asked. "Have you done it before?"

"Yes . . . but that was leading a larger group," he admitted. "We had an Air Mage to keep a cloud around its head while two squads with greatswords hacked at his legs. That kept him busy while the ranged team pounded at him until he went down."

He looked down, remembering. "He's slow and clumsy, but if he hits a person, it's all over for them. And he's so tough, it takes a while for even a large team to bring him down."

"That sounds like the beasts we fight in the forest," Kaito said, brightening. "Though . . . of not so high a threat value. Still, we should be able to use similar tactics."

"Not you, girl," Finley said. "If I'm to be blamed for your death, you're not getting near that thing. Dodging is all very well, but its hand is as big as you are—and it doesn't need to bother making a fist to kill you."

Kaito didn't reply, but gave him a cocky grin which as good as said, "You're not going to be able to keep me away." I interrupted before they could take it further.

"So who do you have with you, then? My lord," I added hastily. He flicked a disparaging glance my way, but I guess he couldn't deny the need for us all to be on the same page if we were going to be fighting together.

"Allen, Master Arcanist. Faulkner, Shadowed Rogue. Coles, Fire Arcanist. They're all level six."

I nodded and checked them out while Kaito introduced his own crew and classes.

Allen was one of the ones wearing the robes. Short and pink-skinned, his light brown hair looked like a bird's nest. Arcanist was a pretty popular profession among adventurers. It gave bonuses to a wide variety of magics, so it allowed for flexibility. *Master* Arcanist was an upgrade to the profession, available at level six.

Fire Arcanist was an upgrade to Janie's Fire Mage. This one looked . . . not cruel exactly, more like harsh. Blond hair and tanned skin suggested he got out a lot, probably adventuring in the open air. I wasn't sure, but I didn't think any of the dungeons gave you a tan. He was one of those people who shouldn't grow facial hair but did anyway, resulting in a scraggly moustache and beard.

The final man in the trio was the Shadowed Rogue. That profession was . . . an upgraded Rogue profession with an additional requirement of Shadow Magic. Which made it better than the regular upgrades (there were a couple of other good ones, Assassin in particular). The benefits . . . mainly went to bonuses to Shadow Magic. Which wasn't bad, really.

Kaito had finished his introductions, so I asked Allen what his magics were.

"Ice, Water and Air," he replied. I nodded. There were some Arcanists that went for every magic type, but most specialized to some extent. That might explain the huge jumps that we'd had trouble following on the earlier level. Then again, they were level six.

"So what is your plan?" I asked the Duke.

"Faulkner was scouting while the others were recovering their mana," he said, making no mention of himself having needed rest. Perhaps he hadn't. "Tell them what you saw," he said to the Rogue.

"The Giant has left floor twenty," Faulkner said. "He was at floor sixteen when I checked; he may be at floor fifteen by now. He's not moving particularly quickly."

Five floors, thirty kilometers to travel, and it had been less than 24 hours since the break had begun. That wasn't *terribly* slow, but I had the feeling the giant could move faster than that if he wanted to.

"Has the dungeon cleared the way for him?" I asked.

"Yes. It hasn't changed the lower exit for this level, but it was already large enough for him to squeeze through."

"The upper exit here, though . . ." I cast my mind back. "That probably isn't large enough?"

"Yes," the duke said. "It's unable to change it since we are here, so this may be the lowest point to serve as a bottleneck. It is . . . somewhat defensible."

Not against birds, I thought but refrained from interrupting. There were birds, on this level and the next, but they hadn't been mentioned as monsters in the lower levels.

"The problem is," Faulkner said, "he's bringing a wave with him. All the monsters in the levels we haven't cleared are being swept before him. That might be part of the reason he's moving so slowly."

I swallowed. Nine floors' worth of monsters, all in one place. "You want to fight them all here?"

"That was the plan," Finley said thoughtfully. "Along with the possibility of a fighting retreat to the redoubt held by my son. Now, I think it might make sense to push on, kill as many monsters as possible before the wave, and then fall back to this level."

"Wait, why now?" I asked.

"Because you are here," he replied. "Your group is—barely—capable of surviving on this floor. You can keep it from changing while we head out and kill what monsters we can."

"Wait," Kaito protested, "We're not just going to sit here while you—"

"You do not have the levels to survive deeper floors," the Duke shot back bluntly. "Here, you can thin out the new spawns and keep this floor defensible. That is of far more use than anything else I can think of you doing."

"But I—"

"If I'm to be held responsible for your deaths, then you need to let me *keep you alive*," Finley continued over him. "If your deaths are to be certain, and I'm going to have to deal with the consequences, I'd rather take the pleasure of killing you myself."

That shut Kaito up. She looked at me pleadingly.

"We don't want to die," I agreed. "But I think the point that Kaito is making is that if we're not in the thick of things, we won't be placed to act out the gods' mysterious design."

"I'm sure the gods, *in their infinite wisdom*, have already planned for that," Finley said with far more sarcasm than I was comfortable with.

"You know they're watching, right?" I asked. "Can lightning strike underground?"

Finley's snort was my only reply.

"Stay here," he repeated. "Kill birds. We'll be back, and you can try figuring out what the gods want you to do then."

We all looked at Kaito, but she didn't protest, just drooped her ears. "Fine," she said.

The duke nodded and without further ceremony gestured for his men to join him. They all grabbed ahold of Faulkner, and shadows, already thick in this cave, swirled around them. Then they were gone. Already jealous of his teleporting, but suspecting that it couldn't be that powerful, I took a look down. Sure enough, they'd only teleported down about a hundred meters, to the next loop of the spiral. They'd saved themselves a lot of walking, but I guess Faulkner couldn't do that too often.

"Um, I have some Earth Magic," Fassi volunteered. "I can make this cave deeper and give it a narrower entrance."

"I can start shooting birds, if we're ready to receive a . . . is charge the right word?" Nori said.

"I'm not sure, but I don't suppose it matters," Kaito replied, her gaze still following the Duke and his party as they made their way down. "Let's get started."

It worked at first. Nori would shoot a bird at a distance of one or two kilometers. It would get mad and bring some of its friends to attack us. She'd maybe get one before it came into Blind range, then I'd get one or two while she tried for her second. That tended to leave two or three for Zichy, Isidre, and Kaito. The entrance to the cave had been narrowed so that only two of them could fight side by side. This meant that our three frontline fighters could take turns having a break, something that Kaito had to insist on, since Zichy didn't want Isidre fighting next to Kaito.

Taking out a small group like this was well within our capacities, especially since we could control the timing and take breaks for healing and rest as needed. We were on our third group when the problem started.

Finley had just about made it to the exit. He hadn't crossed, or even made it to the bottom. He just went along the ramp until he was over the exit, and then shadow-jumped straight down. At which point a few things happened.

For one, a huge bird flew out of the top of the giant tree.

> [Identification]: Eagle Colossus – Threat: 36 – Properties: Flight, Adamant Claws

That . . . was one big bird. Fortunately, it didn't come for us but headed towards the Duke. I, and I'm sure the Duke, had been expecting this. Since the boss didn't reside in the final chamber, getting rid of the chamber didn't eliminate the boss.

The second thing that happened was that all the birds that had been flying around the chamber started heading either for the Duke's party or for us. This . . . was also not totally unexpected. You triggered just about all the birds as you went around or through the floor, but the Duke had taken quite a few shortcuts. It made sense that they'd join their boss for the final fight.

The third thing *was* unexpected. From the exit that Finley had just reached, a huge number of birds started to pour through. These were easily distinguished from the birds of this floor by their more brightly colored plumage. These giant birds were elementally aspected with Fire, Ice and Air magics.

> [Identification]: Giant Fire Swallow – Threat: 33 – Properties: Fire Aspect (ranged attack)
>
> [Identification]: Greater Storm Hawk – Threat: 33 – Properties: Ice Aspect (generate storm)
>
> [Identification]: Shadow Ogre Shrike – Threat: 33 – Properties: Shadow Aspect (concealment)
>
> [Identification]: Colossal Swift Tern – Threat: 33 – Properties: Air Aspect (movement)

Okay, so not just elemental magics. Our guides had not been complete. There were more than just the four types, of course, but I quickly gave up trying to classify them.

Some of them fell to Finley and his men before making it into the chamber. They may have been tougher monsters, but he could still kill them with one blow. Others made it past the gauntlet but wheeled back to attack him or his party.

But some started heading in this direction. We were going to be in for quite a fight.

DUNGEON FUN

D*ungeon rules are off during a break.*
  I pondered this as I watched upwards of twenty giant birds converge on our position. "Charge" didn't seem like the right word, and too many of them were flying *up* for "dive-bomb" to work. None of them were flying in a straight line towards us. Some were coming in high, so they *could* dive at us when they got here, others were swinging wide for a . . . strafe?

A few—too few—of them were either swiftly dropping or twisting in distressed spirals. The result of Nori's arrows and my Improved Blind. That left too many to quickly count, and it was time for us to duck back behind the cover of our front line.

We joined Orino and Fassi at the back. Orino had been furiously casting support spells, and she spared one for me.

"Cat's Grace," she chanted, and I felt the enhancement. *An Agility increase? Feels good.* It probably wouldn't do much, if it came to it, since I was sorely deficient in the physical stats, and these attackers were coming from a lower level.

Dungeon rules are off . . . Not off as in turned off, but *different.* The dungeon had waited until Finley had triggered the boss before bringing in the birds from the lower level. That smacked of a strategy, but then why not attack *our* party with the birds it already had here when we entered?

Fassi crept as close as she dared to the cave entrance and cast a Freezing Mist, projecting it outside. An area effect spell like that was normally good against swarms of attackers, but the giants outside just brushed off the damage as if it were nothing. It *did* manage to drive off the Giant Fire Swallow, which had been generating torrents of flame from under its wings and blowing them in our direction.

Isidre had taken the fore during that attack, blocking it somehow with a golden light. Now she stepped back and let Kaito and Zichy form the front line while she recovered. More of that glowing light was playing over her burns, and Ettalle added her own magic. It looked as if Isidre wanted to say something, but she just exchanged a look with the priestess and let her work.

It was difficult to get a long enough look at an attacker to target a Blind, but I did what I could. Part of me thought I should have stayed outside, invisible, for better targeting, but in here seemed much safer. At least for a while.

I should be outside . . . I rejected the thought and focused on dungeon rules. If I thought about the attack as having been triggered by an *event*, then maybe things made more sense. If the Dungeon hadn't been *able* to act until Finley triggered the boss event, then . . .

Kaito's Dodge skill failed her, and she flew back into the cave, smashing into the back wall and slumping to the ground. Gasps and screams from all the girls, but they kept it professional. Orino and Ettalle moved to heal Kaito's gaping chest wound, while Isidre moved forward to hold the line again.

It reminded me of a badly programmed computer. Or not badly, exactly. I thought about what Fyskel had said, that Ashmor had modified their original design for whatever dungeons had been called in those days. What was that, if not a hack? And the other gods had hacked back, changing what they could to make dungeons safer . . .

What a mess . . . it was no wonder that the dungeon's actions didn't make sense. It did suggest something, though.

"Kaito," I said, coming up to her as she levered herself up. Her wound was healed, and her armor seemed to be healing as well, fibers reaching across the hole and twisting it closed. It was a little disconcerting to watch, but I tore my gaze away. "I think I've got a crazy plan."

Kaito grinned. "Does it involve getting out of this cave?" she asked.

"Yeah," I admitted.

"Then we'll work on that first part for a bit," she said. Getting up, she made her way back to the front. "My turn!" she told Zichy and was back to fighting.

"That's it, I'm out," Fassi said, slumping back against the wall. Freezing Mist was the only area effect spell she had, and it wasn't the most efficient of spells. But she hadn't had the same targeting difficulties that I'd had, so she'd been casting it nonstop, taking some of the pressure off the front line. She was the first to run out of mana, but the rest of us weren't too far behind.

I was the best off, as I was still having trouble landing a Blind spell. I had far fewer mana points than Fassi, but she had been using them at a prodigious rate. Orino and Ettalle were somewhere between our extremes. We'd been keeping one another up to date, but it wasn't like we were sharing status windows.

"They're thinning!" Kaito called back from the entrance. "I think we're past the—"

She was interrupted by a scream from Fassi. A shadow had detached from the wall and formed itself into a claw that had raked across the rabbit-kin woman.

Everyone shouted, screamed, or desperately wished they could turn from the entrance to see what was happening. The claw extended farther out from the wall, and the rest of the bird came out with it.

> [Identification]: Shadow Ogre Shrike – Threat: 33 – Properties: Shadow Aspect (concealment)

Oh, that guy. The shrike was hard to see under all the shadows it was carrying, but it wasn't hard to miss. It was as big as a horse, and its hooked beak must have been a foot long. It looked around, taking us all in, and then made a grab for Fassi with its beak.

[Phantasmal Object]. I cast the spell instinctively, bringing forth the first object I could think of that was large enough. I wasn't sure who was more surprised at the desk that interposed itself between Fassi and her attacker. The modern office furniture looked completely out of place in this cave, but it managed to block the one blow without disappearing. The shrike shook its head in confusion, but I was already following up.

[Light]. I wasn't sure if something covered in shadows would be bothered by Improved Blind, but light seemed an obvious counter. There was already a light spell in the cave, but I hadn't cast it as bright as this one. The shrike shrieked at the blinding brightness, as close to its face as I could manage. Shadows flew off it like leaves under a strong wind.

It didn't seem as if I'd injured it at all, but it was distracted enough for Nori to plunge her swords into its back. She'd switched out her bow when we'd come inside and had been standing backup for the frontliners. Now, she had something to do. She struck, again and again. Abandoning its attack, the shrike tried to slide back into the wall, but it looked as though my bright light was preventing that. It needed shadows.

Once it had finally died, I turned to see how Fassi was doing. She . . . wasn't great. Sitting against the wall again, she was being tended to by Orino, but Orino wasn't casting her usual healing spell.

"Vine Bandage," she said, meeting my gaze. It was easy to confirm, as the spell matched the name. Instead of the glowing gold that I was used to seeing from most healing spells, Fassi had vines wrapping themselves around Fassi's arm and torso. "It's cheaper than healing and will keep her from bleeding. She's not going to be useful in the fight until she gets back her mana and I'm . . . running low as well."

Fassi looked pretty green, but she didn't protest. I didn't say anything, just nodded. Orino looked more upset than I felt, to be honest.

"You ever run out during a fight before?" I asked.

"Not since I was young," she said. "Kaito is fond of taking risks, but never ones this . . . foolish."

I nodded again. Adventuring was all about *reducing* risk. You researched your target dungeon, identified the hazards, and prepared countermeasures, all to reduce the risk to as close to zero as possible. We hadn't, at least, gone into this dungeon blind, but delving into a breaking dungeon was something that went against all advice. Hardly a surprise that we'd gotten in too deep.

"I still have potions," I reassured her. "And Isidre's been too busy fighting to heal much." I hoped that were true. I wasn't sure how much of her pool she was using for damage and protection.

I headed up to the front, where Kaito was taking a quick break.

"I thought you would have known better than to say something like the worst is over," I chided her.

"Sorry, but it really is true," she said, grinning. "I got a bit exuberant when you told me you have a plan."

"Don't get too excited," I told her. "It involves me going on alone."

"Ah! Those are the best plans! I'm so jealous," she complained. "It hinges on your Invisibility, then."

"Yeah," I said cautiously. "If I sent someone down invisible, I might not be able to maintain it long enough, and if I brought someone, they'd be stepping on my toes." Maybe not *one* person. I was pretty practiced at following someone who knew what do to and communicating with them via Unseen Sound. But it was more than just a little bit annoying and I couldn't see a single person making a difference here.

"You chose a very lonely build," Kaito said. "I know you have companions, but even when you are fighting together, it must seem like you are fighting alone."

"Well, not every team can share the same bathtub," I muttered.

"That's—uh—true," Kaito said, suddenly coughing. I looked at her with narrowed eyes as she turned away from my gaze. Had things actually . . . progressed? I'd thought that impossible, but I guess I shouldn't underestimate a girl's determination. Or five of them.

Now I was blushing.

"How much longer, do you think?" I asked, changing the subject. I was looking at the entrance, but it was hard to tell how it was going. Fassi had reshaped the cave entrance to be as narrow as possible, and the front line was a little bit back from the opening. Birds had to fly into the cave, attack, and then fly out, unless they wanted to go toe-to-blade with the defenders. Few did.

Now, as I watched, there came a pause. After a moment, Isidre cautiously stepped forward, sword and shield raised.

"Fassi made sure there wasn't anywhere above that they could perch and ambush us," Kaito remarked. "She does good work."

I nodded but kept watching Isidre. There must be at least one bird out there, because the last attacker had left alive after trading a few blows. Nevertheless, she remained free from attacks as she stepped out onto the cliffside ramp. She looked up and then around.

"I think they're done attacking!" she called back. We all looked at one another, and then carefully came out of the cave.

The first thing that caught my—caught everybody's—eye was the flock of birds circling far above.

"They've gone back to general patrolling?" I said, then looked over to the exit. Thanks to my enhanced vision, I could see that Finley had finished his fight as well. There were a lot of bird corpses, but no human ones that I could see, and no sign of him and his party. He must have gone through already.

"Perhaps the dungeon lost interest once that party passed though?" Kaito speculated.

"Once the boss fight event was over . . ." I mused aloud. It sort of made sense. Kaito looked over at me.

"And now, is it time that we must part? Are you leaving on your mission now?" she asked.

"Are you crazy?" Orino asked her and then turned towards me. "Are you? Not only did the murderous level seven Duke say to stay here, but the monsters below are way too dangerous!"

"She has Invisibility; she'll be fine," Kaito assured her.

"Here's hoping," I agreed, far less confident. This dungeon was more about raw force than cleverness. Nothing that I'd been told in the briefing suggested that there would be something to counter invisibility, but that briefing wasn't perfect.

"What are you even going to do?" Orino asked incredulously.

"Better you don't say," Kaito told me. "Just leave us with a mysterious clue."

"Okay . . ." I said. Weird as it was, her insistence on following anime tropes was working out for me, as I didn't really want to tell them what I was up to. "Have you ever seen *The IT Crowd*?" I asked her.

"No, I don't see much foreign TV," she answered.

"Then I feel safe in saying that I'm going to be following an otaku's advice."

"That's good; we give very good advice!" Kaito said with a grin. "But I thought that otaku was only a Japanese practice."

"Eh, it's close enough," I said. And then I was off.

DUNGEON RUN

I ran down the ramp at close to top speed. I did have to keep my eyes on my footing, so it wasn't *quite* as fast as I could have managed on a flat track. But the slope helped, so maybe it was a wash.

I'd never run this quickly before. Cat's Grace was still in effect, adding to my Agility, so my Run skill total had never been this high. But it had been a while since I'd had a reason to run at full speed, for any length of time. It was exhilarating, and I wondered why I didn't do this more often.

Then I remembered that the delving, banking, enchanting, and politics took up all of my time. Getting the chance to do it now was due to some absurd fluke. How often did you get the chance to run through a cleared floor of a broken dungeon?

Despite being invisible and inaudible, I was fairly sure that the dungeon was aware of me. I didn't think, though, that there was anything it could *do* about me. Finley had triggered the boss trap, for example, and that would stay open until the dungeon reset, which might not be until after the break was over.

Hopefully. Similarly, I was gambling on the idea that the dungeon had reconfigured everything to give its monsters a clear path out— which meant there was a clear path *in*. That did leave the monsters to deal with, but as long as they couldn't see me, I thought I was in with a chance.

It wasn't long before I was over the exit. That meant that there were almost a thousand meters of cliff face between me and it, of course. I didn't have teleportation magic like Faulkner, but I could climb. And it would save me running around this corkscrew a couple of times.

| [Climb] Level 3 acquired through use. |
| For gaining a skill level, you have been awarded 1 XP. |

For a dungeon shortcut, it hadn't been as hard as it might have been. I suppose it would have been more difficult if I'd had fire swallows or whatever dive-bombing me the whole time. I even got to have breaks as the path wound its way around under me twice more.

I jumped the last thirty meters and let my Jump skill absorb my fall. Practicing while in danger was supposed to be worth more skill experience, after all. There were bird corpses all around, but the way forward was clear.

The twelfth floor was just as empty as the eleventh. The dungeon had emptied it trying to take out Finley and, to a lesser extent, us. After fighting his way through, he hadn't hesitated to continue and was now nowhere in sight.

This floor was similar to the previous one. There was the same corkscrewing ramp going down to the bottom of the chamber. However, instead of a single giant tree dominating the center, there was a tapered column rising from the ground to the ceiling. Perhaps a kilometer across at the base, it was maybe a hundred meters at the top. It didn't taper smoothly, though; it rose up with stepped sides, and on those flat places, trees grew.

They weren't as big as the tree upstairs, but they were pretty big for trees, which aren't exactly known for being small. They varied between 200 and 500 meters tall, reaching out so far that they brushed the edges of the chamber in places.

How trees grew in a rock spire was beyond me, but clearly magic was involved, because these were magical trees. Their leaves glittered with colors other than green, reflecting their magical element. Mana Sense confirmed that, yes, they were more magical than normal plants. Not *so* magical that you could gain mana or levels from eating them or anything, but they had to be powerful alchemical reagents. I also saw some fruit hanging here and there that I recognized from the banquets that the King had held.

The boss chamber was, or was supposed to be, in the base of the central pillar, so I would have to make my way down. I followed the path that the Duke had taken, the only path there was.

I knew that Finley had been this way because of the vines. On this level, they covered the walls, growing over the path. Or perhaps they weren't vines, because these plants were hanging down, not climbing up. It was easy to tell because Finley had cut through the . . . stems that were covering the path, causing the plants to fall to the next level.

I wasn't sure why he had done that. We had been warned to be careful of our footing around the vines, but there had been no special danger that we'd been told about. You *could* use them to climb down, but they had a tendency to fall out. Whatever his reasoning—perhaps he'd just been impatient—he had left me with a clear path to follow, so I broke into a run.

Unfortunately, the clear path abruptly ended about halfway around the chamber. There were no corpses, so I assumed the cause wasn't Finley's death.

He probably shadow-jumped, I thought, looking around to see where he might have gone to. There was only one thing that looked promising.

Now that I was farther around the chamber, I could see behind the central pillar. At the bottom of the chamber, in the kilometer gap between the pillar and the walls, the ground had collapsed, leaving a straight scar of broken rock that stood out against the ground cover.

It looked a *bit* too extreme for something that Finley might have done, but then I realized what was going on. There was a tunnel out of the boss chamber to the next floor. This had been collapsed, and that scar led directly to the exit. This floor had been prepared for the exodus that was coming.

Which meant that Finley had already left this level. I started wondering if I was going to catch up to him.

More climbing? I wondered, looking at the cliff face doubtfully. This would be an even longer climb, but there were vines. Cat's Grace had run out, but I'd picked up a level in Climb, so it evened out. The quickest way would be to just take a potion of Feather-fall and jump, but those cost 25 gold, and I wasn't getting paid for this.

You have taken 25 damage!

[Jump] Level 4 acquired through use.

For gaining a skill level, you have been awarded 1 XP.

Ow! Ow ow ow!

It turned out that falling was much like Jumping, at least when skill experience was counting. I had made *some* deliberate jumps going down, but the majority of my skill-up had been due to absorbing short falls.

Fortunately short, due to the path continuing to wind down. The chamber sides *looked* vertical, but there was a small amount of slope. I had managed to make my way down in a series of climbs, jumps, and falls. It hadn't been *fun*, but I'd made it down *and* gotten a skill increase.

I dusted myself off and looked at the exit. It was clear, but I thought I heard some monsters fighting in the distance. It looked as though I would be catching up with Finley after all.

Giant rabbits, mice, and squirrels. It sounded kind of cute, but we had been disabused of that notion by our teachers in our brief training session. We would be fighting mice the size of bears, while squirrels threw acorns that weighed more than us. And then there were the rabbits the size of elephants, with ears that could crush a man with a single flick.

Normally, this was a bit of a hunter's level. There were a lot of animals, and they were very big, but there weren't *that* many of them, and they were spread over a wide area. You could stealth your way through if you wanted. There was a spiral sloping down like before, but instead of corkscrewing down around a mostly empty chamber, it took up the entire volume. You had to hunt mice and squirrels on the way down until you'd made one full revolution and found yourself at a cliff face honeycombed with a rabbit warren.

During a break, it seemed as if the monsters didn't wait to be hunted but came right for you. I found three mouse corpses right at the entrance, but the noise was coming from farther in. I got to running.

It took me a while to catch up to them. The sounds I was hearing were deceptive because they were coming from animals much bigger than I was used to. The grunting and growling was much louder than I thought, and coming from much farther away.

[Run] Level 4 acquired through use.

For gaining a skill level, you have been awarded 1 XP.

Eventually, though, the trees opened up in a clearing, and for the first time, I saw Finley fighting something that challenged him. He wasn't overwhelmed, or seriously troubled, but these rabbits were, despite their looks, monsters he couldn't just cut down with a single swing.

> [Identification]: Emperor Lupus – Threat: 36 – Properties: Fur
> Ablation, Leap

About the same threat as the birds, but they were much bigger. Finley's blade—or, I should say, the coruscating energy around it—was actually having problems cutting through its ridiculously thick fur.

The rest of the party was hanging back, saving their mana. Except for Faulkner, who wasn't even there. A chittering in the treetops, followed by a falling squirrel corpse, suggested a location.

Finley finally finished one of his two opponents, and I decided that I didn't need to help him. These rabbits were too big for Blind anyway, which was troubling.

I headed on. You weren't supposed to encounter the rabbits outside the warren, so I thought it must be close. And so it proved. Once again there was a major difference between the description I had been given and the current reality. The original warren had been . . . bigger than the name would suggest. These were giant rabbits, after all, so they needed tunnels ten feet high to travel down. That would not be enough for the denizens of the lower levels, so some changes had been made.

I gaped at the ten-*meter* tunnel that sank into the cliff face, boring straight through the maze of tunnels that had led to the final boss chamber. It looked as if the boss had been bypassed again.

I moved cautiously forward. As I entered, I saw that there were still plenty of rabbits left. They were sitting in regular giant-rabbit-sized tunnels that led off from the main shaft. Probably from the original warren. I counted at least twelve, probably waiting for someone to step through the tunnel. Finley would have a hell of a fight on his hands.

Unless I did. I gulped silently and started heading forward. Mana Sense didn't show any magical triggers across the tunnel, but I wasn't sure if I could detect all the ways a dungeon could trigger. I should probably have run through. It wasn't as though I would make a sound, however I passed through. But I had to keep my eyes up, looking at the glittering eyes of the rabbits as I walked past them, constantly checking for any movement. When they didn't move, I released a breath that I didn't know I was holding.

The tunnel wasn't lit, but quite a lot of light came through the enormous entrance. It went around a curve and the light level dropped, but I could see the exit ahead. Hopefully, it wouldn't turn out to be an oncoming train.

FİNAL BOSS

L evel fourteen was supposed to be a scaled-up version of a wooded ecosystem. Someone had mentioned during the briefing that the flora and fauna had been enlarged at different scales. The plants were all doubled in size, while the animals—the monsters—were anywhere between four and ten times the size of their natural counterparts.

It wasn't at all apparent to me. The trees were big, sure, but not as big as the giants on floors eleven and twelve. How do you tell a giant small tree from a normal tall tree? I guess there was always . . .

[Identification]: Giant Witch Hazel – Properties: Irritating Sap

Well there you go, it's a giant, I thought. It didn't actually look that big, about six meters high, but I guess the regular version was shorter.

As for the animals, I didn't have to go far to find them. There was a crowd of them just past the initial burst of undergrowth—giant undergrowth—that screened the entrance. It was a collection of animals that wouldn't look out of place in an American or European forest. Bears, wolves, deer. Something that I wasn't familiar with . . .

[Identification]: Giant Wolverine – Threat 37 – Properties: Armored Fur, Extra Attacks

I gulped. It looked meaner than the one in the comics, and it stood about five feet at the shoulder. Like all the others, though, it didn't seem to see me, and it wasn't engaged in any activity. It was . . . just standing there. They all were.

That was not what they were supposed to be doing. They were supposed to be spread out all around this level, getting hunted and hunting in return. This floor was another long spiral leading down to the exit. Unlike the floor above, the ground was a ribbon, twisting around under itself in a helix. As I moved past the crowd of monsters, I got to see it for myself. The ribbon was about a kilometer wide, maybe a little more, and I could walk to the edge and get a good look at the level as a whole.

It was an incredible view, like something out of a computer game. The ground curved down and around, ducking out of sight underneath me. I could see all the way across the lower forest to the outer wall.

And I could see the monsters.

It looked as if the entire population of the floors below had grouped up and was marching forward. Not in formation, but in waves, as if each of the monsters of each floor were being driven out by the monsters of the next lower floor.

First were what looked like a collection of animals from an African wild game hunt. Lions, tigers, elephants, and others. Most of them slipped effortlessly through the trees, but the elephants just crashed forward through them. Watching a giant tree get effortlessly crushed made me realize just how big those creatures were. Ten meters, twelve meters high? It was hard to tell at this distance.

The ogres were next. In any other dungeon, I would be happy to call them giants, but that was a pretty overused term here.

> [Identification]: Ogre – Threat 39 – Properties: Berserk, Armored Skin

They stood a little shorter than the elephants, but that was far too tall for my taste. If it weren't for the relative lack of hair and the horns, I would have thought them to be giant gorillas. Giant, hulking, naked humanoids, they stumbled forward, mostly keeping to the trails created by the elephants. Some of them would absently strip the branches off trees as they passed. Not for clubs, but for something to chew on. They'd take a bite of the leafy end, then throw the rest away.

In this way, the elephant trails were widened for the ogres' betters to pass through.

> [Identification]: Greater Ogre – Threat 40 – Properties: Berserk, Armored Skin, Skilled

The greater ogres were more organized. They wore skins for clothing and carried simple spears and clubs. They had a leader, and someone else . . .

> [Identification]: Greater Ogre Shaman – Threat 42 – Properties: Armored Skin, Skilled, Caster
>
> [Identification] Level 5 acquired through use.
>
> For gaining a skill level, you have been awarded 1 XP.

I wondered idly if Identifying bigger monsters gave me more skill experience. It seemed as though it should. Dismissing the distracting thought, I turned my attention to the monsters from the next floor.

> [Identification]: Dorsan Giant – Threat 41 – Properties: Adamant Skin, Skilled

There weren't many of these, fewer than twenty. But there didn't need to be many. Standing fifteen meters tall, they were armed and armored in steel. They laughed and called out to one another as they marched up the ramp, diverting out of their way to cut down the few trees that remained. A single swipe of those swords was enough to cut a tree down.

I almost mistook the penultimate monsters for their slightly smaller brethren, but Mana Sense made them look different enough to be worth an Identify.

> [Identification]: Giant Lord – Threat 42 – Properties: Adamant Skin, Skilled, Caster

Caster wasn't the only difference, though. Mana Sense was showing me a glow running over their equipment. It was too far away to lock Identify on their swords, but I could make out their armor clearly.

> [Identification]: Steel Chain mail of Elemental Resistance – Quality: Excellent – Properties: Enchantment (Elemental Resistance)

That was a nasty little joke. An enchanted item that no one else could use. And it was steel, so the enchantment would degrade over time. If it had been made out of mithril, at least—but that would have been a lot of mithril.

Finally, there was the Forsaken Giant. He was easy to pick out. At thirty meters tall, he more than stood out. It wouldn't do me any good, but I Identified him anyway. How often would I get the chance?

> [Identification]: The Forsaken Giant – Threat 43 – Properties: Adamant Skin, Skilled, Call of the Forsaken

Could Finley fight all this? I didn't know, but I didn't think so. Maybe back where Kaito was, they could manage some sort of defense. Most of the larger monsters here would need to go up that ramp in single file. Could the monsters climb the cliffs to get around their positions? I found the idea disturbingly plausible.

The real problem was those skilled monsters. Skills were a multiplier for monsters, just like us. When they were multiplying those enormous Threat values, they generated immense skill totals. I had been feeling pretty safe with a 450 skill total in my Invisibility spell. Monsters weren't renowned for their intelligence, so having one generate a higher Perception total than that seemed unlikely.

However, with a skill, a threat forty monster would only need a skill and intelligence of four each to see past my spell. That was much more likely.

The same went for combat skills. Kaito and her company were already being pressed by threat 33 monsters. Taking the threat up to forty would be nasty enough, but even a low skill would double the skill total of a rampaging monster.

If your crazy plan works, they won't have to fight, I reminded myself. I started heading down again, staying fairly close to the edge. The horde below was mostly concentrated in the center of the ramp, so with a bit of luck, I might be able to sneak past them. I didn't stay right on the edge, though, in case I could be spotted from below as I approached.

I wasn't running now. Even if it made no sound, I was too nervous about what was ahead to run towards it. When the first of the giant cats slipped out of the forest ahead, I nearly pissed myself.

The giant tiger that paced its way towards me wasn't that tall. Not compared to what was to come. But it was still *taller than me*, and it was built to be much closer to the ground than I was. Now I knew what a mouse felt like.

It didn't register my presence, though. I moved to the side, and it just kept on walking, its tail lashing from side to side. You can bet I steered well clear of *that*.

The other animals were close behind, though I didn't come close enough to see an elephant. The ogres, too, I was able to avoid. They made so much noise, it was easy to keep my distance.

The greater ogres, though, were organized enough to have scouts, and they were skilled.

"Enemy sighted! Pursuing!" The shout came from ahead of me, I couldn't see from where. I'd been out-stealthed by a giant, how embarrassing. I didn't stop to try and find him. Nor did I pause to note how, again, even monster languages got translated into intelligibility for me. I just ran, as fast as I could, for the edge.

How many skills does he have? I thought to myself. I didn't have any way of figuring it out, but my brain apparently needed something to worry about while I fled. Monsters didn't normally have many skills, but monsters weren't normally this powerful. *Three, five, or maybe even more?*

He had Perception, that was clear. And he probably had a weapon skill. But did he have Run? That was the question of the next five seconds. I wasn't far away from the edge, but the ogre scout had legs that were longer than my entire body—if I stretched my arms out. He *had* to be faster than me. I might have startled him by running; that *might* have given me a second's head start.

I heard a crashing from behind me, but I didn't turn around, didn't even jink to the side. There was no time. If I heard a swoosh of a club, I'd try Jumping, but I didn't think I'd get the chance. There was—

There was clear light in front of me. I jumped. I heard a swoosh behind me, and then I was in the open air.

Jump before you hear the swoosh, that's the way to do it, I thought, crazily. There was a lot of open air below me, but I took the time to glance back. The ogre hadn't followed me. His head was about the same level as mine now, as my Jump had reached the top of its arc. I was already falling, though, and he would soon be far above me.

I took a second to concentrate and materialized a potion into my hand. It wouldn't do to mess up and drop it. Plus, I wanted to get a bit of distance from that ogre. Hitting the ground would hurt, but maybe not as much as getting hit by that club.

He watched me frowning. Actually, that might have been his default expression. It was barely a moment before I was out of reach of anything he might do, so I drank the potion of Feather-fall.

Twenty-five gold down the drain, I thought sourly, but it was better than being pulverized into mush. As the magic took hold, I stopped accelerating downwards and started to coast. I wasn't exactly like a falling feather. I stopped accelerating, but the velocity I'd gained from my few seconds of fall stayed with me. I made a note for future usage. If I took the potion before I fell, then I'd drift down slowly, but if I took it while falling at terminal velocity, I would still be boned. Maybe I'd slow from air resistance?

This . . . wasn't too bad. I had a kilometer or two to fall, so doing it at a decent speed would save me some time. And my current speed wasn't so high that Jump couldn't absorb the landing. Probably.

It looked as though I wouldn't make it all the way to the bottom, anyway. At least, not uninterrupted. I still had my sideways velocity from my jump, and it was taking me slowly across the central shaft. Like dropping something down a stairwell, you had to be careful that you dropped straight down, or you'd bounce off the railings.

In my case, I gently impacted the cliff under the ramp at about two turns down. That wasn't too bad. I used Jump again to push myself off. It gave me a bit of a spin, but I managed to correct it before hitting the ground.

I tried for a proper heroic three-point landing, but it's more difficult than they make it look. Jump doesn't help with looking cool. Instead, I absorbed the impact with a slightly embarrassing tumble and another fifteen hit points.

I looked over at the exit. It was easy to see. There was no sign of a boss chamber, just a gaping hole big enough for the Forsaken Giant to crawl through. If my speculation was right, there should be nothing between me and the final floor.

FİNAL FLOOR

The fifteenth floor started with a waterfall. Two of them, actually. They started from holes in the wall, high up in the chamber, and fell down on either side of the entrance, about a kilometer below. Below the waterfalls, that is. I was right at the entrance staring out at the jungle that spread out before me.

Even without the monsters it normally contained, the jungle would have been an obstacle in its own right. Thick undergrowth to slow me, giant vines to trip me up, and who knows what poisonous or even monstrous plants to deal with. Fortunately, the army of giants had trampled a wide path through all the dangers. Much like I'd seen them doing above, they had cut or knocked down countless trees and trampled the rest of the undergrowth into the mud.

Just as well, since I'm in a hurry.

I started running. There weren't any shortcuts to take on this level, but at least the path was clear. I followed it down the slope of this, the first sub-level, and down the ramp that connected it to the next slope. This floor consisted of four of these sloping sub-levels. The undersides of each sub-level were lit, probably for the plants' benefit. They formed a green and tangled defense in depth and would have prevented me from continuing if it weren't for the path.

Getting to the bottom, I saw that once again, the boss chamber had been removed, and the way forward was clear. I hurried on.

The sixteenth floor consisted of about thirty "islands" that were "suspended" in the air. The reason for those scare quotes was that they all actually jutted out at various angles from the chamber wall. It was still a remarkable feat of engineering—if it wasn't all done with magic—and it made for a remarkable view from the entrance. I think that this was the most amazing sight that I'd seen so far. All the different islands, each with their own distinctive flora . . . they weren't arranged in a spiral leading down this time, they seemed to be arranged in no particular pattern.

Getting from one island to another was via a system of bridges and ladders constructed by the ogres who lived on this level. There were small villages on some of the islands, hunting and edible plants on others. I imagined the bridges were strong enough for the giants to have taken, but I had difficulty imagining that the Forsaken Giant climbed up that way without breaking them.

Then I noticed the vertical trail of pockmarks in the chamber wall nearby. That word makes them sound small, but when I wandered over to take a look at the closest one, it was big enough for me to crawl into.

Fist marks, I realized. The Giant had punched handholds in the wall and climbed up it. I wouldn't be able to take that route, as I wasn't thirty meters tall, so I turned back to the islands. I had to plot a route down, or at least get an idea of one.

I could follow the trail, but the damage wasn't as obvious here. The paths and the bridges were scaled for ogre bodies, and giants weren't that much bigger than them. They *were* that much bigger than me, though, which made traversing the rope bridges somewhat challenging at times.

What was, to an ogre, a series of closely spaced planks to walk on was, to me, a walkway of crudely hewn tree trunks spaced more than two feet apart. At least being supported by ropes two feet thick gave it a comforting feel of stability.

I ran, jumped, and climbed my way down the chain of islands without incident and continued to the level below.

The seventeenth floor was much like the ones previous, except that the ledges were arranged differently and connected with ladders instead of bridges. This was the level of skilled ogres, and it showed in the construction of their village. Instead of crude lean-tos, they had proper primitive huts and cultivated fields. The giants had trampled right through them, but I was sure they'd get rebuilt at some stage.

Getting through this floor wasn't as simple as climbing down endless ladders, though. There were two points where I had to travel *up*, to move along the chamber wall and access the ladders that led farther down. It was a pain, especially since I couldn't climb these ladders normally. Standing on one rung, I couldn't reach the next one if I stretched my arms out. I *could* have jumped, but one mistake would have seen me fall to the bottom. So I climbed down, and occasionally up, the support ropes.

It was hard going, and I eventually ran out of stamina. It wasn't all bad, though.

[Climbing] Level 4 acquired through use.

For gaining a skill level, you have been awarded 1 XP.

I was raking in those skill levels.

By now, I thought, *Finley should have retreated back to where Kaito is.*

Would the Giant have reached them yet? Maybe. He hadn't been moving particularly quickly. If he had reached them, would he take the ramp, or would he just climb up the wall again? The ramp was wide enough for the Giant, but he might want to take a more direct route . . . or he might want to eliminate the annoying insects that were irritating its master.

I worried about them as I watched my stamina tick up. Kaito was no doubt expecting me to come through in the nick of time, but that would be a lot easier if I knew when that was. Could I risk going any faster? I didn't have any more Feather-fall potions. I did have two Spider-climb ones, but they wouldn't make me that much faster going down. And I might need them going up.

It took twenty minutes of resting to get my Stamina pool back to half full. I doubted I could afford the time, but I didn't have any choice. I pressed on.

The giants of the eighteenth level lived in proper houses, each placed on a separate platform. Perhaps the right word was spar. Each spar was relatively narrow, perhaps fifty meters across. They stretched across the entire chamber, crisscrossing it at random angles like swords in the magician's trick box.

There *were* ladders between the spars, but it looked as if they were all at opposite ends. Taking them would have meant running along each spar until I found my way down. Instead, I decided to jump down from spar to spar. They were clustered so thickly, I thought it would be safe.

You have taken 50 damage!

So, not entirely safe, I thought, picking myself off the ground. But I still had healing potions, and this was much faster than running. *Two more floors to go.*

To my surprise, I entered the nineteenth floor at the bottom. Or, almost the bottom. From the way the floor sloped gently away, I couldn't be at the very bottom of the chamber. But, given how high the ceiling was, way above, I knew that I wasn't far from it.

Five castles stood on this gentle slope. Or so they appeared to me. I suppose to the giant lords that normally occupied them, they were just cozy cottages. Filled with loot and magic and enchanted traps; I didn't have time for them today. Walking past them would normally be a sure-fire way of attracting their occupants, but no one was home today.

I started running, headed for the giant door that I could easily see from three kilometers away. The home of the Forsaken Giant, the final boss of bosses for this dungeon.

It was standing open. That was fortunate—I didn't think that I'd be able to open the thing, no matter my magically enhanced strength, or how well it was balanced. It was fifty meters high, taller even than the Giant and almost a meter thick. I gave it an experimental shove as I passed—nothing. Then I noticed there was a gap between it and the floor that I could have crawled through like a mouse.

The door opened onto a Great Hall. Great by giant standards, so ridiculously enormous by mine. There were columns and doors leading off to the side, but I, again, wasn't interested in clearing the place. I needed to go where the final encounter would be, which wasn't this room. I pressed forward, using Run to get across the endless expanse of marble floor.

Another huge door, too big for me to move, would have barred my way if it hadn't already been left open. Behind it was the throne room, easily identified by the massive edifice of stone and iron that was shaped a bit like a throne. It looked more like an architectural conceit by a mad genius . . . but I could see how it could be sat on, if you were thirty meters tall.

That was where the Giant would be found, so my goal would be behind it. I started to Run again, having plenty of room to work up to a good speed. I slowed as I approached, and made sure to examine everything with Mana Sense. It wouldn't do to trigger a trap at this point.

But there were no traps, no magic fields. Just a human-sized door set into the rear of the base of the throne. Beyond that, the core.

I eyed it warily. I had some idea now of how stupid I'd been when I stole my first core. Stupidly lucky, really. I still didn't know what I was doing, but I knew there were a few things I had to avoid.

Taking possession, for one. It wasn't a matter of touching it with bare flesh, I was pretty sure. I'd been wearing gloves and armor when I stole

Rhis, and there had still been a possession attempt. If any of those stories of adventurers disappearing into thin air were true, then most of those adventurers would have been wearing gloves.

It was, I thought, the System at work. It noted when a person had taken, or attempted to take, the core, and acted on that basis. So I needed to avoid triggering that decision.

The second thing I needed to steer clear of was collapsing the mana construct. No one really knew what that would entail, but no one wanted to find out.

Keeping all that in mind, I slowly approached the core. It looked bigger than Rhis had looked, back then, but not by much. It was perched on a pedestal, same as Rhis was then—and was now, back in our makeshift dungeon. I wasn't sure why the core needed to be placed just so—I could see mana connections coming out in all directions—but all the cores I'd seen were like that.

[Phantasmal Object].

I had to cast the spell twice to get what I wanted. With one spell, I created a support column; with another, I constructed a lopsided beam balance. On one side, the beam extended over the core, secured to it by leather straps. On the other side, the more traditional pan that you might expect to see on a set of scales like this.

I paused. I was touching the core with something of mine . . . but I had no real control over it. It was just an object. Static. A decoration, really.

Nothing happened. No notifications, no disappearing. A positive result.

[Phantasmal Object].

I made a bowling ball and dropped it in the pan. The pan jerked down, the core jerked up.

> **Dungeon core has been removed from the external mana construct. Five minutes before the external construct unravels.**

The pan hit the ground, and the bowling ball rolled out of the pan. The core fell back into place.

> **Dungeon core has been replaced. Normal operations will resume.**

This time, there was no notification about losing my corporal form, or of taking over the dungeon. And I remained un-disappeared.

Then another notification came.

Outbreak Defense Completed

Accumulated Experience: 5,749,690

Contribution: 31.41%

Awarded Experience: 1,805,978

You have gained a Level!

You have been awarded 5 Development Points.

You have been awarded 2 Skill Points.

іптеrⲖⲨⅮΕ 2

Kaito watched as Duke Finley and his party reentered the chamber far below. He was about fifteen minutes ahead of the giant beasts that were following him, but he was moving fast. In those fifteen minutes, he'd managed to cover at least a kilometer of distance, some of it straight up. It would only take another ten minutes to reach them.

"Get ready," he told the others, but with no real urgency. The monsters would take longer to arrive. They were taking the long spiral up the side. They moved quickly, but they had about thirty kilometers to travel before reaching them. It was too bad that Nori was out of arrows, or she could have taken potshots at them as they travelled.

There was a murmur from his girls to show him that they'd heard, but they all knew that the most important thing to do now was rest and recover their Stamina and Mana pools. Still, they made the effort to look alert when the Duke arrived. His disapproving gaze swept over them all.

"Where's the King's doxy?" he asked.

It took Kaito a moment to realize who Finley was talking about, and then another moment to choke down his angry words at such disrespect. None of the other girls spoke, they were letting her deal with the matter, but Kaito could feel the furious glares they were giving the Duke. The Duke ignored them, waiting for his answer.

"She . . . went back," Kaito finally said. It was the answer that Kandis would have wanted her to give. She didn't want credit, and she didn't want the Duke to know *anything*. Kaito had once thought that she was exaggerating about the attempts at killing her, but since meeting the Duke, Kaito knew that Finley would have ordered Kandis's death without hesitation.

"You should have followed her," Finley sneered. "We're pulling back."

"Why? Isn't this position defensible?"

"It's being bypassed," Finley said. He stepped back and gestured for Kaito to look. The giants were coming through now, behind the ogres who were now . . . *not* taking the ramp. They were climbing down the rocky cliff, and their lead elements were now walking straight across the chamber floor.

"They'll climb straight up when they reach the other side," Finley said. "Best case is that they attack us from two sides, but it's more likely that they'll just leave us behind."

As Kaito nodded understanding, what had to be the Forsaken Giant came through the lower entrance. He was so large that he had to *crawl* through. Kaito gulped, wondering what it would be like to fight that thing.

"Will we hold the entrance, then?" she asked. "Fight them as they climb the cliff?"

"We'll see," Finley said. "If the dungeon's *thinking*, it will hold them off until the animals can give them cover."

"*Does* it think?" Kaito asked.

"Sometimes it does," Finley answered. "We'll just have to see."

Aghen Shadthe was having a bath. Not, as those familiar with the tales about him might assume, an ice water bath. The water was steaming hot and the tub was not made out of his signature black ice but carved out of a single piece of marble. Given its massive size, it would have been a work of singular craftsmanship, were it not for the fact that it was, like everything in the room and the room itself, a product of his dungeon.

Ice had its uses, to be sure. It made a better construction material than what you might expect, once it was magically prevented from melting. His headquarters wasn't known as Ice Mountain for nothing. He had wrapped acres of ice around his tower, creating a tall, slippery slope. It served as both a physical deterrent and a warning. Any who trespassed farther would feel the icy might of Aghen Shadthe.

However, his dungeon itself used very little ice. He didn't feel the cold, but his *attendants* definitely did. Like the two lovely ladies washing him right now. As the idle thought crossed his mind, he cast the barest whisper of a spell on them. After all, he might forbid any of his people from taking Cold Resistance, and his school might inculcate total obedience and loyalty into his attendants from birth, but it never hurt to *check*.

The girls squealed as the icy cold rippled across their naked bodies, but they never stopped sopping his body, and they certainly didn't complain.

He watched them closely for their more *physical* reactions. Anyone could squeal but hardened nipples and goosebumps were much harder to fake.

Satisfied, he allowed them to warm their bodies against his. Had there been time, he would have taken advantage of their increased fervor, but he was expecting a report. Correctly identifying his lack of interest, the girls held off and finished rinsing and drying him without further attempts at arousing him.

He made an approving note to himself as they dressed him. The school ensured loyalty, but not every one of its products were *bright* enough to serve him independently. It took close observation over a period of time to determine just how well a particular attendant could identify his needs. Those that could identify whatever he happened to want at the moment were sufficient to serve him in the tower. Much rarer were those who could *anticipate* his desires. These few were sent out as his emissaries.

As for those who failed, well, there was always a need for more people to toil in the lower reaches of his dungeon. They also served.

Once his robes were properly arranged around him, the girls quickly slipped on some revealing silk dresses. One wore a pale red, the other a turquoise blue. Nodding in satisfaction, he gestured for them to follow him. It was time for another test.

Sitting down in front of the communication item, he waited for Manuela to make contact. His attendants draped themselves decoratively at his side, intuiting that he wanted them to observe this conversation.

Manuela was prompt, of course.

"Master," she said, dropping her gaze to the ground once she had seen his face.

"Manuela. Report," he said warmly.

"Alexandros has sent all the Champions into Duke Finley's dungeon. There's no official word coming out of the castle, but the assumption there is that the Duke has entered the dungeon as well."

"Perhaps this will start a new trend. Going into a breaking dungeon? How amusing."

Manuela smiled at his small jest, and his two attendants shifted slightly to let him know they were amused without interrupting him with something as indecorous as laughter. Seeing that her master had no further comment, Manuela continued her report.

"The majority of the King's elites are no longer to be found in the palace," she said. "Kayla reports sighting twelve intense magical pulses from the central palace. I can't prove anything, but . . ."

"That suggests that the elites have gone to help defend King's Isle," Aghen finished for her.

"Yes, my Master," Manuela agreed. "If twelve were sent, it suggests that no one higher than level five is left in the castle. Aside from the King, of course—he's been sighted."

"Of course. There would be no way he could leave his capital at such a delicate time. Everything seems to be proceeding according to plan. Instruct Kayla to proceed with the second obelisk at the arranged time. That is all."

"Yes, Master," Manuela said reverently. She bowed and ended the communication.

"So," Aghen addressed his girls. "*Are* things proceeding to plan?"

The one in blue frowned with concentration. "Isn't it bad that the Champions are moving in concert? And against us, at that."

"The dungeon break was Lord Ashmor's play," the one in red replied. "It's only natural that the gods would make a move against it . . . but it was only ever a distraction on our part."

"Won't Lord Ashmor require more effort from Master to help with his ploy?"

"No . . ." the one in red looked uncertain, glancing at Aghen for confirmation. "Lord Ashmor's deal was strictly confined to that one action, was it not?"

Aghen nodded. "He has already fulfilled his half of the bargain. Quickly, as is his wont. He may come back with another deal, but if the terms are too onerous, we can always complain to the others."

The one in red nodded, satisfied. "Then, having the Champions in the dungeon only helps us. Either they will die and take themselves out of the equation, or they will be stuck in the dungeon for days, unable to interfere."

"We still don't know if the elites have actually left," the attendant in blue warned. "He might have sent any twelve of his men to fool us."

"Perhaps," the one in red agreed. "But he can hardly ignore the threat to his home territories. With Master able to project his magic through the portal, he can project a considerable threat without leaving his tower."

"True," Aghen agreed. That was the true value of the Order. Every one of his emissaries possessed the means to summon his attention, which dealt with most matters. More serious situations might require his magic, delivered from a portal at a safe distance from the conflict. Since he had set up this system, there had never been an occasion requiring him to actually step through the portal, leaving his precious dungeon.

The King also had his teleportation network, of course. But this would be a naval battle, and the King was never going to risk one of his nodes by putting it on a ship. His men would teleport out to the island and then set sail. Every hour they travelled would be another hour that they could not come to the King's aid.

"That still leaves the King," Red warned. "He is supposed to be level eight, yes?"

"I wouldn't want to face him in a sword fight, true," Aghen said. "But his primary abilities lie in empowering his followers. With no real power-houses at his disposal, his own power is greatly constrained. And he has not yet divined how this conflict is being fought. He should be easily dealt with."

The fortifications had seemed so impressive to Zichy when they'd arrived at the dinosaur level. Zichy wasn't sure how Kaito knew they were dino-saurs. She had said that there *weren't* any where she came from. Zichy had Identified them, of course, and while some of them had "saur" in their names, not all of them had. And none of them had "dino." So that was a mystery.

The fortifications had seemed good, though. She didn't know much about defenses, but when they'd all arrived at the fort, Vassi had worked with the Duke's Stone Mage to build the walls even higher. Then Finley's Arcanist had reinforced them with ice, making the outsides slick and cold and spiky.

Things had gone well at first. The beasts tried jumping up, but the walls were too high and slick. The ogres didn't fare much better. The walls were now taller than them, almost reaching to the ceiling. The ones with clubs could shatter the ice, but it just grew back. They were holding, but they weren't doing much killing. The ogres were just too tough! Any wounds Zichy managed to make were just light cuts. Given enough time, that would take an ogre down, but the giants were right behind.

The ones with axes took the lead, shoving the ogres aside and cutting into the wall with axes. Axes were for wood, not stone, but that rule prob-ably didn't apply when the axe head was bigger than she was.

The wall Zichy was on exploded under the blows, like a particularly flaky pastry. This was a lot messier than that. Stone, ice, and blood was fly-ing everywhere, and Nori could only hope that the blood didn't belong to anyone she knew. The wall disappeared from under her and things started looking bad.

Then Ettalle was there. Grabbing Zichy as she fell and snatching her out of the way of a big piece of wall that had somehow gotten *above* her. They landed on the ground with bits of rubble falling around them.

"Get out of here," Ettalle ordered. "You can't dodge!"

That seemed like a great idea, so Zichy didn't bother pointing out that all the rocks were on the ground now, or that Ettalle's Agility wasn't *that* much better than hers. The ogres were clambering through the gaps in the wall now, towering over Zichy, and looking as if they'd want to grab her up and eat her like a pastry.

Then the notification came. Zichy couldn't read, so she didn't know what it said. But she knew what it meant, or thereabouts. It was telling her that she had done a good job and that the dungeon event was now over and that she had gotten her experience as a reward. That seemed nice.

Not everyone seemed as pleased, though. Zichy's attention was mostly on the ogres and giants, who had turned around and were heading back down into the dungeon. Zichy didn't know monsters would do that, and she wasn't entirely sure they wouldn't turn around. But Duke Finley was worth paying attention to, especially when he seemed mad.

Now he was staring at thin air and looked madder than Zichy had seen him so far.

"Twenty-five percent!" he yelled, but Zichy didn't know what he was talking about.

TRIUMPHANT RETURN

I blinked for a little bit at the notification. Only a short while, but longer than I should have. Dungeons were dangerous places, after all.

I could feel my Mana and Stamina return with a rush, as well as the few points of Health that I hadn't bothered taking a potion for. The notification was real. I was level six, far faster than planned. Oh, and there was the small matter of saving Dorsay from the Giant. Had he disappeared, or was he just now starting to head back into his proper position?

Either way, there was no reason to stay here. I left the core room and started to jog back around the throne. When I got to the front, I stopped looking at the reward chest that was there.

Had that . . . been there before?

I hadn't been paying attention, but a quick use of Memorize showed me that no, it hadn't. It must be the reward for defeating the Giant?

Neither my past life nor my current life as an adventurer had taught me to leave money lying around, so I quickly stepped over to open it. There were two objects inside, sitting on a large pile of platinum coins. I restrained myself from grabbing them, and did a quick Identify.

The first one was a crude clay figurine of a human—or humanoid.

[Identification]: Token of the Forsaken Giant - Quality: Perfect –
Properties: Teleport to Entrance

It had been a while since I'd seen one of those. Rhis—or Oakway dungeon, rather—had used a similar system, but all of the dungeons since had made me slog all the way through the easier levels each time. Though from the sound of it, this only helped you get out, it didn't negate the need to kill your way down.

The other one was a small shield. It was too small to use as a shield, maybe twenty centimeters wide. But the shape was unmistakable. As for what it actually was . . .

> **[Identification]: Spatial Aegis – Quality: Perfect – Properties: Ward against Spatial Manipulation**
>
> **When activated, prevents or disrupts any form of Spatial Manipulation, including Teleportation and Portal Magic. The delimited space of a Mana construct is not included in the Spatial Aegis's field, but if the Shield is used inside a delimited space, it will affect any spatial manipulation within the space. Pocket dimensions with entrances within the field cannot be accessed, but are otherwise unaffected.**
>
> **Range: A radius of one meter for each point of mana in the primary mana store when activated.**
>
> **Duration: One second for each point of mana in the secondary mana store when activated.**

What the . . .

When did the descriptions start being useful? I quickly checked the Token again, along with the rest of my equipment. But the descriptions were still the same. A name, a few stats. Not . . . whatever this was.

I checked it again to make sure I hadn't been imagining things. It was still the same. I thought about checking it out but remembered that I was in a dungeon, and I didn't know if this space was spatially expanded. Preventing or disrupting that sounded bad.

Was this thing even useful? Aside from wrecking dungeons, that is, which wasn't something I had a lot of use for. I suppose it would work as additional security for my vault—it would be nice if people couldn't teleport in. Not being able to use spatial items would be annoying, though. They were very useful.

Reminded of their usefulness, I swept the coins up with my own spatial ring, after using Identify for a quick count. Twelve hundred, very nice. I put the Aegis in there as well. Unactivated, it posed no danger to the pocket dimension. Then I grabbed the Token.

I made a face that no one could see, but I didn't really have a choice here. I didn't want to leave Kaito and the others, but I *also* didn't want to face the Forsaken Giant and all his smaller friends. I'd done all I could. I activated the Token and walked out of the dungeon.

Into the sounds of cheering and celebration, which confused me for a bit. Then I realized that all the soldiers here were part of the event, and would have been notified about it ending. A celebration was to be expected.

What was less expected was them ignoring me, standing in the corpse-strewn courtyard, locked in and surrounded by the defenses. It took a moment for me to realize that I was still invisible. I started to cancel the spell but reconsidered.

Was it possible for me to get out of here, *without* letting them know that I was here? It was going to take the others hours to get out of the dungeon. Since they didn't actually know where I was, it would be hours more before anyone started looking for me. I could have a whole day before the King found me to throw me at some other pressing problem. He still had this Aghen Shadthe attack and who knows what other problems.

I eyed the wall judiciously. It wasn't designed for climbing, quite the opposite. Quite a lot of it was covered in blood, or ichor, or both, which only made things harder. But its main anti-climbing feature—lots of men with pointy objects poking climbers—wasn't applicable in my case.

Looking up, I could see a lot of gouges in the wall. They would make good handholds. I found what looked like a good place and climbed right up. I listened out for any cries of "What's that!" but no one was paying attention.

Nice work, I told myself as I stood on the battlements—or were they crenellations? *I can just walk out of here.*

And so it proved. There was a clear path from the inner courtyard to the outer gate. Blocked by gates, but these were wide open at the moment. The actual outer gate was closed, but there was a smaller one that stood open, letting supplies in under the watchful eye of a guard.

Not watchful enough, of course. I slipped past, through a gap in the traffic, and I was back in the city. Rather than report to the King, I headed straight for my dungeon.

The streets were remarkably normal, considering all that was going on. People were going about their business as normal, with maybe just a bit of extra gossip. I got to overhear a lot of speculation about just what was going on. They didn't seem to have announced the Dungeon Break, or who had been sent to stop it. Nor had any announcement been made about the fighting . . . was it two nights earlier, or three? I had lost track of time.

I let Greater Invisibility end somewhere along the way. I attracted a few looks, but that was better than constantly dodging foot traffic. Once I was visible, people cleared out of my way. I was dressed in my adventuring gear, and while I wasn't covered in blood, I wasn't exactly clean. I must have looked pretty dangerous, and I still hadn't worked out how to restrain my level six aura.

There were two kids keeping watch at the front door of the Gilded Lily. They started when they saw me and disappeared inside.

"Headmistress is back!" I heard them yelling from behind the door. I raised an eyebrow but decided to just keep walking. They hadn't *shut* the door, so I closed it behind me. Then I remembered about the lights.

I left one Light spell in the lobby and then took another with me. I could see maybe five kids hiding on the staircase and in what had been shadowed corners.

"Shouldn't you be at lessons?" I said mildly, which triggered a stampede for the dungeon entrance.

[Intimidate] Level 3 acquired through use.

For gaining a skill level, you have been awarded 1 XP.

I face down a Duke and stop him from killing me, but I get the point for sending a bunch of kids running. That's messed up.

I knew it was probably the case that I'd gotten the *majority* of the level for facing off with Finley, and it was only the last few points that had come from the children. But it still felt bad.

I pressed on, looking for a responsible adult. Rhis appeared as soon as I crossed the threshold. So I was still looking. I kept walking and he fell in beside me.

"Mistress! You've returned! Welcome back to your domain!"

"Thanks, Rhis," I said wearily. "Have you managed to avoid killing anyone since I left?"

"Yes, Mistress, I can report no casualties!" he said proudly.

"Well done," I said warmly. "Injuries?"

"I thought casualties included injuries," he said, frowning. "But nonetheless, while there have been some bumps and scrapes, Mistress Felicia was on hand to eliminate them."

"That's good." People here had a different attitude towards injuries than I was used to, and I couldn't say it was wrong—at least when there was a Healer at hand. "What doesn't kill you raises your Body Development" wasn't a real saying, but it should have been.

Rhis leaned in conspiratorially. I'm not sure why, since I was the only one that could see him. "I think she's trying to gain favor with the children—as part of a plot to take over your role of Headmistress."

"She can have it," I said easily, knowing that Felicia was trying no such thing. "Who is here right now?"

"All but four of the children are at their assigned duties," he told me. "The Fire Mage is taking people through the monster section, along with her servant. Cutter is playing in the weapons room, and the jumping one is in the main classroom."

"Jumping one? You mean Isabel," I said, working it out just as I reached the main classroom.

"If you say so. She's been here more than the others . . . trying to learn your secrets."

I nodded absently, then entered the room. Isabel was there, going over some of the texts with the children. She wasn't startled by my entrance— the kids had provided some warning. She did get a little nervous as she took in my appearance.

"Hi, Isabel," I said. "I'm just passing through on my way to bed. Can you get Cutter to take a message to Felicity and Kyle, to let them know that I'm out of the dungeon and everything's about as fine as can be expected."

"I think they'll want to know more than *that*," Isabel said. "Are the other Champions all right? Is the monster defeated? Shouldn't you be at the palace?"

"Just let me get a few hours sleep, and I'll be ready to answer questions," I pleaded. "Or maybe a few days."

"If you say so," she agreed, doubtfully. I grinned and made my retreat to the next floor.

"My room is where I left it?" I asked Rhis.

"Of course," he said. "I've taken the liberty of adding a few improvements. Did you want me to get the bath ready before bed?"

"I don't think—wait, no, I absolutely do," I told him, after checking my state. Sure, I could conceal all this with a Disguise spell, but a hot bath was a much better solution.

"Then your stateroom awaits," Rhis said grandly, gesturing at the door. I glanced at him warily before opening it. The room inside was different from before.

He'd decorated it to my tastes. The wood paneling that was the definition of good taste here had been replaced by the cool white expanse of plastered walls. There was a modern wall-to-wall carpet. The bed, which had been a fairly spartan affair before was now a sinfully thick mattress, contained within an intricately carved mahogany frame. Soft pillows and sheets called out to me, but my attention was stolen by the half-open door at the other end. Steam was wafting out from my ensuite bathroom.

I sighed. "Can you take care of my armor? Clean it and stuff?" I asked.

"Like it was new," Rhis assured me.

"That sounds great," I said, heading to the bathroom while undoing straps. "And this . . ." I stopped, half undressed, and picked up a glass bottle of pink goo. "Is this shampoo?"

"There is a wide selection of . . . lesser treasure available in my catalogues," Rhis explained. "I'm not sure if you'll find this suitable, but it should be adequate."

"Well, I'll just have to try it out," I said, glancing over at the other bottles. "This is really nice, Rhis; you've done well."

"Thank you, Mistress."

"And now, I think I'd like some quiet time." The last of my clothes fell to the floor, disappearing when they touched it. It felt a little odd to be naked in front of Rhis, but I knew the presence of his avatar didn't actually affect his ability to sense me. "Can you remove your avatar and don't communicate with me until I ask for you, or it's an emergency."

"As you wish, Mistress," Rhis said and faded from view.

I sank into the bath and gave another sigh of contentment.

Hopefully, I thought, *I can go eight hours without another emergency.*

EMERGENCY

This is *hardly* an emergency. The situation is actually highly beneficial."

"To you, maybe, but all you care about is guzzling up mana." That was Janie's voice. Coming from behind the door . . . to my room . . . where I was . . . had been sleeping.

Damn.

I looked around. The first thing that I saw was my clothes, cleaned and neatly folded. My armor was there as well, but I didn't think I'd need that right away.

"Why am I arguing with an illusion anyway?" Janie asked rhetorically. She started banging on the door. "Kandis!"

"Stop that, you lunatic!"

"I'm up!" I called out as I pulled on my shirt. That and pants would have to do. Until I found out what was going on, I was going to stay here and enjoy clean carpet under bare feet. I headed to the door, still a bit groggy. I'd gotten *some* rest, at least.

Opening the door revealed Rhis and Janie, the latter fully armored up. I smiled at her in greeting, and then directed a question at Rhis.

"How long was I sleeping for?"

"Five hours and nine minutes, Mistress," he said. "I tried to stop this maniac from waking you, but I was unable to use lethal force." He gave me some of his puppy-fox eyes, as if that was going to make me give him permission to murder my friends.

Janie, meanwhile, was looking past me. "Nice!" she said, glancing over at Rhis. "Sucking up to the Mistress, huh?"

"Of course!" Rhis said, sounding offended "I exist to serve her, after all." He let the illusion end, leaving behind his avatar, visible only to me.

"Mistress," he said. "I suspect that if I hadn't stopped them, this one would have attempted to assassinate you. Her stated reasons for approaching you were farcical, and—"

"That's enough, Rhis," I said wearily. I looked Janie up and down and said, "I guess you'd better come in and tell me about this emergency. Wait—are your shoes clean?"

"Of course," she said, grinning. "There's nothing like a burst of cleansing fire to take care of monster bits."

I looked at her suspiciously, and then down the corridor. Ash was just as bad, if not worse, for my carpet, but she hadn't left any blackened footprints.

"All right," I said, and let her into my room. I led her over to Rhis's best approximation of a modern couch that was gracing one corner of the room. It wasn't an illusion—he'd spent real mana on this—so he'd had to work with existing designs of this world. Janie gave it a long look, but sat down without incident. Rhis stood next to her, looking as if he would like to tackle her.

"The problem is, there's been another case of sabotage of one of the obelisks."

I prodded my sleepy brain into operation. "That's . . . not my problem?" I tried. "I don't mind if the nobles are getting less mana. The general populace barely even noticed the first one."

"They'll notice this one," Janie said darkly. "But something you've missed—the mana doesn't go to the nobles, it goes to their *dungeons*. Remember how they were worried about whatshisfaces's broken dungeon running out of mana? If they lose enough mana, that could happen to any of the dungeons."

"This is nonsense," Rhis interjected. "I've never seen so much mana as we have right now."

"Rhis, make an appearance if you want to take part in this discussion," I said. He pouted, but did so, and repeated his objection.

"I thought you'd taken off," was all that Janie said.

"As if I'd let you confuse Mistress with your foolishness," he spat back.

I sighed. "He wanted to talk to me without you hearing, and he knows I don't like it when he doubles up. It gives me a headache."

"Right. Anyway, you might be getting more mana, but those other dungeons are getting mana spoon-fed to them. If that feed cuts off, having a bit more ambient mana isn't going to save them."

"Rhis, could you maintain twenty levels with what you're getting right now?" I asked.

"No," he admitted.

"So another dungeon collapse is a real possibility," I said. "Still, I don't see what I can do about that, especially if the King's people can't manage to."

Janie nodded. "The other problem, well, it's easier to show you than tell you. We need to go up on the roof."

I sighed. It looked as though I would be putting on shoes after all.

I'd been expecting something like it from Janie's description, but actually *seeing* it was a slap in the face. Having *two* massive mana conduits spewing the building blocks of magic all over the place was much more than just twice the mess. Even more amazing were the people on the streets, most of them going about their day as if nothing was happening.

"You see it, don't you?" Janie asked, standing beside me on the roof.

"Yeah," I said, looking at the mess.

One loose mana conduit had been like vomiting on the floor. Or perhaps a better analogy, given the inherent *stringiness* of some of the mana, was an endless stream of pasta and sauce. It had poured out over the city, some of it dispersing, some of it sticking, some of it just . . . flowing around. *Clean* and *orderly* weren't terms you could use for the process, but it essentially flowed from one point and dispersed.

With *two* sources . . . they mixed. Waves of mana crashed into one another; strings of mana twisted around one another. It was turbulent, a whole other order of confusion and mixing mana.

"When mana gets twisted up into knots," I said, recalling one of the first things I'd learned about this world. "You get spawn points."

"Big ones, too," Janie agreed. "They haven't spawned yet, but it won't be rats like they get in the sewers. I reckon anywhere up to threat twenty."

I shuddered to think about it. The guards must be preparing a response, but even so . . . there would be a massacre.

"I guess we need to head to the Guild," I said.

I did a few other things as I got my armor on. I instructed Rhis to use his extra mana to construct weapons for the kids, but to distribute them only through Isabel. I told Isabel what was going on, and that she might have to lead the kids to fight off invading monsters.

"Can't we just hide in the dungeon?"

"No," I said with a grimace. "You need to protect Rhis, and keep any monsters from getting in. If any of them do, Rhis will probably go mad and try to kill everyone."

If she looked nervous before, she looked distinctly worried now.

"Thick walls," I said reassuringly. "You've got strong stone walls, which will help. Barricade everything, arm anyone who will fight. We're going to see if there's anything we can do about this, but if we *can't*, we'll come back to defend you. If you think you've got somewhere safer to run to, then by all means go there."

Isabel nodded, and I could tell that she was frantically thinking of somewhere she *could* run to. I gave her a moment to come up with something, only acting when I saw despair bloom across her face.

Fuck it. I didn't want to do stuff like this, but it was going to increase her—and everyone's—chances of survival.

"You can do this," I said with the intensity that only Persuasion could give. "You're strong, and these kids are depending on you. You won't let them down."

Determination replaced distress on her face. It would only last a day, but that should be long enough. I gave a few last minute orders, and then we headed out.

"Congratulations on the level, by the way," Janie said as we jogged through the streets. "I guess that was part of what you meant by things going well?"

"I did all right," I admitted. "I doubt the Duke will be pleased when he figures out it was me that took a third of the experience for the break."

Janie whistled. "That'd do it, all right. Did you actually beat the Giant?"

I quickly filled Janie in on what I'd actually done, to her amusement. As we got closer to the Guild, I saw more worried looks on faces. People were talking urgently to one another, and I heard "monster attack" being said more than once.

"People are starting to talk," I said. "The palace had better make an announcement soon or there'll be panic."

Things were decidedly more panicky in the Guild Hall. A large proportion of adventurers had Mana Sense and had worked out what was going on. The receptionist was stonewalling a group of people demanding answers. They were a mixed bunch of fives and sixes, but they didn't have my Charisma.

"Make way, please," I said. The words were mild, but Persuasion turned them into a whip. The crowd parted hastily, but Persuasion crashed ineffectually into the Guild's Bureaucracy.

"The Guild Master is unavailable at this time," she repeated primly. I smiled and switched to my own Bureaucracy skill.

"I think you'll find that the Guild Master left instructions that I was to have access to him in an emergency," I said. "My name is Kandis Hammond."

"Ah ... yes ... Member Hammond ..." The girl twitched as her defenses abandoned her and left her open to Persuasion. Bullying the lower levels wasn't my style, but I really didn't have time for this.

"I'm afraid that the Guild Master isn't here," she admitted.

"Where is he?" I pressed.

"He's . . . on a quest for the King," she said, the words dragged out of her.

A quest? What on earth—oh. It took me a second to figure it out, but I managed not to blurt out what I'd just worked out. The Guild Master was one of the King's high-level elites. He'd been sent to face Aghen over at the King's Isle.

That meant that the King had access to teleportation, or some other way of fast travel. I doubted even griffins would get his forces there in time. That was hardly a surprise, though. Who else was more likely to have teleportation than the King? This put us in a bit of a spot, though.

"Who's in charge, then?" I asked, staying within the range of questions Bureaucracy told me were kosher.

"The . . . his deputy went on the quest as well. Until one of them gets back, there's no one with authority to do more than accept job completion notices."

I kept my face impassive, but inwardly I was cursing the Guild's flat command structure. *No backups? No succession planning? Management fail.*

"You need to issue a quest—get everyone available on the streets to disrupt the monster spawning," I told her. The look on her face told me I wasn't going to like her answer.

In theory, adventurers could just go out on their own to kill monsters. However, a lot of them wouldn't bother if they weren't getting paid for it. Some of them *did* have the basic decency to act to save people, but many of them were just in it for the money. Even if we did rely only on volunteers, the guild would still be needed to organize the horde. We needed an even distribution of patrols, not a bunch of vandals wandering about.

"I can't do that," the receptionist said, her voice firming as she fell back into Bureaucracy's embrace. "After the . . . the King has forbidden any mass action on the streets. I can't . . ."

I took a deep breath. "Plan it," I said, pushing both Persuasion and Intimidate to their limits. "Unless you want to be the one responsible for the slaughter that's going to take place tonight, get everything ready. Get the word out, work out the costs, get your numbers, and assign patrol routes."

"That's all . . ." she said helplessly.

"You're not doing anything else now, right? Plan it. I'll get you your authorization."

She nodded meekly. I looked around at the crowd, who had been looking on in confusion.

"Spread the word," I told them. "Let civilians know to get to shelter, let everyone else know to be here in . . . two hours." I glanced back at the receptionist who had gone white at the idea of getting everything I'd asked her to do in two hours. I didn't wait for a response, I just strode out of there, Janie falling in by my side.

I'd barely taken three steps out of the building when I heard a familiar voice.

"Well, well, how my stars have fallen! Fancy meeting you here!" I looked over to see who was addressing me. Leaning out of a carriage was a fancily dressed man waving at me frantically. Vodurn, the Royal Fool.

ПOT SVCH A FOOL

Janie and I got into the carriage at Vodurn's invitation. I *could* have run to the palace faster, but I suspected that any time I saved would have been lost in convincing the guards to let me in. Vodurn sat across from us, wearing a genial smile.

"This is a surprise, Councillor," he said. "I was under the impression that you were saving us all in the Maze of the Forsaken Giant."

"Everyone in the castle got notified that the break was over," I said. "I got out sometime last night, and went straight to bed."

"Have the rest of your party been hiding themselves as well? The King is most eager to hear the tale of your bravery."

"We met up with Duke Finley but got separated after that," I admitted. "I managed to acquire a token that teleported me out, so I don't know how they fared."

"I see." He paused, looking at me intently.

"You've dropped your rhyming thing," I said, to fill up the gap. He smirked.

"I had thought my affectation was seen by you more as an affliction," he said. "If it's not amusing, then alterations must be made, to retain your affections."

I grimaced. I could hear it that time, though I still didn't see it as funny. A glance over at Janie, though, told me that he still had it.

"That wasn't a complaint, and I'm not sure that now is the time for wordplay," I said.

"Oh? Is not now a time for celebration?" he asked.

I stared at him. "Do you . . . not know that another obelisk was sabotaged?"

"Ah, that. While it is concerning, it's a matter for the King and his Order of the Long Name. Reserves are dwindling, but I'm assured they will have things fixed before things get desperate."

"Will they?" I asked. "How long has it been since the first one failed?"

He shrugged. "The King has made his displeasure known—all efforts are being turned to the problem, I am assured."

"The King . . . I need to speak with him, right away."

Vodurn waved a lazy hand, "He wishes to speak with you as well."

"*Not* at his earliest convenience. I need him to authorize a Guild deployment on the streets."

"The Guild are not entirely in favor at the moment," Vodurn said with a thin smile. "The Guild Master's actions may have proved necessary, but they were hasty and ill-thought. Many of his men are still under arrest from that night."

"He'll need to release them; we'll need everyone for this," I muttered.

"I find that idea highly unlikely. And what would he need them for?" Vodurn asked.

"You're not a mage, you can't see it . . . but the King has mages, right? To advise him?"

"Of course, but . . ." Vodurn hesitated. "His most trusted magical advisors were sent to King's Isle, to fight off Shadthe."

"Of course," I groaned. "Well, the problem is that all this loose mana spilling about is causing knots and vortexes, which are going to start spawning monsters soon."

"Oh, I wouldn't worry about that," Vodurn said with relief. "The wards on the walls prevent any spawn points from forming."

"Wards on the *walls*," I said, as if this wasn't news to me. "That filter *incoming* mana. They don't do anything if you dump a load of mixed mana *inside* the walls."

Vodurn looked at me, his air of unconcern slowly fading away.

"Perhaps we can go a little faster," he said, standing up and thumping three times on the carriage roof.

Despite the urgency, I still had to wait for a while in the dining hall. It meant I got to eat, at least. The rest of my crew found me, and I caught them all up on what had gone down.

"Which reminds me . . . can everyone Identify this?" I asked, pulling out the Aegis. There was a long pause as everyone with the skill took in the description. The long, useful description.

"That can't be right, can it?" Felicia said. "I've never seen an Identify like that."

"It seems powerful . . . if expensive to use," Janie mused. "And . . . not very useful, under most circumstances."

"Yeah. If I had to guess, this is—" I was going to say more but Felicia gave me a significant look. Turning to look in that direction, I saw that Aubert was approaching the edge of our Privacy bubble. He started when I looked at him, but swallowed and kept moving forward.

"Lord Aubert," I said, when he had come close enough to hear me. "You're looking well."

I kept the bubble up—no reason not to, and you never knew when someone might say something that shouldn't be overheard. Particularly when that someone was Aubey.

"I heard," he said, "that you might have news of Lord Finley. Did he really stage a coup?"

I blinked. The coup was such old news that I'd forgotten about it.

"Is the King keeping everyone in the dark?" I asked.

"Yes," he said, simply. "Ever since the fighting, there's been no announcements. People—important people—are just missing, and there's been no word on what's going on."

"I see . . ." I thought for a minute about whether I wanted to spill the beans. It wasn't as if I'd signed an NDA or anything. *His Majesty really should be getting ahead of this*, I thought.

"The short version," I said, "is that his coup was sprung early. The Guild Master attacked Finley's men and they defended themselves . . . but despite what the Guild Master thought, the soldiers weren't on the streets to start the coup. So it's all a bit of a wash, and I think Finley will get away with it."

"What? Why? Surely the King won't . . ."

"You were the one who told me," I explained. "No evidence . . . if Finley says the men were there to help with the break, then no one gets to deny that, right? So he'll walk."

"Walk where?"

"Walk away from this, without any consequences," I said, irritated at having to explain the idiom.

Aubert cursed furiously. "His majesty can't let him get away with this! An attempt on the throne . . ."

"Don't ask me what the throne is going to do," I said. "But his Majesty has bigger problems at the moment."

"What could be a bigger problem than treachery?" Aubert asked.

I paused before answering him, struck by a sudden thought.

"You've got guards with you, right?"

"They're not necessary in the palace, but I have ten men as an honor guard in case I need to go anywhere," he replied.

"And there are a lot of useless nobles like yourself, just sitting around Court waiting for the King to notice you."

He bristled at being called useless, but he didn't actually protest. "There are a number of nobles waiting at Court for one reason or another—as are you."

"How many of them are you on speaking terms with?"

"Perhaps fifteen or twenty? Where are you going with this?"

"In a few hours, or maybe less, monsters are going to start spawning in the city," I told him. He stiffened with shock.

"What? How?"

"Never mind that right now. I'm trying to get the King to approve deployment of the Adventurers Guild . . . but if you and your buddies can get 200 guards out on the streets *right now*, you can save a lot of lives."

"I don't think . . ." He glanced at my expression, and quickly qualified, "Yes, yes, saving lives, I'm all for it. But most of my peers . . ."

"Fine. Three things," I said, ticking them off on my fingers. "One—I'm guessing most of them don't have slots in the local dungeons, so this is experience there for the taking."

Aubey nodded thoughtfully. "Most of us are a bit stuck while they stay here."

"Two. Being seen on the streets, saving people, will make them seem like heroes to the people," I said. "Whatever it is they're here to achieve, will be easier for them if there are people cheering their name. Save enough people, and the King might notice."

Aubey pursed his lips, but nodded thoughtfully. I could see the idea blooming in his eyes. Making a name for himself with the people might just be enough to get the King to confirm his title.

"And finally," I added, "if they do this through the Guild, and I get this deployment authorized, they can get paid for it. It might be not much, compared to what they're used to, but it will be more than they normally get for killing monsters."

"I will gather them, my lady," Aubey said. From the look on his face, he seemed to immediately realize his slip, but he pressed on. "I'm not sure how many yet, but we will be on the streets in two hours."

He started to bow, caught himself, then turned on his heel and left.

"Remember when you asked if your level was showing?" Janie asked as we watched him leave.

"What of it?"

She pointed to his retreating figure. "I'll admit, you had him eating out of your hand before, but he would never have called you lady before. You took control at the Guild like you were Voight himself. And you've got the King's Fool running off to let the King know what you've got to say."

"I'm being a bit more forceful, is what you mean?"

She snickered, and the rest of my team broke into chuckles.

"Just a tad, yeah. The tiniest little bit," she said.

"Well, you may have a point," I admitted. "It's just that since I woke up, there's been this crisis and nobody except me seems to know about it, or what to do. Present company excluded, of course."

"So, what do we do, then?" Kyle asked. "All this urgency, it seems strange to be sitting in a dining hall."

"Yeah," I sighed. "I have to stay here, in case the King wants to see me, but can you all go and defend my dungeon?"

"Are you sure?" Felicia asked. Janie didn't say anything but looked mulish.

"I'm sure," I said. "I'll be safer here than anywhere, but Isabel's all alone, defending those kids. Plus, if any of the creatures gets into the tower, Rhis will go insane."

"Ugh, when you put it that way," Janie said, "I guess we don't have a choice."

I never actually saw the King, at least not that day. A messenger from Vodurn found me after about an hour, letting me know that authorization had been sent. Breathing a sigh of relief, I headed for the palace wall to see the results.

The palace had its own wards, apparently, which ensured no spawn points would form within them. I could see with my own eyes that what little mana made it this far became thinned and orderly. So I focused on the rest of the city.

It was chaos. Cities—at least cities in this era—were designed to keep threats like monsters out. They weren't equipped to deal with them once they got inside. By the time I got to the wall, monsters had started spawning, slowly at first, but with increasing speed.

Many of the points had an adventurer, or a team, there beforehand. Those locations were a bit of a gamble. You didn't know what kind of threat would come out, at least not at first. A few teams were overwhelmed by the monster that spawned, falling back or dying. That monster then had free range to terrorize until a higher-levelled defender could be found.

Most of the Guild members knew what they were doing, though. Once formed, spawn points were fairly stable, putting out monsters at a constant rate and within a range of threat values. As information came back to the Guild, patrols became more focused, and bad matchups became fewer.

The worst ones, though, were the ones where no one got to them in time. There just weren't enough people. Between the town guards, the adventurers, and the roving bands of nobles, there were perhaps 700 people to cover a huge, twisting network of streets and houses.

I wondered why the King's guard weren't being sent on the street, and from the looks on the faces of the men next to me on the wall, I wasn't the only one. Discipline was held, though, and I didn't make things worse for them by voicing an opinion.

Things were . . . mostly under control, or getting there, when I spotted a small procession approaching the palace. A small team of ten, moving with purpose. They weren't patrolling randomly—though they did take care of a monster that happened to be nearby. It was only when they started fighting that I recognized them.

Kaito and her harem were out of the dungeon.

REUNION

I held my breath until I could count every one of Kaito's girls. If one had been missing, I would have had to make myself scarce. I wasn't sure what the rules were for replacing dead members, and I didn't want to find out.

That entirely selfish concern dealt with, I was glad to see that they were okay. They walked up to the front gate and went out of my line of sight. Presumably, they were let in. It wasn't long after that a messenger found me, asking me to accompany them to see the King.

Oh, now he wants to see me.

That thought was a bit unworthy of me. The King *had* responded to my message and gotten the Guild out on the streets. With everything that was going on and key people out of the city, he was probably pretty busy. It made sense to wait and see all of the Chosen in one go.

I followed the messenger and found myself in a waiting room with the other girls. Squeals and hugs were had all around. It seemed that the girls had decided they liked me, and that meant hugs. I wondered if all beast-kin were this touchy-feely, or if it was just them.

Only Isidre and Kaito held themselves apart, though they did smile at seeing me. Once I'd wrested myself free, Kaito greeted me.

"It's good to see you made it out, Miss Kandis; we were all quite worried!" she said. The "Miss" meant that she was using the Japanese *-san* suffix, which . . . I was okay with. "How did you make it out before us?"

"I managed to get a token that teleported me to the entrance," I explained. "*Only* to the entrance, or I would have tried to check up on you. Then . . . I didn't really feel like dealing with Finley's men, so I slipped through the castle."

Kaito frowned. "The castle wasn't manned by Duke Finley's forces when we came through," she said. "The Duke was quite upset by that."

"What? Did the King's forces take over?" I tried to figure out if that had been the case when I had come through. It had been . . . a mix, I thought? Soldiers here wore a bewildering array of uniforms depending on their allegiance, rank, and unit, but I was pretty sure that I'd seen uniforms belonging both to the Duke and to the King.

If that was the case, then it might explain why the King's guard wasn't out on the streets. Half of the forces in the city were keeping the other half under arrest.

"They did," Kaito confirmed. "The Duke was arrested when he came out . . . at least nominally. He's been confined to his quarters."

"He agreed to that?" I asked. I didn't think there was anyone in the city right now who could *make* the Duke do anything—aside from the King.

"Yes . . ." Kaito said. She dropped her gaze to the ground. "He was . . . somewhat subdued after what happened in the dungeon. His son . . ."

"Didn't make it?" I suggested when Kaito didn't look as if she wanted to continue. She nodded.

"One of the Duke's companions, his son, and one of his son's companions," she said, sighing. "We held off the ogres, but the giants disposed of our fortifications like they were made of sand. It happened so quickly, we might all have died if the break hadn't ended at that moment."

"Some of us would have survived," Ettalle put in. The cat-kin grabbed ahold of Kaito's arm and held herself close. "We've got good dodgers, and the back line could have fled. But . . . it wouldn't have been good."

"Yeah! It was real lucky the break ended right then!" Nori said, coming up on Kaito's other side. "So how'd you do it, huh?"

"Yes, how *did* you do it?" a voice said from behind me. I turned. The King was here.

We arranged ourselves decorously to face the King. Two couches were not quite enough to fit eight people, but the harem was used to fitting large groups in tight spaces. Ettalle, Nori, and Fassi squeezed onto one couch with Kaito, while Zichy stood behind. That left one couch for Isidre, Orino, and me.

Once we were all settled, the King started speaking.

"First of all, while your modesty does you credit, Councillor Hammond, there is no point in denying that you were responsible for ending the break. Even if Duke Finley wasn't complaining about only receiving 25 percent of the total, I can *see* that you've gone up a level."

I really needed to learn how to hide that aura. The King's words set off a bunch of gasps and exclamations from the girls, and one smug look from Fassi. *She'd* noticed, apparently. Isidre, sitting next to me, touched me on the arm to attract my attention.

"Congratulations," she said and managed to make it sound sincere.

"Ah, well, you'll all get there soon enough," I said.

"I'm sure," the King agreed. "Now, as to how?"

He was keeping it polite, which I appreciated, but that monstrous Intimidation was at his fingertips any time he wanted. I would have to play this very carefully.

"There are Guild secrets involved with that story, Your Majesty," I said carefully.

He frowned. "I wasn't aware you were fully initiated," he said.

"I'm not," I agreed. "I came upon these secrets through my own investigations, and was later informed by the Guild that I was trespassing on their domain."

"Then you're not bound by oaths," he said, leaning forward.

"No, but it puts me in a delicate situation. I'm dependent on the goodwill of the Guild for a lot of my agenda in Talnier. In the interest of maintaining that, I've agreed to not spill their secrets—but I don't know what they actually are."

"Wait, you don't know their secrets?"

"I know what I know," I explained. "And I know that some of what I found out is considered a secret. But they weren't willing to *tell* me what they were keeping secret. Without the Guild Master here to guide me, I don't know what I can say that doesn't infringe upon that trust."

"The Guild—and the Guild Master—answer to me," the King said with a frown.

"However—and correct me if I'm wrong on this—you have allowed the Guild to keep its secrets. As part of the grand balance established by your grandfather."

The King glowered at me for a moment and then sighed. "So you want to wait for Voight to get back before you talk. Why did I bother summoning you then?"

"With respect," Kaito put in, "there are matters more important to discuss that require Miss Hammond's presence."

"Oh? And what makes you think you can judge *importance*, girl?" Irritated, the King's Intimidation skill flared up. I winced, even though it wasn't directed at me. Isidre flinched and grabbed my arm and the other girls quailed, but Kaito was unbowed. Her ears drooped, and she swallowed nervously, but she kept talking.

"The break is over, so information about how to end it can wait a few days. The burgeoning spawn points are a *current* concern."

"If you want to go and sign up with the Adventurers Guild to fight monsters, that's no concern of mine," the King said dismissively.

"I have a different suggestion," Kaito said politely. "While no one doubts the competency of your Theurges—"

"Despite the fact that they haven't managed to repair those obelisks yet," I interjected. Both the King and Kaito shot me a look. The King's was irritated, Kaito's more imploring.

"I suspect that their *style* of mana manipulation is less suited to the current situation than one would like," she continued.

"Explain," the King said.

"Ah . . . as I am not a mage, it is difficult for me to explain," she said. She looked over at Ettalle, but she was still whimpering from the King's earlier bout of irritation. I decided to step up.

"I'm not sure where she's going with this, but Kingdom Theurgy is mostly about moving mana efficiently from one point to another," I said. "It avoids spawn points by draining the mana out of an area."

"Yes, and in the current situation in the city?" Kaito said, half of her attention on me, the rest on trying to revive Ettalle's spirits.

"It's . . . got nowhere to go," I said, thinking about it. "The free mana is penned in the city by the wards, and without a dedicated obelisk to suck up the mana, it just sloshes around until it gets sucked up by a dungeon or a spell."

Obelisks must absorb mana more efficiently than dungeons, I realized, or over a wider area. I'd never seen a vortex over an obelisk as I had for dungeons.

"Yes, it is a turbulent pool, when what we need is a river!" She shook Ettalle, finally convincing her to participate.

"Uh, that's how we do it in the Great Forest, your Majesty," Ettalle said nervously. "The shamans concentrate the mana in a stream that flows naturally. Done right, the river absorbs nearby ambient mana, and keeps buildups from forming."

"And so you want to try this . . . barbarian technique on our streets," the King said.

"Well, we're not shamans," Ettalle explained. "Orino and I might become such, eventually, so we've had some training, but we don't have Theurgy. We were hoping that if we explained the technique to your people, they could manage it.

"My Scholars of the Sacred Breath are a little busy right now," the King said wryly.

"Are they? Because they don't seem to be accomplishing much. Couldn't they spare a few people to try this out?" I shot back.

"I suppose that's true," he conceded. The look he gave me wasn't friendly, though.

"So if you could put something down to show your support of the idea, we could try and convince them to try it?" Kaito said hopefully. "If we could take Miss Kandis along as well, she's very good at getting people to accept new things."

Royal warrants weren't just hastily scribbled notes with a seal attached. They had to be constructed. So there was a brief wait, while the King went off for other meetings, and we waited for the document to be delivered.

"Are you sure you're not going to get into trouble for sharing your people's secrets?" I asked.

"They're not secrets," Ettalle said. "They're sacraments."

I raised an eyebrow in response, so she continued.

"The way the Kingdom constrains mana is an offense to Naldyna," she said. Despite her words, she didn't look offended. She was just too good-natured to pull it off. "I'm more worried that, after we show them how to do it *properly*, they'll just write it off as barbarian stuff and throw the technique away."

I nodded in agreement, but I suspected that the truth was less one-sided than that. Latora's methods worked well for Latora and the Tribes' way worked well for the Tribes. The current failures here didn't look good for the Scholars, but I knew that the Tribal method was not without failures. Moving mana naturally meant that sometimes the mana moved on its own. I had heard that villages occasionally had to be evacuated because a mana stream had decided to pass through, bringing monsters with it.

There was more than one reason that the Tribal villages were little more than glorified campsites. They weren't nomadic, but they lived as if they were, always ready to pack up at a moment's notice. Not that they were complaining about such a life, but it wasn't for everyone.

To our surprise, when the King's warrant came, it was accompanied by another, which had a note attached. This second warrant was given to me. The note said:

Consider this both a reward for your help but also a sign that I've decided that I don't want to keep you here any longer than necessary.

It wasn't signed, but the warrant was actually my—Talnier's—Charter, all properly signed and sealed. He must have had it all ready to go.

I tsked under my breath. If he thought this was all the reward I was going to require, he had another coming. The others looked at me, but I didn't say anything, just stored the note and the scroll in my ring.

"Let's go and see the wizards," I said.

FIXING IT

"Absolutely not." The man glared at me from beneath his hood. "No one of this order is going to waste time following instructions from a barbarian."

He glanced disdainfully at Kaito's crew. They huddled together, somewhat crestfallen at their reception. Isidre was the only harem member not there. She had joined up with her people to mount a more physical response to the monster problem. She didn't have enough knights to *solve* it, but every little helped.

"Brother Laurent," I cut in. My voice was friendly, but that meant absolutely nothing in this world. "Is your order really in a position to refuse orders from the King?"

His attention snapped to me, both because of my question and because he could feel my Persuasion wrapping around him. Brother Laurent was a fairly political animal, I'd guess. He'd introduced himself as of the "third grade," and the trim on his robe was more ornate than the Brothers gathered around the obelisk. But the Scholars were about skills, not levels. They weren't the sort to go haring off into dungeons, and while you could get experience from Theurgy and Enchanting, you couldn't get much.

I judged Brother Laurent to be about fourth level, and with decently high Charisma and Persuasion. Maybe sevens in each? Four times 49 was 196, a respectable total. But it was dwarfed by my own 300 Persuasion total.

Most people backed off, or looked for a compromise at this point, in the same way that no one wanted to *start* a fight with the six-foot-tall bruiser. And since I didn't want to get a reputation as a bully, I normally let them. This guy, though, definitely wanted a fight.

"The King does not get to dictate to us how to do our jobs!" he spluttered. "We are the experts here—he needs us more than ever right now!"

His words were accompanied by all the social skill totals he could muster. Not just Persuasion, he was trying to get an Intimidate in there. I was unimpressed. Did he really imagine that I would think that withdrawing the Scholars' service was a credible threat?

"The King needs people that can solve his problems," I said calmly. "Which you have been failing at of late."

I held out the King's warrant. "If you can't solve the King's problems, it's only natural that you would be replaced by people who *can*."

I didn't know where the King might find such people—I wasn't volunteering—but that didn't really matter. What mattered was the grip my overwhelming Persuasion had on him. From my own experience, I knew that it felt a lot like having the oxygen sucked out of the room. He tried to fight back, but he was outmatched. When I held out the warrant, he took it.

You have defeated André Laurent in a Tier 2 Social Contest! You have earned 40 XP.

Tier two? He must have really *not wanted to comply*, I thought, brushing past him to take a look at the obelisk. Then I caught the glances that his fellow Scholars gave him and understood. *Ah, he's lost face with his subordinates.*

The Scholars made way for me as I approached the obelisk, scuttling to the side while glaring at me impotently.

"What seems to be the problem?" I asked. We weren't here for the obelisks, but as long as we were here, it seemed worthwhile to take a look. No one wanted to answer me, and Brother Laurent was still spluttering over his warrant, so I singled one out.

"It's . . . difficult to explain to a layman—laywoman," he said evasively. "I can't exactly *show* you the mana . . ."

"I'm an Enchanter, myself," I said. I didn't want to give away that I had Theurgy if I didn't have to. "This all looks like it's working properly."

It actually *did* look as if it was working properly. The Scholars had done something to the stone monolith that made it transparent like glass. This made it easy to see the enchantments running through it. The transparency spell was something that *would* have been a low-level Stone Magic spell, if it was on the list. A spell that was right in the wheelhouse of Theurgy, then.

The enchantment was a little trickier to decipher. They didn't use runes, so I couldn't see what they were doing, exactly. Twisted three-dimensional scribbles were embedded in the rock somehow. They seemed to function *like* runes, but if runes were a science, this was an art. No two of the scribbles were alike, and their function seemed to work on feelings.

I could feel Theurgy radiating its approval of the glowing scribbles. I couldn't tell what they did, but they seemed *right*. As well, much like with a runic circle, I could see the mana running through the design. There were no missing or malformed sigils that would have spoiled the flow.

"That's the problem," my unnamed interlocutor said. "There's nothing wrong to fix, but it's not channeling the mana."

I didn't get what he meant at first; it seemed to be channeling mana just fine, but then I remembered what obelisks were supposed to *do*. There was supposed to be a torrent of mana flowing through this enchantment—a conduit in and a conduit out.

Looking at the wider picture, I could make out a weak, tenuous connection to the loose mana conduit that floated above. That conduit should be down here, being redirected to flow to the palace's central distribution point. The enchantment was clearly broken, but it wasn't clear *how*.

I looked up at the conduit again, then back down at the obelisk. Could it be that simple? I looked back at Brother Laurent, now getting lectured by the girls on how to direct mana.

Better to ask for forgiveness than seek permission, was the old saying. Better yet was to not get caught in the first place. If nothing happened, no one would know, and if it did work, I could take credit.

[Dispel Image].

I cast it silently, but the effects were dramatic. Not the effect on the actual target—the illusion just faded without a fuss. All the people watching, though, started screaming.

"What did you do? What did you do?" the man next to me yelled. He was pointing at the enchantment, which now looked very different.

Now, half the sigils were gone, and a few more were there but damaged. The mana was no longer flowing but leaking out of the squiggles as if they were flawed runes.

"There was an illusion," I said. "I removed it. You should be able to see the problem now?"

The Brother stared at me and then whipped his head around to look at the obelisk again. "It's been ruined all this time, and we couldn't see . . ." he whined. "This damage, it will take so long to fix."

"I'm sure it will," I said with the easy manner of someone who wasn't going to be working on it. Something caught the attention of my Mana Sense on top of the obelisk. "Hang on," I said.

I couldn't jump to the top of the twelve-foot monolith, but I could get high enough to grab on. With that accomplished, Climbing helped me lift myself to the top. There was . . . something there. I could see it with Mana Sense but . . .

[Dispel Image].

I grabbed the small disk that appeared and examined it closely. Then I jumped down again.

"Here's your problem!" I said brightly, channeling the mechanic who had fixed my brakes. I showed them the enchanted amulet that had been placed there. "This is what was concealing the damage. Its mana must have been concealed by the first spell I broke, and it had another to keep it from being seen."

I handed the amulet to Brother Laurent, who had joined the others in gaping at the damage.

"This . . . is what caused the damage?" he said numbly.

"This is what *concealed* the damage," I said. "There's probably a rogue Theurge out there actually doing the sabotage."

Did it have to be a Theurge? I didn't know. If those sigils had a physical component, then an Earth mage could probably disrupt them without showing signs on the surface. I thought. It really wasn't my problem.

"Now that you can see the damage, how long will it take to get fixed?" I asked.

"Two, three days?" Brother Laurent said, answering me promptly, as he had to. Perhaps realizing that he hadn't meant to answer me, he looked over at me, alarmed.

"We can't do it any faster than that, I swear!"

I nodded. "Then it sounds like Kaito's idea will still need to be tried. Have you figured out how many of your people need to go with them?"

He nodded, warily.

"Then if someone can show me to the other obelisk, I think I've got some more dispelling to do."

* * *

"So that was the reason for the delays," I said to the King. I was pretty sure that he hadn't wanted to talk to me again today, but this was important enough to make an exception. I showed him one of the amulets. "I left the other one with the Scholars to examine, but I figured you'd want this one."

I had already picked up a Conceal Mana rune from it. I'd thought that it was doing my trick of maintaining a spell cast by the enchanter, but it looked like runes could do illusions as well.

The King reached for it but changed his mind and gestured for one of his attendants to take it.

"It seems the Kingdom is in your debt once more," he said.

"*More* in my debt," I said. "That Town Charter barely counts as a reward; that was *owed* to the people of Talnier."

The King raised an eyebrow, and with a flex of his displeasure reminded me that having the second-highest social skill total was still only the *second-highest* skill total.

"And Talnier thanks you for your generosity, Your Majesty," I hastily added.

"Hmm. Regardless, you *are* deserving of further rewards," he said, trailing the sentence off. Leaving it to me to ask?

My first instinct was to ask for money, but I had a number of different ways to make more of that.

"I'm starting a new business," I tried instead. It was a little late to be asking, but he probably had not yet heard about the Bank of Talnier. "What are the laws on things like that?"

"What sort of business?" he asked.

"A new sort," I said and started to explain about banks. He stopped me about halfway through.

"There are no rules on lending; the nobles would never hear of it," he said. "Since you're not a noble, you'll pay tax on your profits, of course."

"Of course," I said, one eye twitching. Of course, nobles got tax breaks. "On profits."

He looked at me suspiciously, but I kept my face open and innocent. Between a millennium of tax evasion techniques and the fact that I was part of the government of Talnier and *responsible* for collecting tax, I was quite sure he'd find my accounts were in order, should he check.

"Then, I do have another project I'd like *official* recognition of," I said. He caught my meaning and frowned.

"I *know* you're not planning on leaving that here," he said. "Especially since you've arranged things so it will starve in a few more days."

"Right. I still need to find a place. But I also need to ensure that it won't be stolen by adventurers, or confiscated by other nobles who say they're acting in your name."

"Not willing to strike it out in the wilderness? That's the traditional method."

"I'm a city girl at heart," I told him. "I've got a council to serve on and a business to maintain."

"Talnier can't support *three* dungeons," he said. "Frontier or not, it can barely manage the two that it has."

"It could, if the Scholars in the area were a *little* less conscientious about how much mana they drained out of the area."

"You want my mana," he said flatly.

"We're talking about a reward, are we not? Whatever reward you're giving, it's going to be something you own."

He sighed. "How much mana are we talking about?"

I smiled back. I could feel Bargain coming into play. It was likely I would be as overmatched in this as I was in Intimidate, but it would be good practice.

Just then, one of the King's functionaries burst into the room.

"Your Majesty, there's an urgent problem, down at the docks!"

INTERLUDE 3

The fear started as soon as her ladyship left. Her ladyship—Kandis, as she insisted Issey call her—had an aura about her that Issey associated with nobles. It made everything that Kandis said seem right, and sensible. It was only after Kandis had left that everything collapsed, taking Issey with it.

Defend the dungeon! Keep other monsters out of it! Protect the kids!

It was easy to say, but Issey was just a dancer, and a barely employed one at that. One step away from being a whore, two houses down from the whorehouse. She couldn't take care of one kid, let alone organize a bunch of orphans into a fighting force. It was impossible.

And yet . . . she had to try. Aside from the fact that these kids needed to be protected, she couldn't bear the thought of Lady Kandis coming back and having to tell her that Issey had failed. Being exposed to that aura, an aura that made everything *right*, when Issey was *wrong* . . . would she stop existing? Would she die?

It was a foolish notion. Lady Kandis had been nothing but kind to Issey, the kids, and even those louts that had been harassing her. Issey knew that. She was just unwilling to countenance a future where Lady Kandis looked at her with *disappointment*.

So she did her best to follow the instructions she had been given. The first ones, at least, weren't so hard to follow. The kids were counted. The dungeon provided weapons—real ones this time. Some of the kids were level three, the same as Issey. They looked like kids, but they fought like adults. Issey made sure she knew who they were and then split them into groups, making sure that at least one level three was in each group.

She knew her home better than anyone, of course. It *did* have stout walls, having been constructed by crafters better than anyone that Issey could find today. But there were weak spots. Places that had been damaged and repaired by lesser crafters. Places where the damage hadn't been fixed at all. Issey made sure to cover the gaps with people.

Her first challenge came from the sewers. The Gilded Lily had always had a rat problem, a neglected spawner in the sewers. Going down there on the occasional rat extermination had gotten Issey to level three. Pretty good, for someone whose profession didn't give experience.

Not even Kandis had predicted that the rat spawner would be energized by the raw mana, but when the first three rats had poked their heads up in the kitchen, Issey knew that her siege had started.

The kids dealt with those three rather easily. The fifteen that followed were more of a challenge, but for most of the fight, the hole in the floor served as a useful choke point, limiting the creatures' numbers. By the time they fought through, the kids had thinned them out to something that proved manageable. The kids were in high spirits from their victory, ignoring their injuries, and tried to convince her to let them follow the trail back to the spawner.

It was then that the first monster attacked the front door. It was some kind of wolf, standing four feet high at the shoulder, with black and vivid blue fur. Issey paled when she Identified it. She didn't have her numbers, but the impression she got was that this was a higher threat monster than anything she'd seen before.

It snarled and roared and tried to break its way in. The spears that they had—or the spear *wielders* that they had—were not enough to harm it, but they did discourage it. It growled and spat, and then *disappeared* with a flash of light, only to reappear at a boarded-up window and start to tear at it. A fresh team raced to stick their spears through at it, but it flashed again, this time scratching ineffectually at an undamaged, shuttered window.

Am I going to fail so soon? Issey asked herself. She wondered how much of a gap it would take for the wolf to flash itself in there with them. If that happened . . .

Before it could, there was a yelp, and the wolf was engulfed in flames. It flashed, but the flames followed them. It flashed again, and this time it went somewhere Issey couldn't see it, but it was close enough that she could hear its snarls and the sound of fighting. When it ended, Issey carefully opened the door and looked outside.

"How's it going, kiddos?" Janie said, standing out in the middle of the street. "Guess who your reinforcements are?"

Behind her were the rest of Lady Kandis's companions. Felicia was already cutting the beast open while Kyle stood watch over her.

Issey gave a sigh of relief. It was going to be all right.

Isidre was feeling left out. She was supposed to be the Champion of Duit, but lately she'd been feeling more like a supporting character. Just another one of Kaito's women . . . Isidre shook her head. That wasn't fair to Kaito; she'd never treated Isidre with anything less than respect. And if Kandis got on better with Kaito than she did Isidre, well, Isidre had to admit that she was the one at fault there.

Isidre had split her small force three ways, to cover more ground. Five men were with her, and two more squads were within signaling distance. They were all mounted. They didn't have clearance to fly over Dorsay, but the Head Constable had allowed that, under the circumstances, going mounted on griffins would make them more effective. Griffins were perfectly capable of being ridden on the ground, and there would be no complaints as long as none of their long, wing-assisted jumps took them higher than the roofline.

The griffins' speed, and their senses, were definitely helping. Helping them *save lives*. It was chaos out here. Monsters were appearing completely randomly. In the streets, or in people's houses, it didn't seem to make any difference to the spawn points. It was *good* that she was out here. She couldn't think of anything else she should be doing, but . . .

Her contribution to clearing the break had been minor. Half a percentage point, while Kandis had come up with some trick that snared her an entire level! Now Kaito had come up with some clever plan involving mana that was going to end this whole problem, while Isidre was left to just clean up the symptoms.

You are saving lives. Defending the weak. Do not discount the value of those actions.

Fortunately—no, Duit would never leave something like that to chance—the voice came during a lull in the fighting, at a moment when Isidre had let her thoughts run free.

"Thanks, my lady," Isidre murmured. If any of her people heard her, they'd know who she was talking to. "But . . . I've been hearing so much about the mysterious plans of the gods . . . I just wanted to be the linchpin of one, instead of a supporter."

I understand.

A shock of joy and well-being pulsed through Isidre. More than just words, there was a feeling that the *words were true*.

A scream came from up ahead. Something like a giant spider, but with long squirmy tentacles in addition to its eight legs, was perched on the side of the building and had dragged a struggling woman from inside. Isidre and her troops leapt to the attack.

The battle was short but furious. Eventually, the spider-thing was dragged down by griffin claws and finished off with lances. It was too late for the woman, though; she'd been torn in half in the first few seconds.

I am known as the God of Life because I seek to preserve the lives of all mortals, Duit told her as she stared down at the body. *You cannot save everybody. Ultimately, you can save nobody. But every time you save a life, you preserve their uniqueness, and their ability to experience uniqueness for a little longer.*

"Right," Isidre said to the air. To her companions, she said, "Take care of the body; we can't leave it out here. Ten minutes, and then we move on."

As they saluted her, she felt a strange chill in the air.

It had been a while since Kaito was not the center of attention, and he was trying to determine if he welcomed it or not.

Once, he would have absolutely preferred to be ignored, whether by the bullies at school or his slightly less obnoxious co-workers at the string of dead-end jobs that he had gone through in his previous life. Since coming here, though, he had been the focus of attention for a crowd of beautiful, affirming, huggable young ladies. He would have been quite insane to not enjoy that.

Now there were other concerns. Ettalle and Orino were trying to explain mana rivers to a group of three Theurges. The hooded men were not what Kaito would call receptive to the idea. Kaito would have called them sulky, if that wouldn't have been exceedingly impolite.

The rest of the group was either watching out for incoming monsters—as Kaito was—or contributing to the discussion with a supportive yell or a disparaging jeer. Kaito winced to think that the discussion had devolved to the point where such things might be considered helpful.

"It's not a conduit!" Orino exclaimed for the third time. "It's a loose braid—it's *supposed* to leak mana."

"That's inefficient, and way more complicated than it needs to be," another one objected.

"Yeah, but . . . but, it's not about moving mana, is it?" Ettalle put in. "It's about collecting it and letting it move *naturally*. That way you don't need strong enchantments to keep it in place."

"This will attract those monsters, though."

Orino rolled her eyes. "Cleaning up the mana will stop them from forming, you—"

Kaito cleared his throat. He didn't like it when the girls got coarse or rude. Orino winced but recognized that name-calling was going to be unproductive.

"The monsters are attracted, yes," she said. "They're attracted to the middle of the streets, instead of people's *houses*."

"But this is so much harder than the normal way," the third one whined.

Kaito sighed and held up the King's order once again. "Should we go back and tell your superiors that you couldn't follow our instructions, or should we skip a step and go directly to the King?"

The Scholars looked at the order warily, sighed, and then started weaving mana the way Orino had said.

Kaito smiled warmly and wondered if that was how Kandis would have handled it. The men had known all along that they were going to do it Orino's way; they just wanted to complain. There had been no social contest, just Kaito's Persuasion convincing them of what they already knew.

Kaito shivered at a sudden cold breeze. Hopefully, they would soon be able to get moving again.

It was time.

Manuela looked out over Lake Dunlead. There was nothing there, but she looked anyway. There wasn't much where she was, either. Just the docks, mostly empty of ships. They had all taken off when the troubles had started, leaving only the smell of fish and waste behind. The ones that remained now were those with owners, or crews, that were stuck in the city for some reason. They—or others—would return soon, when the situation stabilized.

Or not.

She looked over at Kaypa. An odd man with sallow skin that looked greenish, even though he was in good health. He had come a long way to find Manuela's master, and travelled farther in his service. She nodded, and he started to weave.

It did nothing well, but it could do *anything*, badly. That was how Theurgy had been explained to her. Kaypa's task today was a minor one. It could have been easily handled by Water Magic or Air Magic, but those tools were not available to her today. She didn't have Mana Sense, so she waited for the weave to become visible as a slight distortion before her.

She placed her master's token inside it and watched as Kaypa made it drift out onto the lake. It got out to about fifty meters, far enough that Manuela couldn't see the spell anymore, and could barely make out the token against the dark water.

It was time. The ice began to grow.

ICY RELATIONS

I didn't get invited to join the procession, so much as I just tagged along. Procession might be the wrong term. It wasn't as if the King and all his Court proceeded down the main streets to the docks with all due pomp and circumstance. There were no bands or cheering crowds—the streets were still empty except for patrolling adventurers and the monsters they were hunting.

But when the King decides to go down to the docks, he doesn't get to just stroll out the front gate on his own. So when he announced his intention, called for his arms and armor to be made ready, and strode off towards his inner apartments, I just waited around where the rest of the entourage was starting to form up. They weren't going to let him go on his own after all.

I got a few puzzled looks, but I was already *in* the private part of the palace. No one really had the authority to tell me to get out, and I gave a stern glare to anyone that looked like trying.

It looked as though he would be travelling light, not more than twenty people all told. Most of them were guards. They were lower level than me, but not that much lower. The worst of them could probably take me in a straight fight. There were a few scared looking officials with low levels and lower importance. I think they were there in case the King wanted something sent for. The most important official was the Steward of Dorsay. I hadn't talked to him before, but I knew who he was.

At the last minute, an important-looking figure dashed up to the group. I didn't recognize him, so I buttonholed one of the lesser officials and asked him who the man was.

"The Harbormaster, Kimlet Athean."

Oh, okay. That *was* where we were headed. The man himself looked like a foreigner, with dark, slicked-back hair and sallow skin. He looked about as nervous as the other officials. My reluctant informant looked as if he was about to say more, but at that moment the King walked in.

He was dressed for battle, wearing some *very* fancy plate mail. It wasn't as . . . elaborately complete as I'd seen in documentaries back home, making me think that armor hadn't *quite* developed as far here as it had in Europe. Needless to say, though, as it was made from magical metal, and enchanted, it was far more protective than European armor would have been. I imagined it could stop a tank shell.

He glanced at me as part of his survey of all those that were coming with him, but he didn't say anything. I assume he knew that the difference between him giving me permission or not was about forty meters of distance as I tagged along, invisible.

He brought two more people with him, squires or stewards or something. I felt that there were a number of people missing here. Military or magical advisors who would have been part of the party that headed out to Risurn Island. He didn't say anything about it, though, just nodded and strode out towards the front gate.

We all fell into line behind him, the guards spreading out to form a perimeter. As protection, they were fairly nominal. Perhaps the squishy Court officials needed defending from wandering monsters, but the King could take care of those fairly easily. Perhaps the idea was that he was too important to be bothered by lesser threats.

That was how it proved as we headed down to the docks. The two monsters that we saw were immediately engaged by a squad of guards. The King didn't even glance in their direction and just kept walking. The officials followed, huddled in the center.

We started to feel the chill as we got closer to the lake. Not that it was a particularly warm autumn day, but there was an icy breeze brushing past us. As we got closer, we could finally see what it was.

Someone—one guess as to who—had parked a mountain of ice in the lake. Black ice. Seeing it for the first time, I now knew why they called it that. It was actually clear, just like regular ice without cracks or bubbles. Maybe not *perfectly* clear. I wasn't sure if it was darker than regular ice, or if just the sheer thickness of it was enough to absorb the sunlight. But the edifice before us seemed to drink in the light, leaving only shadows beneath the cold surface.

I'd called it a mountain, but it wasn't quite that high. Perhaps fifty meters or so. Flat topped, with some kind of structure on top. Columns all around, supporting a roof of ice. A huge stairway ran all the way from the top down to one of the piers, encasing it in ice, and possibly anchoring it in place.

The King held his silence until we had made our way to the very edge of the ice. Even then, he kept silent and just glared at the person standing at the foot of the stairway. Manuela Fisher.

"Your Majesty," she said, bowing. "My Master is ready to treat with you."

The King took a long look at the ice staircase stretching above us. It looked slippery.

"I think not," he said and drew his sword. I blinked and almost missed my chance to Identify it.

> [Identification]: Shattering Sword – Quality: Perfect – Properties: Unknown – Origin: Lair of the Spider Queen

He took one swing, and the stairway shattered. About twenty meters of ice, pulverized as if he'd struck it with a club big enough for the Forsaken Giant. The sound of it was like an acre of fancy glassware getting smashed.

Manuela winced from the blow, even though it came nowhere near her. So did the officials and stewards of our party, cowering back in fear. I was pleased to count myself, along with our guards, as someone who didn't take a step back. I think I would have normally, but the physics here was a little weird. It was magic that shattered the ice, not kinetic energy, so there wasn't actually the sort of blowback that I instinctively expected from such a mighty blow.

"If your master wishes to threaten us from behind his portal, he will have to shout," the King said wryly. With a quick movement, he sheathed his sword again.

It was a good line, but I wasn't sure his point was entirely made. Looking at it, he'd destroyed a good number of stairs, but that was only the surface. The bulk of Aghen's construction was still intact. Even as I watched, the ice started to flow, reshaping itself.

"Your Majesty, I—" Manuela started, but she was interrupted.

"Never mind, Manuela, I can accommodate His Majesty's fear of heights."

The voice came from above, but we couldn't see exactly where. That was soon rectified, as what could only be a portal gracefully slid down the icy slope towards us.

It was encased in ice. Clear, dark ice enveloped what looked like a golden arch, big enough to pass through. Within the arch, an oval shaped ring of blue energy hung, free floating in the air.

Behind the ring was someone I could only presume to be Aghen Shadth. He had dark, coffee-colored skin and black hair with the tips dyed green. His face looked . . . overindulged, and he was wearing makeup—obvious greens and purples around his dark brown eyes. He was sitting on a chair that looked a lot like a throne.

"So," the King drawled. "The criminal finally reveals himself."

Aghen's voice was deep and rich, and he spoke slowly, ponderously. "To call me a criminal is to claim that your laws affect me in any way. I am beyond them, as much as any nation is."

"You come to my city, assault it, and claim immunity? You will find that you are not immune to my law, or my wrath."

"Oh? Step forward through the portal, and see how far your wrath reaches."

Looking closer, I thought that I could see that it wasn't just empty air between the two of them. Behind the portal, I thought I could see the sheen of more black ice. I wondered if Aghen might not be really there, and we were just seeing an image reflected, or somehow magically projected from the ice.

Whether or not he shared my suspicions, the King was not so stupid as to pass through the enemy's portal on his own. He just snorted in derision.

"Just tell me what brings you to darken my docks," he said.

Aghen smiled. "Why, greed, Your Majesty. Yours and mine. You've managed to accumulate more mana in one spot than many countries would think safe. Small wonder that someone would come looking to share in that bounty."

"Naturally, you think it's greed. Dorsay's dungeons make this country strong and secure. That mana is for the good of the whole country, not whatever self-aggrandizing project you have in mind."

The King gripped his sword, looking as though he wanted to use it against the portal.

Would that work? I wondered. *Maybe that's what the ice is for, to protect it.*

I took a look using Mana Sense, but there was a lot of powerful magic there that I didn't understand. It wasn't all Ice Magic, I was pretty sure.

"You say that," Aghen continued, "but you've proved unable to handle the demands that come with such a concentration. Really, I'd be doing you a favor."

"We've found your sabotage," the King said. He held up the enchanted amulet I'd given him. "Your tricks aren't going to work anymore."

Aghen didn't lose his smile, but it slipped a bit. "How unfortunate. It seems that your city won't be paralyzed for much longer. Still, you seem to be quite helpless *right now.*"

"Anything but, you wretched parasite," the King snarled.

"You're handling things adequately at the moment," Aghen admitted, "But how will you fare once my agent strikes a third time? Do you think you can repair your connections before that happens?"

"Of course we can," the King said. I knew that was a bluff. Did Aghen? Probably.

"You'll lose a dungeon if that happens," he warned, still wearing that smile. "Or perhaps I should cause another break? Have you been enjoying the one you have?"

It seemed that Aghen wasn't quite up to speed on the local news. The King didn't speak to correct him, just glared some more.

"I should have known that was you. Underhanded, cowardly—"

"Come, come," Aghen said smarmily. "All is fair in such conflicts. And there's no need for further action. Just agree to my terms, and we can—"

"There will be no agreement!" the King yelled and struck out again. With one swift move, he drew and swung at the portal. Once again, an invisible force flashed out, shattering the wall of ice behind the portal. The ice holding the artifact, though, was made of sterner stuff.

"You had to try, I understand," Aghen said smugly. Some of the force had gone through the portal and had cracked the ice there. But even as Aghen spoke, it reformed itself. The image of Aghen, though temporarily distorted, did not go away. "But your physical force is useless. I was going to give you more time to come to terms with your situation, but under the circumstances, I will have to accelerate my timetable. You have until tomorrow at noon to give me your answer."

Aghen's smile grew wider. "At that time, if you have not submitted, I will release another of your precious conduits. I'll also do so if you actually manage to fix one of them. Just to keep you on the edge."

The King snarled and looked over at Manuela. "I can at least—" he said, raising his sword again.

"If you harm one of my Agents," Aghen said icily, "My terms will not be anywhere near so generous."

The King thought about it . . . but lowered his sword. "Tomorrow, then," he said and turned away.

GAME RESET

As we headed back, the King gestured for me to come closer. Guessing his intent, I cast Privacy Bubble—aloud, just on the off chance that there were some watchers who didn't know I could silent cast.

"Can you intercept the saboteur?" he asked. He didn't mention the spell, which I took to mean that I'd read him correctly.

I grimaced. "I need a target for Dispel Image," I said. "If it was a confined area, I could hope to get lucky, but . . ."

"At least fifteen key menhirs, more if they decide to strike outside the city," the King confirmed. "All spread out around the walls and inner city."

"So no chance then," I concluded. The King didn't say anything for a moment, and I started to worry that he was going to have me try anyway.

"There was an Illusionist working for Duke Finley," I said. If I was going to be press-ganged into a job with no chance of success, another colleague would double my chances. "Somebody . . . Archambault?"

He frowned. "If an Illusionist had been picked up when we invested the castle, I would have been informed."

"So he's skipped out, then?"

"Illusionists are a shifty and unreliable bunch," he said wryly. "I'll make inquiries as to the name; he may have just failed to volunteer his class."

"What's going to happen with his boss? The Duke, I mean." I added, in case it wasn't clear.

"Mmmnn, I have not yet decided. This current matter takes precedence, and I need to . . . take the temperature of the other dukes. At this stage, though, I would say not much."

"Really?" I asked with just a hint of incredulity. "All that, and he walks free?"

"The Duke cannot be blamed for the break; we've learned that it was caused by his so-called ally, Shadthe. His defenses held, so his ancient family obligation has been fulfilled. For me to take his holding away at this time would be . . . impolitic."

"He tried to launch a coup, though?" I protested.

"Who is to say what those extra men were there for? He can claim that he was building up his forces due to fears of the dungeon's safety. He can claim that Voight's interference with his reinforcements endangered the town. I'd be forced to discipline Voight, instead."

"That's f—messed up," I complained.

"Voight is in need of *some* discipline," he countered. "How much depends on how well he does out at Risurn."

He looked off into the distance. "Only a distraction, but one I could not ignore. The fact that Shadthe is focused here will hopefully mean his presence in that domain is weaker."

He snapped out of it and looked back at me. "Of course, things might go differently, if you were to testify."

"I thought a commoner's word wasn't worth anything against a noble's," I said warily.

"True, but the word of a Champion is a different matter," he replied.

"Really?"

"Not just any Champion," he mused. "That barbarian woman, for example, would never be accepted by the lords. A Champion who risked her life saving the city, though, who had been elevated to nobility for her deeds . . ."

"I *just* got Talnier's status as a free city confirmed," I objected. "You want me to become the Baroness of it?"

"Marquess, actually," he corrected, "If we are to recognize the tribes as a nation, then the territory becomes a border region, rather than a frontier. As for your Council, if you don't wish the income from taxes, you can continue the present arrangement, with yourself as a purely nominal head."

"Remind me how this would help?" I asked.

"Binding yourself to the realm like that would go a long way towards convincing the other lords of your . . . soundness. That's the sort of thing you'd need to get your testimony accepted. That and marriage, of course."

"Marriage?" I exclaimed. My voice *may* have gone up slightly, but it was a calm and considered request for clarification, and not at all a shriek or a squeak.

"That shouldn't be a problem for you," he said with an amused smirk. "I understand there's already a young Captain in Talnier who's set his cap at you. If he doesn't suit you, once word gets out of how *eligible* you are, you should be inundated with suitors."

"I already am, at least when I'm not delving or sneaking about town," I said sourly. "Quite a number of lordlings have offered to overlook my humble origins."

"Oh, you can do better than those fools," The King said, that smirk still on his face.

"This *is* a joke, right?"

"Partly," he admitted. "You'd never get a proper marriage done before the trial."

I glared at him while trying to figure out how to say no. You weren't supposed to say no to a King, so Etiquette wasn't as much help as it should be.

"Think it over," he said. "Or, rather, forget about it for now. Our current emergency takes precedence, and a trial requires that I still have a city to hold it in."

"What are you going to do?" I asked.

"What I can. We're assuming that this saboteur is invisible, but the spell is part of the item, not cast. They may not have the spell, and may simply be relying on stealth. And even if they are using Invisibility, the spell is not impenetrable. I can get those of my men, and available adventurers, who have high Perception totals to search them out. While that goes on, I can muster an assault on the portal itself."

"It seemed pretty invulnerable," I said. "He put it right out the front and everything."

"Nothing is proof against a determined enough effort," he assured me. "It won't be easy, though. He gave me that hit because he was confident that his spell would hold. When I come back, he'll be putting all his effort into stopping me."

"Did you know that when you took the swing?"

"No, I was hoping that he'd overlooked the possibility that some sudden violence in the right place could put an end to his plan."

"So he's winning the strategy game here."

"Not . . . entirely." The King looked at me thoughtfully. "He thought, when he arrived, that we'd still be dealing with the break. That you—that all the Champions—would be dealing with that. We've broken his trick with the sabotage earlier than he expected."

I raised an eyebrow. *We broke the trick?* Apparently, being a King gave you partial credit for your subjects' accomplishments, because he proceeded without a shred of guilt displayed.

"He's running out of time," the King declared. "His feints have been exposed, and now he's right out there in the lake where I can get to him."

"I see. Good luck with that, I guess." I hesitated for a bit, second-guessing myself. Was this really the best move I had? Then I remembered a piece of wisdom that had been passed down in the trading room since time immemorial.

If the decision is risky, pass it to management to make the call.

"Actually, your Majesty, there is one other thing I could do . . ."

Even after clearing it with the King, I was still nervous about it. The individual steps were easy enough to do, though, so I started going through each one. I could always back out at the last minute if I got cold feet.

"Rhis, I'm going to need you to expand into the roof."

"Yesss, expansion! It's about time!"

"Try not to get too excited. This isn't for more levels; I need some sort of roof access made."

"Another entrance? Mistress, that will severely compromise security! Especially if it's on the roof! It will bypass half of our defenses!"

"It's just temporary," I assured him, but he kept the pout up. "I suppose . . . we could not connect it to the top? Have another staircase leading to it from the first floor?"

"That . . . could work," Rhis said thoughtfully. "As long as I can expand into the walls to get the extra room."

"Fine, fine, just get it done." By now, I had faith that Rhis would sense my intentions and construct a roof entrance that fit my needs without further details.

This bit wasn't strictly necessary. I could do it from the existing entrance, but it didn't feel right. I wanted to see the city when I did this, not the lobby of a decrepit building. While I waited for Rhis to finish, I continued catching up with the gang, getting a report of what monsters had come, and congratulating the kids on their victories.

All of the kids were level three now. Cutter was on level five, having gained experience both from the action here and from making a number of runs through my fighting level over the past few days. He was going to wait until he could talk with Cloridan again before taking a new profession.

When Rhis reported that he was done, I excused myself and stumped up the newly appeared spiral stairs all the way to the roof. Rhis had done me proud; the stairs came up in a freshly constructed cupola perched on the top of the roofline. Arches all around, each barely big enough to hold a walkway around the stairs I'd just come up by, supported a small dome. Most of the open arches were open windows, but one was built to be walked through, leading out to the roof.

I took a single step out onto the roof. Now that I knew what I was looking for, the "denominated space" of the dungeon was easy to spot. Right now I had one foot in it and one foot out. I checked to make sure that I still had access.

[Dungeon Status], I thought.

Dungeon Name	Tower of Learning		
Level: 7	XP: 38,095,541	Next Level: 100,000,000	Floors: 4
Current Mana: 1,368	Mana Cap: 1,500	Mana Regeneration: 150	Upkeep: 15,954
Dungeon Traits	[Expand]	Invaders: 0/0/0/0	
Monsters: 24	[Expand]		

No real surprises there, though I was glad to see that everyone was out of the dungeon at the moment. We still had that monster spawning emergency. At the thought, I glanced uneasily back at the open stairwell behind me. Maybe Rhis had a point about security. Most of the monsters being spawned couldn't fly, but some *could*, and some could *climb*. This cupola was hard to get to, but if something *did*, Rhis would break.

At my thought, the window arches started closing up with stone. The doorway I was standing in remained open, of course, but that would be temporary. I thought about having the windows be glassed in but rejected it in favor of additional defense. I didn't need a view.

It wasn't that great, anyway. All the buildings in this area were about the same height, so an uninspiring vista of rooftops was spread out before me. Still, better than street level, I supposed.

I returned my attention to Rhis's status. His 1,368 mana was plenty for my purposes, especially when you considered that, in human terms, it was a thousand times that.

I pulled out the item I received from the bottom of the Maze of the Forsaken Giant. Thanks to the unusually verbose Identification, I knew exactly how to use it. Was that a clue from my patron, about what I would have to do? It must have been. Without the mana from my dungeon, it would have been a powerful item with limited use. With that mana . . .

I held the Spatial Aegis and let the mana flow. Out of me, to start with, then from the dungeon, into me, and then into the Aegis. First, the duration. I'd suggested an hour, but once I'd explained what my capacity was, the King had decided on a day. Long enough that Shadthe would give up trying to reconnect, but not *too* disruptive for spatial items used by Dorsan citizens.

The cost for that was 86,400 mana, and I let it flow through me. An unending torrent, flowing into a seemingly bottomless black hole.

[Mana Development] Level 5 acquired through use.

For gaining a skill level, you have been awarded 1 XP.

[Mana Development] Level 6 acquired through use.

For gaining a skill level, you have been awarded 1 XP.

Dungeons are cheating, I thought, not for the first time. I wasn't finished, though. Next was the area. I went with fifty kilometers. Fifty thousand mana.

[Mana Development] Level 7 acquired through use.

For gaining a skill level, you have been awarded 1 XP.

The Aegis held it all without complaint. Even with Mana Sense, there was just the faintest of glows about it. Shaking my head in disbelief, I stepped fully out of the dungeon, onto the roof.

I triggered the Spatial Aegis.

Now it glowed, quickly becoming too bright to look at. No heat, though, thankfully. I closed my eyes and turned my head away from the light. It lasted for about ten seconds, fading just as quickly.

I looked out over the city. Aside from some shouts from below, nothing seemed to have changed. I suspected it would be a different story down on the docks, though.

ISOLATED

By the time we got down to the docks, it was all gone. I didn't know whether the ice had melted or just disappeared, but there was nothing left of Shadthe's ice ziggurat. There were some guards present, keeping everyone away from the pier where the construction had "docked." Thanks to Memorize, I recognized the officer in charge. He had been one of the ones to accompany the King on his last trip down here.

I didn't know his name, but I hardly needed it for an update. I walked straight up to him and gave him a warm smile.

"Has the artifact been secured yet?" I asked without preamble. Browbeating a soldier for operational details would *probably* get me in trouble, but there was no harm in just asking. And he had *seen* me talking with the King. He struggled with it, but not for long.

"No, my lady," he admitted. I carefully did not correct his form of address. "It fell into the lake—we have divers searching."

I eyed the waters. As I watched, one of the divers came up for breath and then dived down again. There was probably some sort of System wackiness that governed how long you could hold your breath that I hadn't investigated. A Water Mage would help, but I wasn't much of one. And the water looked cold—and smelly.

I made a note to myself to practice Water Magic back in the tower.

"What about Envoy Fisher?" I asked. "What happened to her?"

"She fled," the man replied. "Pursuing her wasn't my—my priority."

"I'm sure," I murmured thoughtfully. Were there others that were doing the pursuing? They might have hoped that she would lead them to the saboteur, but I had the feeling that Manuela's tradecraft was better than that. It was better than *mine*, after all, and I knew better.

"Well, thank you for your time," I said. "I'll be sure to tell His Majesty that you're doing a wonderful job."

He flinched slightly and saluted me, and I went back to rejoin my companions. I'd left Janie back at the dungeon, but Felicia and Kyle had insisted on joining me. It was still pretty dangerous on the streets, even with the various efforts of the monster extermination squads. Since I didn't really *want* to skulk around like an invisible thief, I had gratefully accepted their support.

"I guess back to the palace," I said. "It's the best place for news, and I might be needed to undo an invisibility spell."

The palace compound was buzzing with guards, but it wasn't under lockdown. We had our passes, so we were able to get in. My spatial ring wasn't working, but I'd thought ahead, emptying it of things I thought I might need while I was in the tower.

Wait, does that mean Shadthe's portal would work from within a dungeon? I thought to myself. I was willing to bet that the other end of the connection was in Shadthe's dungeon, so it must work from within a dungeon.

I made another note to bring that up if I ended up talking with the King, or got asked about strategy. It didn't seem likely, nor did it seem particularly urgent. Manuela hadn't gotten a look at the Aegis, so she wouldn't have seen its Identification.

We headed back to our apartments, but I couldn't stay there for long. There wasn't anything for us to do, but I couldn't sit still and wait for everyone else to play their roles. Would the saboteur strike again, or would the guards catch them? Eventually, I decided to go up on the walls. From there, I would have the earliest notice of any mana conduit sabotage, and I could follow the progress of Kaito's plan.

It looked as if it was working. It was doing *something*, at least. I'd never gotten a good look at how the Tribal mana workings worked. They ran through the forest, so you couldn't see one until you were *in* one.

Looking down at the city, I could see something that had to be the mana river that they were forming. It ran in a rough circle around the city, mostly keeping to the streets. It didn't run *straight*, taking turns according to some hidden logic of geography or its own internal dynamics. Overall, though, it described a rough circle.

It looked quite different from the mana conduits. While they looked like physical constructions, this looked . . . like mist. It was one type of mana, I realized, allowed to leak out of the construction and fill the air around with homogeneously smooth mana.

I wasn't sure what its purpose was, but it seemed to slowly dissolve the tangled spaghetti weaves of the existing mana mess. The loose mana was getting drawn in and was being forced to circulate . . . around and around, I guessed. Maybe at some point, they could link it into a conduit and pipe it into one of the dungeons.

"Looks like they've gotten the hang of it," a voice came from beside me. I turned to see Fassi, looking down at the streets below.

"Shouldn't you be down there?" I asked. "Or with Kaito?"

She flicked an ear at me. "We're not actually doing the work; we were just showing the Scholars *how*," she said. "And Kaito is reporting to the King how it all went. I thought I'd come up here and see for myself how it's going."

She looked over at me. "They said we should ask *you* why our spatial items aren't working," she said with a scowl.

"I shut down Aghen Shadthe's portal," I said, as if it were no big deal. "No spatial manipulation for another twenty hours. Your items are still in there, you just can't access them until the effect ends."

She snapped her fingers. "That item!" she said. "But where'd you get the mana?"

"Trade secret," I said. "But it's not like there's a shortage." I pointed down at the city.

"As if," she snorted. "Wild mana like that, it's not as if a mortal could absorb a thousandth of it."

"I suppose that if we could absorb mana more efficiently, we wouldn't have this problem."

"True, we'd just suck up all this extra mana and put it in some gems." She sighed and looked down again at the city. "But if we could do that, we'd keep sucking it down until it was all gone."

"Isn't that what the Kingdom actually does?" I asked. "I know you're ideologically opposed to that, but it seems to be working for them."

"Theurgy enchantments can only go so far," she said. "They need a certain amount of magic to work, so they have to shut down when the mana drops to a certain point."

"Interesting," I said. "Is that—" but I was interrupted by an approaching guard.

"My apologies, Councillor, but you're needed in the inner compound."

* * *

"Of course, Your Majesty, I was happy to help."

"And without negotiating a reward first; that is very unlike you."

The noblewoman he was addressing curtsied gracefully. To my surprise, I recognized her as my one-time dinner companion. Lady Rankin. Next to her was another surprise.

"I knew time was of the essence, your Majesty," Lady Rankin continued, "And your generosity is renowned."

"I'm sure that it is. Ah, Councillor Hammond." The King turned to me, and I gave a little jump as Etiquette gave me a nudge. I had been too busy staring at the new arrival to pay attention.

What is Reynard Moore doing here? I wondered, but the King was talking.

"Councillor, I've called you here to identify these three." He gestured to the far side of the room. I blinked and glanced over to see three people in manacles and gags. One of them I recognized.

"I, uh, think you've already met Envoy Fisher?" I said, confused.

"Yes," he said patiently. "But since illusions are in play, and since Fisher—and all envoys—are notoriously slippery, I thought it best that you confirm that these people are who we think they are."

"Oh! Of course . . . [Dispel Image, Dispel Image, Dispel Image]."

No one flickered and changed before our eyes, so it looked as though we had the real ones. I glanced back at Reynard. He was trying to keep his cool in front of the King, but he did look back at me, and I could see his anger. Yeah, he recognized me. I remembered that he'd been able to see through the Katherine Meland illusion that I'd used back then.

Now, though, we were both level six. He could probably still beat me up, but I doubt he could stand up to my illusions or social skills. I returned his glare with a calm, icy gaze.

I beat you once, when you out-levelled me, I thought. *Now, we're on more even terms.*

"Congratulations, it seems you've caught your culprits," I said aloud. "Or . . . Lady Rankin has?" That seemed to be what was going on here, the reason for her presence. I had thought her just a socialite, but it seemed she was something more. Maybe *she* was the spymaster.

"We must all do our part in the defense of the realm," she simpered. "It just so happened I had a man in my service with a knack for seeing through illusions." She gestured at Reynard. "He was able to track them down and alert His Majesty's forces."

"I see." I looked back at the prisoners. The two I didn't know were looking pretty scared, but Manuela was maintaining a defiant stance. I felt a little bad, looking at her. She'd never done anything to *me*, and it felt weird going from fending off her amorous advances to watching her get carted off to . . . wherever. "What's going to happen to them?"

"Nothing too onerous for the envoy, at least for now," the King said grimly. "She shall serve as a hostage until this situation is resolved. The other two . . . we still need to confirm that one of these is the saboteur."

"I'm sure they are," Lady Rankin said with a thin smile. "Shadthe cannot have that many hirelings in the city. And that one was found with one of the enchanted amulets."

"Perhaps," the King said. "We shall put them to the question and see what is revealed."

Well, none of that sounded good, but I didn't want to step into it. "Then, if there's nothing else, Your Majesty . . ."

"One more thing," he said, his eyes remaining on the prisoners. "Since it seems that this crisis is now close to being resolved, Duke Finley's trial will be held soon. Have you given any thought about whether you'll testify?"

My eyes flicked over to Rankin, who kept her face studiously neutral. The King was really asking if I wanted to be ennobled, and I didn't see her as being a fan of that idea. For one, I was fairly sure she was an ally of Finley's and for another, she didn't seem the type to welcome a jumped-up commoner as a peer.

"With respect, Your Majesty, I'd prefer to keep my current status. If that means my testimony won't be heeded, then the problem lies with your Court, not my status."

Now he looked at me, surprised, and just a little bit offended. "I was under the impression that you had your own problems with the man." His voice had gotten a bit sterner.

"Sure," I said. "But it wasn't me he plotted a coup against. To be honest, I don't think you're going to let that stand, no matter what testimony gets heard."

This time it was his eyes that flicked towards Lady Rankin, who was staying very quiet. No doubt she would have preferred to be actually invisible.

"Perhaps," was all he said, followed by "You can go."

I curtsied again and got the hell out of there, only sparing a last glance at Manuela.

Sorry, there's really not a lot I can do. Hostage wasn't *too* bad; maybe Shadthe would pay up.

As I left, I made another note. I really should ask Voight how Reynard came to be working for Lady Rankin.

THE TRIAL

I t took two days to organize the trial. To be fair, there was a lot of organizing to be done, and I was glad that I wasn't a part of it. I had my own preparations to make, and they kept me busy. I was pretty much done with Dorsay—I'd gotten what I came here for and the longer I waited, the more likely it was I'd come back to a disaster in Talnier.

But tying up loose ends can take a lot of time. In my case, I had my tower, and my school, and lots of questions from Voight when he finally returned. The Kingdom had other concerns. Fixing the menhirs, cleaning up the lost mana, rounding up Finley's troops—both official and unofficial.

They weren't finished with all of that by the time the trial was announced, but things were clearly getting better. I was not asked to testify, but I *did* get to attend. I was a bit conflicted about showing my face because I couldn't see this as a *real* trial. The only judge was the King, who was hardly a disinterested party. There wasn't a jury, but there *was* an audience of lords that the King needed the support of. If they didn't like the King's judgment, then things would be . . . bad, I was told.

So there would be only a vague nod in the direction of justice. With no nobles to testify against him, the King's verdict and sentence would be based entirely on the politics of the situation. Some nobles would want Finley to fall, of course. Others would support him. Others still wouldn't care about *Finley*, but they would care about what this trial said about their privileges and the relative power balance between the King and the nobility.

None of the other participants even rated a trial. The Lyran ambassador had been expelled, or would be once the Lyran fleet had removed itself from Latorran waters. I had heard that the battle had been hard fought, and not entirely a victory for the Kingdom. However, without anything to gain here, Shadthe had removed his influence from the battle, causing the Lyrans to retreat.

One of the men that had been captured with Manuela had confessed to being the one who had caused the Forsaken Giant break. Or so the King had announced. There was no trial for him; his execution had been announced at the same time as his crime. Nothing had been mentioned about Manuela or the other man, presumably the saboteur. No doubt, negotiations with them or Aghen Shadthe were continuing.

I wasn't sure what was going to happen on the Aghen Shadthe front. Without his portal, or his agents, there wasn't much he could *do*. However, he hadn't been defeated, only pushed back. No mention had been made of his other agents, such as Tom back in Talnier. I supposed that it would depend on how negotiations over Manuela proceeded. Was the Kingdom going to be at war with the wizard, or were they going to paper over the differences and let bygones be bygones?

One person who seemed to have come through this smelling of roses was the Chancellor. Despite the fact that this all started from one of his schemes going wrong, he was still on the dais next to the King. I would have liked to imagine that he faced *some* censure, but if that was the case, it wasn't being publicized.

The trial was being held outside, in the outer court of the palace compound. Unlike most of the indoor spaces, it was large enough to hold the 300 prisoners that were being tried along with the Duke. Not all of his forces were being prosecuted, just the ones that he'd illegally smuggled in. I wasn't sure what crime they were supposed to have committed, but again, this wasn't a real trial, just an attempt for the King to show his dominance while trying not to overstep his bounds.

Since the courtyard wasn't normally where trials were held, they'd had to make a few changes. The King, his officials, and Duke Finley were all up on a dais against one of the walls. The rest of the courtyard was set up in much the same way as my first audience had been. There were stands at the sides for the spectators. One side for nobles and one side for commoner guests like myself, because of course the nobles didn't want to mix.

The prisoners knelt on the stone flagstones in the middle of the courtyard. They were surrounded by guards armed with spears. Occasionally, one of the prisoners would try to shift their weight off their knees and get "reprimanded" by the butt of a spear.

I mostly ignored a lot of what was being said, preferring to observe Duke Finley's face as the proceedings went on. He wasn't happy, and I had to admit to feeling good about that. I couldn't claim to be responsible for any part of that expression, though. If anything, my actions had saved his life. From what Kaito had told me, the giants, let alone the Forsaken one, would have wiped the floor with them.

Despite being lucky to be alive, the Duke's face was a mixture of sadness and anger. Sadness at losing his son, and anger at being held to account by the King he'd tried to depose. Talk about entitlement.

The first person to testify was the Lyran ambassador. From the fact that he appeared willingly and testified with no signs of distress, I judged that the fix was in, as far as that country was concerned. His testimony was carefully crafted, leaving the Chancellor's involvement out of it. Instead, he made out that he'd made contact with Finley on his own initiative.

Finley's response to this was simple. "He lies," was all that he said.

Then Manuela was brought out, confirming the ambassador's words. She seemed subdued, far from her normal exuberant self. She had a few details to add, mainly about how Shadthe had betrayed the conspirators and caused the dungeon to break. There was a flash of anger on the Duke's face when he learned about that, but he kept his composure.

"Lies, all lies," was all that he said.

Finally, there was the matter of the soldiers, brought in for the coup. Not all of them were present. Quite a lot of them had died on that night of chaos, and more of them had turned and run when things turned against them. Still, there were something like 300 of them here, shackled and kneeling on the stones of the courtyard.

"These are not men of mine," Duke Finley said. "Who they are sworn to, I don't know."

That wasn't in the script. There was a murmur from the crowd and a sudden stir from the captured soldiers. The Chancellor, serving as the prosecutor up to now, paused and looked to his King for instructions. The King called him over and they conferred quietly. When they broke off, the Chancellor left the dais to speak with other Court officials. He looked grey with shock.

The King spoke up for the first time, resuming the prosecution.

"That's not what they claim," he said, his voice ringing out. I didn't think it was magic amplification, just good lungs.

"I care not what they claim," the Duke replied, just as loudly. "They are not sworn to me, and if they say they are, they lie."

"My lord, no!" one of the soldiers exclaimed, struggling to his feet. He was struck down by the guards, as were five more who had the same idea.

"It's us! Your sworn—" Another prisoner was cut off by a brutal blow by a guard, forcing the captive to the ground. More and more of the soldiers were struggling with the guards now. It was a one-sided struggle, as the prisoners were shackled in iron, but there weren't that many guards . . .

Until there were. A troop of guardsmen marched in, perhaps a hundred of them. The prisoners were soon quelled, and the King continued.

"They seem convinced otherwise," he said wryly. His attention was on the audience, perhaps trying to judge if Finley's peers were going to back such an obvious lie.

"Clearly, they are mercenaries hired by Shadthe to discredit me," the Duke said coldly. "To drive a wedge between the pillars that hold this nation together."

"I see," the King said calmly. "Soldiers for hire who break the law have no protections under it. They are nothing but common bandits."

He paused, perhaps to give Finley a chance to respond, perhaps to lend a bit of gravity to what came next. Finley's eyes narrowed, as if he sensed something was going to happen, but wasn't sure what it was.

"Captain, execute these bandits."

Now there was an uproar. A lot of the spectators rose from their seats in protest, myself among them. We weren't quite dumb enough to go down and confront the King's guards, though. Enough of them were facing the stands with spears at the ready to enforce decorum.

Most of the prisoners didn't stand still to be executed, but they didn't have a chance. The guards weren't striking with the blunt end of their spears this time. They hewed into the prisoners with brutal efficiency.

Duke Finley watched as his men were chopped down in front of him. He must have been shocked, but his face didn't show it. He wasn't showing anything now; the anger and sorrow were covered over by a blank mask.

It was over appallingly quickly. I still hadn't grasped the idea that it was happening before they started dragging corpses away. The flagstones were red with blood.

"With that small matter cleared up, it seems that there are no charges left to bring against you," the King said. "All that remains is to congratulate you on your successful defense of the break."

The Duke took a deep breath and slowly turned away from the bloody flagstones.

"Thank you, Your Majesty. It is gratifying to be proved innocent, as I knew that I would be." He gave me a quick satisfied glance and seemed satisfied with what he saw. He might have mistaken my horror at the atrocity I'd just witnessed as being upset about him getting off scot-free.

A voice came from the stands where the nobles were seated.

"Your Majesty, may I speak?"

I looked—we all looked—over to where it came from. To my surprise, it was Aubey—Lord Duvost—stepping out onto the main floor. He walked towards the dais where the participants were, walking through the pooled blood without a care. He stopped before the first step and bowed.

"You would speak on this matter?" The King asked. Finley didn't say anything, just looked at Aubey like something that had crawled out of a gutter.

"I would, your Majesty. I would speak against this man, and be heard by my peers. However, while I have claimed a title, I have not been confirmed in it."

Aubey's voice wasn't as loud as the King's, but he wasn't at all quiet. He was speaking as loudly as he could without shouting.

"Then, Lord Duvost, may it be so. I confirm your right to your title before all your peers."

I wondered if this was scripted as well, or if the King was just going along with whatever Aubey had planned.

Lord Duvost bowed to the King and then straightened. "I accuse Duke Finley of killing my father and attempting to kill me."

"What testimony do you bring to this accusation?" The King asked.

"The testimony of my father, as he lay dying in my arms," Aubey said bitterly. "And the word of the Status, notifying me of Duke Finley's failed Intrigue against me."

"I see," the King said. He turned to Finley. "And what do you have to say to this accusation?"

Finley had fully recovered his composure by now. He was back to showing carefully controlled anger, but there was a certain amount of triumph.

"When nobles disagree, there is only one way to determine who is in the right," he declared smugly. "I invoke my right to trial by combat."

"I accept," Aubert replied immediately. "As the wronged party, I choose steel weapons and armor."

"What a shame," the King sighed. "For a second there, I thought you had a plan."

THE DUEL

Y ou're an idiot."
     I said those words to, who else, Aubert Duvost after allowing him to enter my apartments. He shrank a bit under my gaze, as well as at the looks that everyone else were giving him. Most of the disdain was coming from Janie, while Felicia and Kyle's were more curious. The kids looked on with that predatory interest that kids got when the adults were going to do something entertaining.

"I—I don't see why you'd say that," Aubert said defensively.

"You had to know that he'd call for trial by combat," I said. I would have liked to complain about such an archaic method of determining justice, but it wasn't much worse than the other methods commonly used here. After seeing how those other, supposedly more civilized methods worked out, I was having second thoughts about even the loose association I had with the royal house. Other than leaving the country, however, there wasn't much I could do.

The thing that really got under my skin was that if I had accepted that title and testified against Finley . . . would those men not have died? If my testimony had been enough to sway the lords enough for the King to convict . . . would he have? With Finley convicted of treason, there would have been no need to execute the troops. Or would there be? I had to admit, I didn't see any kind of reason evident in that incident.

The King had surmised that Finley would claim the men as his, part of an overzealous plan to defend against a break. A minor offense with a good cause behind it, hardly worth prosecuting. Instead, Finley had disowned his men as bandits in a fit of pique.

The King's response had been no less childish, in my own, carefully unstated, opinion. One kid says he doesn't want his toy anymore, so the other kid breaks it.

"I knew he would call for a duel," Aubert admitted, breaking me out of the thoughts that had been running through my head ever since I'd had to wipe the blood off my shoes before returning to the apartment.

"And you know he's going to—" I stopped, struck by the inappropriateness of the expression I was about to use. Wipe the floor worked for fistfights, but the floor was going to be much bloodier by the time the Duke was done. "—cut you down like a dog," I tried instead.

"Not . . . necessarily," Aubert said weakly. "But I couldn't let his evil acts stand!"

"Seems to me they'll be standing just fine when you're bleeding out on the floor and Duke Finley is getting cleared of all charges."

"The gods . . ." Aubert started, mumbling the words. "A trial by combat, it puts the matter in the hands of the gods. They sometimes act to correct injustice."

"And how often do they do that?" I asked skeptically.

"Not often," he admitted. "But there are three Champions in the city! They must be paying attention right now."

"Of course they are," I said. "And how might they interfere with this duel?"

"Well . . . generally they act through their Champions."

"So you want me to help you cheat in this duel."

"It's not—it's not cheating if a god does it," he said hesitantly.

"What about me, is it cheating if I do it?"

"Probably," he admitted sheepishly. "Especially since no one knows you're a Champion. Maybe one of the others?"

I sighed. Fortunately, Kaito and Isidre had not attended the trial. They had been delving the King's dungeon at his invitation. An invitation that had not been extended to me. I hadn't thought much of it at the time—I was far too busy with logistical concerns to go—but now I wondered if the King had made sure that they were out of the way when things got bad.

On the one hand, it was nice that the King didn't think I was loose cannon enough to disrupt the trial. On the other, it was more evidence that the mass execution had been a message to *me*, as much as the Duke.

Play the Game properly, or people will die.

If that *was* the message, then I rejected it. People were going to die regardless of what I did. I'd save them if I could, but I couldn't have saved those poor souls. The Game—the rules that all these nobles played among themselves. That was the real problem and that was what had to come crumbling down.

"Aubert," I said, giving him his full name while he was still around to hear it. "If this was your plan, why didn't you come to me—or the others—*before* the trial?"

He looked to the side shiftily. "If I'd confirmed divine intervention before I spoke up, it wouldn't have been an act of standing up heroically for justice . . . and that's what it takes to get an intervention."

"That's true," Felicia spoke up. "That's what's in all the stories."

"Don't encourage him!" I groaned.

"Well, I just thought you might not know about the stories," she pointed out.

"Leaving the stories aside—far, far aside—Aubert, I don't know of a way to interfere with your duel."

"You don't?" Janie asked, surprised. "What about all the fancy finger-twiddling?"

"Oh, I could make you win the *fight*, but the problem is that people will be watching. If I make you or your sword appear where it's not, or disappear entirely, people will *notice*."

"You've thought about this," Kyle stated.

"Of course I've thought about this! The very idea of this trial offends me, and I'd want to interfere even if I didn't have a stake."

"You have a stake?" Aubert asked suspiciously.

I stared at him. "You may not be the best of neighbors," I said. "But if you lose and Finley wins, who takes your title?"

"My younger brother?" he asked, confused.

"Does he? Or will it go to your cousin, Guillaume? Finley's loyal servant."

"But he's in prison," Aubert objected.

I sighed again. "People can come out of prisons," I told him. "With Finley emerging from this more powerful than ever, how is the King going to resist his petition?"

"I didn't think of that," he said glumly.

"You didn't think, period. And now you're going to die."

"Isn't there anything you can do?" he asked plaintively.

"I do have *one* spell that only Finley will see," I said. "The problem is, as soon as something happens that contradicts the spell, it ends."

"I don't understand," Aubert said.

"If I use that spell to make your sword disappear, then when you stick him with it, that will contradict the spell, and the spell will end," I explained. "Do you think, if I give you a chance, that you can finish him with one blow?"

He thought about it. "No," he finally said. "Even if he was unaware, I don't have Rogue bonuses that would let me do enough damage."

"So, you get one strike in, he calls foul, and I get carted off to prison. You get to redo the duel without me, and die."

"It would be a forfeit," he corrected me. "He would be awarded the victory, and I wouldn't die?"

"I'd be so happy for you, as I rotted in prison," I said sarcastically. "We won't be doing that."

"What about the others?"

"I don't like your chances. Neither of them are good at what you'd call tricks, and they're still level five—not up to dealing with the Duke directly."

He slumped in his chair. "So I'm really going to die, then?"

I looked at him sympathetically. "I'm afraid so."

The duel was held in the same courtyard that had seen the execution of 300 men just two days ago. The stones had been cleaned, but to my eye, they were still stained. This was the last of my engagements in Dorsay. I'd gotten my Charter, and the last of the loose ends, if not tied up, were being left behind. I didn't want to attend this duel, but I really did have a stake in who won. I didn't want to wait a week for the news to come via regular channels.

I was the only one of my party here. I was all packed up and would be taking a griffin out of here as soon as possible after the duel was done. Rhis was safely tucked away in my spatial ring, now freed of a lot of the coin that had been there a few days ago. The Tower of Learning was no more but would hopefully be resurrected soon in Talnier.

There was just this duel—or call it another execution—to get through. This time, the dais had been set between the two stands, and the stands were set up closer together, for a better view of the fight. The King, the judges, and the two combatants were standing there at the moment.

"The terms of the duel are that it continues until one fighter is unable to," the King said, his voice ringing out. "They shall fight using steel weapons and wearing steel armor."

This was . . . not code exactly, but the traditional term used for unenchanted weapons and armor. You *could* enchant steel, but only for a short time before it degraded. Similarly, the terms mentioned only arms and armor, but it apparently included other enchanted items. Both fighters were scanned by a mage before the fight started, but I gave Finley a scan of my own, just to be sure.

Not that he needed help from an enchantment.

The King was looking pretty grim as the officials left the platform. If I were Finley, I wouldn't have wanted him adjudicating my duel. Of course, the King wasn't doing that directly, but it was his officials who were filling the role. If the fight had been more even, he might well have managed to tip the scales somehow.

The King gave Aubert's hand a friendly shake as he prepared to dismount from the dais, clapping one hand to Aubert's shoulder. At first, Aubert looked pleased at the attention from his liege. Finley had been pointedly snubbed.

Then Aubert got a pained look on his face. He said something, but too quietly to be heard at this distance over the crowd. The King kept on smiling and shaking his hand.

Then Aubert screamed. There was a second screech as the armor covering Aubert's shoulder deformed under the friendly-seeming grip of the King.

The crowd went silent at the sound, and at the sight. Aubert fell to the ground, still screaming, as the King released his grip.

"Healers!" he called out, and two men in military uniforms rushed onto the dais. Rather than cast spells on the King's victim, they picked him up and carried him off.

"How careless of me," the King announced calmly. "I do forget my own strength sometimes. It seems that Lord Duvost is unable to fight this duel."

"Healers can—" Finley tried to interject.

"I'm afraid his armor has been pressed too hard into his shoulder for an easy recovery," the King said with a sad frown. "It will have to be removed before healing . . . which will take some time. Master of Ceremonies, what is the proper course of action under such circumstances?"

He was speaking to the main judge, who looked far too composed, given what had just happened. He must have been tipped off by the King.

"With the accuser unfit for the trial, a Champion must be selected from—"

"Excellent," the King said. "Since his injury was my fault, it is only right I step up into his place." Finley started to object, but he was stilled by what had to be the King's Intimidation let loose far enough away for me to not feel it.

"Let's see . . . steel weapons and armor," he said. He dropped his cloak to the ground and there was a shimmer as a breastplate and mail appeared around him. A sword shortly followed, appearing naked in his hand. All of it was unenchanted.

The crowd's murmur grew, as it viewed what was more clear evidence that this was all pre-mediated by the King. No one spoke too loudly, though. We had come here expecting an execution, but we had clearly been mistaken as to the victim. No one wanted to be added to the list.

Finley was frozen in place, his teeth bared in a grimace. He was already wearing his armor. Now, he drew his sword.

"Someone said to me," the King mused, stepping into position opposite Finley, "that when the rules prevent treachery being unmasked, the problem is in the rules. Or words to that effect. You thought I was weak, constrained by the rules that bind us all. You forgot that the rules *serve* *me.*"

His sword flashed as the duel began.

You have defeated Finley Arryen in an Intrigue. You have earned 245 XP.

Two hours later, I was on a griffin flying back to Talnier.

I never want to go back to that damn town.

RETURN

From above, Talnier looked like a picture postcard of a fantasy town. From here, you could barely see the nasty spikes that covered every wall and roof. They just looked like decorations. You couldn't smell the fish markets or the semi-open sewers that ran through the main streets. And you definitely couldn't make out the less savory parts of the town. Criminals liked to work in narrow streets, covered from the light of the sun by high buildings and jutting eaves.

That was how you could tell the difference between a banker and a criminal—a banker needs good lighting.

Talnier looked much the same as it had when I left. I asked the rider to circle the town so I could get a good look. There was some new construction going on—both in the town center and outside the walls. The town center would hold the new administration building while the market outside was going to be a more commercial district. It looked as if it was going to be behind a wall, but the small wooden structure barely compared to the high stone walls of the main town.

At least it isn't on fire, I told myself. *I'm sure everything will be fine when I get down there.*

I was travelling alone, and by griffin, for a number of reasons. Number one, of course, was that I couldn't get out of Dorsay fast enough. The other reason was to serve as a lightning rod for the remaining discontent that the noble faction felt about me.

I say remaining, but while they had lost one of their main standard-bearers, the actual amount of resentment hadn't subsided in any way. The new Duke, one of Finley's other sons, wasn't going to be confirmed quickly, but I'm sure he would inherit a certain amount of suspicion of my role in his father's death. Since he couldn't go after the King or the other Champions, at least openly, he might well decide to come after me.

As for the other faction of nobles that wanted me, if not dead, then firmly put in my place, I'd been warned about them already by Aubey, just before I left.

"It seems I'm not dead after all," he had said, wincing at the pain. The King's healers had been wittering about, claiming that there was nothing they could do at the moment. Whether that was true, or if they were just sandbagging so that the King's story held up, I didn't know. It was also possible that the King had ordered them to *not* save the arm—as part of some cost that Aubey had to bear as the price of the King saving his life.

"I didn't predict it, and if I had, I'm not sure I would have recommended it," I had told him.

"Better injured than dead, and I got my confirmation."

"You know, they're already spreading rumors about why he did it? Lady Rankin was saying that he was so taken with your bravery fighting the spawned monsters that he couldn't bear to see you perish."

"It's as good an explanation as any," Aubey had mused. "I still don't know why he intervened. If that's true, then I owe you for suggesting it."

His eyes had darkened as he considered what to say next. "This isn't over, though. Finley's heir, and my lord Duke, they both want Talnier."

"They can't have it, not legally."

He had shrugged, instantly regretting it as the metal dug in deeper. "They'll find a way. And when they do . . . at least when my lord does . . . I'll be the head of his spear."

"You're going to lead an armed force against me?" I was less shocked that they were willing to countenance such flagrant law-breaking than I was at the fact that Aubey was willing to admit it.

"I'm your closest neighbor . . . and I owe my loyalty to Duke Victor. If he gives me an illegal order, I can report it to the King, but there will be some pretext to give them cover."

"I see. Thanks for the warning."

"Sorry."

I left him there, then, in the good hands of the healers. Well, the hands at least. I guess I'd see how good they were the next time we met.

So there was resentment, but I thought that it would take some time to crystallize yet. Travelling alone meant that I could get back to my power base more quickly before something manifested. And it meant that everyone else could get back unmolested by any "bandits."

Say what you like about nobles, but they did have a refreshing tendency to focus on their principal enemy. Janie and her caravan weren't a threat to the nobles, so if I wasn't with them, they should be ignored. While they didn't care about collateral damage, the notion of going after an enemy's dependents *deliberately* was too dishonorable to be even considered by most nobles.

Janie's caravan was going to take much longer to get here. Three carts' worth of kids and supplies didn't move very fast. I hadn't wanted to bring the kids with me, but I hadn't had much of a choice. Most of them had realized that they didn't have much future in Dorsay and had clamored to come with me. They were mostly at level three now, so they could take care of themselves to an extent.

Not all of them wanted to be Adventurers, to my relief. Some did, but others were saving skill points for Crafting skills. I'd promised to see if I could find them apprenticeships in Talnier. Others were interested in Scribe, and the jobs that could come from that.

To my surprise, Issey had also asked if I had a place for her. I'd thought that she was married to her dream of dancing . . . and she was, but she'd accepted that there wasn't a living in it. She'd developed an interest in teaching, which I was happy to encourage, and I promised to teach her the skill when I got a chance. I'd also promised to find her a space, either in the tower or someplace in town, where she could both practice and perform. There might not be a living to be made dancing in Dorsay, but everything was much cheaper in Talnier, and there wasn't much entertainment beyond drinking.

Between a couple of runs through the dungeon with Janie and the spawn night, Issey had managed to make level four. Once I set up the new Tower of Learning, she'd be one of my key personnel.

That meant we had to do something about the Gilded Lily. Issey didn't want to sell or abandon it. Rhis had withdrawn carefully from it, leaving the parts he had occupied in better shape than he had found it. The addition of a cupola hadn't done any harm. He hadn't occupied all of it, though, and the place was in disrepair. If we stopped occupying it, some lowlife would be squatting in minutes.

Fortunately, Guild Master Voight had owed me a few favors and was willing to rent it as accommodation for Guild members. It would need renovations, of course, but the building had required repairs already, and they could keep the basic structure. The main ballroom was a little big for a bar, but Voight had assured me that wasn't a critical problem. Nor was its proximity to the various whorehouses in the area.

Given the absurd price differentials between Dorsay and Talnier, Issey should be able to live quite comfortably on the rent payments, even if she didn't get a job. As long as the payments came through. Someone running between towns with a bag of gold was no substitute for electronic funds transfer. It might take approximately forever before I was able to set that up, though.

Another loose end, the Digger brothers, would *not* be joining us. While it would be nice to tell a story about how they'd seen the light of gainful employment and left their life of debauchery and petty crime behind, they hadn't noticeably changed. I avoided the discussion entirely by paying their tab at the Rose and enabling them to be customers once again. The mistress there wasn't going to extend them *credit* again but, thanks to me, they had a little money. They were just philosophically opposed to paying their debts.

Access to the Rose got them out of our hair for long enough to pack everything up. Well, for Rhis to pack everything up. Quite a lot of the dungeon was Phantasmal, of course, and could be dismissed at will. There were some actual items and monsters that had to be packed away or slain.

Rhis claimed, with no actual evidence that I could see, that *withdrawing* from a volume that it had taken was something that no dungeon had ever done before. He dropped all his objections, though, once I reminded him that this was just a practice dungeon, and we'd have a chance to construct a new, better tower.

Despite never having done it before, Rhis took care of the task with his customary perfectionism, emptying the spaces before undoing the spatial expansion and carefully withdrawing his influence from the parts of the structure that he'd occupied. Then he voluntarily dissolved the mana construct, leaving his core lying on the floor. Not for long, of course, as I quickly secured it. It was going to be tough to find a place close to Talnier without disrupting the two dungeons already there, but at least I could operate in the open now.

The griffin dropped at the rider's command, heading for the central yard in the Griffin Riders Academy. We landed with a rush of air as the griffin flared its wings as we neared the ground.

Cloridan was there, waiting for me. I'd sent word ahead of when I was coming. Since I wanted my opponents to know I'd left, I hadn't cared who might intercept the message.

"So it all went well, then?" he asked doubtfully, as I watched myself get unstrapped from my harness. "I kind of expected you to arrive covered in blood, or ash."

I gave him a glare to hide how glad I was to see him. "I had a bath—several, in fact."

He snickered. "Your suitors will be glad to hear it, I'm sure. They're already lined up—I told them you were going to rest for today and you'd see them tomorrow."

"Suitors? Plural?" I asked. "I would have thought Tom would have legged it out of town by now, and Hector . . . Hector Rodakis must know that I firmly rejected Finley's offer."

"Hope springs eternal," Cloridan said loftily. "I dunno why they're still here, but they are. I don't imagine you coming back as an even more ridiculously good-looking version of yourself is going to dissuade them."

"My Charisma hasn't changed," I objected. Cloridan just gave me a look. "But I might have gained a level," I admitted.

"I'm sure there's a story behind that," he said.

"So you got me one day to rest," I returned, ignoring the question.

"Ah, well, about that," he said awkwardly. "There's a tiny bit of a crisis."

EPİLOGUE

Reynard bowed as gracefully as his Agility would let him. He hadn't done anything *wrong*, as far as he was aware, but that didn't matter. His mistress, for want of a better word, was angry. Angry with someone she couldn't lash out at, and so now was a very dangerous moment for anyone that happened to be convenient for her to expend her rage on.

Lady Rankin ignored him as he rose from his bow. He didn't say or do anything that might distract from her most important correspondence, lest he attract her ire. Instead, he found himself contemplating just what the right word for their relationship was.

Not *employer*, though she did pay him. There was an aspect of voluntary service to employment that was missing here. He wasn't a slave, but he was bound more closely to her than he would like. Nor could he call her "my lady"—he had sworn no oaths of fealty, and she would have only laughed if he'd offered to. As someone without noble blood, they would have been worth nothing.

Mistress did seem like the closest fit. Not in the sexual sense, of course. While Lady Rankin *was* beautiful, Reynard saw himself as a strong man who dominated his partners. If the Countess ever did decide to take him to bed, Reynard imagined that she would order him drugged and chained down for her to make use of.

Carefully keeping any sign of it off his face, Reynard allowed himself to imagine what that would be like. She *was* beautiful, after all. Why was it that all his problems were caused by beautiful women? He hadn't even slept with any of them!

Marianne Rankin's slight smile twitched at the reminder of the current fly in her ointment. The man in front of her stood completely still, slipping back into his crude fantasy, unaware that every part of it was visible to the person he was imagining. She allowed him the time to detail it further, pretending to be interested in letters that she'd already read.

It wasn't *completely* inaccurate, she supposed. Such indulgences were rare, as they had to be completed out of the eye of her husband, the Earl. Occasionally, though, circumstances managed to align themselves. She wondered if they ever would for this man. She would need to have strong precautions in place, of course. He already out-levelled her, and she had promised to get him to level six.

A promise she actually meant to keep, as she had a use for a more powerful version of him. After that, well . . . anything was possible. She smirked to herself as the fantasy progressed. He would probably find the real-life version to be less enjoyable. More painful, certainly, but some people turned out to like that.

Nobody so far had liked how the sessions had ended, though. She didn't blame them for that, but she was amused by how it always seemed to take them by surprise. It should have been obvious—what was the point of having someone at your mercy, beneath you, trembling with pain and vulnerability . . . and not take advantage of that?

There was also the fact that she couldn't leave any witnesses to her . . . indiscretions.

Tiring of the game, she elected to end it by speaking.

"The King still hasn't seen fit to award me my dungeon back," she said waspishly. Technically, it was her husband's dungeon, but there was no chance that Reynard was going to correct her. "After all the efforts we made on his behalf, he still wishes to leave it in the hands of your Adventurers Guild."

Reynard eyed her warily, wondering if he was going to be blamed for this. She had considered it, but his performance had actually been exemplary during that episode, so she elected to be generous.

"You did well, nonetheless," she allowed, and watched his thoughts relax. At the back of his mind was a list of questions about that night, but he kept them there where they belonged. Marianne was as pleased about *that* as she was about his actual performance.

It had been a simple matter to locate Shadthe's agents. Manuela hadn't expected a noble to have Mind Magic, so she hadn't taken the precautions that she needed to. Marianne had known the locations of every safe-house and contact that Manuela had, long before the first obelisk had been sabotaged.

She hadn't *done* anything about it because that would have revealed her secret. In the chaos of that night, with the King desperate for salvation . . . a single ranger getting lucky and seeing through a few paltry illusions wasn't something that was going to be questioned.

Clearly, though, the King hadn't been desperate *enough*. Not for the first time, Marianne was tempted to go beyond reading minds and start changing them. She had the spells for it . . . but she resisted the temptation. As attractive as turning the King into a puppet was, other mages could see her spells. See her casting them, and see her mana twisting around the King. Not many of them could *break* the spell, but there was a foolproof method of ending any mage's spell.

So as always, she set the thought aside and addressed the matter at hand. "I'm sending you to Talnier," she said and watched as he almost—*almost*—allowed his dismay to show on his face.

"My lady . . . please don't take this as refusal, but there are a number of . . . *problems* with that idea."

"Oh?" she said, as close to innocently as she could manage. Since she was an *excellent* actor, her imitation was quite good.

"I know that you're aware, the Guild has a strong presence in Talnier," Reynard said. "They'll be looking for me."

"Perhaps, but the Guild no longer has authority over you," she told him. "You've withdrawn from their ranks and no longer answer to them."

"They don't let you leave, once you get to level five," he mumbled, nervous about contradicting her.

"The geas prevents you from leaving," she corrected. "As long as you wear that amulet, the geas won't affect you."

He touched the spot where the amulet lay under his clothes. That wasn't the actual purpose of the enchanted item. She had broken the geas herself with a spell. The amulet connected him to her, allowing her to read his thoughts at a distance. That did mean there was a mana connection between them, but as long as he was out of Dorsay, it looked exactly like the connection between high-ranking guild members and the main Guild Hall.

"They'll accept that?" he asked doubtfully.

"They'll have to. If they don't, you'll have papers that show you're working for me now. That should make you untouchable by the likes of them."

He nodded slowly. "But what about Katherine—I mean Councillor Hammond? She knows who I am."

"Some bad blood between you?" the Countess asked with a smile.

"You might say that," he agreed.

"That is not a problem," she assured him. "The good Councillor does not hold a grudge. However, she will assume that *you* do."

"That . . . wouldn't be an incorrect assumption," he admitted. "What is it that you want me to do there?"

"Nothing at all, really," Marianne said idly. "Oh, observe—spy, if you prefer that term. Delve in one of the dungeons. We do want to get you to level seven."

"The Guild won't . . ."

"We needn't go through the Guild," Marianne said, smiling. "Talnier has some sort of access arrangement with the Tribals; we shall negotiate with them on your behalf."

"Will that . . . work?" Reynard said doubtfully.

"Who knows? But I expect so. In any case, it gives you an excuse to be there. If it does work, it should be deliciously annoying to the Guild to have a renegade delving in a dungeon they regard as theirs."

"I suppose that's true. But surely that's not all you're sending me there for?"

"I may send you further instructions in time, but for now: keep your head down, delve as much as you are able. You may show as much animosity towards Hammond as you like, just don't do anything that will get you arrested."

"I'm not *that* dumb," he asserted. "From what I've heard, she's got half the town eating out of her pocket. There are too many level sixes with an axe to grind for me to give them an excuse."

"I'm not sure she has that much control," Marianne said. "But find out for yourself."

That was a dismissal, but he didn't immediately turn to leave. Marianne knew why. If she wasn't reading his thoughts, she could have read it on his face. He knew better than to directly question her orders, though, so he didn't want to say it.

Marianne decided to take pity on him. "The point, Reynard, is for you to attract her attention. The longer you stay, without taking any action against her, the more she will want to know what you are up to."

He nodded, but the confusion was still there. She sighed. "It's the oldest charlatan's trick in the book. If she's watching you, then she's not watching *anything else.*"

With that, his expression cleared. He bowed again.

"Yes, Mistress."

* * *

The man struggled, but he had no chance against the two guardsmen holding him.

"This is a stitch-up!" he protested. "I haven't done anything!"

"I'm sure you're right," Hector said mildly, "But that just confirms that you're the person I'm looking for, Marlon Tougas."

The man froze. "What's that supposed to mean?"

"Haven't done anything," he quoted. "You said it properly, you're a cut above most of the lowlifes in this quarter."

"Fuck you, it's still true," Marlon spat.

"Ah well, you must have mistaken us for guards. We guard the walls; we're not here to solve crimes."

"So dragging me off the street is some kind of mugging, then? Didn't think you toffs were so hard up."

Hector laughed. "Hard up, but not for money. It took us a while to find out, but you're the best snitch in town."

"There's no law against knowing stuff," Marlon said.

"Of course, but it seems odd that when my men were out looking for information, you steered well clear of them. Instead, they've been speaking to a gaggle of inferior informants, getting conflicting information and just plain lies. Don't you like making money?"

"Not from the likes of you."

"Well, that's too bad," Hector said, smiling. "Because I require the best, and you don't get a choice. Starting tomorrow, you work for me—and only for me."

Marlon's eyes narrowed. "Tomorrow?" he asked suspiciously.

Hector nodded. "You'll need a little time to recover," he said sympathetically. "Next time, don't make it so hard to find you."

"Wh—uff!" was all that Marlon had time to say before the beating started. Hector left them to it.

When he returned to his guardhouse, there was an urgent message waiting for him. He read it with increasing incredulity. Fighting in the streets? Lord Finley arrested for treason?

Word of Aghen Shadthe's duplicity seemed almost an afterthought, but it did have immediate implications. He quickly dashed off a note asking for permission to capture or kill the envoy living in this town. That would be a nice benefit from this madness.

Less pleasant to imagine was Lord Finley's fall from grace. His faction must be seething. As a *very* junior member, he'd have to make sure to not step on any toes.

It made his offer to Kandis more problematic . . . but if Lord Finley was gone, surely whoever replaced him would still see the value of it? He needed more information. He quickly started drafting letters to his sponsors, pleading for more news. Once that irritating Parkes was out of the way . . .

You will be mine, Kandis, I promise you.

ABOUT THE AUTHOR

Christopher Hall, also known as Maxlex, is the author of the Phantasm series. Hall started writing his first novel while sailing the Tyrrhenian Sea one summer, the salty night air flavoring and enriching his worldbuilding. Since then, he has continued to hone his craft while holding down diverse jobs in metalworking, marketing, perfume sales, and briefly, modeling. In addition to writing, Hall's interests include illuminated lettering and artisanal brewing. He endeavors to convey a sense of l'esprit in all his creative pursuits.

DISCOVER
STORIES UNBOUND

PodiumAudio.com